THE JACK REACHER CASES

Books #1, #2 and #3

DAN AMES

A HARD MAN TO FORGET

SET IN THE REACHER UNIVERSE
BY PERMISSION OF LEE CHILD

DAN AMES

USA TODAY BESTSELLING AUTHOR

FREE BOOKS AND MORE

Would you like a FREE book and the chance to win a FREE KINDLE?

Then sign up for the DAN AMES BOOK CLUB:

For special offers and new releases, sign up here

PRAISE FOR DAN AMES

"Fast-paced, engaging, original."

— NEW YORK TIMES BESTSELLING AUTHOR THOMAS PERRY

"Ames is a sensation among readers who love fast-paced thrillers."

— MYSTERY TRIBUNE

"Cuts like a knife."

— SAVANNAH MORNING NEWS

"Furiously paced. Great action."

— NEW YORK TIMES BESTSELLING AUTHOR BEN LIEBERMAN

Published by Slogan Books, Inc., New York, NY.

AN AWARD-WINNING, BESTSELLING MYSTERY SERIES

A HARD MAN TO FORGET

The Jack Reacher Cases

Book One

Written by Dan Ames

CHAPTER ONE

The two men with guns walked behind the man carrying the shovel. They knew what they were doing. A shovel was sometimes as good a weapon as any. A man with a shovel and nothing to lose was bound to make an effort with whatever he had.

So they kept their distance.

Should the man turn and swing the shovel with arms extended, his reach would cover eight feet or so.

The men with the guns maintained a ten-foot distance.

The man with the shovel gave no indication of a desire to attack, however. His shoulders were slumped. His feet shuffled along in the sand. He said nothing.

It was night in the desert. The stars were out. The wind was blowing steadily from the southwest but it had no power. It was cool and the men with the guns were chilly. Above them, the night sky was littered with stars.

The man with the shovel was sweating. He trudged along, and his face was slick, glinting in the pale moonlight. Occasionally, he stumbled on a large rock. Without bothering to look at what had impeded his path, he simply moved forward.

The men with the guns neatly avoided the stones the man with the shovel stumbled upon. He was their trailblazer, even though he was the only one who had no idea where they were going.

When the trio was at least a mile from the road, the men with guns glanced at each other, nodded and stopped abruptly.

The man with the shovel initially kept stumbling forward, but eventually, he noticed that his escorts had stopped.

He stopped. Turned and faced them.

One of the men with guns pointed his pistol at a spot on the ground and lifted his chin toward the shovel.

The man with the shovel glanced down at the spot on the ground. He saw nothing special. Sand. Some loose gravel. A weed.

He glanced back up at the men.

They waited.

"You bastards," he said. His words carried no force. No threat. A simple statement, accepted by all.

The man with the shovel put the point of the blade in a spot in front of him. He stepped forward, placed his foot on the shovel and pushed it into the ground.

He started digging.

In the distance a coyote howled. The sound of the steel shovel echoed in the empty desert air. When it hit a loose rock or a layer of gravel, the reverberation seemed to hang in the space above the men.

The men with guns paid no attention to the desert or its distant inhabitants. They were solely focused on the man with the shovel. They continued to keep their distance. A shovel full of sand flung at them was always a possibility. So they stood well back. Close enough to be able to shoot and kill their target with complete confidence, yet far enough to cause a spade full of sand to dissipate over the distance it had to travel.

The man with the shovel showed no signs of a plan to attack.

He was mechanical. Insert shovel. Scoop. Toss sand. Repeat.

His sweating had stopped.

His hands were unsteady. At times, the shovel wobbled in his hands.

It seemed that he was about to say something, but his mouth moved without producing any sound. One of the men with guns was very tall and as he watched the digger's face, it reminded him of a freshly caught fish tossed onto the bank, gasping for air.

When the floor of the desert was level with the middle of the shoveling man's thigh, one of the men with guns spoke. It wasn't the tall one. The other one was short and stocky, with a bull neck.

His voice carried no emotion.

"Toss the shovel. Sit down."

The man in the shallow grave paused. He leaned on the shovel and looked toward the dark purple sky. His lips continued to move, but no sound came out.

One of the men with guns was curious if the man was praying. But the voice was so soft, and with the ten-foot safety zone, he couldn't hear. But his educated guess was that a prayer was being recited.

The man with the shovel put one hand on the bottom of the tool's handle and threw it into the darkness. It sailed on an arc and rotated slightly, like a perfectly thrown football.

It landed in the sand and made a soft, distant thud.

The man sat down, pulled his knees up toward him and wrapped his arms around them. He buried his face into the space between his arms and his chest.

He was crying.

One of the men with guns stepped forward, lifted his pistol, and fired twice. The pistol was equipped with a silencer and the sound of the shots was little more than a soft *huff*. It made no echo and quickly faded.

The hair on top of the shoveling man's head puffed upward as each bullet entered his skull. He tipped backward and slumped onto his back.

The shooter tilted his head to the side, and judged how well his shots had laid out the man in the grave.

He seemed disappointed with the result.

He unscrewed the silencer and slipped it into a pocket. He placed the gun in a concealed holster underneath his left arm.

He then reached forward and pulled the dead

man's feet toward him, so the body was flat in the grave.

The other man retrieved the shovel and joined his partner at the foot of the grave.

He withdrew a quarter from his pocket and let the shovel handle rest against his stomach.

"Call it."

"Heads."

The man with the coin tossed it, caught it and slapped it down on top of his other hand. He then pulled his hand away with a flourish.

He showed it to the other man, who then grabbed the shovel and began tossing sand on top of the dead man.

In the distance, the coyote howled once more.

CHAPTER TWO

It wouldn't be until much later, long after the bodies had begun to pile up and all hell had broken fully loose, that Lauren Pauling would begin to wonder just why she had been thinking about Jack Reacher that morning.

It had been a fairly routine start to the day.

Early coffee. Quick skim of the New York Times. A brutal workout in the gym housed in the basement of her apartment building. It was a ferocious routine that included a punishing cardio segment followed by an extensive free weight program. As Pauling was nearing the age of fifty, she took special pride in knowing that her fitness regimen would leave much younger women begging for mercy.

A shower, light breakfast and the start of her work day.

For Pauling, that meant leaving her apartment on Barrow Street and heading over to her office on West 4th. As she walked, she glanced at her reflection in the store windows. She was a little taller than average, with goldish blonde hair. Her startling green eyes weren't discernible in the reflection, but they were often the first thing people noticed about her. She could use them strategically when she needed to.

She reached her office building, climbed the narrow staircase, and let herself into the two-room office suite.

There was a casual lounge area at the front with two chairs and a table. Magazines were neatly arranged on the table's surface, and the chairs each held an accent pillow. The walls were home to art prints. Not expensive. Professional.

The second part, her actual office, was in the back.

Pauling was a private investigator. Her top-of-the-line business card gave a little bit more information: Lauren Pauling. Private Investigator. Ex-Special Agent, Federal Bureau of Investigation. At the bottom was an address with 212 and 917 phone numbers for landline and cell, plus e-mail and a website URL.

Like the woman herself, the business card was professional, elegant and direct. The same held true for her website and the office.

It was the picture of efficiency and prestige. Not over-the-top luxurious, but with high-end finishes that would impress clients.

Pauling wasn't cheap.

Her professional habitat reflected that fact.

She cruised through her email with practiced efficiency. Within thirty minutes every issue had been addressed, every necessary action taken, and all inconsequential messages filed.

Maybe it was then, during the momentary lull when her mind turned to Reacher.

Of course, the truth was, it often did.

Pauling's last case with the FBI had been the worst period of her life. A kidnapping turned murder. She had felt like a failure, that she had let the victim down. It wasn't until Jack Reacher arrived that eventually the case of Anne Lane reappeared in her life. Working with Reacher, she'd eventually found justice for Anne.

And then Reacher was gone.

It was his way, she understood that.

But the resulting justice that finally arrived, along with the knowledge that she, Pauling, had done nothing wrong, had breathed new life into her.

She had returned to her company and her career with renewed vigor. As a result, her business had soared to the point where she often turned down work, or referred cases to other investigators.

Now, she shook off thoughts of Reacher.

He was a hard man, and a hard man to forget.

But she had been trying to move on. It just wasn't easy to do. Pauling was well past the point of romantic infatuations. There had been men. Successful. Impressive. Kind.

But none of them had been like Jack Reacher.

And she knew without a doubt that there never would be. There was Jack Reacher, and there was everyone else.

The thought of moving on gave her the motivation to get up from behind her desk, and walk toward her front door. She was going to swing by the mailbox and see if anything had been delivered. She tried not to spend more than a half hour at a time sitting behind her desk. She had a second desk to the right of her main workstation that could be lifted so she could stand and work.

But now, she wanted to move. Thoughts of

Reacher always prompted her to take an action of some sort.

As she prepared to leave her office, Pauling spotted a letter that had already arrived, placed neatly under her door.

She hadn't heard anyone stop by.

It was a little early for mail, so she assumed it was an overnight envelope.

But it wasn't.

It was a plain white letter.

With one word emblazoned across its front.

Reacher.

CHAPTER THREE

Despite having worked for an organization known to have a vague and fluid set of guidelines, Michael Tallon lived by a very specific set of rules.

The saying went that the world was not black-and-white. Plenty of shades of grey, that sort of thing.

While sometimes true, Tallon preferred to live in the black-and-white as much as possible. He detested vague boundaries and shadowy borders. Maybe it was an innate desire to be able to quickly deduce a threat. Split-second decisions between right and wrong. Life and death.

Tallon's mind went to those rules when the man in the restaurant began behaving badly.

It wasn't much of a place, the restaurant. A

chain eatery serving generic Mexican food, barely one step up from fast food.

It featured an open seating area, mostly tables separated here and there with a stand of booths. A giant drink dispenser was on one side, the serving counter in the middle, the entrance on the other side. The walls held posters advertising the latest meal special with a soft drink the size of a city's water tower.

A row of plaques touted employees of the month, as well as awards for customer satisfaction, given by the restaurant itself.

The place was half-full, mostly locals, Tallon guessed. His eyes had scanned the customers when he'd entered, and the only person who'd caught his eye was the man now demanding the attention of just about everyone in the place.

"You're a nightmare," the man barked at the young woman sitting across from him. She recoiled at the volume of the man's voice, and the proximity of his face. Tallon figured she probably caught a little spittle on that exclamation.

He tried to ignore the man. He was here only because he was hungry and needed a quick stop before continuing his drive. Tallon had just finished a project and was on his way home.

Ordinarily, he would have pushed through but

his need for food had grown to the point of distraction and knew that he still had six hours of driving ahead of him.

He'd ordered the least offensive item on the menu, grilled chicken tacos. The chicken was rubbery, the tortilla soggy. But the coffee was good and surprisingly strong. It was fuel, nothing more.

Tallon had eaten all of the tacos he'd planned to, and was about to take the rest of his coffee and go, when the man's voice cut through the monotonous drone of the restaurant yet again.

"You're worthless, just like your mother," the man said. "Both of you are useless."

All of which brought Tallon's mind around to his rules.

One of which dealt with bad parents.

Tallon had seen his fair share of them and been tempted to intervene on previous occasions. But Tallon believed in perseverance. His own parents had been fair and generous people. But he'd known others who had been cruel and vicious. Yet, he'd seen their children survive and in some cases, even thrive.

The world could be a cold and dark place. At some point, everyone had to learn that donning armor and entering combat was an occasional necessity.

So Tallon had decided not to get involved. The man was big, well over six feet, with greasy hair tied into a ponytail. He wore a sleeveless shirt, revealing thick arms wrapped with barbed wire tattoos.

He had thick hands, with large silver rings on nearly every finger. They looked like skull rings, one of them featured some kind of colored glass pieces for the eyes.

Tallon saw movement to his left and before the older woman rose from her booth, he knew exactly what was going to happen, long before it did.

He'd seen the older couple sitting in the booth near the window. The woman had one of those open, caring faces that denoted a love of family and goodness in others. She also had wide, expressive eyes that revealed an intensity of personality typically seen in someone much younger. It was a face and a demeanor that meant action. This was a woman who preferred to get involved sooner than later.

The man Tallon assumed was the woman's husband did not share this intensity. He was speaking quietly to the woman and Tallon knew he was urging his wife of many years to not get involved.

She would have none of it.

Tallon watched as the woman crossed the dining area. She had on a pair of blue slacks, a white blouse buttoned up to the neck, and sensible black shoes. She was tall, maybe a former athlete.

A woman of action, Tallon thought.

Most of the humdrum, muted conversations taking place in the restaurant stopped. It seemed to Tallon that even the requisite kitchen noise from behind the service counter had suddenly diminished to a quiet lull.

The older woman arrived at the table of the man and the young girl.

"You're teaching your daughter to accept being abused by a man," the old woman said. "If you continue, she'll look for someone just like you. A thug who berates her and probably beats her. Is that what you want?"

In the background, Tallon saw a worker at the counter dart back into the kitchen, most likely looking for a manager. The old woman's husband began to slide out of his booth. It wasn't a neat, quick move. He wasn't as spry as his wife.

But Tallon knew the big man wasn't going to

hesitate. Those rings weren't for display. The guy was a brawler. He had it written all over his face, and his hands.

"Fuck off, you old bitch," the big man roared. He lunged to his feet and the old woman retreated halfway back to her husband. They collided, and the woman fell to the floor.

"No, Dad! Leave her alone," the young girl screamed. Her face had turned red and she had started to cry. It was terror that had given her the courage to talk. And a compassion for someone other than herself. Her father had probably beaten down the ability to care for herself, but the inherent goodness was still there, as long as it was reserved for others.

But the big man wasn't listening.

He moved quickly toward the woman and her husband.

Tallon noted the big man's dirty blue jeans and his thick, black leather steel-toed boots. He was walking toward the woman and Tallon knew with utmost certainty that he planned to punch and then stomp the woman before she got to her feet. He'd probably try to clobber the old husband, too.

Had to impress his daughter, his pea brain probably told him.

Tallon's rules about bad parents were one thing.

Innocent bystanders were a whole different ballgame. There were no blurry lines on that one.

He was out of his booth and between the big man and the older couple before anyone had a chance to react.

Tallon was face-to-face with the big man.

"Turn around, go back and apologize to your daughter," Tallon said.

The man laughed, his face incredulous. He looked behind him, wondering, Tallon supposed, if a bevy of cops had suddenly arrived to supply backup.

But there was no one. Just a scared girl and a restaurant staff all peering out from behind the counter with blank stares.

Tallon read the story that was on the man's face. A cruel man, wanting to prove his superiority, and single-handedly destroy everyone who got in his path, in a little chain restaurant on the outskirts of nowhere, U.S.A.

The eyes changed, turned almost gleeful, and Tallon knew the punch was on its way before the big man even did.

The man's blow was slightly unorthodox, slow, but with a fair amount of power behind it.

Rather than avoid it, Tallon simply stepped into it, deflected the arm wide, caught it in both hands and slammed it down on the back of one of the restaurant's fixed chairs.

The arm snapped like a medium-sized piece of driftwood.

The man screamed and staggered, almost falling to his knees.

Tallon drove his elbow into the man's throat, cutting off the scream, and then as the man continued to drop, followed it with a knee to the face. Tallon both felt and heard the cartilage squish like fresh roadkill beneath a truck tire.

The man's eyes rolled back into his head.

Behind them, the manager disconnected from a call he had just made. 9-1-1, Tallon knew.

He had just enough time, so he began pulling the rings from the man's fingers.

He wasn't sure why, exactly.

A part of him recognized the rings were old, and that the man's fingers had grown fat around them. They were the man's armor. Something about the way they had looked made Tallon feel like the man got some kind of special confidence from them. And had felt that way for a long time.

So they didn't come off easily.

One pulled most of the skin off the finger it was attached to.

Tallon had to break three fingers to get the accompanying rings free.

With all of the rings now in his right hand, he forced them into the man's mouth, breaking several teeth in the process.

Tallon then returned to his table, took his tray and slid the plate and remaining food into the waste bin. He took an extra napkin and wiped off his hands.

He walked over to the young girl and pulled out a wad of cash from his front pocket. He guessed there was nearly a thousand dollars there. Using his body to shield the view of the man on the ground even though he was completely unconscious, he handed the girl the money.

"Get on a bus. Take your Mom if she loves you. Get out of here. He probably didn't learn the lesson."

The girl mumbled something soft but she slipped the money into her pocket and stood to leave.

With a nod to the old couple, Tallon left.

He still had a six-hour drive ahead of him.

CHAPTER FOUR

Miles from the dead man who'd been forced to dig his own grave, another project was being undertaken.

This, too, was being performed under the cover of darkness, with only modest lighting required.

The coyote who had serenaded the dead man during his execution was now nowhere to be found.

Instead, the same two men with guns were now present, along with a half-dozen others.

The activity took place behind a gated entrance off a dirt road in the middle of the desert, surrounded by razor wire and signs proclaiming private property. There were a half-dozen buildings, spread out in the style of a quasi-military complex. The biggest of the structures was the size of an airplane hangar.

Bundles of desert camouflage netting were littered throughout the complex, some in place, others waiting to be utilized as circumstances arose.

Unlike their activity hours earlier, the two men with guns were not burying a human being.

This time, a large piece of machinery was slowly making its way into a new home.

Underground.

In the large, hangar-like building, a huge retractable door was raised, revealing a tunnel the width of three traffic lanes. Everything was painted military gray, and the path was illuminated with lights protected by metal screens.

There was some hushed talking, subtle yet unmistakable hand gestures being made, and a delicate job was in the process of precise completion. The air smelled of gasoline, motor oil and fresh paint.

Near the back of the hangar, a man stood silently. He was very tall. Very thin. With a bald head that caught the harsh light of the hangar's interior. The men working did not look at him directly, instead, they seemed to note his presence in their peripheral vision.

Once the large item was securely deposited and the huge door rolled back into place, the bald man turned and entered an elevator with buttons showing two floors beneath ground level.

He entered the elevator and pressed the button for the lowest level.

Outside, the lights of the complex were shut off and the camouflage netting was moved into place by an automated system, like a football stadium with a retractable roof.

In the dark, with the netting in place, the entire structure was nearly invisible.

Along the dirt road, the tire tracks from the vehicles were slowly being erased by the night's desert wind.

CHAPTER FIVE

When the situation demanded it, Lauren Pauling could move with a quickness and agility that often surprised the people around her. Her fast-twitch muscle fibers were always primed, and her reflexes as well as her endurance were a bit of a legend at the Bureau.

Her preference, however, was to always proceed when possible with deliberation.

Survey. Analyze. Intuit.

Which is how she handled the arrival of the mysterious white envelope.

The one that simply read *Reacher*.

She stood still in her office, her head cocked slightly to one side as she ran a series of rapid observations and calculations through her mind.

Definitely not delivered by the mail.

Too early.

Definitely not delivered via one of the overnight services as the envelope was plain, with no labels bearing the name of a shipping company.

She also rapidly discounted the notion that it had been incorrectly delivered to another address and brought to her office by the resident of the wrong address.

There was no address at all on the front.

Nor was her name included.

All of which told Pauling that the letter had been hand-delivered.

A courier, maybe.

Still, most couriers had instructions on whether or not to obtain proof of delivery. In the majority of cases, that was the norm.

Which meant if the envelope had been brought by courier, the instructions had been to simply deliver the envelope without obtaining a signature.

Why?

Had the courier been told not to be seen? To simply slide the letter under the door and disappear?

Pauling took a step closer to the mysterious

guest on the floor of her office.

Living in New York, the favorite target of various terrorists groups, tended to make a person suspicious of generic packages being delivered. And Pauling was no exception.

Added to that, she was ex-FBI and had performed her share of duties involving foreign enemies of the state.

If that weren't enough, she and Jack Reacher had done some serious damage to a crooked mercenary. Maybe one of his gang was back and wanted revenge.

Pauling discounted that as well.

Even a letter bomb would have some kind of shape.

This was slim. Pauling guessed it held one piece of paper. Probably not even a full sheet. Notecard sized.

Pauling also ruled out the notion that Jack Reacher had delivered the message. Not Reacher's style. He was direct and to the point. Yes, he moved around the country anonymously, but there was no way he would have arrived at her door and dropped off a piece of paper without announcing his presence.

Pauling had gathered all of this intelligence by assessing the front side of the envelope only. Now she stepped forward, leaned down and turned the letter over before picking it up.

There was nothing on the back.

That, too, confirmed her previous theories.

A hand-delivered letter.

She picked it up, brought it to her desk and set it before her. She sat down. Leaned forward. Smelled the envelope.

Only the vague smell of paper, a kind of unimpressive scent one associated with a tiny copy room in a corporation. Or an office supply store when it first receives its shipments of back-to-school supplies.

A trace of New York car exhaust as well.

That was it.

Deciding she had gathered all of the information she could, Pauling used a letter opener and sliced the envelope open.

One slip of paper eased itself out onto her desk.

It was notecard sized.

Folded in half.

No fancy trim. Or bold lettering. Or heavy linen stock.

Just a garden-variety notecard.

Pauling opened it.

Written in black ink with a firm hand, was a phone number.

The number meant nothing to her.

CHAPTER SIX

Nearly two thousand miles from the mysterious activity in the desert, a group of people assembled around a large table made of a dark wood polished to perfection. It was nearly black, and reflected the recessed lighting above, as well as the anguished faces seated around its perimeter.

There were file folders on the table. Laptops with multiple wires running into neatly camouflaged openings. Paper cups filled with industrial-strength coffee.

Very few words were spoken.

A large screen at one end of the room displayed a satellite map. There were no cities listed. No roads with electronic labels attached. Any clearly delineated location was absent.

What little activity was taking place stopped when the door opened and a man entered.

He was older than most, but with square shoulders, a neat buzz cut, and a posture that implied confidence, assertiveness and total command.

Without hesitation, he walked to the head of the table. He looked down at the chair, but chose to stand. He appraised the various men and women seated around the table.

He spoke in a clipped manner, with a timbre that betrayed authority.

"I want the person in the room with most current information to tell me in as few words as possible..." he said.

His eyes went from person to person before he finished the thought.

"...just what in the hell is going on."

CHAPTER SEVEN

Death was home to Michael Tallon.

The small town of Independence Springs was nestled in the south-western crook of Death Valley.

It was situated between Los Angeles and Las Vegas, in an area most people saw from the very distant highway.

Tallon owned a decent-sized chunk of land and a small adobe house. Some referred to it as a casita. Others, a ranch.

To Tallon, it wasn't a home. He thought of it as headquarters.

From the outside, it appeared to be a typical California gentleman's ranch. Someone who might prefer to play cowboy on the weekends. Or the kind of home a retired couple who couldn't afford the lavish homes of a bigger city might turn to for a warm and low-cost option.

Because of Tallon's background, the home had some interesting features.

Multiple security cameras. An alarm system with two backup generators. An armory. A weightlifting room that occupied the entire garage. A landscape that appeared to be ordinary, but was in fact strategically laid out to prevent cover for an attacking force while also providing advantageous shooting lanes for someone inside the structure.

Likewise, the home's electronics were significantly out of the ordinary. There was a hardwired landline. A wireless radio unit. Two satellite phones with multiple batteries and chargers. A hardwired communication system for cable and Internet, along with a satellite-based stream that could continue to feed the home information without power and if the physical cables were somehow severed.

The windows were bulletproof, the entry doors made of specific construction designed to withstand explosives and fire.

One might assume Michael Tallon was a man with a great deal of enemies.

While that was true, it was also true that most of them were dead.

Still, Tallon had taken some precautions because he could afford to, and it made more sense to install fortifications than to skimp.

When he did things, Tallon tried to do them the right way.

Now, he disarmed the security system, walked through the house and satisfied with the results, unloaded his gear. He stashed his weapons, showered, and splashed a finger's worth of whiskey into a glass.

He sat in the living room, with the picture window looking out over the broad expanse of desert to the mountains beyond. The interior of the room was darker than the outside, and a film of reflective material adorned the exterior. No one could see in, but Tallon could see out.

It was good to be back, he thought.

His project had been completed with neat efficiency, and all had gone as planned.

Except for the confrontation in the restaurant.

Tallon's mind went to the young girl. She had a challenge in front of her, that was for certain. The police would come. They would do a half-hearted search for the man who had injured the original assailant. But they wouldn't find anything. Tallon was quite gifted when it came to leaving no trace of his presence.

But the girl. He hoped she would take his money and leave. Find a friend. Or a family member. Maybe her Mom wasn't so bad. Maybe they just needed a break.

Maybe consider the intervention of a stranger a sign to forge a new path.

He hoped so.

But it was a guarded kind of hope. He wished he had a way to follow up, but he knew he couldn't. To have given the girl any kind of information would have been a mistake. She would have been forced to give the same information to the police, and then there would be issues.

He had done the right thing.

But a part of him wondered...had he done enough?

CHAPTER EIGHT

The deliberations continued.

Pauling had lunch with a contact at the United Nations. She was a woman, too. She and Pauling had a professional relationship. But they recognized in each other the same trials and tribulations that always came with being a strong and intelligent woman in the world.

Their friendship had benefits.

Pauling sometimes used the woman for information. Information she couldn't get from her regular contacts at the Bureau. Or the State Department. Or even her databases for which she paid significantly large sums of money every month.

There simply was no substitute sometimes for boots on the ground.

It was something she knew Jack Reacher strongly believed in as well.

The woman from the UN also received benefits. Mostly career advice and world experience. The woman from the UN spoke multiple languages, had traveled far and wide but not in the same circles that Pauling had traveled in. Therefore, she often used Pauling as a sounding board. Pauling's analytical mind was razor-sharp and the woman had recognized a resource when she saw it.

For Pauling, lunch was delightful. A refreshing break. A wonderful salad of field greens, candied walnuts and smoked salmon. With a glass of sparkling water. And excellent, thought-provoking conversation.

In the back of her mind, however, Pauling was thinking about the phone number and the mysterious envelope with Reacher's name on it.

Pauling loved mysteries. And puzzles. It was why she had gone into law enforcement in the first place.

She'd always enjoyed challenges, and so she'd made a career out of them. The more complex the task, the better.

After lunch Pauling walked back to her office. It was a sunny day in New York, the shadows of the buildings diminished the warmth, but Pauling stayed in the sun when she could. Most of the office dwellers were back at their desks and the sidewalks were relatively light with foot traffic. It was one of the pleasures of being self-employed. The opportunity to set one's own schedule and guarantee a moment, here and there, to relax.

In her office, Pauling got behind her desk and opened one of her databases. She used a reverse lookup service and searched for information on the mystery number.

The results were immediate.

It was a cell phone.

Registered to someone in Albuquerque, New Mexico.

That was interesting.

Pauling had never been to Albuquerque. She'd been to Las Cruces, New Mexico to chase a drug dealer who'd slipped into the country near El Paso. Eventually, she'd caught him near the Mescalero Indian Reservation hiding in a dilapidated RV being driven by a pair of eighty-year-old hippies.

But she'd never been to Albuquerque. Her mind instantly went to Reacher. His travels took him everywhere, she knew. Had he been in Albuquerque? Had he sent the message from there to her office in New York?

For a moment, she wondered if Reacher needed help.

And then she laughed at herself over the silliness of that thought.

Reacher never needed anyone's help, as far as she knew.

Still, the question of the envelope was a puzzle, and she was enjoying the diversion.

Finally, she decided the time for contemplation was over.

Pauling picked up her phone, punched in the numbers and waited for a voice at the other end of the line.

CHAPTER NINE

The prisoner's IQ was in the low-rent neighborhood of 75 or so. Five points below the lowest end of the average spectrum of human intelligence.

IQ and personality are not intertwined, however.

His antisocial and sociopathic tendencies had originated all on their own. They weren't caused by his low mental capacity; rather, they were exposed by it.

In other words, his innate nature fated him to a life of crime. His diminished intelligence guaranteed he would be caught. And quickly.

By the time the day's test subject was fifteen, he had been incarcerated multiple times. Upon his latest release, he had been sentenced to a halfway house. Adding to his repertoire of less than savory characteristics, he soon included addiction.

Heroin, to be exact.

An offer of free drugs led to his abduction, and he now found himself strapped to a straight-backed wooden chair whose legs were bolted to the concrete floor.

The room was all concrete, with a single overhead light, and a pipe that ran the length of the wall, up to the ceiling, to an austere shower head, poised directly over the test subject's head.

The prisoner had a strange intuition that he was underground. Maybe it was the quality of the acoustics. Or the lack of windows. Or the slightly damp, musty smell. Like a basement.

Behind a thick window made of one-way glass, a small group watched the prisoner. They observed him with great interest. They each held a clipboard with a sheet filled with lines and boxes meant to be utilized once the experiment began.

Standing at the rear of the group was a bald man of impressive stature. He stood nearly six and a half feet tall, with broad shoulders and a face comprised of razor-sharp angles. The man's head was shaved, revealing several blood vessels protruding with great visibility. His eyes were clear and blue, and a little wider than normal as if he was either mildly surprised, or watching the world around him with great intensity.

Those who knew him well, knew it was the latter.

They also knew his blood vessels were dilated for a reason. He was both a medical doctor as well as a doctor of philosophy. His medical degree allowed him a large amount of latitude in prescribing himself unusual and unique pharmaceutical products designed to increase his musculature, as well as his intellect.

The physical side effects were all too apparent.

The psychological ramifications were not.

The group in front of the man had no intention of making their observations known, however. They were solely focused on the prisoner on the other side of the wall. Each and every one of them knew as well that the man behind them was observing *them*, as much as the unfortunate victim strapped to the chair. They much preferred to be observed in their current setting than in the space on the other side of the protected wall.

Somewhere behind them a mechanical thunk

reverberated throughout the room. As a group, they all straightened in their chairs and moved their pens into position over their papers. The man at the rear of the room remained immobile.

A gurgling sound echoed throughout the space, followed by a hiss and then from the shower head a stream of muddy brown liquid sprang, showering down on the prisoner below.

The man struggled against his straps, but to no avail. They were industrial-grade and impossible for a human being of even superhuman strength to break. The chair itself was extremely sturdy and could withstand any amount of panicked torque.

The man in the chair bucked and heaved, screamed and cursed. Initially, they were protestations of fear, however, as the liquid continued to rain down upon the man, his skin turned red and blisters began to appear. The fear turned to anger, followed by hostile shouting and cursing. Gradually, his voice lost volume and his throat and vocal cords burned.

His head slumped forward.

The liquid continued to pour down onto his now inert form.

Soon, the effects on his body would be severe and irreversible.

Behind the wall, the people with the clipboards began to write.

The man at the back of the room leaned forward.

He was smiling.

CHAPTER TEN

"Hello?"

The voice on the other end of the line belonged to a woman. Voices were always difficult to assess age, but Pauling guessed the woman was younger. Somewhere between mid-twenties and mid-thirties.

"Hello, this is Lauren Pauling, I'm a private investigator. With whom am I speaking?"

"Who? Who are you?"

The woman sounded exasperated and harried. In the background, Pauling could hear the sound of other voices and possibly someone typing on a keyboard.

Pauling answered by speaking a little more slowly, and a tad louder. "Lauren Pauling, I'm a private investigator. Someone delivered a letter to me with this phone number."

"Hold on," the woman said.

Pauling listened and heard the swish of fabric, which probably meant the woman had placed the phone against herself. Most likely, the woman was at work, in an office, and needed to go somewhere private to take the call.

Moments later, Pauling heard the sound of a door closing and the woman came back on the line.

"Okay," the woman said.

Pauling waited but the woman apparently had no intention of precipitating conversation.

"First off, did you send me this letter?" Pauling asked.

"No, I didn't send any letter to anyone." Her voice was guarded. As if she was being questioned by an authority figure.

"Okay," Pauling said. "Are you in need of a private investigator for any reason?"

Silence on the other end of the line. There was the vague sound of traffic and Pauling figured the woman had left her office building and was now taking the call outside, which seemed a little extreme.

Why the need for such intense privacy?

"Hello?" Pauling asked.

"I'm here," the woman said.

"Do you know a Jack Reacher?" Pauling asked.

"Who?"

"Jack Reacher."

"No."

A prank, Pauling thought. *It had to be a prank*. Someone must have read about her exploits with Reacher on the Anne Lane case. Why they would have gone to the trouble of doing something as annoying and petty as this was beyond the realm of her imagination. But stranger things had happened.

Still, the behavior of the woman on the other end of the line was odd. Usually, a prank had some sort of punchline.

So far, there was nothing.

Well, she had work to do. If no one needed her help, she was happy to move on to the next task for the day.

"I'm sorry," Pauling said. "There must have been some mistake. I sincerely apologize for the intrusion–"

There was a muffled sound and Pauling stopped talking.

She listened intently.

The sound came again.

Had the woman gasped?

"Hello?" Pauling asked.

Another sound.

And then Pauling realized what she was hearing.

The woman was crying.

CHAPTER ELEVEN

The man in charge of the group of people seated around the big black conference table went by the name of Rollins. He had a first name. And a fairly impressive title. But he preferred to be called Rollins. Nothing more. Nothing less.

He waited patiently while the individuals around the table weighed their response to his request for someone to tell him what the hell was going on.

However, Rollins knew they weren't just organizing their thoughts before speaking, they were also assessing their competitive rank in the room.

The lower a person's rank in the hierarchy, the less need there was to speak. Those with laptops vacillated between peering intently at their screen, while also trying to acknowledge the boss had just issued a statement someone in the room needed to address.

The longer the silence went on, the more charged the air in the room became.

Eventually, barely perceptible shifts in body language had everyone leaning slightly toward the man centrally seated along the edge of the table.

His name was Petrie.

Unlike the square shouldered, silvery buzz cut presence of Rollins, Petrie was a small man. He had a head that was very narrow, as if someone had squeezed it together like a loaf of bread being pinched between firmer items in the grocery cart. His nose was long, with a high Roman arch. His eyes were set back in his head.

The effect was that of a small predatory bird.

"Since the initial notification, we have been gathering data. That process continues. It's still too early to draw any conclusions," Petrie finally said.

"Please state your early conclusions," Rollins said. It was a rebuke. Stalling was not acceptable. Theories needed to be formulated. Hypotheses tested. Insights discovered.

The room lapsed into silence.

Rollins swiveled his head slowly, letting his

gaze fall on every individual for at least a few seconds.

Finally, it settled on a woman seated last at the table. She had short, auburn hair cut into a hip wedge shape. Her face was guileless, but it was the kind of openness that held an advantage. Many had trusted the countenance, only to discover that it had been a tripwire.

She lifted her head, taking her gaze from the laptop in front of her and fastening her eyes directly onto Rollins.

"Someone is so far ahead of us we can't even see their taillights," she said.

CHAPTER TWELVE

The sun was merciless, but mercy was the last thing Tallon wanted.

His goal was punitive in nature. What didn't kill you made you stronger.

He began the run with a sprint, to break the sweat and to jump start his heart rate. There was a trail that meandered from a canyon entrance several miles from his house. He had driven there, parked, and embarked on his training run.

What was he training for?

He often asked himself that question. He was training for any eventuality, he told himself. The unexpected. The upcoming. The unforeseen enemy around the corner.

It was his way of life.

He'd been taught that reflexes came down to

training. When presented with split-second decisions, under duress, most individuals reverted to their most basic instincts. In other words, in order for the desired behavior to occur, it had to be second nature. And it could only become that deeply ingrained through repeated training. Over and over and over. Until a person did it without thinking.

Because in the heat of battle, there usually wasn't time for intellectualizing.

A person reacted quickly, or they died.

It was that simple.

Tallon wore a weighted vest to simulate a pack or a weapon. He wore a lightweight T-shirt, camouflage cargo pants, hiking boots, a baseball cap and sunglasses. On his wrist was a multifunction watch. On the inside of his pants was a concealed holster with a 9mm pistol. Opposite the pistol was a folding knife, honed to a razor edge.

Once his breath was coming in gasps, Tallon slowed the pace to a steady jog, one that would eat up the miles and that he could maintain for hours. It was his default pace.

The canyons were rimmed with red, the sand a dirty brown that showed darker where the wind or an animal had disturbed the ground. An occasional field mouse darted out of Tallon's way and overhead a hawk was watching his progress.

Routine was never a good thing. Tallon knew that patterns were bad. As a hunter, he had used them extensively himself. On days like this, Tallon never took the same route twice, but he had a general idea in mind for the length of the run. He usually aimed for around ten miles and by alternating his choices to avoid uneven terrain, he was able to not only vary his path but extend or shorten the distance based on his current preference.

Today was a longer day.

All of the time on the road, trapped in a vehicle had left him restless and irritable. The open desert calmed him. The extremes of nearby Death Valley helped him maintain his perspective and focus.

As he ran, the calm that so often quickly arrived on these excursions failed to materialize. He was off. Something felt foreign to him.

His eyes and mind sought out differences in the surrounding terrain. Maybe there was someone else out in the desert. Hikers. Campers. Meth manufacturers. It wouldn't be the first time he'd come across others seeking refuge in the desert, for various reasons.

But he saw no one.

Tallon continued on.

The hawk had left his holding pattern and was gone. A snake crossed Tallon's path a hundred yards ahead.

His stride ate up the miles and less than ninety minutes later, he was nearing the completion of his route.

Tallon was satisfied with his performance.

But the outing had left him troubled.

As if he had missed something.

Something out there in the desert.

CHAPTER THIRTEEN

"Who are you?" the woman asked. "I know you said your name. But, like, who are you? Really?" She sniffled. Her voice trembled and Pauling knew the effort to utter even those words had been significant.

Pauling gave the woman a moment and then said, "My name is Lauren Pauling. I'm a private investigator based in New York City. Your phone number was delivered to my office via a letter."

"I don't understand," the woman said.

"Why don't we start with your name?" Pauling said. She had a fresh pad of paper in front of her, her pen ready to start writing.

"I don't know," the woman said.

"You don't know your name?"

"No, I mean I don't know if I should talk to you. I don't know what to do." The woman's voice had risen in tone, and Pauling knew she was about to burst into tears. Probably trying to keep it in check since she would have to go back to her desk. A face ruined by tears would be noticed by coworkers.

The young woman was desperately trying to keep it together.

"Why are you afraid to tell me your name?" Pauling asked.

"Yes. I mean. I'm afraid to talk to you. I don't know who you are or why you're calling me. I don't know if it's some kind of trick. Or a test. I just don't know."

The woman's voice had grown softer, to almost a whisper. She was panicked. Scared.

Pauling tried to be as soothing as possible. "Look, why don't we start over. First, tell me if you're in any immediate danger."

A long pause and then, "I don't know."

Pauling idly tapped the end of the pen against the sheet of paper. It was the only sound in the office. Tap. Tap. Tap.

A thought occurred to her.

"Are you worried someone is listening to this phone call?"

The woman gasped. Pauling took that as confirmation.

"Do you have children?" Pauling asked.

"No."

"Are you married?"

"Yes," the woman said, but the answer triggered another round of sobbing.

Pauling patiently waited for the woman to catch her breath.

"Did something happen to your husband?"

"I don't...know," the woman choked out. "I can't do this. Can't talk. On the phone. I have to go. They're going to wonder where I am."

The thought occurred to Pauling that she could simply leave the woman her phone number and tell her to call her if she felt like she needed help. Ordinarily, she would have given serious consideration to going in that direction.

Leaving the matter in someone else's hands.

Except for one thing.

Reacher.

The name had been on the envelope. Why? Who had written it? Clearly not this woman. She was scared of her own shadow. Plus, she claimed she'd never heard the name Jack Reacher.

Pauling had gotten to know Reacher very well. She recognized in him an almost pathological need to fight for the little guy. The innocent being victimized by those in power abusing their position.

Was this woman one of those people?

Was Reacher unable to help this woman and so somehow had managed to send a message to Pauling?

Too many questions.

No answers whatsoever.

"According to your cell phone number, you live in the Albuquerque area?" Pauling asked.

"Yes."

"Is there a safe place we can meet? A public place?"

"Probably. I mean, yes. There's my office. Where I work."

Pauling ran through the time it would take her to get to the airport, and her best guess at flights out of New York.

"Okay, I tell you what," Pauling said. She hesitated for just a moment, a little surprised at herself for reaching the decision she was about to make. "I'm going to get on a plane, and come out and see if I can help you. If I can, great. If not, no harm done."

"Umm," the woman said.

"I'll try to get there late tonight if possible. If not, first thing in the morning."

"It's just that–"

"Just what?"

Another long pause and then the woman whispered.

"I think they're coming for me, too."

CHAPTER FOURTEEN

The prisoner with the low IQ looked down at the mess on the floor. Blood. But with something mixed in. He kept looking at it, but nothing registered. It felt oddly familiar yet totally foreign.

And then he realized what it was.

His hair.

Almost all of it. Most of it had come off in small chunks, literally melting from his head like an ice dam in a river finally breaking up in the spring.

Along with the hair there were several chunks of skin.

He screamed, or at least he thought he did, but he couldn't hear anything. Great waves of red and yellow lights flashed in his eyes. His skin was on fire. Pressure from within his skull made him feel like his eyes were going to burst from their sockets.

He'd known pain before.

But nothing like this.

He'd inflicted pain on others. Some of their faces flashed across his consciousness. There was the first woman he'd ever attacked. A former friend he'd nearly beaten to death. That, too, had been an attack he'd started. A cowardly blow from behind with a hammer.

The screams in his mind echoed the screams that struggled to escape his burned throat and mouth.

He couldn't tell which agony was real and which were memories.

With a lunge, his body surged against his restraints, but to no avail.

He was trapped.

And he was dying.

Like every other time in his life when he had desperately needed someone, anyone, there had been no one.

It was up to him

If he couldn't help himself, then there was no help at all.

Another light flashed before his eyes, but this

one was different. It didn't register with him as one associated with pain.

He wondered if it was God.

He'd been to church as a kid, before all of the troubles began, and he wondered if he'd died and was going to see Jesus. Or heaven. Or maybe it was hell. Maybe he had died and this was hell.

There had been no doubt in his mind that he would not be going to heaven. Then again he had stopped believing in God a long time ago. So it didn't really matter.

All he knew was that this kind of pain was pure hell.

The real kind.

More pain, this time in his arm and his neck. Sharp, stabbing pain.

He recognized the sensation, even his full-throated agony.

Needles.

They were sticking needles into him.

CHAPTER FIFTEEN

Pauling flew first class, one of the perks of owning her own business. There was no one in accounting to question her spending.

The buck stopped with her.

When she had been a young FBI agent, on the government dime, accommodations had usually been less than premium. Despite public perception of government agencies being extravagant spenders - $800 toilet seats, anyone? – they had always been conscious of the fact they were funded by taxpayer dollars. So usually they were on the cheapest flights, in the worst hotel rooms, with the shoddiest rental cars. And with an extremely low per diem for meals, restaurants were usually fast and cheap.

As a private investigator, a successful one at that, Pauling had become extremely well-versed in the business aspect of expense reporting and tax deductions.

Now, she insisted on first-class flights, and first tier hotels. Rental cars she didn't care about. And she still usually opted for quick, healthy meals.

After the plane took off and they leveled at altitude, Pauling took out her laptop, connected to her paid in-flight Wi-Fi account, and launched her browser.

After a lot of teeth-pulling and crying, she had been able to get the woman's name in Albuquerque.

It was Cassady Simmons.

Cassady with an 'a' the woman had told her.

Now, Pauling began to search for what she could find out about the mystery woman who had some connection to Reacher, and appeared to be in a great deal of trouble.

Or, more accurately, in a great deal of fear.

Whether or not that anxiety had any basis in reality, Pauling was about to find out.

There was scant information on Cassady Simmons. The only social media account she had was a Facebook profile marked private. No way to hack around that. Pauling was able to look up tax records and parse through them, until she came to a Cassady Simmons who was married to a Rick Simmons. Their ages were 29 and 31, respectively. They had purchased a house two years ago. There was no employment information on paper, but Cassady had given Pauling her work address. It was for a supply company, Pauling discovered backtracking from the address, and it looked like a fairly mundane operation.

She continued to search, but could find little else.

Pauling closed her laptop and thought about the potential of what she might find. The flight went quickly, and she got up once to stretch her legs, use the restroom, and work out the kinks in her neck from sitting so long. Business travel was never the glamorous enterprise so often portrayed in the media or in films.

She got back to her seat and her thoughts inevitably turned to Jack Reacher. The thought had occurred to her that she might see him in Albuquerque. Maybe he had taken on Cassady Simmons' case and needed her help. She caught herself again. Jack Reacher was a one-man army who never called for backup.

And Pauling was too realistic to think that he simply wanted to see her again.

No, there was something else going on in Albuquerque.

Cassady Simmons either was in trouble, or for some reason deeply believed she was in some sort of danger.

Pauling was slightly torn. On the one hand, she hoped this woman wasn't in any kind of trouble. On the other hand, that would mean she would be wasting the better part of two days flying back and forth across the country.

The plane eventually reached its destination and after a smooth landing, Pauling hit the terminal, heading fast for the rental car shuttle.

It was time to meet Cassady Simmons.

CHAPTER SIXTEEN

"Who do we have out there?" Rollins asked the group.

They were still sitting around the long, black table. They'd been at it for hours and fatigue had set in. Irritability. Answers had become more clipped. Impatient.

"The SAC is Ray Ostertag," said Petrie, the small man with the hooked nose. "He's a good man. But obviously the initial call came to us because of the potential situation."

"Ostertag's qualifications," Rollins stated.

"He's a good man," Petrie continued. His voice had become more enthusiastic, reflecting his satisfaction in being able to supply an answer. Even if it was to something fairly mundane like the qualifications of the people underneath him.

"Ostertag spent a lot of time in Chicago working gangs. Also a fair amount of intelligence background."

"Good, he may need it," Rollins said.

He shifted his attention from Petrie and looked around the room.

His gaze settled briefly on the woman who'd made the comment about the taillights. He moved on from her and once again landed on Petrie. The others around the table again shifted slightly in their chairs, waiting for what came next.

Just as Petrie was about to offer a suggestion, Rollins spoke, cutting him off.

"Agent Hess," Rollins said. The woman seated last at the table lifted her gaze.

"Sir," she answered.

"Get out there. Assess the situation. Report back to us within twenty-four hours."

Without waiting for a reply, he turned to Petrie.

"You need to have a full threat assessment on my desk by noon tomorrow. I want every possibility researched with specific counter measures and damage estimates. This has the potential to get out of control fast. We can't let that happen."

He left the room.

Petrie looked at Hess. "We'll give Ostertag a heads up. The minute you're there and have done an initial download, call me. Tell me what they've got, what they can and can't do, and what you need."

Hess closed her laptop and stood.

"Will do," she said.

CHAPTER SEVENTEEN

Pauling's rental car was a white Impala. A big, roomy four-door. Some habits died hard. She'd spent so many hours riding in and driving the Lincoln Town Cars that she was simply used to the size.

Now, she let it cruise down the freeway toward Albuquerque. Cassady Simmons had told her that she worked for a company called Industrial Supply & Wholesale. According to Google, it was on the south side of the city, on the other side of the Rio Grande.

Pauling always marveled at cities of this size. About a million people if you included the suburbs.

Cities of this size were always nice. Very contained. Being a frequent traveler, she always enjoyed the smaller airports which tended to be cleaner and much faster to get through.

Albuquerque also enjoyed a picturesque setting. The mountains in the background, shouldering shadows down to the banks of the big river. It was easy to see why someone had stopped here and decided to stay.

Pauling recognized that she liked the feel of a smaller city, but wasn't fooling herself. She was a big fan of New York. It was her home.

The allure of going somewhere smaller, cheaper, and more accessible was understandable. Pauling had no real hometown to speak of. Her father had been in the military and they'd traveled far and wide. It was probably the military life that had nudged her toward the Bureau, a quasi-military operation. And maybe it explained why she'd had such a powerful attraction to Jack Reacher.

It took Pauling less than twenty minutes to reach Industrial Supply & Wholesale's office. It was a brick building, cream-colored, that looked like it was at least fifty years old. Probably part warehouse with a section that had been converted into offices.

The area in general was a warehouse district that appeared to be at the beginning of some gentrification attempts. Sandwiched in around the warehouses were converted factory buildings that now housed condos. On one corner, she saw a brewpub and an organic coffee shop. Maybe the gentrification was further along than she'd first reckoned.

Pauling found a parking spot a block from the office building and eased the Impala into its space. She left the car running with the air conditioning on. It was hot. It was time to get ready to meet Cassady Simmons.

Pauling got out of the car, went to the trunk, and opened her lone suitcase. She had supplied all of the necessary permits to check her handgun. Now, she retrieved the case and brought it back into the car in the front seat, opened it, and removed her gun. She loaded it, cocked and locked it, and slipped it into a holster on her left hip.

Next, she retrieved a small notebook and pen from her briefcase and looked at her phone. She had added Cassady as a contact and sent her a text. They had agreed to meet on Cassady's lunch hour. Apparently there was a park nearby with a picnic table where they could chat.

Pauling's phone buzzed and she saw the response.

Coming now.

She got out of the car, locked it, and headed toward the entrance of the supply company. She was near the front door when it opened and a fresh-faced young woman with light brown hair, blue eyes and a mask of intense stress stepped out.

Pauling immediately knew it was Cassady.

The woman turned and barely glanced at Pauling as she hurried down the sidewalk, her shoulders hunched forward like she was expecting a raincloud to open up and dump a torrential downpour at any minute.

But the sky was blue.

Not a cloud to be seen.

Pauling turned as well and walked on the opposite side of the street until Cassady turned onto a side street and eventually arrived at the small park she'd mentioned. There was a stand of trees isolating the park from the busy nearby road. A small play structure. A walking path. A family of squirrels scampering around the base of a tree.

The need for subterfuge seemed a little overboard to Pauling, but the fear and anxiety on the woman's face was very real.

Pauling watched Cassady Simmons choose a picnic table on the far side of the park, where she could sit and see the entrance. A little light blue lunch bag was in the woman's hand and she set it on the picnic table.

Good place for a weapon, Pauling thought as she carefully approached.

She slid onto the bench seat across from Cassady.

"Cassady," Pauling said. More of a statement than a question.

The woman closed her eyes. Nodded.

"Tell me what's wrong," Pauling said.

Cassady opened her baby blues and for the first time, the fear dissipated for just a moment.

"I'm surprised I've lived long enough to meet you," she said.

CHAPTER EIGHTEEN

"Now that you see me face-to-face, why don't we start at the beginning?" Pauling asked.

She had her notebook, pen, and cell phone in front of her.

Cassady glanced around, as if someone might be standing nearby with a hyperbolic microphone.

"There's no one here," Pauling assured her. "Just you and me."

Cassady dipped her head as if she was about to literally plunge forward. A long, shaky, breath and then, "It's my husband," she said.

"Rick."

"How did you know?"

"Public records," Pauling said. "I did a little homework."

"Okay, I guess," Cassady said. "He said he thought he was being followed. He got more and more paranoid and then one day, he just didn't come home."

"Come home from where?"

"From work."

"Did you go to the police?"

"No."

"Why not?"

"Because Rick told me not to."

Pauling knitted her brow. "He told you not to? When? Before he disappeared?"

Cassady nodded. "He said that if he ever didn't contact me for awhile, that I shouldn't worry. And he said the police wouldn't be able to help."

"What does he do?"

"He's a truck driver."

Pauling started writing.

"For who?"

"It's called Rio Grande Trucking."

"Did he say who he thought was following him?"

"No."

"Did anyone you know of want to hurt him?

Did he have enemies?"

"No. He's an easy going guy," Cassady said. "He hates trouble. It was hard to make him mad, even when we were fighting."

Pauling was tempted to ask how often they fought, but she decided to hold off on that one for now.

"How are your finances? Any money trouble?" Pauling knew more often than not, money was the root of the crime. Or, the lack of money, more accurately.

"Fine," Cassady said. "We're fairly frugal."

"What about drugs and alcohol? Any problems there?"

"Rick likes to drink beer on the weekends, but that's about it. I like white wine. Maybe a mojito when I'm getting crazy," she said. This time, she laughed a little bit and Pauling felt a swell of compassion.

Despite that, she had to ask the next question. "I just have to ask this, I'm sure the answer is no, but was there any infidelity on either side? I don't care one way or the other, I just have to know if I'm going to look into this for you."

"I can't pay you," Cassady said, quickly.

"I understand," Pauling replied.

"And no, no infidelity. That would be–"

She stopped herself, but Pauling instantly intuited what she was going to say. Maybe it was the way Cassady had caught herself, or the insinuation.

"Oh," she said.

Cassady looked at her. "Oh, what?"

"You're pregnant, aren't you?" Pauling asked.

Cassady burst into tears.

CHAPTER NINETEEN

In the desert, nothing goes to waste. Every drop of water. Every ounce of protein. Every opportunity to obtain sustenance is utilized.

So when the coyote smelled something in the air, its instincts immediately kicked in. She was hungry, and the smell was familiar.

Blood.

Where there was the smell of blood, usually, there was meat.

It took the coyote the better part of ten minutes to triangulate the location of the scent and there, she found the first drop of blood.

One drop led to the next.

And the next.

Soon, there were multiple scent markers

telling the coyote a meal was most likely close at hand.

It was a trail for the coyote.

It led her to a clear disturbance in the sand.

An alarm rose within the coyote. This was the smell of something foreign. Something to be feared.

It was the same kind of scent she had discovered around places where bad things happened.

But mixed in with the sense of danger was a delicious smell.

Food.

Life.

The coyote lifted her head and peered into the darkness around her.

She saw no threats. She backed off from the discovery, circled, and then came back.

Nothing had threatened her.

Nothing had leapt out from the darkness to attack.

For the moment, she felt safe enough to investigate further.

She planted a front paw at the edge of the disturbance in the sand.

And then she began to dig.

CHAPTER TWENTY

Luckily, probably because she had been crying so often lately, Cassady had a tissue in her purse. She used it to catch the tears before they completely ruined her makeup.

"I really have to get back to the office," she said.

Pauling checked the time and made a decision.

"Do you trust me now?" she asked. "Enough to have a longer conversation?"

Cassady nodded, still wiping her eyes.

"Okay, since you have to get back to work and don't want to look like you had the worst lunch of your life, why don't we continue this conversation at your home?" Pauling asked. "I want to see the house, and maybe we can talk more and start to get some insights into what may have happened."

"Okay," Cassady said. She gave Pauling her address, and Pauling didn't bother to tell her she already had it. It would just freak the girl out even more.

They walked back together and parted in front of the door Cassady had emerged from earlier.

"I still don't understand something, though," Cassady said. "If you're not involved in whatever happened to Rick, how did you get involved? I mean, I didn't contact you. So who did?"

"That's part of why I'm here," Pauling said. "I don't know the answer to that, either. But the way I'm looking at it, once I have my answer, you'll probably have yours, too."

Cassady nodded and Pauling put a hand on her shoulder.

"We'll figure this thing out together, okay?" she said.

Cassady gave a half-hearted smile and walked through the door back into her building.

Pauling's words of encouragement had sounded even hollow to her. The truth was, she had no idea how she was going to get to the bottom of Rick Simmons' disappearance. Already, she was having doubts about Cassady's ability to help and figured the meeting tonight with her would probably produce very little.

Still, she had to remain positive.

And most of all, she wanted to find out Jack Reacher's involvement.

Pauling went back to her Impala, put the car in gear and drove away.

She would check into a hotel, hook up her laptop, do some more research and then head out to meet Cassady.

There was something about the girl and the situation that just didn't add up. Pauling felt like she was missing something, something obvious but she couldn't force it to crystallize. It was like a memory you just couldn't place.

Pauling headed into downtown Albuquerque.

She felt like staying in a nice hotel with a gym.

Maybe she had just enough time to work out some of the kinks from the flight.

CHAPTER TWENTY-ONE

The plane was being flown by a sixty-year-old man who'd left the advertising business to pursue his passion for aviation. Often times, in long meetings at the agency, he would daydream about being in his little plane, taking to the skies, flying over and above everything. A quiet and peaceful world where he was in control.

His office had sported all things aviation. An airplane clock. A paper clip holder in the shape of a fuselage. A coffee table featuring landing gear for supports.

Eventually, he'd saved enough money to lease a little hangar and keep his pride and joy, a Piper Cherokee from the 1970s, in excellent flying condition. He planned to fly as long as he possibly could. He was only sixty years old, and his savvy investing had paid off with a retirement fund that kicked off more than enough to keep what was normally a fairly expensive hobby from draining him dry.

Now, he'd spent a good amount of the afternoon crisscrossing the desert and the mountains, doing a big loop and enjoying near-perfect weather.

He never felt more at peace than he did in the air.

It seemed to put all of the world's issues into perspective. Made them seem smaller somehow.

Now, he was on his way back to the airstrip just outside of Albuquerque. He would land, stow the plane, maybe hang out in his little hangar for an hour or two, nursing a whiskey and replaying the flight in his mind.

But his reverie was interrupted when he spotted something in the desert below.

With casual ease, he maneuvered the plane around for a closer look, dropping in altitude as he made his run.

The ground flew past him in a blur, but ahead, he saw a shape on the ground.

As his plane sped forward, the image came

closer and closer until he was able to confirm what he thought he'd seen.

A body.

There was a definite shape of a torso, along with some limbs.

A pack of coyotes scattered as he flew overhead.

There was no doubt in his mind as he prepared to call in what he'd seen.

It had been a body.

Or at least, what was left of it.

CHAPTER TWENTY-TWO

Pauling chose an upscale hotel that belonged to a family of luxury properties, mainly because she knew they would have some of the amenities most important to her.

Room service coffee, twenty-four hours a day. A gym. And reliable Internet service.

She checked in, didn't bother unpacking, plugged in her laptop and put on workout clothes. She headed down to the fitness center, was pleasantly surprised by its extensive collection of machines and free weights, and put in forty-five minutes of intense exertion.

Afterward, she showered, dressed and checked the time.

She had an hour to kill before she had to

rendezvous with Cassady. Pauling decided to use the time to plow through her always-accruing email.

There were status updates from subcontractors on other active cases. Initial queries on new investigations. Purchase order requests. And then there was yet another email from a huge competitor who wanted to buy Pauling's company, along with her services.

They were pursuing her mostly because they kept losing business to her.

If you can't beat 'em, buy 'em. That was their strategy. It had worked for a lot of holding companies, Pauling knew.

They also wanted her because of her pedigree. They were apparently having a hard time matching it, when it came to selling themselves to new clients.

Pauling politely declined their offer.

The money was certainly attention-getting, however. She could sell her private investigative company, buy a villa in the south of France...and what? Sit on the beach all day? Go through a bunch of lovers on vacation? Develop a drinking problem?

The fact was, her job was important to her.

She had family, sure. A sister in Portland with three children.

It was good to visit them. Pauling even looked forward to seeing everybody.

They were as close as two sisters could be who'd chosen distinctly different life paths.

Pauling could still have kids, through adoption. Maybe one day she would. She certainly had the financial resources to give a child everything they could need.

But her job demanded travel.

And the ability to drop everything on a moment's notice and just go. The last time she'd checked, that wasn't a good lifestyle for a single mother.

That spontaneity was essential to the life of a private investigator.

Just like this case.

The Reacher File.

That's how she thought of it. She didn't consider it the Cassady Simmons Case.

It was the Reacher File.

Pauling had taken the mystery letter with the phone number, put it in a folder, and filed it under the name "Reacher."

Perhaps she'd done it because she felt wistful thinking of Jack Reacher.

Or, perhaps it just made sense.

Checking the clock on her laptop, Pauling saw it was time to go.

She snapped her laptop shut. Put on her holster and slipped her gun into its spot. She double-checked her keys and phone and then left the room. She put the Do Not Disturb sign on the door handle.

Pauling retrieved the Impala, pulled out of the hotel parking garage and pointed the big vehicle toward the home of Cassady Simmons.

She would be there in fifteen minutes.

CHAPTER TWENTY-THREE

Petrie was summoned to Rollins' office. It was a corner space, with a window on each side. The view wasn't much, just the side of another building, but at least natural light made its way in.

Which seemed misplaced. In contrast to the content of the discussion.

"How good is Hess?" Rollins asked.

"She's good. Sharp. Ivy League. Not afraid to do what has to be done."

Rollins was sitting in his chair, his cell phone on the desk in front of him. Petrie remained standing.

"Have you read the safeguards that were in place to prevent this exact kind of thing from happening?"

"I have."

"And?"

Petrie sighed. "Nearly all preventive measures in this type of situation are to minimize the impact of human error."

"This wasn't error."

"The side product of this approach is that it also eliminates windows of opportunity for folks with bad intentions. The more processes that are automated and regulated, remove bad actors from the equation."

"A good theory."

"The one drawback nearly every operation of this type has is that the human element can never be fully removed," Petrie said. "Otherwise it becomes Artificial Intelligence. Which has its own worst-case scenarios."

"Indeed," Rollins asserted.

"Suffice to say, this was a combination of human interaction combined with technologic savvy."

"Had to be," Rollins agreed.

"So unless you are willing to take human beings completely out of the equation, you will always be dancing with the devil."

Rollins raised an eyebrow at Petrie.

"Dancing with the devil?"

"It's all about odds. You limit the number of people with access to certain things, but you always have to have someone there. And no matter how much you lower the odds, mathematically, there's always the potential for the dice to land on the wrong spot."

"And now we're adding someone else to the equation," Rollins said. "I hope Hess can handle this."

"She's not alone, sir," Petrie pointed out. "I'm monitoring this thing from start to finish. And like I said, Ostertag is capable. He and his team can accomplish whatever Hess asks them to do. If need be, we can provide more support to Hess once she makes an initial assessment."

Rollins swiped his cell phone from his desk and looked at the screen.

"Okay. Let's get this thing taken care of. No more surprises."

Petrie was about to answer, but Rollins had put the phone to his ear.

He let himself out of the office.

CHAPTER TWENTY-FOUR

Pauling turned down the street that Cassady Simmons called home, and began looking for the correct house number.

It was a modest neighborhood, full of single-story homes, many with Spanish tile roofs and white stucco. Some had garages, most didn't. Cars were parked in driveways and landscapes featured mostly rock and thin shrubbery, punctuated by the occasional cactus plant. Walkways were paved with dark red stones, often bordered with white edging.

Ahead, she saw a full-sized sedan parked along the curb. Something about it gave Pauling pause.

It looked like a cop car.

Or a Bureau car.

And it appeared to be parked in front of the house bearing Cassady's address.

Pauling parked behind the car, noted its license plate number and exited the Impala. She walked to the front door. Before ringing the bell, she listened. There was no sound. Pauling turned around and looked back at the car.

Okay, decision time.

One, it could be that the owners of the mystery car weren't here, at Cassady's house. Maybe they were visiting the home across the street. Two, maybe Cassady herself wasn't even home yet. Three, if Cassady was home, and there was someone inside with her, would ringing the bell make sense?

Pauling weighed her options.

Suddenly, it occurred to her that maybe she had slightly discounted Cassady's fear. Had the young woman finally called the police? Had she ignored her husband's advice not to call them? Had they sent out a pair of detectives?

At times like this, Pauling trusted her instincts. And right now, they told her to test the door first and see if it was unlocked. She reached forward, and turned the doorknob. The latch clicked open.

Unlocked.

Now she knew.

There was no way Cassady Simmons in her current state of mind would leave the front door unlocked.

Pauling gently pushed the door open and stepped inside the house.

Staring back at her, with a disappointed look on his face, was a man with a gun.

CHAPTER TWENTY-FIVE

Michael Tallon's behavior wasn't governed by money. Most of what he'd done professionally in his life had been because he believed in something. His father had been a bit of a genius with numbers and had found a home in the accounting industry. His son had shared some of the ability, but none of the desire.

He had been captivated at an early age by a belief in his country. It was something he'd come to organically, and it had blossomed within him as a young man.

It was why he'd chosen to enter the military.

Still, money was money.

You had to respect it.

Or it would make you pay.

Tallon kept close tabs on his modest investment portfolio, and particularly focused monitoring of his liquid investments. It was something his father had taught him.

He had done well in his career so far and through various efforts, had achieved a steady income from both his military and government work. He had invested shrewdly and his return was steady. Some now might even say he was fairly well off.

But Tallon lived for something more.

So, he logged out of his banking and investment accounts, went to the kitchen and grabbed a beer.

His casita featured an open kitchen, with clean lines and high-end finishes. Tallon had sprung to have a professional designer do his space, with certain adaptions that he needed for his line of work.

A sliding glass door opened out onto a rear deck, with a stone fire pit in the middle. Tallon loved to sit out here when the evening cooled down, with a small fire, a beer in hand, looking out at the distant mountains.

He sat in a chair, and put his feet up on the edge of the fire pit, contemplated building a fire.

He used juniper wood and the scent was oddly comforting to him.

He drank his beer and thought about his run in the desert.

How something had troubled him.

It was still there, in the back of his mind.

The sense that something was about to happen.

When it did, he knew he would be ready.

And as always, he hoped he would be given the opportunity to do something good. Maybe even, to right a wrong.

CHAPTER TWENTY-SIX

The man with the gun didn't hesitate.

And neither did Pauling.

As he raised his gun to fire, she dove left, into a space off the hallway that turned out to be a living room.

Something exploded behind her and Pauling knew that the front door had received the round meant for her. She heard plaster explode and chunks of it landed on the floor.

Pauling got to her feet with her gun in hand as the sound of gunshots continued to echo in the hallway.

Well, the car outside didn't belong to cops, she knew that now. And she felt a sudden surge of anger, not just at the shooter in the hall, but at herself. Cassady had been right to fear for her life.

Pauling felt awful that she had simply sent the woman back to work.

Now, Pauling scooted close to the edge of the wall and took a quick peek around into the hallway.

The man was gone.

Pauling darted back into the living room and looked to the other end of the space. There was a pass-through to the kitchen and an opening to the right of the room that no doubt doubled back to the hallway.

That's where the man with the gun would be if he planned to ambush her again. Or, it would be the way he would come for her.

It was the obvious choice.

Maybe he was hoping she would stay looking toward the hallway which would mean he'd have a clear chance to shoot her in the back.

Well, that wasn't going to happen.

Pauling ducked down and crossed the living area to the edge of the pass-through. She took a quick look.

It was a narrow kitchen, with an opening on the other side into a dining room. It was a basic setup. Stove. Refrigerator. A little bit of counter space and some cabinets. A small table with two chairs.

No sign of the shooter.

Pauling kept moving, crossed the pass-through into the kitchen with her gun extended in front of her.

The kitchen was empty and so was the hallway.

Pauling ducked into the dining room. Empty.

She could see through the kitchen into the living room but there was no one there.

Which left the hallway and the rooms beyond.

Suddenly, at the rear of the house, Pauling heard a thump and then a door slammed.

She carefully moved forward, using the edge of the wall for protection. She darted through the hallway into an open door across from the kitchen and in her peripheral vision, she saw the man with the gun at the end of the hallway.

His pistol was raised and he shot, but Pauling had already flung herself forward. Chunks of plaster from the wall behind her flew in all directions.

Pauling wheeled around and was about to fire.

But the man was gone.

The door at the end of the hallway was wide open.

She moved quickly forward.

It was a small house. The first room on the right was a bathroom.

It was empty.

Pauling leaned against the bathroom's doorjamb. Outside, she heard a car start up, followed by the sound of squealing tires and an engine racing.

Pauling ducked back into the hallway, moved quickly down the hall to the door on the right. She took a quick look inside.

It was a bedroom with a dresser, two windows, and a body on the floor.

It was Cassady.

She wasn't moving.

CHAPTER TWENTY-SEVEN

The car emblazoned with the logo of the New Mexico State Police pulled off the highway and its driver looked into the distance.

His name was Paul Veasy and he'd gotten the call that an aircraft had notified dispatch a body had been seen out in the desert.

Not exactly big news in this area. The desert was a harsh and unrelenting place. Homeless people. Drug addicts. Folks suffering from mental illness. When they went into the desert they usually didn't come back.

Now, Veasy looked at the sun in the sky, and mentally ran through the past few days, weather-wise. It had been hot with very little cloud cover.

Great for the golfers, not so good for a person lost and perhaps in a weakened state.

The pilot had been fastidious with pinpointing its location, and Veasy had gotten the call.

Veasy debated about driving his vehicle into the desert, but decided against it. One, even though the terrain was obviously flat, there were occasional boulders, well camouflaged to completely blend into the landscape. More than one trooper had managed to rip out pieces of his squad car's underpinnings by being too aggressive in taking his vehicle off-road. In cop shows on television, a character's penchant for ruining squad cars was often a lighthearted joke. Not so in the real world. Your car was your responsibility. You could get a black mark in your employee file if you were careless with it.

Two, Veasy was on a diet. He'd joined Weight Watchers, was now down fifteen pounds, and was constantly looking for reasons to exercise. On the program, food was correlated to a point system and the more he exercised, the more points he earned. The more points he earned, the more food he could eat. And Paul Veasy loved food. It was how he'd ended up in Weight Watchers in the first place.

So, Trooper Veasy shut off his vehicle, pocketed the keys, locked her up and walked toward a patch of land currently being overseen by two vultures circling overhead.

It took him about fifteen minutes to reach the corpse.

It had been torn apart, but Veasy could see it was a man. The work boots, jeans and shirt all told him the deceased was male. What was left of the face and other areas of exposed skin were all charred black.

Ethnicity was impossible to estimate.

Veasy carefully stepped around the body, and slipped a hand into the front pockets. They were empty.

He gently lifted the body and found a wallet.

He opened it and studied its contents.

There was a New Mexico driver's license.

With a photo and a name.

Rick Simmons.

CHAPTER TWENTY-EIGHT

Pauling went to Cassady, pivoted so she was facing the doorway and couldn't be ambushed, and knelt down next to her. She saw the duct tape around the woman's wrists, and quickly turned her so she could see her face. Cassady's wide eyes stared out at her in terror, another strip of duct tape was across her mouth.

Pauling held up her finger to indicate she needed a second. She then left the room, checked the bedroom across the hall, and raced to the front of the house.

The mystery car was gone.

Pauling grabbed a small paring knife from the kitchen, went back to Cassady, and cut her hands free.

"This is going to hurt a little bit," Pauling said,

and then pulled the tape from Cassady's mouth.

"Owwwww," Cassady said, and then burst into tears.

Pauling helped her to her feet, and guided her toward the kitchen.

"We need to call the police," Pauling said, and reached for her cell phone.

"No!" Cassady barked at her. "No. They have Rick."

"Did they say that?"

"No."

"Then how do you know?"

"Why else would they be here trying to get me, too?"

Pauling wasn't sure she could answer that. She hadn't gotten a very good look at the man who'd shot at her. He'd been a white guy, in jeans and a dark jacket. Black shoes.

"Why don't you tell me what happened?"

Cassady sat in one of the chairs at the kitchen table and Pauling got her a glass of water, then sat across from her.

"That's just it, I don't know what happened," Cassady said. She took a drink of water and then gulped the rest.

"Why don't you start with when you came home from work?"

Cassady nodded.

Pauling knew that someone had heard the gunshots and the cops would most likely be arriving soon, despite Cassady's desire not to call them.

"I came home from work, changed, and was getting ready for your visit when someone grabbed me from behind. I don't know how they got into the house."

Pauling knew. If they had Rick Simmons, they no doubt had his keys to the house. No need to break in. Just use the key and let yourself in. Easy.

They took me back to my room and I thought they were going to rape me."

"You said 'they.' Why do you think there was more than one person?"

"When I came to I could hear them talking."

"What were they saying?"

"I don't know. I thought I heard them say Rick's name, but I can't be sure."

In the distance, Pauling heard a siren.

"Cassady, I need you to think. Why would someone be after you and Rick? You're absolutely right. If they already have Rick, why do they want you?"

The young woman burst into tears.

"I have no idea," she said.

CHAPTER TWENTY-NINE

The bald man with the bulging veins was not pleased. He didn't show it to his subordinates, however. Any sign of negative emotion was not helpful. It was its own form of weakness.

He simply remained staring at them.

"It was supposed to be a grab and go," the smaller of the two men said. He was thin and wiry. A relatively new employee. He was also the most nervous of the two. The other one, a tall man, knew better than to speak. He'd been working for the bald man for quite some time.

"How were we supposed to know that some chick would show up? She was some kind of cop, too."

"So you failed to bring Cassady Simmons here," the bald man said.

"Well, yeah. But it wasn't our fault." The shorter man looked at his coworker for support and possible vindication, but he was greeted with silence.

These were excuses, and everyone in the room knew it.

The bald man contemplated the human beings before him. That was one of the intrinsic failures of evolution. It didn't create perfection. People died all the time, mostly because of gaps in the evolutionary process. A lack of knowledge. A momentary lapse of awareness. One had to recognize the fallibility of their own minds and bodies. Too few did.

Hundreds of years ago, a failure to recognize a danger in the environment meant certain death. Genetic material that played any kind of role in that failure, was also eliminated. It couldn't be passed along.

It was the beauty of evolution.

Natural selection.

The two men stood waiting for their superior's response.

He was still contemplating the laws of nature.

In the wild, a human being could wander out into the night, get snatched up by a tiger, and that particular personality trait would become less apparent in the population.

The bald man did not believe in God. He believed in science. In physics. In the power of the natural world.

He understood, however, that at this moment he was a part of that evolutionary process. He could either be the tiger in the night who eliminated the weakness in these two men, or he could allow the undesirable trait to continue. Perhaps the fear they were obviously experiencing right now would curb that predilection.

That might be true.

It also seemed like the best approach was to split the difference.

The bald man pulled the gun from its resting spot in the small of his back, raised it and fired. The bullet struck the short man on the right, and blew off the top of his head.

The body sagged to the ground.

The tall man hadn't moved, despite blood spray flecking his face.

Although he didn't show it, he felt vindicated by his decision not to speak. Unless his boss was going to shoot him, too, it had been a life-and-death decision.

Instead of a bullet, he received an order.

"Throw him in the incinerator."

CHAPTER THIRTY

"Let's try to work this out," Pauling said.

She had finally gotten Cassady under control. The tears had stopped, but the young woman was still shaking. Pauling had poured her a glass of water from the kitchen counter, and let her drink while she performed some security.

Pauling went to the doors and windows and made sure everything was locked. She dead bolted the door.

While she went through the house, she studied the belongings. It was all to be expected. Basic furniture, probably from one of the big warehouse furniture stores. Nothing very expensive. Nothing unique.

There were a few framed prints of desert

flowers on the walls, and the rest were pictures of Cassady and Rick. Some of their parents and extended family as well.

It looked like the home of a relatively young couple about to start a family.

Pauling made her way back to Cassady.

"What am I supposed to do?" the young woman asked her. Her voice was more steady, but still a little shaky. She looked like someone whose world had been turned upside down, more than once.

There was no doubt how awful Cassady must feel, Pauling thought. Her husband's missing, no family nearby, her home invaded, attacked, and now the only person here to help is someone she just met. Someone who Cassady doesn't even really know.

Pauling decided the wrong way to go about this was to start telling Cassady what to do. For starters, she didn't even know where to begin. And to start listing things for the young woman to do would only overwhelm her more.

So she decided to take a different approach, and get Cassady's mind off of herself.

"Let me tell you a little bit about myself," Pauling said. She gave Cassady the rundown on her background, including her work at the FBI with kidnapping and other types of cases. She also told her a little about the Anne Lane case, leaving out the part about Jack Reacher.

"But I still don't know how you found me," Cassady said. "How do I know you're not one of them?"

"Well, for starters, I didn't try to kidnap you," Pauling pointed out. "If I was one of them, I would have helped them get you into their car or something. And they shot at me, I didn't shoot at them."

"Yeah," Cassady said. "Unless you just want to appear to be my friend to get something from me."

"Something like what?" Pauling asked. She wasn't being a smart-ass. The fact was, there was a possibility that Rick Simmons had been taken in an effort to get something. That attempt had failed. So now they were coming to Cassady for whatever it might be.

Pauling didn't think so, but since it had come up, she thought she would pursue it.

"It can't be anything. I would have given them whatever they asked for to get Rick back. But we don't have anything," she said, her voice on the verge of breaking into sobs again. "We have, like, five hundred dollars in our checking account."

"Right," Pauling said. "So if you don't have anything, what could I possibly be after?"

"That's true," Cassady admitted.

"Also, I wanted to go to the police. You didn't. If I were doing something illegal or trying to harm you, I highly doubt I would have suggested the cops."

"I'm sorry, I do trust you," Cassady said. "I'm just scared. And sick of this shit. And I miss Rick."

She started crying again.

Pauling was about to say something when the doorbell rang. She got up, walked to the living room, with her hand on her gun.

What the hell was it now, she thought.

Pauling looked out toward the front and saw exactly what she had hoped she wouldn't.

Two police cars.

CHAPTER THIRTY-ONE

"Cassady Simmons?"

The cop peering in at Pauling was young, with big brown eyes, a hawk nose, and thick black hair swept straight back. There was another man in back, an older cop. They both looked solemn.

Pauling immediately knew what that meant.

Oh no.

She hesitated before answering the cops, but there was no other way. There wasn't time to soften the blow she knew with certainty was coming.

"Sure, let me get her. Come in," she said.

Pauling walked back to the kitchen and Cassady looked up at her. It was a horrible moment for Pauling, because she knew what was about to happen and felt incredibly guilty that Cassady didn't. There was no way to prepare her, though.

"The police are here," Pauling said.

"I said not to call them!" Cassady hissed at her. A mixture of terror and anger swirled behind Cassady's big blue eyes. Her mouth was set in a tight, grim line.

"I didn't call them," Pauling said.

"Well who did?"

"Someone probably heard the gunshots. Or maybe nobody called them and they're here for a different reason," Pauling said, trying to prepare Cassady for what was most likely to transpire.

Cassady's eyes went wide and she jumped up from her chair and practically ran down the hallway to the police.

Pauling trailed her, heard the cops break the news.

Cassady let out a long wail, a painful scream, and collapsed.

The two cops caught her in their arms.

Pauling pointed to the couch in the living room.

They carried the young woman to the couch and Pauling grabbed a pillow, to rest Cassady's head. There was a throw blanket on one of the chairs. Pauling put that over Cassady.

She turned to the older cop and gestured for him to follow her into the hallway.

"Tell me what you found," Pauling said.

The old cop looked at her with bemused skepticism.

"And exactly who are you?"

"Lauren Pauling."

"Okay, Lauren Pauling. Now tell me who you are and why you're here. Family? Friend?"

"A friend."

The cop had taken out a notebook and pen, ready to take notes.

"Do you know her husband? Rick Simmons?"

"Never met him," Pauling said. "I'm a friend of Cassady. She called me because she was worried about Rick. Do you know anything about that?"

The old cop tapped his pen against the notepad, weighed his options.

"You have some ID?" the cop asked.

Pauling showed him her driver's license.

"New York, huh?"

"So what's the deal with Rick?" Pauling asked, ignoring his question.

Finally, he glanced toward the living room and

then back at Pauling. “Rick was found deceased in the desert.” His voice was low, but Pauling could tell he’d done this before. Probably many times.

Pauling just nodded. She had figured that was the reason for the police stopping by, and from their body language. Breaking this kind of news never put a bounce in anyone’s step.

“Cause of death?” she asked.

The older cop looked at her. He had a weathered face, deeply lined and tan. His eyes were blue, and accepted no bullshit.

“Are you sure you’re just a friend of the family?” he asked.

“Friend. And private investigator,” Pauling said. “We can talk about that later, though. Cause of death?”

He shook his head. “Not for public consumption. Were you a cop? You seem like it.”

“FBI,” Pauling said. “Formerly.”

The old cop gave a little smirk. “Figures.”

He brushed past her and walked toward the living room. Pauling followed him and watched as he joined his young partner standing next to Cassady, who was now curled up on the couch. In the fetal position, numb with shock. Her worst nightmare had come true.

Pauling knew what was going to happen next. They would want to bring Cassady to the station to identify the body. They would probably put her in an interview room afterward and ask her a ton of questions. Pauling was confident Cassady had nothing to hide, but she still thought about finding the young woman an attorney. She filed the thought away for the moment.

Instead, it was Pauling's intention to take Cassady to the police station. The poor woman had no one now. Maybe there was extended family, but in the meantime, Pauling was it.

She really wanted someone to go out to the crime scene. She wanted to find out where the body had been found and look at it before nature ran its course. She was licking her investigative chops but couldn't do anything, as she had to protect Cassady from further harm.

Pauling ran through the people with whom she had worked previously in the area. Immediately, one named jumped out way ahead of the rest.

They had worked together several times, once when she was still with the Bureau.

Pauling almost smiled at herself.

It would be good to see Michael Tallon again.

CHAPTER THIRTY-TWO

Tallon looked at his phone. A call was coming in and the number was linked to a contact in his phone's database.

Lauren Pauling.

A small smirk tugged at the corner of his mouth.

Now there was a woman, he thought. He pictured her in his mind. Really quite beautiful, with golden hair, a killer body and gorgeous eyes. A little older than him, she had a timeless look about her. Not to mention that she could pass for a woman probably ten maybe even fifteen years younger.

But it was that voice.

The voice is what he remembered.

A little raspy. Like a blues singer just before her first cup of coffee in the morning.

He slid his thumb along the phone's screen to answer the call.

"Pauling," he said.

"Are you out in the middle of the desert?" she asked him. "Running for your life with vultures circling overhead?"

They had worked together a few times previously, both in official capacities with the government, and later, when they both went into private contract work.

Pauling had even been to his house and witnessed his intense physical regimen firsthand. It had been all business, though, despite his best efforts.

"Nope. Middle of the garage," he said.

It was true, he had fashioned a home gym in the garage and was in the middle of lifting. There was a window, but he kept it shut. He liked the heat and the sweat. As the saying went, the only easy day was yesterday.

"Squats or bench press?" she asked him.

"Deadlifts."

There was a pause, and then Pauling said, "So you're not on a job at the moment, I can assume?"

"You assume correctly," Tallon answered. He

sat down on the end of the weight bench. A puddle of sweat was forming beneath him and he snatched a towel from one of the barbells, used it to wipe his face so he wouldn't smear it all over his phone.

"How about you join me in Albuquerque?" Pauling asked.

"Albuquerque?" Tallon asked. "What the hell's in Albuquerque?"

"That's what I'm trying to figure out," Pauling answered. "I need someone who can do some investigating, as well as possibly performing asset protection. The situation is rather fluid at the moment."

Tallon ran through the calendar in his head. He had a job tentatively on the books for next month, but nothing at the moment. He'd planned to catch up on paperwork and put in extra time in the desert as well as on the gun range.

Well, that could wait.

"When do you need me there?" he asked. They would figure out the financial aspects later. Tallon knew that Pauling would pay him fairly.

"Yesterday," she said.

Tallon ran through what he needed to do before he could leave, and his best guess at the length of the trip. "I can be there in about eight hours," he said. "I'm going to drive so I don't have to deal with airport restrictions." Meaning, he planned to bring more firepower than certain regulations allowed.

"Good. I'll text you the address," she said.

"Looking forward to it," he said, and he had a small smile on his face. He was looking forward to seeing her again. And hearing that voice.

He didn't expect a response and when she disconnected, he wasn't surprised. Pauling was smart and tough. She didn't have time to play games and neither did Tallon.

The thought of time prompted him to check his watch.

It would take him fifteen minutes to finish his workout and then he would start to assemble his gear. His vehicle already had a full tank of gas and he kept everything neat and tidy. It was his way of always being ready to leave at a moment's notice.

The workout, however, was not something he would cut short.

Tallon always finished what he started.

CHAPTER THIRTY-THREE

Special Agent Jacqueline Hess arrived in Albuquerque.

The flight had been efficient and relatively painless. She'd spent the majority of her time reviewing all of the files and documents Petrie had given her on her way out the door.

It had been a lot.

But Hess was a fast reader and a quick learner. Data was power. Her mind was a model of efficiency and precision. She was born to be an analyst and she knew it.

Hess also knew that her beliefs and convictions were just as powerful as the best kind of analysis.

The moment the plane's wheels touched ground, her phone lit up.

There were messages from Petrie, back at headquarters, as well as from the head of the Albuquerque office, SAC Ray Ostertag.

Hess breezed through the messages from headquarters as they were mostly request for status updates. This always amused her when requests for updates were placed with no attention paid to time. Did Petrie want an update on how the flight went? Hardly.

The message she focused on was from Ostertag and it told her that a car was waiting for her outside of baggage claim.

Hess used the restroom, retrieved her gear, grabbed a coffee to go and stepped out into the warm, dry air of New Mexico.

She recognized the power of the moment. That first breath of fresh air, not stale and recycled like in the airplane and the airport itself. This was real. She was here, and Hess couldn't shake the fact that it felt like all of her life had been leading up to this point. There was a lot riding on this.

Like her entire future.

Well, she couldn't let it get to her. She had to perform. And perform well. So she shook off any jitters and focused on the task at hand.

Hess spotted her ride immediately. A Crown

Vic, charcoal gray, with light gray interior. Direct from the FBI car pool, she was sure.

A young agent in a white shirt, dark jacket and tie, sat behind the wheel. He glanced over and nodded at her, then got out and popped the trunk.

"Agent Hess," he said. "I'm McIlroy."

She shook his hand and then slid into the front passenger seat.

They didn't speak as McIlroy put the car into gear and pointed it toward downtown.

"We should be there in ten minutes or so," McIlroy said.

Hess ignored him and watched the scenery change from airport industrial to desert with a freeway running through it.

She wondered how long she would be stuck in Albuquerque.

For some reason, her guess was that it would be longer than the good folks back at headquarters were assuming.

CHAPTER THIRTY-FOUR

The good news for Cassady was that identifying the body was not necessary. Pauling knew it was probably because of the condition of the corpse and it would have to be accomplished through dental records.

The bad news was, she was indeed questioned at the police station by the two detectives who had arrived at the house.

During the process, Cassady was barely holding it together. Although because Pauling wasn't allowed into the interview room, she had no real idea of how it went.

As Pauling waited, she saw a man enter the squad room, and make his way over to the interview room where Cassady was being questioned.

He was an older man, with a dark suit and a crewcut.

Pauling recognized the FBI when she saw it.

Why was the FBI involved? Pauling thought.

The questioning continued until eventually the older cop brought Cassady out. No one else came out of the interview room.

"What's with the Feebie?" Pauling asked.

The cop ignored her.

"We'll touch base with you if we have any more questions, Cassady," he said. "In the meantime, do you need a ride home? Or will Ms. Pauling here be taking you?"

"I've got it," Pauling said.

She steered Cassady out of the squad room, out of the building and into her rental car.

Pauling knew better than to ask Cassady what they had discussed. Pauling knew exactly what kind of questions they would have trotted out. However, she was extremely interested in the FBI man.

But Cassady was in no shape to answer any more questions.

They would simply have to wait.

Pauling felt a deep compassion for the young woman who had left the police with nothing at all. Since Rick's death was ruled a homicide, all evidence collected was kept with the cops. She had nothing from her husband now, but memories.

Pauling took her back to her house, and found some Benadryl in the medicine chest. It would have been better to have a Valium, but not for a pregnant woman.

Cassady went to bed, exhausted, and on the verge of both a physical and mental collapse. Pauling had told her she was bringing in some extra security for her until things settled down. She wasn't sure Cassady even heard her as she was in a total and complete fog.

Pauling buttoned up the security of the house and got a text message.

She glanced at her phone.

Tallon was pulling up in the driveway.

Pauling went to the front door, glanced out from a side window as she never trusted peepholes.

It was too easy for a perp to stand at a front door, put his gun to the peephole, and wait for the light beneath the door to change slightly. Pull the trigger, shoot the person on the other side of the door through the eye.

It had happened before.

This time, however, instead of an assassin

waiting to fire a round, Pauling saw Tallon watching her from the front step.

He was looking over at the side window with a smile on his face.

It gave her a moment of relief from the drama of the day to see him.

She smiled, in spite of herself, and opened the door.

"I don't trust peepholes, either," he said.

CHAPTER THIRTY-FIVE

"Heads are going to roll for this one," Rollins said.

He had just walked into Petrie's office, a much smaller, much less impressive space than his own.

Petrie was at his desk, reading through a status report he'd already reviewed twice. There was no new information, but sometimes a second and even a third look bring something new to the surface.

Not this time.

He watched Rollins sink into a chair across from him.

"Anything?" Rollins asked.

Petrie stifled the urge to frown. Hess had just gotten to Albuquerque and was en route to meet with Ostertag. What could she possibly have accomplished this soon?

"We'll know more when Hess files her first update," Petrie said, his voice cautious. He had carefully phrased his response to include the words 'know more' when the truth was they didn't know anything just yet.

Other than what had already transpired.

Petrie was also struggling to make out the nuances of his boss's expression. That phrase about heads were going to roll could be taken many ways. It all depended on the expression. A threat? An urge to cooperate? Stating the obvious? Most importantly, exactly *whose* heads were going to roll?

Petrie resisted the urge to rub his neck.

"We can still get ahead of this thing," Petrie said. It was something he sort of believed, but it sounded like the perfect thing to say. The truth was, he had no idea if there was time to be proactive.

Rollins rocked back in his chair. He put his feet up on his desk and Petrie absentmindedly noted the brand. Cole Haan.

"Worst-case scenario?" Rollins asked.

Petrie contemplated the question.

"About as bad as it could possibly get. For everyone involved."

Meaning, not just the actual people responsible. But even those with indirect responsibility would pay the price.

"How do you see the worst-case scenario playing out?" Rollins persisted.

Petrie sighed. "It depends what you mean. Are we talking total numbers? Areas affected? The usual political fallout and blame game?"

Rollins grimaced.

"Even in general terms it's horrible," he said. "I imagine the specifics would be even worse."

"They are," Petrie said.

"Let's start with the area affected. What are your thoughts?"

"Let's start with the most difficult."

"That would be when. We have no idea of a timetable, or even if there is one. There has been no communication. No ultimatums. Nothing."

"Okay, so we don't know when. What about where? Best guesses?"

Petrie let out a long, slow whistle.

"Huge. A huge area." Petrie said.

"I know. But which huge area. There's gotta be some indication."

"It would be a guess. Based on nothing other

than proximity, access and value of target. And it's my guess, not the team's. We've still got a lot of data to collect."

Rollins raised an eyebrow, waiting for Petrie's answer.

"Los Angeles."

CHAPTER THIRTY-SIX

"Have you ever met Jack Reacher?" Pauling asked. She had filled Tallon in on what had happened back in New York, starting with the mystery letter emblazoned with Jack Reacher's name.

Cassady was resting in the other room and Pauling had taken Tallon out to the back patio to talk privately. Even though the young woman was asleep, Pauling wanted to make sure their conversation couldn't be overheard.

It was a warm night, with stars scattered across the night sky. The house wasn't too far from a busy street, and they could occasionally hear the sound of traffic, a horn honking in anger or warning.

Pauling couldn't remember if Tallon had ever

come across Reacher in his time in the military, or in some of the investigative cases he'd taken on since he'd left. Their world, ex-military working as civilian investigators, was a small one. Technically, Reacher wasn't an investigator, Pauling knew. His cases were simply instances of Reacher walking into something...and someone...who needed help.

"No, never met Jack Reacher," Tallon said. "I've heard a few stories, though," he said.

"Good stories or bad?"

"Good, mostly. But they aren't really stories. More like rumors along the grapevine, you know. One guy heard from another guy about this thing that happened," Tallon said. "You know how it goes. Military guys are a bunch of gossips."

Pauling laughed. She enjoyed Michael Tallon's presence. He was smaller than Reacher, but then again, who wasn't? A little over six feet, but solid muscle. He had brown hair, cut short, a strong jaw and light green eyes. More often than not, the eyes contained a trace of humor. But when they turned to flint, she could tell they'd seen more than their fair share of violence.

"I didn't realize you guys were a bunch of gossips," she said. "Maybe I'll have to watch what I say around you."

"Is Reacher really involved in this?" Tallon asked.

"I really have no idea," Pauling said. "In an indirect way, he's the reason I'm out here. Somehow he's involved in this, but I have no idea how or why. However, if his name hadn't been included, I probably wouldn't have come out here."

"He was an MP, right?" Tallon asked? "An investigator?"

Pauling nodded. "Yes. Army. One of the best I've ever seen."

"Does the woman here..."

"Cassady."

"Cassady. Does she know him?"

"No. She says she never heard the name before. And that her husband, Rick, had never mentioned him, either."

"Okay, a mystery on top of a mystery."

"Wrapped in an enigma."

They both sat in silence for a moment.

"So they took her husband," Tallon said. "Killed him. And then they came after her. So why didn't they take them together?"

"Opportunity," Pauling said. "He's a truck driver, right? Rarely home? They had to do it separately. The odds of them being together at an opportune time were probably pretty slim. Better to take one and get the other one later."

"Why the time difference?" Tallon asked. "Why not two separate grab teams? Do them simultaneously? That's what I would do. Have the teams be in constant communication so they can synchronize their movements. No way for one victim to warn the other."

Pauling had thought the same thing herself. They were just brainstorming, though. And it was always good to have someone else to bounce ideas around with.

"Maybe it was a lack of manpower," Pauling said. "Maybe we're dealing with a small crew.

"Could be," Tallon said. "Maybe one main guy and a couple of sidekicks."

"Could be, but I don't think so," Pauling said. "That Crown Vic was new. Well-taken care of. The men were well-dressed. He fired without hesitation. This isn't an amateur operation."

"So what's our plan of attack?" Tallon asked.

"First things first," Pauling said. "You stay here, keep an eye on Cassady. I'm going back to my hotel room, get a few hours rest, and then I'm going to head out to the crime scene. I need to see firsthand where Rick Simmons met his end. And why there."

"Roger that," Tallon said.

Pauling got to her feet.

"Let me know when she's up, and how she's doing. I'll be back mid-morning."

Pauling left, went to her car and headed toward the hotel.

Moments later, a black Crown Vic cruised past the Simmons house, and followed Pauling onto the freeway.

CHAPTER THIRTY-SEVEN

At first light, Pauling was back on the road.

A few hours' sleep.

A good cup of dark roast.

The city was just waking up, the freeway mostly full of truck drivers and road warrior sales people. The occasional tourist family putted along in the slow lane, with the minivan packed, along with a luggage carrier strapped to the top. A hippie couple here or there off to camp in the mountains. Smoke dope and drink coffee, contemplate the universe.

Pauling was contemplating the situation.

Rick Simmons, murdered in the desert.

An attempted abduction of Cassady Simmons.

She decided to start there. Why an abduction? Why kill her husband, and not her? Why kill him, but only kidnap her?

That didn't make sense to Pauling.

Unless they wanted something from the husband, who refused to give it up, and died in the process.

So then they moved on to Cassady.

That was a possibility.

Another angle was that they planned to kill Cassady, too, eventually. The abduction may have only been step one in the process. They'd been interrupted. Maybe the plan had been to kidnap Cassady, take her somewhere, and torture her. Clearly, they were after something. The problem was, Pauling didn't know what. And even worse, she believed Cassady didn't know, either.

Pauling continued to cruise down the highway, to the west. Her sleep had been brief, but solid. The coffee had woken her up, and she was excited to have turned in the babysitting part of the job for the actual investigation work.

It suited her better.

She'd gotten an idea of the location of the crime scene from the cops who'd arrived at Cassady's house.

It didn't take long for her to find the spot. There were several orange cones pulled off to the side of the road. Behind them were tire marks and loose debris. Out of the corner of her eye, far off in the desert, she thought she could see the flutter of crime scene tape.

Pauling pulled the car off the road and parked. She checked her cell phone to make sure she had a good signal and it was fully charged. Her gun was in its holster. She locked the car up, slipped the keys into her front pocket and began the hike across the desert to the spot where Rick Simmons had most likely been killed.

She couldn't be accused of tampering with a crime scene, as it was basically abandoned, and too big an area to keep contained. Plus, since it was the local cops who'd let slip the location of the crime, they wouldn't be in any kind of a big hurry to admit their mistake.

As she walked, Pauling had to admit that she didn't know exactly what she was looking for. Just trying to get a feel for what may have happened and why this location.

The morning sky was just beginning to turn from orange to blue, and the cool desert breeze felt good on her face. She'd put on trail running shoes and blue jeans, with a black t-shirt and light jacket. Her pistol was snug on her hip.

She spotted a small mound of dirt, a shallow

depression, and the remains of two flags of crime scene tape.

This was the spot.

Where Cassady's husband met his fate.

She slowly approached the site of Rick Simmons' final resting place and scanned the area. Not much. A few scrub bushes, rocks and sand. A stand of cactus off to the north. A bird flew overhead, looking for a meal, no doubt.

Pauling knew the cops would leave the crime scene like this for the time being. Eventually, someone would come and take down the signs, after the investigation was over. Or maybe not. Maybe they'd leave it all for the desert to reclaim. Cassady might come out and somehow mark the spot with a cross.

Then again, Pauling didn't know if the young woman was strong enough for that kind of thing. Certainly not for awhile.

Pauling wondered about the time of the murder. She imagined the killers had waited to do it at night. Far from the road. They would have needed to eliminate the possibility of being seen by the occasional passing car. They were far enough from the city to the point where there was very little traffic. But there was enough that it would have been a factor to some degree.

The first insight she gained was that the killers were brazen.

They must have parked their car. But where? She walked back and studied the tire tracks. There were too many. She wondered if the cops had noticed the tracks.

Had the killers simply pulled their car off the road and parked on the shoulder? That would have taken some nerve. A parked car on the side of the highway at night? Say a cop just happened to cruise by and notice the vehicle. They would stop, jot down the license. Call it in. Proof that the car was there.

No, they would have driven the car all the way off the highway, into the desert, far enough from the road to make sure no one had seen them.

Which meant their tracks were in the sand.

Pauling hoped the cops had taken good photos of the tracks. They would possibly come in handy. She thought of the Crown Vic from Cassady's house. No way to tell if the tires were a match just looking at them.

The other thing about the crime scene was that it seemed sudden. Like, they hadn't had a good plan of where to take Rick Simmons.

It seemed like a location chosen by means of opportunity.

They grabbed him here, killed him here, and left him here.

It just didn't seem like the kind of place to dump bodies. Too close to the city. Not far enough from the road.

They had a huge desert to choose from, yet they chose this spot.

Maybe they were just lazy.

And not as professional as she might have first assumed.

The other mistake they made was that they hadn't dug the grave deep enough. The coyote found it. The plane saw it. It should have been dug much deeper with a lot more sand on it. And then some rocks should have been scattered on top. Big enough that a small mammal couldn't push the rocks off.

Again, maybe lazy.

Or maybe amateurs.

Or both.

Pauling stayed another twenty minutes, walking and thinking, taking some photos of the scene for later examination and to confirm details.

She decided she'd gotten all she could, so Pauling started walking back to her car. When her vehicle was in sight, she saw another car drive by her rented Impala.

It was going at a slow, steady speed. Perhaps a bit slower than normal, which is what caught Pauling's attention.

It was past then, and sped up noticeably.

Pauling got a glimpse of two people in the car. One driver. One passenger.

She couldn't tell if they were men or women.

Or if they were the same two men who had tried to grab Cassady.

But the car was a Crown Vic.

Pauling considered chasing after them, but they had already crested the horizon by the time she got to her car and a high-speed chase would have been pointless.

Instead, she headed for Cassady's house.

And Michael Tallon.

CHAPTER THIRTY-EIGHT

"Is this what normal people do?" Tallon asked.

He was sitting in Cassady's living room. The bullet holes from the failed abduction were still visible, but he had cleaned up the plaster and dust on the floor.

Pauling had just arrived, fresh from her foray into the desert.

Tallon thought she looked especially good. Perfectly fitting blue jeans, a light cotton short-sleeved shirt and hiking shoes.

"Yeah, but most people have the television on," Pauling pointed out.

"I tried that but it was annoying," Tallon answered. "Much better this way. Quiet."

The couch was so soft he felt like he was

sinking into it. Becoming a part of it.

"I read somewhere that the average person watches something like five hours a day of television," Tallon continued. "How is that even possible?"

"It's called binge-watching," Pauling said. "Where's Cassady?"

"She's in her room," Tallon said. "Crying."

He had tried to talk to her, but she wasn't very responsive. Tallon had figured that role might be better suited for Pauling, anyway.

"There's coffee," he added.

"Let me check on her first," Pauling said.

Tallon waited. He could smell Pauling's perfume. It was nice. Clean. Refreshing. A little citrus in there. Pauling was even better looking than he'd remembered. He wondered about her background with the FBI. He knew she'd handled some high-profile cases, even been involved with one that involved some mercenaries. The soldiers of fortune were people Tallon had known of vaguely, which was why the case had stuck with him, probably. He also recalled that was the situation where Jack Reacher had gotten involved.

Tallon had a feeling there'd been more between Reacher and Pauling than just detective work. Something about the way she looked when Reacher's name was mentioned.

That thought was interrupted when Pauling came back out of Cassady's room.

"We need to talk," she said.

They each took up a corner of the kitchen table, a fresh cup of coffee now in front of Pauling.

"What did you find?" Tallon asked. "Anything the cops missed?"

He watched Pauling as she formulated her response.

"Death in the desert, and not much else," she said. "They found whatever they were going to find. It wasn't like I was going to come across a spent shell casing they'd overlooked or something. I just wanted to see where it happened."

She had a tablet and opened up the map app, tapped a few times with her finger and showed it to Tallon.

"Here's where it happened," she said. She set the tablet on the table and spun it around for Tallon to see.

He looked at the map.

"So we're here," he said. He put his finger near the location of Cassady's house.

"And she works here," Pauling said, pointing out Cassady's office building.

"What about the husband?" Tallon asked.

"He was a truck driver. Rio Grande Trucking," Pauling said. She dug through her notes from her first conversation with Cassady and came up with an address, which she copied down by hand.

She pushed it across the table to Tallon.

He called it up on the tablet and the three locations made a nice little triangle.

"Why don't you go check Rio Grande Trucking?" Pauling said. "I'll stay with her for the time being," Pauling said. "I'm not too worried about them coming for her again."

Tallon snatched up the address and headed for the door.

He wondered if Pauling would start getting some of her five hours of required television viewing in while he was gone.

Probably not.

Like him, she liked action.

And now, he was very glad to be back in action.

CHAPTER THIRTY-NINE

Tallon liked the tag-team approach. He'd done a fair amount of personal security jobs. They paid well but weren't his favorite task.

Usually, he felt like a babysitter with a gun.

So he was more than happy to let Pauling stay with the woman.

The house was secure. Pauling was good. He wasn't worried about it.

Tallon plugged Rio Grande Trucking's address into his phone's navigation and followed it west out of Albuquerque. He drove past a strip mall with a mega store, gas station and fast food restaurant.

Later on, he passed a mobile home dealership.

He realized he'd never seen a mobile home

dealership. But of course there would be such a thing. It's not like people would buy them online.

A long stretch of desert followed until he came to an intersection where his navigation told him to turn.

He did so and found himself in front of an abandoned gas station. There was ancient plywood over the windows. The gas pumps were long gone, filled over with concrete. Scrub weeds were everywhere.

It had the look of a business that had gone belly up at least a decade or two ago.

Tallon parked and looked at the ghostly setting in front of him.

If Rio Grande Trucking existed, this certainly wasn't it. There was no way this place had been in existence until a few weeks ago.

This enterprise had gone out of business a long time ago.

He texted Pauling and asked her to confirm the address, which she did. She even said it was the correct address according to the business information listed on the Internet, which they both knew didn't mean a lot. But still. For some reason, this address was linked with Rio Grande Trucking.

Now curious, Tallon got out of his vehicle and

walked up to the door. There was some graffiti, and it looked like someone had tried to pry the door open, to no avail. Litter was strewn around but looked like most of it had been investigated and discarded by the local rodent population.

Tallon walked around to the side of the building.

Everything was gone.

The foundation for a small air conditioning unit was there, but the unit itself had been removed, along with any piping and electrical conditions. Anything of scrap value looked like it had been severed with a cutting instrument, probably a reciprocating saw. The kind that goes through wood and metal.

Not stolen, just methodically removed with very little effort at conservation. Which told Tallon this was possibly a bankruptcy and foreclosure situation. Parts stripped off for what little money the bank could get.

In the rear of the building was a small parking lot, a few spaces probably for the employees, and maybe a few for repaired cars or two.

Not a very ambitious parking lot. Maybe that lack of purpose was one of the reasons the place had gone kaput.

All of the parking spaces were empty now. Just cracked asphalt. Loose gravel. And weeds.

Tallon had quickly dismissed the idea that Rick Simmons had been working here until recently. There was no Rio Grande Trucking here. Maybe they'd moved. He thought about calling Pauling and seeing if there was perhaps another Rio Grande Trucking. But he figured she was a pro and would have already done that.

He stood looking at the sad sight in front of him.

It was all wrong for a trucking company, too. They would need a big loading dock. Places to park the big rigs. Sure, there was plenty of empty space around, but not the kind a trucking company would need. Even if it was a tiny company, say, with only a truck or two. This still wouldn't fit the bill.

Tallon continued his walk around the building. Above a side door he spotted an under-mounted black dome of glass. Small, just big enough for a camera. Probably disconnected and not powered.

Still, a little odd the dome of glass hadn't been smashed. It looked like the area was home to more than a few vandals. Everything else had been pretty much torn away, covered up, or left in ruin.

Tallon thought about the idea of a fake address being used for Rio Grande Trucking.

In his experience, fake addresses were a lot like fake names.

Often, they held a clue to the truth. People on the run often chose a new identity using the same initials as their real name. John Smith became Joe Sullivan. That sort of thing.

Maybe this abandoned gas station had something to do with Rick Simmons' murder.

Then two things happened.

Pauling called and said that it was possible to take a different road from the address of Rio Grande Trucking to the area where Rick Simmons' body had been found. A shortcut of sort. Not only was it a straight shot, but it meant the distance between the two locations was less than a mile. Which seemed like a huge coincidence to Pauling.

And it seemed that way to Tallon, too.

The other thing he realized was a bit more immediate.

Tallon suddenly realized he wasn't alone.

CHAPTER FORTY

"I have a question about Rick's job," Pauling said.

Cassady was flat on her back in bed. Her eyes were rimmed with red. A box of Kleenex was next to her. She had a pillow in her arms and was hugging it close to her body. Using it like an inadequate shield.

"What?" Cassady asked.

"Have you ever been to his job? His place of work?"

"He was a truck driver," Cassady said. "He didn't have an office. His cab was his place of work."

She sniffled and pushed a wad of Kleenex up against the base of her nose.

"Did he ever say anything about having to visit the company's office?" Pauling asked. "You know, like its headquarters?"

"No."

"What about paperwork?" Pauling asked. "Most truck companies have a physical office where they keep the paperwork, if nothing else. Did he ever say anything about having to drop off paperwork, or pick up a load. Anything like that?"

Cassady shook her head. A flash of irritation crossed her face.

"What does this have to do with what happened?" Cassady said. She sounded angry, and Pauling realized a lot of the emotion was simple fatigue and shock. Mixed together with a devastating depression.

"Why are you asking me about this? He was a truck driver," Cassady said. "Nobody does this to somebody because they drive a truck."

Pauling decided not to tell her what Tallon had found. Not yet, anyway.

"I guess I was just wondering if he ever had to go and meet with a boss. Or a secretary. Or a dispatcher or something like that. Was there ever a reason he had to go to the physical office of Rio Grande Trucking?"

"Nope. Never," Cassady said.

Like everything else on this case, it was a dead end. Was there a Rio Grande Trucking? Had Rick made the whole thing up? If so, who did he work for? And who did he work with?

"Did he ever talk about anyone at work? Any names? Any coworkers?" she asked. Her voice betrayed the incredibly low odds of receiving a positive response. It was a long shot, through and through.

Now the irritation in Cassady's face morphed into something else.

"Sandy." Cassady said it with far too much emotion.

"Sandy?" Pauling replied. "Who's Sandy?"

Cassady waved a hand clutching a Kleenex like she was dismissing the thought.

"I assumed it was a dispatcher or something," she said. "Somebody who would actually have a reason to talk with the drivers," Cassady said.

Pauling caught the undercurrent of emotion.

"Rick didn't say who she was?"

"Nope."

It was definitely not adding up. Pauling decided to press the issue.

"He just said her name? Without any context?"

Cassady's mouth narrowed to a severe, thin

line. She turned to Pauling and her eyes cleared, shining with an intensity that hadn't been there before.

"Yeah," Cassady. "In his sleep."

CHAPTER FORTY-ONE

"Help you?"

Tallon turned and saw two men watching him.

They were both big in their own way. One was very tall, at least 6'6" with a pear-shaped body. The other was average height but twice as wide as his partner. His shoulders were massive, his arms were thick, but very short. A wrestler, not a puncher. The tall one would be the striker. He would fire from a distance allowing the other one to get in close.

If it came to that.

They wore jeans, hiking boots and t-shirts. The short, wide one had on a baseball cap. Tallon thought of the term 'shit-kicker' and how it was highly applicable here.

The short, stocky guy was also the one who'd spoken.

Tallon slid his phone into his front pocket, having just finished talking with Pauling. The men must have pulled up quietly and parked behind Tallon's vehicle.

"You deaf?"

That was the tall one. He had a high-pitched voice. Not in the least intimidating. In fact, Tallon smiled at the sound of it.

It was like being threatened by Pee-Wee Herman.

The two men shifted slightly, putting more room between them.

"So the camera works?" Tallon asked. He'd noticed the little dome of dark glass, that it was the only thing that looked like it survived. Which had been odd. Considering the general decrepit state of everything else. His suspicions had clearly been confirmed.

Neither guy answered.

"What do you guys do, sit together in some little office somewhere, keeping close tabs on the abandoned gas station?" Tallon said with a laugh. "That's what your lives have come to? You must have been real stars in the classroom. Do you jerk each other off if someone shows up here?"

His tone and attitude took them by surprise.

The tall one glanced down at the stocky one. Clearly, he was looking for his shorter counterpart to take the lead.

The stocky one pulled out an extendable baton and snapped it all the way open with a flick of his wrist.

Tallon almost smiled.

The gesture was meant to scare him. To fill him with terror. Maybe make him submissive and do what they asked.

It had the opposite effect.

For a couple of reasons.

One, the extendable baton as a weapon was best used to disarm someone. Slashing strikes downward that connected with bone, wrist or fingers, designed to knock a weapon from someone's grip was the best way to use it. That's what it had been designed for. A lot of would-be toughs didn't know that, of course. They tended to use it the incorrect way. Trying to clobber someone over the head, for instance. Something told Tallon that the man in front of him hadn't done his homework. In fact, he'd probably never done any homework, ever.

Tallon had yet to draw a weapon.

Two, an extendable baton was a good way to

keep distance from a potential threat. Again, that was the impetus for its creation in the first place. If the tall one had the baton, it would be even better. Very difficult for Tallon to strike the tall man with his long arms, extended even farther with the baton.

Now, the instrument also had some disadvantages. It required a good amount of energy to wind up and unleash a strike. It could be used to jab, but that wasn't the best move.

The only way their current setup would work was if Tallon attacked the stocky man with a weapon extended in front of him.

He wasn't about to do that.

However, getting in close first to the guy with the baton was the way to go.

"This is going to be fun," the baton-wielding man said.

And then they made their move.

The tall one came in first and the move revealed the plan. The tall one would attack with a long-distance punch, and the stocky guy would pound Tallon with the baton while he fought with the big guy.

Tallon's reaction was instantaneous.

He launched himself at the stocky one who

attempted to draw back the baton in a big sweeping strike.

Wrong move and he was both way too slow and way too late.

Tallon's straight kick caught him in the solar plexus and the man seemed to momentarily hang in the air as the power and viciousness of the kick left him stunned, gasping for air.

The baton's backswing stopped and the stocky man's upper body leaned forward. Tallon's momentum carried him forward and he drove a straight right into the middle of the man's face, squashing the nose and driving the cartilage back and upward, directly into the frontal lobe of the man's brain.

He flew backward, falling on his back and his skull made a loud cracking sound as it hit the asphalt.

The baton flew from the man's hand and Tallon caught it with his right hand, still on the follow through from the terrific blow he'd just delivered. He turned on his heel, pivoted his hips and swung the baton.

The tall man was still coming, too late to adjust his course, and the baton hit him in the neck, just under the jaw line. Its knobbed end drove into the nerves of the tall man's spine. His eyes rolled over to white, and his body jolted like he'd stepped on a live wire.

Tallon brought the baton back, twisting the other way in a backhand with a short arc that connected with the tall man's temple.

It was a terrible blow and the man tottered, as if he was checking his shoelaces, and then he fell face-first into the blacktop.

In some states, Tallon knew that an extendable baton used to strike the head area was considered lethal force in a court of law.

Oh well.

Self-defense was a beautiful thing.

Tallon used his shirt to wipe off the handle of the baton, and he threw it into the distance of the parking lot where it rolled into a clump of weeds.

The whole process had taken less than thirty seconds and in the meantime, no one else had driven by the area.

Tallon approached the stocky man and put his fingers to the man's throat.

He was dead.

Tallon relieved the man of his wallet and went to his partner, who was clearly still breathing. Tallon took his wallet, too. He went to his vehicle, noted his opponents had arrived in a Crown Vic.

Wasn't that what Pauling had said the men who tried to grab Cassady had been driving?

Tallon climbed into his vehicle and drove away.

CHAPTER FORTY-TWO

Cassady was no longer any help.

Pauling recognized that.

There always came a time when a witness or family member could no longer contribute anything meaningful to an investigation. They had been wrung for any and all information. Any new insights would only come with brand-new questions. But those would have to come later, when new information arrived that prompted new questions.

So when the person was no longer a resource, and when that person was also in danger, there were two approaches.

One, use them as bait.

Two, get them to a safe house.

Pauling had a hotel room. It would only be

considered a safe room for Cassady if she or Tallon were there, too. It would provide no protection to stash Cassady there and leave her by herself. So, guarding her at the hotel was really no different than guarding her at the house. If the bad guys knew to come here, they could probably figure out where Pauling was.

Using Cassady as bait, on the other hand, wasn't a bad idea. A tried and true technique. Sometimes the bait was killed, however.

Also, they had tried once to grab Cassady and failed. The odds of them trying again were slim. Sure, they could assemble a huge strike force but Pauling didn't think that would be the case. Especially now that the bad guys knew Cassady was being guarded.

The other thing Pauling hated about using her client as bait was that it was a passive approach. She hated taking a passive angle on an investigation. It was always, for her, the last resort. Only used after she'd exhausted every other avenue. Being active was the key. Pushing forward, always seeking progress.

Sure, there were times when you had to play a waiting game. But this wasn't one of them. At least, not now.

She, Pauling, was a very good investigator, if

she thought so herself. So was Tallon. Using either one as a bodyguard was a misallocation of resources, in Bureau terminology.

No, she needed to be actively solving the case.

Having a third person was a luxury she couldn't afford. It was always a possibility, Pauling had been in charge of teams numbering in the dozens. But this case, she was only here because of Reacher. Or his name, more accurately. If it hadn't been splashed across the front of that envelope, she would have ignored Cassady Simmons and her plight.

Instead, she came out here, hoping to see Reacher.

And now, she was working a case pro bono. Which was a fancy way of saying she was working for free.

Which meant she needed to wrap this thing up, but like everything else that was easier said than done.

Tallon interrupted her train of thought with a text that he was here and about to enter the house. Letting her know so his arrival didn't startle anyone. Namely, Cassady.

Pauling went to the door and let him in.

"How is she?" he asked.

"Sleeping," Pauling said and nodded her head toward the closed door of Cassady's bedroom.

"So are these guys," Tallon said, and handed her two wallets.

Pauling took them, and glanced at the IDs.

"What happened?" she said.

Pauling listened as Tallon walked her through the scene at the abandoned gas station. She found it particularly interesting the location was under surveillance, and that the two men were driving a Crown Vic.

"So not only did they publish a fake address for Rio Grande Trucking, they figured somebody would eventually come looking for it. Hence, the camera," Pauling said.

"Which means their plan wasn't very long-term," Tallon said.

"Good point," Pauling said. The long-term play would have been to make sure no one ever came looking. By putting up a camera, they had pretty much planned somebody would be investigating. Which meant they were working on a limited time frame."

"I killed one of them, just so you know," Tallon said.

He said it with about as much emotion as

someone stating there were leftovers in the fridge.

"Was the other one mobile?" Pauling asked.

"Not right away," he answered. "But he's probably awake by now."

"They won't go to the cops," Pauling said. "They have the camera so they watched it all. Probably sent a clean-up team the minute you left."

She thought it interesting the lack of reaction on Tallon's face. That was one thing he and Reacher had in common. They never went looking for trouble but if someone came at them, they didn't mind levying a very high price.

"Let's see what I can find on these names," Pauling said. She took the wallets to her computer and spent a few minutes accessing her databases remotely.

"Whoever they were, they certainly weren't the A-Team," Tallon said. "More like the C-minus team."

"Local help, most likely," Pauling said. "Hired cheap."

"Overconfident, too. Bringing your wallets to a beat down."

Pauling scanned the information her programs had recovered. "Yep," she said. "Locals. Minor criminal histories. No signs of employment. Freelance thugs."

"You get what you pay for."

Pauling snapped her laptop shut and looked at Tallon.

He raised an eyebrow.

"You look like you have a plan," he said.

"I do," she answered. "Here's what we're going to do."

CHAPTER FORTY-THREE

"Mr. Walker, I'm afraid Brooks is dead," the tall man said.

The bald man with the bulging veins kept his face impassive. They stood in the underground room, with a window looking into the chamber where the experiments took place. There was a person in restraints, most of his skin gone, and blood splattered around the floor.

"I know Brooks is dead," Walker said. "I watched him die."

Walker had made sure to put a surveillance camera on the gas station, just in case anyone started poking around about Rio Grande Trucking, after the disappearance of Rick Simmons. The world was full of people asking questions.

The problem was, they were usually asking the wrong questions.

"So you saw it all?" the tall man said, his high-pitched voice sounding squeaky to his boss. Walker thought the big man sounded like a mouse. An overgrown mouse.

"Of course I did," Walker said. "The joy of seeing you two morons getting your asses kicked was negated by the realization of how severely I've overpaid you."

A vein on the side of the bald man's head was throbbing, and the tall man knew that was a bad sign.

"I've got Brooks' body in the car. Want me to throw it in the incinerator?"

Walker shook his head.

"Not yet. Go get that one first," he said, nodding toward the dead test subject in the chamber. "Throw both of them in there together and then meet me up at the command center. We've got to make some moves and make them fast."

The tall man was buoyed by his boss's forgiveness. He opened the door to the chamber and went to the chair. He wondered about putting on some protective gear but he was afraid to ask.

Behind him, he heard the door slam shut and the heavy locking mechanism rammed into place.

Above him, he heard a gurgle of liquid begin heading toward the shower head.

"No!" he shouted.

He ran back to the door and heaved on it, but he knew firsthand it was impregnable. He'd watched many unfortunate souls do what he was doing just then.

The fluid erupted from the shower head and began spraying in a 360 degree pattern. It splashed onto his face and hands igniting a burning pain the kind he'd never experienced before.

On the other side of the glass, Walker watched the tall man screaming at him.

He smiled.

"Another mouse dies in the name of science," he said and laughed.

CHAPTER FORTY-FOUR

Chicago. That's where Pauling's plan started.

She had a friend, a nurse, who specialized in obstetrics. Pauling knew she could stash Cassady there, safely.

Pauling had a long history of investigation and over that time had developed a sixth sense for when it was time to get one's hands dirty.

Now was the time.

Just to be sure, she booked a flight out of Phoenix for Cassady, instead of Albuquerque, just in case anyone was watching the airport. Who knew? Someone had put a camera at an abandoned gas station. Having a watcher at the airport wasn't out of the question.

Pauling was confident they wouldn't be watching in Phoenix, though.

"Why do I have to leave again?" Cassady said. She sat on the edge of her bed, her shoulders slumped.

"It won't be for long," Pauling assured her. "Just a few days, probably, until we get this thing sorted out."

"What about my work?"

"We'll have you call in sick. Do you have sick time?"

Cassady nodded.

"Okay, that's what we'll do."

Pauling hugged Cassady and handed her an envelope. "There's three thousand dollars in here in cash. Keep it on you. It's yours. Don't worry about it."

"What about the police, though? They said I should tell them if I planned to travel anywhere."

"I have to talk to them anyway," Pauling said. "I'll let them know you stepped out for a bit but that you'll be back in a few days. It won't be a problem."

"Okay," Cassady said.

She looked around the house and Pauling knew what she was thinking. That this had been her home. Where she thought she was going to raise a family.

Instead, she was left alone.

"Make sure she gets on the plane safely," Pauling said to Tallon.

"You got it," he said.

Tallon and Cassady left and Pauling wondered about the local cops. About how exactly she would handle that. She'd told Cassady she would take care of it.

It was mostly true.

She just didn't know *when* she would share Cassady's whereabouts.

Pauling locked up Cassady's house and drove down to her hotel room, showered, changed, and thought about her next steps.

Tallon would be back once Cassady was safely on the plane.

In the meantime, her plan was to dig deeper on the IDs of the men Tallon had dealt with at the abandoned gas station. She'd already run the basics through her software programs, but was waiting for information from one of her backchannel searches. The kind that didn't appear in normal Internet traffic and therefore couldn't be traced.

A message was waiting in her inbox telling her

that the information had arrived. She scanned through it, noting that it contained most of what she'd already learned.

With one exception.

Employment.

In her initial background search, it had showed both men were unemployed. But this database, a back door into the IRS, traced payments to both men from an entity called S & S Security.

What really caught Pauling's eye, though, was the address associated with S & S Security. It was the same as Rio Grande Trucking.

The exact same address as Rio Grande Trucking.

Which Pauling already knew was an abandoned gas station west of the city.

Reacher, what did you get me into? Pauling wondered. *More accurately, what had Rick Simmons been into? Why him?*

She stood and began to pace. Sometimes, she thought better on her feet.

What would Reacher do? He would explore the avenues. Think about who stood to gain. There were always commonalities. Cornerstone motivations at the root of most evil done by mankind.

So far, Pauling had been unable to find out who would want to target Rick Simmons. And his wife.

There had been no financial problems.

No extramarital affairs.

Except for a mysterious coworker named Sandy, whose name had been whispered during the night. Not much to go on. Certainly not much to take to the cops.

Plus, Cassady was pregnant.

The more she thought about it, the more she felt Rick Simmons was the key. Cassady was just a distraction. Or maybe insurance.

Rick's story was tied up with Rio Grande Trucking, which shared an address with two thugs in a Crown Vic.

Pauling's thoughts returned to Sandy.

How could she find the woman if she couldn't even find the company itself? Pauling paced and thought. She rolled her head from side to side. She wished Reacher was there to provide some physical distraction.

But he wasn't.

Well, one option would be to call every trucking company in Albuquerque and ask for Sandy. See if anyone answered in the positive. And then what? Ask Sandy if she knew a Rick

Simmons who might have mentioned her name in his sleep? Sandy would probably know that Rick was missing. Maybe Sandy was missing too. Or maybe she was involved.

It was a horrible plan, but it was all she had. So Pauling spent the next three hours calling every trucking company in the Albuquerque area.

There was no one named Sandy.

She went down to the hotel's café and ordered a coffee. She was tempted to add a brownie out of frustration but decided against it.

Without Sandy, the only other thing that stood out to her about this case was Reacher. Why was his name used? Who wrote it on the envelope? Why was it sent to her?

What did she know about Reacher that might apply to this case?

He was former Army. An MP often placed in charge of homicide investigations. He was a tough guy who hated to see injustice done. Who tended to stand up for those who were being bullied.

Everything about Reacher screamed ex-military.

For some reason, the word 'military' resonated with Pauling.

She felt something akin to a vibration.

The military.

How did the military and Albuquerque interact? What would have involved Reacher out here?

Pauling's jaw suddenly dropped open.

"Oh my God," she said out loud. Much louder than she expected because several people in the hotel coffee shop turned to look at her.

She jumped to her feet and headed for her room, dialing Tallon on her phone.

Why hadn't she seen it sooner?

Suddenly, she knew *exactly* who Sandy was.

CHAPTER FORTY-FIVE

"Any chance you're going to tell us what the hell is going on?" the man with the thinning blond hair and ruddy complexion asked Agent Hess. They were in a conference room in the Albuquerque FBI office. Ostertag was at the head of the table. To his right was an older man with perfectly combed gray hair. To his left, a Hispanic man with thick black glasses.

Hess sat at the other end of the table.

"I can tell you some of what we know," she replied. "But there's a reason we were alerted back in DC, instead of you."

"Yeah, that's what I figured," Ostertag said, his voice thick with sarcasm. "I get a call that some hotshot agent from HQ is coming out here and I have to have a team assembled. No indication what it's about. You know, we've got our own stuff to deal with here. We've got a huge ring of meth dealers. A truck full of illegal immigrants was found yesterday. They were all dead. Nine bodies roasting in the desert like meat in an oven."

Hess let out a slow breath.

"I appreciate your current responsibilities," she said. "I've been given strict instructions to ensure the reason I'm here today receives your top priority."

Ostertag rolled his eyes. He was an impatient man, Hess could see. "Of course it is. That's why we're here."

"It starts with a man named Rick Simmons," Hess said.

Ostertag shook his head, and looked at the other two men in the room. They gave him blank looks.

"Never heard of him," Ostertag said.

"Well, you won't be hearing anything," Hess said. "Because he's dead. Murdered in the desert yesterday."

"Okay," Ostertag said.

"He was a truck driver. Working for a company called Rio Grande Trucking."

Ostertag's irritated demeanor instantly vanished.

"Oh shit," he said.

Hess smiled at him. "Exactly."

CHAPTER FORTY-SIX

"Sandia," Pauling said to Tallon. "As in Sandia Nuclear Laboratories."

"The nuke guys? What about them?" he answered.

Pauling relayed the conversation she'd had with Cassady. The one where she said Rick Simmons had been talking about 'Sandy' in his sleep.

"That's it?" he asked. "You think just because he's a truck driver and he mentioned a Sandy that he was involved with the nukes?"

"Rick Simmons wasn't talking about a mysterious Sandy," Pauling said. "He was talking about Sandia. His real employer."

"Sandia uses truck drivers? I thought they

built nuclear missiles. A bunch of geeky scientists and stuff."

"They do both."

They were sitting at a table in the coffee shop of Pauling's hotel. Tallon was back from dropping off Cassady, without incident. He was hungry and had ordered two ham and cheese croissant sandwiches with black coffee.

"Nothing like microwaved bread," he said as they were delivered. He had devoured both of the sandwiches in minutes, after offering Pauling one. She had declined.

Pauling thought he looked eager. Babysitting didn't sit well with him, either apparently.

"What do you mean both? They do all the scientific stuff and they truck the shit around the country? That seems dangerous."

"That's why they do it themselves," Pauling explained.

"For security reasons," Tallon said.

"Right. They can't subcontract trucking with something like that. Could you imagine the public outcry if they found out some joe-trucking-operation-off-the-street was hauling around nuclear material? Maybe the guy takes a break at a truck stop, gets a prostitute and dies. The hooker drives off with a load of nukes."

"Yeah, that wouldn't be good," Tallon said. "Hookers and nuclear warheads are a bad combination. Trust me." He smiled at Pauling.

"How much do you know about Sandia?" she asked him.

"Just that they do the nuke stuff. Related to the Manhattan Project, right? Had a role in building the A-bomb?"

"Right, sort of," Pauling said. She sat back in her chair and studied Tallon. "Let me give you what I know. It's not everything, but for our purposes, it will do. Sandia National Laboratories was developed a little after Los Alamos. Los Alamos – where they built the bomb, needed a place to build non-nuclear materials that supported their efforts. It was decided to keep them separate. Thus, Sandia was born. Eventually, they became involved in nuclear operations, too, all in support of Los Alamos."

"So you're telling me Sandia has a fake address? And a camera? The goons are from the government?" Tallon asked. He drained the rest of his coffee, glanced at Pauling. She didn't want anymore, anyway. She was pumped. This was progress.

Pauling shook her head. "No. Sandia is not bush-league. The gas station, the guys you dealt with, all scream locals. Someone locally planted that address. Sandia has probably never heard of Rio Grande Trucking. This whole Rick Simmons angle was probably a surprise to them, too. They're a major military player. Which is probably how Jack Reacher is mixed up in all of this."

"Yeah, what's the deal with Reacher?" Tallon asked. "What's his story, anyway? Where is he?"

"I keep wondering that, too," Pauling said. "At least now I know why he was involved. This is exactly the kind of thing he would get mixed up in. But, for now, we've got to move forward assuming that Rick Simmons was driving for Sandia. And he was killed. And whoever killed him, wanted Cassady for something."

"For what, though? That's the big question," Tallon said. "It's not like Cassady Simmons is walking around with nuclear codes or something."

"No, that isn't the big question," Pauling answered.

"What is?"

She sighed. "Where in the hell is Rick Simmons' truck?"

CHAPTER FORTY-SEVEN

"So this Rick Simmons is dead?" Ostertag asked.

"That's correct," Hess said. "Shot in the desert. And buried. Although they were thorough in killing him, they weren't so fastidious in the burial process. A coyote dug him up, and then a plane spotted the body in the desert."

"What about the truck?"

"Well, that's where it gets interesting. How much do you know about the trucks used to deploy nuclear materials?"

Ostertag glanced around the room. No one volunteered to admit their lack of knowledge. "I know a little bit. There are a couple of factories that make the bombs, and then they have to be delivered. Usually to air force bases. I'd heard the trucks had armed guards and such. Was that not the case?"

Hess smiled at him. "Very good. However, these trucks usually have a lot more security measures than armed guards. Typically, there's an additional armed guard in the cab with the driver, who is also armed. There's usually a tail vehicle. If it's a really big delivery, there might be a lead car as well. But that's not all. The truck itself, even though it looks pretty much like your average tractor trailer, is loaded with electronic gear. Satellite-based GPS devices. Remote access driver controls."

"Then how the hell...?" one of the agents asked.

"Additionally, there are small explosive charges placed at the wheels," Hess said. "Should the driver determine it necessary, he can literally blow the wheels off the trailer, rendering it completely immobile."

"What about the tracking devices then?" Ostertag said. "If it was designed to avoid all of this, we should know exactly where it is."

"The internal security team at Sandia doesn't know what happened, either. But they're cooperating," Hess said. "They called us in."

"Local police?" an agent said.

"Cooperating as well," Hess said. "We already knew Rick Simmons was missing, so as soon as they got the call, we intervened. No problems there. They know all about Sandia and Los Alamos. They know where their bread is buttered. No territorial pissing matches here. The only issue is a lack of evidence. No one's got anything so far."

"So what are we doing now?" Ostertag asked.

"We've got to pursue this thing 24/7. Rick Simmons had a wife, Cassady Simmons, who somehow managed to hire a private investigator before we got involved. I need someone to handle that situation," Hess said. "Ostertag, you and your team also need to work the local angles. Everyone here knows someone involved with military industries north and west of here. It's not so much a question of who would have taken the material. It's more, who would have the intelligence and the capability to even deal with it. This isn't a bunch of M-13 gangbangers we're dealing with. There has to be at least a baseline of knowledge to understand what they're dealing with. See what you can find out."

"I'm still having trouble understanding how a

semi-truck full of nuclear material could simply vanish," Ostertag said.

It was the obvious question, and Hess hesitated to speculate, but providing a good answer would help the team focus.

"Most likely, there was cooperation from the team. Maybe the driver. Maybe additional folks. Essentially, carjacking a nuclear truck is impossible. It could have only been done with someone helping from the inside. The question is, why? What was their motivation to steal a truck full of nukes?" she said.

One of the more junior agents at the table cleared his throat.

"I'm sure there are other people here wondering the same thing. But I have to ask, just so I know what kind of threat we're talking about." He glanced down at the notepad in front of him, as if he was afraid to ask the question while making direct eye contact with Hess.

"So what kind of payload did Simmons have in his truck?"

Ostertag nearly winced at the directness of the question.

He looked around at his team, who were also suddenly studying the notepads in front of them.

Finally, he glanced at Hess.

She shrugged her shoulders and answered with a tone that was casually informative.

"Enough to wipe out most of California."

CHAPTER FORTY-EIGHT

"I knew a military guy who drove a nuke truck. He was a bad ass. Told me all about the vehicle," Tallon said.

He and Pauling were parked a half mile from the entrance to Sandia Labs. It was the closest they could get, a mega gas station barely in sight of the entrance to the complex. They'd had to buy waters and snacks to justify staying in the parking lot. Before long, they would be noticed.

"Yep. I did some research on those suckers. It's like Fort Knox on wheels," Pauling said. "They look like civilian vehicles, but they're 100% military grade. Total defensive measures, including the axles being wired with explosives to blow the wheels off so no one can drive off with it."

"Didn't work, apparently," Tallon said.

"Rick Simmons wasn't ex-military, though," Pauling pointed out. "Or at least he told his wife he wasn't. Maybe he was lying and he did some time in the Army. Maybe that's how Reacher was involved," Pauling said.

"Could be," Tallon admitted. "How many drivers does Sandia have?"

"I don't know," Pauling said. "Probably not that many. But Sandia is just one operator within the whole nuclear program. There are probably a dozen fleets of trucks, driving all over the United States with nuclear material. From factories to military bases, to nuclear waste sites."

"That's my point then," Tallon said. "Multiple trucking operators. Multiple sites, right? A fleet of hundreds of trucks? That means there are hundreds of drivers and assorted personnel. It's not like Rick Simmons was the only one in charge of one of these rigs."

"No, I'm sure you're right. Lots of drivers. Lots of guards. Lots of support personnel. Could you imagine the risks involved?" Pauling asked. "What if one of these was driving through an ice storm and slid off the road?"

"They must have all kinds of emergency procedures in place."

"And they've probably planned for a scenario where someone tries to steal a truck. It would be a terrorist's wet dream," she said, looking at Tallon. "Why were you estimating the number of drivers?"

"Well, in addition to the question of where his truck is, I can't stop thinking about something else. Why Rick Simmons?"

"Nothing has jumped out at us," Pauling said.

"Usually you find some kind of weak link," Tallon said. "Drug addiction. Alcohol. Gambling. Prostitution. Affairs. We didn't find out anything about the guy. Other than the fact that he's got a pregnant wife who loves him very much."

Pauling was about to answer when a semi-truck pulled out of the side gate of the Sandia complex.

A white pickup truck was in front of it.

A plain sedan was behind it.

"So they have their security caravan in place," Tallon said. "I wonder if Rick Simmons had one? And if he did, how in the hell did they get the truck from him?"

"Or, how did they get him to cooperate? Give them the truck and what? Send him on his way?"

They were in Pauling's car, but Tallon was driving and he waited until the convoy was on the road and then he put the Impala in gear and followed.

He was good at being subtle in his approach to the truck.

But apparently, not subtle enough.

Not more than two miles into the pursuit, a siren erupted behind them, and Tallon was forced to pull off the road.

A plain sedan was behind them.

A man in a suit and tie walked up to the car. Tallon watched him, making sure his hands were out in the open. He rolled down the window.

"FBI," the man said and he showed Tallon his ID, which was legit.

The FBI man slid into the backseat of Pauling's car.

"Thanks for the ID, but I know a Feebie when I see one," Pauling said.

"Lauren Pauling," the man said. "Good to meet you. I'm Ray Ostertag. SAC of Albuquerque. Officially asking you to stand down. We are on the case."

"What case would that be?" Pauling asked.

"The same case you came out here for. Cassady Simmons. Her murdered husband."

"Let's not forget his missing truck," Tallon chimed in.

"I'm not going to ask again," Ostertag said. "We've got a lot of eyes on this thing."

"I can imagine," Pauling said. "It really wouldn't hurt, though, to have some extra intelligence to keep the bosses in Washington happy. We can help you out. Free of charge."

"No, absolutely not," Ostertag said. "Appreciate the offer, but we've got this. Rick Simmons is our problem now."

"Well, if you change your mind," Pauling said. She had her business card in hand and offered it to Ostertag.

He ignored it, opened the back door and got out, then stuck his head back in before closing the door.

"I won't ask again," he said and slammed the door shut.

CHAPTER FORTY-NINE

"I have an idea," Pauling said.

"Let's hear it."

"The idea starts with a question."

"Shoot."

"If Rick Simmons had a truckload of nuclear material someone killed him for, why, after they killed Rick and apparently stole his truck, would they then go after Cassady? Didn't they already have what they wanted?"

Tallon played along. "Maybe she knew something. She could have blown the whistle on them. Sure, they already had what they wanted, but maybe they wanted to make sure they could get away with it, too."

"Maybe," Pauling said.

"But you don't think so?"

"Could be. Or not. My idea is, since we've been warned off of pursuing Rick Simmons, why not turn our attention back to Cassady?"

"Because we just stashed her hundreds of miles away," Tallon said. "If you recall, I personally drove her to the Phoenix airport and put her on a plane to Chicago."

"I'm not talking about questioning her again," Pauling said. "We tried that and got nowhere. That well has run dry. She can't *tell* us anything more. So we'll have to learn what we can without her now. But I also wonder if we were asking the wrong questions."

"What do you mean?"

"Well, we were looking at reasons why someone would want to kidnap Rick. But we never asked about her. Specifically, would someone use Rick to get to Cassady?"

Tallon nodded. "Yeah, I never really looked at it that way. It was either Rick. Or Rick and Cassady. Never just Cassady."

Pauling felt a surge of excitement. Intuition. Something felt right about this. Like when a puzzle couldn't be solved, realizing it wasn't the puzzle itself, but one's approach that was all wrong.

"Where did you say she worked?" Tallon asked.

"Industrial Supply & Wholesale. Why?"

"Honestly, there was nothing to Cassady personally," he said. "No family in the area. Pregnant. And if she was faking all of that drama over her missing husband, she deserves an Academy Award. Hell, the one for Lifetime Achievement, because she played that role to the hilt."

"Look, we're five minutes from her employer," Pauling said. "I know exactly where it is because that's where I met her the first time. Let's see what we can find out in person, and then we'll go from there."

Pauling directed Tallon and as they drove, Tallon said, "Plus what's great about this approach is we're not disobeying that FBI guy's orders. He told us not to pursue the Rick Simmons angle. See?" he said. "We're the epitome of well-behaved citizens."

"Sounds good to me," Pauling said, as they arrived at the building from which Cassady Simmons had emerged just days before. To Pauling, it seemed like a long time ago.

They went inside and told the woman at the front desk they were looking for some information regarding one of their employees. The receptionist asked them to wait. Fifteen minutes later, a woman appeared.

She was overweight, with red hair that had been put back into a bun but had now started to fray.

“I’m Debbie Macomb, Head of Human Resources here at ISW,” she said. “I understand you have some questions about an employee. You must understand that any information of that nature is private.”

Pauling got the impression the woman was off-script and not happy about it. She guessed Human Resources personnel weren’t asked to improvise very often.

“Yes, I understand that, but this is a very important matter,” Pauling said. She handed the woman her business card, where FBI was featured prominently.

Debbie Macomb seemed to consider it and then she said, “There’s a small conference room down the hall, let’s talk in there.”

She led them to the room which featured a small round table, four chairs, and a plant in the corner. Its leaves were drooping and covered in dust.

“I can only provide information to you that is already public. Nothing that is confidential to the company. With that in mind, please go ahead and ask your questions. I'll do my best to be helpful."

"OK, we appreciate that," Pauling said. "I guess for starters, what does ISW do?"

"We supply a variety of products and services to the healthcare industry."

"Is this the only office or do you have other locations?"

"This is headquarters and the only office," Macomb said.

"How many employees?"

"A little over two hundred as of the start of the year."

Pauling was trying to keep a rhythm to the interview. Keeping the questions easy to answer and hopefully let the woman relax.

"Are you an independent company?"

"Yes."

"Owned by an individual? Or a holding company?"

"Our parent company is called Vanguard Holdings. This is all public information. And as much as I want to help, I have a meeting in five minutes. Is there anything else I can do for you?"

"Well, I'm not sure if you're aware of this but there's been a tragedy. I'm not at liberty to go into the details," Pauling said. "However, if there's anything you could do to help me understand more about Cassady Simmons and her time here, that would be great."

Debbie stood up.

"I'm afraid I have another meeting scheduled, and that is definitely not information I can provide. Sorry. I wish you luck in your efforts. Now, I'm afraid I'll have to escort you out of the building.

She didn't wait for a reply, and ushered them first from the conference room and then out the front door.

Pauling looked at Tallon.

"Was it just me or did she become anxious once the name Vanguard Holdings came up?"

"Definitely," he answered. "Right after it was mentioned, she suddenly had an urgent meeting."

Pauling started walking back toward the Impala.

"Let's see what we can find out about Vanguard Holdings."

CHAPTER FIFTY

Vance Walker loved globes. He loved looking at the world, miniaturized.

He didn't know why. At one point, he'd amassed a fairly large collection of expensive, antique globes.

And then he'd set them all on fire as he watched with a dry martini in hand.

There was only one he spared. A miniature that sat on his desk. Nothing valuable about it. He'd just liked having it on his desk.

Now, he watched it.

Imagined it with a population reduced by 99 percent.

The thought electrified him.

His cell phone rang and he looked at the screen, and then answered.

"Yes," he said.

The voice on the other end of the line spoke for some time. The person described the current situation and provided a best guess on the timing of certain logistical realities.

"I see," Walker said.

They spoke for several more minutes, and discussed an area near the western border before disconnecting.

Walker got to his feet.

Many, many years had brought him to this point in time and he wouldn't have done it any other way. It was his vision that had created a new reality. Changing the world required that sort of single-mindedness, guided by proprietary knowledge. No one else had it and even if they did, they wouldn't know what to do with it.

Now, he went to a hook next to the door to his private office and removed the shoulder holster equipped with a .45 semiautomatic handgun. He shrugged on the rig, and followed that with a light camouflage jacket.

He stepped outside and listened. There was the hum of machinery, a few voices in the machine shop, and his armed guards near the entrance.

Walker found his second-in-command. A

former Marine who'd lost a leg in Iraq and added a heroin addiction once he'd come back home.

He was clean now, and owed it all to Walker.

"Spread the word," Walker told him. "We're moving out in one hour. Make sure everyone follows the proper procedure. No mistakes."

With that done, Walker went down to the truck. It held everything he needed to begin what he considered to be his very own genesis. A fresh start. A chance to guide humankind back to the path from which it had deviated so long ago.

For the first time in his life, he could imagine a scenario in which human beings achieved their full potential.

Walker reached the oversized hangar door and breathed deeply. The scent of oil, gasoline and cigarette smoke filled the air.

Along with an excitement that hummed with more power than the multiple generators running in unison.

It was time, Walker thought.

His time.

CHAPTER FIFTY-ONE

Tallon again drove, as Pauling worked her iPad and phone.

"Okay, Vanguard Holdings," she said, reading aloud. "Headquarters are listed as Las Vegas, for obvious tax reasons, I'm guessing."

"And just think of how much more fun their holiday parties would be in Vegas, than here."

"Hmm, interesting," Pauling said. "Very difficult to find a publicly listed board of directors or executive leadership."

"Red flag," Tallon said.

Pauling picked up her phone. "I try not to use this source very much, but this calls for it."

She dialed a number and spoke briefly to someone on the other end of the line. She waited. While doing so, she tapped away at the iPad.

"Yeah," she said into the phone, after several minutes of waiting.

"Vance Walker," she said, turning to Tallon. "Okay, thanks. I owe you a drink when you're in New York." Pauling laughed and disconnected from the call.

"I didn't know you buy drinks when people do you favors," Tallon said. "I would have exploited that a long time ago."

"Federal tax records show a man named Vance Walker is the owner of Vanguard Holdings," Pauling said. "Looks like he's a very wealthy man."

She was reading an article about Walker from several years ago. "Very wealthy."

Tallon tapped his fingers on the steering wheel. "Sure, those medical inventors make millions, as long as they hold the original patent, right? Every time someone uses their widget, they get a cut. It can add up, especially considering what hospitals charge nowadays."

"The question is, what, if anything, a medical company might have to do with a truck driver hauling around nuclear materials," Pauling wondered.

"Do hospitals use nuclear stuff? For tests or something?"

"Not that I know of. Maybe X-rays."

"So the question is, we know Cassady and Rick were both targets of abduction."

"Rick first, Cassady second."

"But what if it was the other way around?" Tallon asked. "Sandia information is highly classified, right? So how was Rick Simmons found in the first place? What if they located him through his wife? What if she filled out the paperwork at Industrial Supplies and put down Rick Simmons and then listed his current employer as Rio Grande trucking?"

"That would mean that someone knew Rio Grande Trucking was actually Sandia."

They drove, and Tallon realized he was heading back toward Pauling's hotel.

"Holy shit," Pauling said as she continued to read on her iPad.

"What?"

"I found an old medical journal where Walker said he was developing a new method for treating exposure."

"Exposure to what?" Tallon asked.

Pauling looked at him.

"Nuclear radiation."

CHAPTER FIFTY-TWO

Pauling's phone buzzed a block from her hotel. She glanced at it and then spoke to Tallon.

"Ok. My contact just sent me the address for Vanguard Holdings. It's west of here. Just beyond the abandoned gas station, not far from where Rick Simmons' body was found," she said.

"Let's go," Tallon said.

He turned the car and pointed it west.

"Why am I not surprised at its location?" Tallon said. "It always seemed odd that Rick's body and the gas station were in the same rough vicinity."

"Now we know why," Pauling agreed.

It took them less than fifteen minutes to get

there, but when they approached the entrance, several squad cars had the road blocked.

"Well, that's not a good sign," Tallon said.

"Someone else may have beaten us to the punch."

An unmarked sedan was there, too. Either undercover cop, or FBI, Pauling thought.

"No way to get around them," Tallon said. "I'm going to pull over and see if someone notices we're here."

He drove onto the shoulder and before he was able to put the Impala into Park, one of the plain sedan's car doors opened.

"Feebie alert," Pauling said as she and Tallon watched the car.

"It's that Ostertag," Tallon said.

Along with him, Pauling saw a woman. Tall, with the build of a former athlete.

"She's FBI, too. But not local."

Ostertag waved them out of the car.

Pauling approached them first.

"Pauling, I thought I told you to stay away from this case," Ostertag said.

"I have been," she said. "We were just getting some things from Cassady's office and they told us she might have something out at her company's holding company. That's why we're here."

"What a load of bullshit," Ostertag said.

"It's the truth," Tallon said. "Odd we should bump into you out here. What's going on?"

"And is this your boss?" Pauling asked, lifting her chin toward the woman.

"This is Agent Hess," Ostertag said. "By the way, they have your friend Cassady. Stashing her in Chicago didn't work out very well."

He wasn't being smug, but the criticism still stung Pauling.

She was about to answer when the sound of a chopper roaring in from the south interrupted her.

Sand kicked up around them.

"Let's go," Hess said. She looked at Tallon and Pauling. "You're coming, too."

CHAPTER FIFTY-THREE

"There's no way they have Cassady," Pauling said after she'd put on her headset.

"Nice job protecting your client," Hess answered, her voice dripping with sarcasm.

They were airborne and roaring to the west. Pauling wondered why they'd been brought aboard. Definitely against standard FBI procedure. But she wasn't going to point that out to anyone.

It looked like she was finally going to get to the bottom of who had killed Rick Simmons. And she couldn't help but wonder if a rendezvous with Jack Reacher was in her immediate future.

"You're in way over your head," Ostertag said. "You two have no idea what you're dealing with.

You really should have listened to my advice and gotten out of Dodge."

"What do you mean we're in over our heads?" Pauling asked. "We found out about Vance Walker. We know he used information from Cassady's personnel record to discover her husband was a driver for Sandia. He must have killed Rick in order to get his hands on some nuclear material. That's what he's all about, right?"

Ostertag glanced around from the seat in front of Pauling. "I'm impressed," he said. "You had part of it."

"They don't need to know anything else," Hess said. "They're here just so we can keep an eye on them."

"Bullshit," Tallon said. "We're in it this far. You might as well use us."

"Use you for what?" Hess said. "You've got an overblown sense of self-importance. Just shut up and enjoy the ride."

"I don't think so," Pauling said. "How's this? Vance Walker is an inventor," she said. "What if he developed a treatment for radiation exposure. In other words, in a nuclear blast, cockroaches and Walker's patients would survive. Maybe he even injected Cassady with his secret formula. How's that, Agent Hess? Am I close?"

Hess turned around and looked at her. "Not bad," she said. "But again, that's only part of it."

"So arrest him," Tallon said. "You keep talking like you're one step ahead of everyone, but it sure doesn't look like it."

"We were planning to," Hess said. "We had our eye on him but he proved to be a little more industrious than we realized. Turns out he'd built that underground complex back there and was doing all kinds of stuff. And then he whacked Rick Simmons and stole a truck full of nuclear material."

"Why? Did he run out of the stuff for his medical experiments?" Tallon asked.

Ostertag and Hess didn't answer.

Pauling suddenly knew why.

"Holy shit, he's going to set it off somewhere as a huge medical experiment, isn't he?" Pauling asked.

"Not quite," Hess said. "It seems Mr. Walker went from an interest in medicine to genetics."

"Like what? Starting a new race?"

"He may have a bizarre plan to set off a nuclear war and that way, only he and the people he's vaccinated will survive," Hess said. "He'll own everything, once everyone dies from the fallout. He'll be the king of the world. Or, at least, what's left of it."

"That's crazy," Tallon said. "Where is this bomb of his?"

"We think he's heading for Los Angeles," Ostertag said.

"Does he really think a nuclear bomb in L.A. will start World War III?" Pauling asked. "No one's going to believe that."

"Doesn't matter," Hess said. "He believes it will. And now we've got to deal with it."

"We've got an FBI SWAT team en route to where we're hoping to cut off the truck," Ostertag said.

"Let's get this party started," Hess said.

CHAPTER FIFTY-FOUR

"There," Ostertag said.

A single Crown Vic was parked on the side of the freeway. Pauling estimated they were maybe a hundred or a hundred and fifty miles from Albuquerque. Which meant that Walker and his truck had gotten a couple hours head start on them. She was surprised they had come that close to their operational launch.

Pauling wasn't a big fan of coincidence.

Why had Walker pulled out just before they'd gotten there?

"It's about ten hours to Los Angeles from here," Ostertag said. "We're at the foot of the El Malpais Conservation Area. Nothing here. This is where we're going to stop the truck."

Hess had directed the chopper to fly far enough away from the freeway to avoid being seen by Walker and his convoy.

"Put her down!" Ostertag yelled to the pilot.

They landed and Pauling removed her headset. She followed Ostertag out of the chopper, with Tallon behind.

The chopper then took off and flew behind a line of mountains to the north. There was grit in Pauling's mouth and she spat it out. As the sound of the helicopter faded, it was met with silence.

Pauling wondered how everyone could be so sure of the truck's location if all of the GPS technology had been removed previously.

"Tell them what they need to do here," Hess said to Ostertag, gesturing toward Pauling and Tallon. "I'm going to call into the HazMat and SWAT teams and check on their status. They should be here within fifteen minutes."

Hess turned toward the Crown Vic and its driver, putting a cell phone to her ear.

Ostertag turned to Pauling and Tallon.

"You are to be witnesses only," he said. "You are not to engage in any–"

Suddenly, the front of his face exploded outward in a shower of blood and brain matter.

He folded to the ground and Pauling was reaching for her gun when she froze.

Hess stepped out from behind Ostertag's fallen body with her gun raised, a small curlicue of smoke rising from the muzzle, now pointed directly at Tallon and Pauling.

"He was right," she said. "You are only to be witnesses."

The driver of the vehicle got out of the plain sedan. Pauling felt like she'd seen him before. Maybe one of the thugs who had tried to grab Cassady at her house. The one who'd taken a shot at her.

Pauling watched as he went to the back of the car and popped the trunk.

He hoisted Cassady out of the rear of the vehicle, none too gently. Her hands were tied behind her back, a piece of duct tape was across her mouth, and her feet were duct taped together, too.

At least she's alive, Pauling thought.

"Getting rid of evidence, I see," Pauling said to Hess.

"Sure. Loose ends aren't a good thing in this kind of situation," Hess said. "It should have been taken care of much earlier but we weren't exactly working with the A-team."

An off-road vehicle emerged from behind one of the towering sandstone cliffs. It drove toward them and Pauling knew who was in it before the vehicle stopped.

A tall bald man emerged from the front passenger seat.

He walked with an exaggerated posture, and wore gold-rimmed aviator glasses with yellow tinted lenses.

Vance Walker, Pauling thought

He looked like a delusional cyborg. His body was lean and taut, and he moved with the easy grace of an athlete. It reminded Pauling of someone.

And then it hit her.

"Do we have a little father/daughter reunion going on here?" Pauling asked. "How touching."

"You're fairly perceptive," Hess said. "I'm kind of surprised you were such a failure at the FBI. That place is full of simpletons. You should have fit right in."

"Spoken like Daddy's little girl," Pauling said.

"The SWAT team was a nice touch," Tallon said. "You've thought of everything, except this plan will never work. Your old man's a crackpot and you're brainwashed."

"We have thought of everything," Walker said.

"And I consider the label crackpot to be a good one. We've got a truck full of goodies for the city of Los Angeles. They deserve it."

"How many millions are going to die because of your experiment?" Pauling asked. "Do you really think it's going to incite a war?"

Walker rolled his eyes.

"How many people will die?" Walker asked. "The answer to that question is whatever the number, it won't be nearly enough. Which is why this is only the opening salvo in the war to remake the world."

"And while you accomplished nothing at the FBI," Hess said to Pauling. "At least you're going to finally get the credit you deserve."

Pauling had a sudden, stunning revelation.

"You sent me the letter with Reacher's name on it, didn't you?" Pauling asked.

Hess smirked at her.

"You saw my file," Pauling continued. "You knew I had worked with Reacher previously. Why? Why did you lure me out here?"

"I needed someone to blame for all of these murders. And to generally fuck everything else up," Hess said. "You seemed perfectly qualified. A former FBI agent, a bit of a rogue. A private investigator. I knew if I brought you out here, I'd have another chess piece to play with. It worked perfectly."

"No one is going to believe you," Pauling said.

"Aw, were you hoping to roll around the hay some more with Reacher?" Hess asked.

Pauling felt her face burn.

Hess leaned forward and whispered to Pauling. "Yeah, that was in the file, too."

Walker stepped around Hess. The other man, the one who'd shot at Pauling in Cassady's house, had now walked up to them. He pushed Cassady toward them and leveled his gun at them.

"Ah, here we are," Walker said.

Pauling had heard a rumble in the distance and now the convoy arrived. A Crown Vic in front, followed by a semi-truck pulling an extra wide trailer behind it. On the trailer was a large metal shipping container.

Two men got out of the Crown Vic and walked toward them. One of them was very tall and Pauling remembered that Tallon had described one of his beating victims at the gas station as being of impressive height.

The tall man smirked at Tallon.

"Showtime," Walker said.

CHAPTER FIFTY-FIVE

Rollins and Petrie had dismissed the other members of the team. Now, they were on a live video link with an Air Force base whose location had not been fully disclosed.

The footage was grainy, but then again, it was being beamed from a UAV tens of thousands of feet above where Pauling and Tallon now stood.

"She's gone rogue," Petrie said. "Final confirmation."

The shit had hit the fan once Hess had been in Albuquerque. After her initial check-in, she had stopped providing any updates to the team. They'd been able to track her movements, but all communication had ceased. There hadn't been time to send in a second team.

All they had managed to do was confirm with Ostertag that Hess was leading the operation, but had stopped short of asking him to intervene and update them on her behalf. It would have raised too many red flags.

Now, they realized their mistake.

"How? Why?" Petrie asked.

"Oh, we'll get to the bottom of that," Rollins said. "But we've got to move on this now. And move fast."

He spoke into the headset.

"Agent down," he said. "Recommend we strike now. That truck cannot be allowed to go anywhere."

Rollins listened to his military counterpart on the other end of the line.

"Confirmed. Contents of vehicle must not be agitated," he said.

Petrie watched the figures on the screen. It looked like there was movement and he stifled the urge to shout an alarm.

"Roger that," Rollins said into his headset.

He turned to Petrie.

"Warn Pauling," he said. "She's got an incoming in about ten seconds."

CHAPTER FIFTY-SIX

Pauling felt the phone buzz in her pocket. They'd taken the guns but not her phone. And now, the three of them were separated from the main group. Walker and Hess had approached the big truck, while the man with the gun kept his distance from them.

Her phone buzzed again and she waited until the man with the gun wasn't looking at her.

She was able to glance at the screen.

There were only two words and the message had come from an area code she recognized as Washington, D.C.

The message was clear.

Drone. Incoming.

She glanced up at Tallon, who was watching

her. Pauling looked at the bluff where Walker had been hidden during Hess's ambush.

Pauling glanced back at Tallon and nodded.

She turned and began running for the bluff. Behind her, she knew Tallon would grab Cassady and follow.

Her feet dug into the sand and at any minute she expected a bullet in the back, between her shoulder blades.

She heard someone shout and Pauling glanced back over her shoulder.

Tallon was carrying Cassady like a sack of groceries, and running at an angle, cutting every five steps to throw off the aim of the man with the gun. Pauling pivoted and changed direction just as the shooter fired another round.

Sand kicked up in front of her.

Pauling hoped they wouldn't be too eager to pursue them. After all, the only thing in front of them was a vast stretch of sand. Dozens of square miles of nothing but parched desert.

There was another shot and more sand kicked up in front of Pauling.

"Quit shooting, just run them down, you moron," Pauling heard Walker yell.

An engine roared to life behind them, but the bluff was less than a hundred yards away. Tallon passed her, which pissed off Pauling. Even worse, she could have sworn she saw him smile as he raced past her. An impressive feat considering he was carrying a human being under his arm.

Behind them, Pauling heard the sound of an engine grow louder. Since the desert was flat, with no obstacles to maneuver around, the driver could easily catch them. But not before they made it to the bluff.

But just then, Pauling heard the sound of a second engine. This one had a tone that was much softer, much slower, and quite distant.

Instantly, she knew what it was.

She'd spent some time overseas, and had seen, and heard, her fair share of drones.

The sound was unmistakable.

It was reminiscent of a distant lawn mower.

The sound grew and then she saw Tallon disappear behind the bluff and she followed. There was a large rock outcropping and Tallon must have recognized the sound, too, because he threw Cassady behind the rock and waited for Pauling, who dove in on top of Cassady and then Tallon landed on top of her.

Just in time.

An explosion shook the ground and instantly falling dirt and rock rained down upon them.

Pauling could hear Cassady screaming underneath her.

The sound of the drone was gone.

And so was the sound of the car behind them.

Silence.

CHAPTER FIFTY-SEVEN

They got to their feet and Pauling freed Cassady from her restraints.

"Wait here," Pauling said. Cassady was a wreck, with tears smearing the reddish sand on her face. She slumped over and leaned against the base of a boulder. Pauling figured she couldn't even stand if she tried.

"It's going to be fine," Pauling told her. "I'll be right back. I promise."

She joined Tallon at the base of the bluff, and they both readied themselves to see what damage had been done.

"I'm impressed, Pauling," Tallon said to her. "Calling in a drone strike? You've got some pull, don't you?"

"I wish," she said. "I would have called it in a lot sooner."

They came out from behind the bluff and saw that the car pursuing them, and its driver, were gone.

In its place was a wrecked, burning shell of metal. The smell of burned flesh filled the air, along with acrid smoke and burning fuel.

Just beyond the wrecked car was a grisly collection of body parts, scattered like they'd been spilled from above.

Pauling spotted what was left of Hess. She'd been ripped in two. Carefully, Pauling approached, knelt down and used her fingers to extract Hess's gun from its holster.

Someone behind her yelled and Pauling turned just as Walker leapt from the ground, his face a bloody mask, and raised a gun, pointed at Tallon.

But Tallon was already moving. He simply stepped inside Walker's outstretched arm and punched him in the throat. He followed that with a terrific blow, an elbow to Walker's jaw that made a horrible popping sound and then Walker sank to the ground.

Tallon caught his arm and pulled the gun from his hand. Tallon checked the pistol and held it in front of him, looking off toward the shipping container still on the truck.

It was intact.

Pauling thought for a moment that Tallon was going to shoot Walker, but instead, he stepped back and turned to Pauling. "That was precise–"

Suddenly, a gunshot rang out and Tallon threw himself to the left, rolled and sprang to his feet, the gun held in front of him, his finger on the trigger.

Pauling looked and saw Cassady standing six feet away from Walker, whose bald head was now sporting a big hole from which blood was gushing. He sank to his knees, and then fell face-first in the sand.

Cassady had a gun in her hand, which she now looked at as if it was a foreign object someone had placed there.

Pauling figured she must have found it in the wrecked car. She'd probably gotten it from the driver, the man who'd held them briefly at gunpoint.

Pauling walked toward Cassady, who stared at the dead body of Walker.

Finally, Cassady spoke.

"That was for Rick," she said.

CHAPTER FIFTY-EIGHT

Tallon stood next to his vehicle. It was late, and he had given serious consideration to spending the night in Albuquerque and heading back home in the morning.

But he decided against it.

It had been a strange ride, and he was looking forward to getting back to "his" desert. The thought of running free and being lost in his own thoughts was highly motivating. He was anxious to get on the road.

He and Pauling had waited with Cassady for the Feds to arrive, as Pauling knew they would. It took about an hour of them waiting before it happened. Eventually, after some long hours being questioned, they were released.

Cassady had been taken to a local hospital and

was under care for some minor bumps and bruises. A distant aunt had agreed to come and help her get back on her feet.

And now, Tallon was just waiting for Pauling.

They had come back to her hotel and she had run in to get something for him. Now, she came back out and walked over to where he had parked.

"Pauling," Tallon said, "You sure know how to show a guy a good time."

"I appreciate that," she said. Tallon again marveled at her voice. That low, jazz-singer-the-next-morning rasp that was incredibly sexy. This was now another job where he'd worked with her and hadn't been able to make any progress romantically.

Well, maybe next time.

"But honestly, what did you think?" she asked. "That I would call you in for a divorce case? A cheating spouse?"

"No, I figured it would be good. Just didn't think it would be on this scale," he answered.

"Here," she said. She handed Tallon a check. He didn't even look at it.

"Until next time?" he asked.

"Sounds like a plan," she said. He leaned in, then, and kissed her. It was a hell of a kiss, the kind that made him wonder why he hadn't tried it sooner.

She must have read his mind because after, she said, "Well, I've got a flight to catch in two hours. Drive safely, Tallon."

He smiled at her. Those green eyes were something else. Next time, he'd be a little more bold.

"Later, Pauling," he said. "You know where to find me."

He drove away and saw her turn and walk back into her hotel.

That's a hell of a woman, he thought.

EPILOGUE

Two Days Later

New York welcomed her back with a mailbox stuffed with letters, an email folder full of messages, and an office in need of some fresh air.

Pauling was back on her regular schedule. She'd already worked out, gotten her coffee, and unlocked the office. She cracked a window and then attacked her mail with gusto.

She'd also put in a call to Cassady and spoken with the aunt as well as the doctor to make sure the young woman and her unborn baby were both doing fine. She would recover, and hopefully start putting her life back together.

Tallon had sent her a photo from the backyard of his house. It had been last evening, and there was a small fire in the fire pit, with a mountain range in the background framed by a beautiful orange glow from the setting sun.

It had been an invitation of sorts, and Pauling was giving it some serious consideration.

Once she was caught up with her various bills, purchase orders and invoices, she worked until her little red icon for unread email messages finally blinked off.

She was officially caught up.

With her desk clear, she brought out the folder with Reacher's name on it.

For a long time, she simply stared at it.

It was this cheap little folder that had started it all.

She'd definitely wanted to see Reacher again, but she wondered how much of that was leftover physical attraction. And curiosity.

Pauling considered that. It wasn't like she was a young twenty-something, looking for love. At this point, she had made some choices and was comfortable with the results.

But who really knew what was going to happen? What the future might bring?

It was like she had told Tallon, life was just full of surprises.

Maybe one of them would turn out to be Jack Reacher.

THE JACK REACHER CASES (BOOK TWO)

THE RIGHT MAN FOR REVENGE

A USA TODAY BESTSELLER

CLICK HERE TO BUY

FREE BOOKS AND MORE

Would you like a FREE book and the chance to win a FREE KINDLE?

Then sign up for the DAN AMES BOOK CLUB:

For special offers and new releases, sign up here

ABOUT THE AUTHOR

Dan Ames is an international bestselling author and winner of the Independent Book Award for Crime Fiction.

www.AuthorDanAmes.com
dan@authordanames.com

ALSO BY DAN AMES

THE JACK REACHER CASES

The JACK REACHER Cases #1 (A Hard Man To Forget)

The JACK REACHER Cases #2 (The Right Man For Revenge)

The JACK REACHER Cases #3 (A Man Made For Killing)

The JACK REACHER Cases #4 (The Last Man To Murder)

The JACK REACHER Cases #5 (The Man With No Mercy)

The JACK REACHER Cases #6 (A Man Out For Blood)

The JACK REACHER Cases #7 (A Man Beyond The Law)

The JACK REACHER Cases #8 (The Man Who Walks Away)

The JACK REACHER Cases (The Man Who Strikes Fear)

The JACK REACHER Cases (The Man Who Stands Tall)

The JACK REACHER Cases (The Man Who Works Alone)

The Jack Reacher Cases (A Man Built For Justice)

The JACK REACHER Cases #13 (A Man Born for Battle)

The JACK REACHER Cases #14 (The Perfect Man for Payback)

The JACK REACHER Cases #15 (The Man Whose Aim Is True)

The JACK REACHER Cases #16 (The Man Who Dies Here)

The JACK REACHER Cases #17 (The Man With Nothing To Lose)

The JACK REACHER Cases #18 (The Man Who Never Goes Back)

The JACK REACHER Cases #19 (The Man From The Shadows)

The JACK REACHER CASES #20 (The Man Behind The Gun)

JACK REACHER'S SPECIAL INVESTIGATORS

THE JOHN ROCKNE MYSTERIES

DEAD WOOD (John Rockne Mystery #1)

HARD ROCK (John Rockne Mystery #2)

COLD JADE (John Rockne Mystery #3)

LONG SHOT (John Rockne Mystery #4)

EASY PREY (John Rockne Mystery #5)

BODY BLOW (John Rockne Mystery #6)

THE WADE CARVER THRILLERS

MOLLY (Wade Carver Thriller #1)

SUGAR (Wade Carver Thriller #2)

ANGEL (Wade Carver Thriller #3)

THE WALLACE MACK THRILLERS

THE KILLING LEAGUE (Wallace Mack Thriller #1)

THE MURDER STORE (Wallace Mack Thriller #2)

FINDERS KILLERS (Wallace Mack Thriller #3)

THE MARY COOPER MYSTERIES

DEATH BY SARCASM (Mary Cooper Mystery #1)

MURDER WITH SARCASTIC INTENT (Mary Cooper Mystery #2)

GROSS SARCASTIC HOMICIDE (Mary Cooper Mystery #3)

THE CIRCUIT RIDER (WESTERNS)

THE CIRCUIT RIDER (Circuit Rider #1)

KILLER'S DRAW (Circuit Rider #2)

THE RAY MITCHELL THRILLERS

THE RECRUITER

KILLING THE RAT

HEAD SHOT

STANDALONE THRILLERS

KILLER GROOVE (Rockne & Cooper Mystery #1)

BEER MONEY (Burr Ashland Mystery #1)

TO FIND A MOUNTAIN (A WWII Thriller)

BOX SETS

GROSSE POINTE PULP

GROSSE POINTE PULP 2

TOTAL SARCASM

WALLACE MACK THRILLER COLLECTION

SHORT STORIES

THE GARBAGE COLLECTOR

BULLET RIVER

SCHOOL GIRL

HANGING CURVE

SCALE OF JUSTICE

THE RIGHT MAN FOR REVENGE

SET IN THE REACHER UNIVERSE
BY PERMISSION OF LEE CHILD

DAN AMES

USA TODAY BESTSELLING AUTHOR

PRAISE FOR DAN AMES

"Fast-paced, engaging, original."

— NEW YORK TIMES BESTSELLING AUTHOR THOMAS PERRY

"Ames is a sensation among readers who love fast-paced thrillers."

— MYSTERY TRIBUNE

"Cuts like a knife."

— SAVANNAH MORNING NEWS

"Furiously paced. Great action."

— NEW YORK TIMES BESTSELLING AUTHOR BEN LIEBERMAN

Published by Slogan Books, Inc., New York, NY.

FREE BOOKS AND MORE

Would you like a FREE book and the chance to win a FREE KINDLE?

Then sign up for the DAN AMES BOOK CLUB:

For special offers and new releases, sign up here

THE RIGHT MAN FOR REVENGE

The Jack Reacher Cases

by

Dan Ames

“The more laws, the less justice.”

-Cicero

CHAPTER ONE

The big man didn't hear the sound of the rifle being fired. He didn't have a sense that a bullet was hurtling toward him at thousands of feet per second. For him, it was a day like any other.

On the road, moving from one town to the next.

A vague destination in mind, maybe a cup of coffee and breakfast in a local diner, the soundtrack provided by the locals discussing politics or the high school sports team's victory or loss with the appropriate level of enthusiasm.

As the bullet bore down on him, the big man's mind reverted to the road ahead of him.

How different it was than the typical highway he was used to traversing. Instead of long, straight patches of sunbaked asphalt, this was a mountain road in the Pacific Northwest, well saturated with frequent rain. Towering evergreens flanked both sides of the road and prevented the sun from heating and drying the pavement.

The big man was running calculations in his mind, a comparison between distance traveled when elevation was a factor. It wasn't as easy as walking a long, flat stretch, but the big man was in excellent shape.

He shrugged his massive shoulders. He was at least 6'5" with a deep chest and narrow waist. Lean. Tough. He had on blue jeans. A shirt with a toothbrush in the pocket. Both looked like they were brand-new. His shoes were English.

His last thought was a statistical analysis of what the view ahead would look like when he topped the rise and the road curved back down toward a valley, most likely.

When the bullet hit the back of his head, it blew it apart with a velocity that drove his upper body forward.

The sound of the shot startled a trio of ravens who flocked to the sky.

The man folded at the waist and toppled forward. He landed on the side of the road amid hard-packed gravel and a few hardy weeds.

While his immense body was intact, most of his head was gone. Blood gushed from the stem of his neck, pooled, and ran down the slope of the embankment.

No human being heard the sound of the rifle, except for the shooter, who looked down from above at what was left of the target. Satisfied, the killer stood, retrieved the shell casing, and placed the rifle back in its case.

While the lonely road saw little traffic, eventually someone would see the body. The shooter planned to be well down the road before that happened.

Down on the embankment, the last of the big man's blood had finished spilling from his body.

Nothing moved and nothing happened until the next morning, when a car carrying a pair of hikers driving toward the trailhead slowed at the sight of a small group of turkey vultures gathered around the remains of a human being.

The hikers called the authorities and when the police arrived, they summoned a crime scene team and notified dispatch that initial observations pointed toward a homicide.

First responders instantly surmised the likelihood of a gunshot to the back of the victim's head, resulting in chunks of the man's unrecognizable face decorating the ground a few feet from the body.

At least, the pieces that hadn't been snatched up by the hungry birds.

The crime scene technicians were fast but thorough, and one of them soon managed to extract the contents of the dead man's pocket, which consisted of two items.

A toothbrush.

And an ATM card.

A slight rain had begun to fall, and it began to wash away some of the blood splatter covering the dirt and gravel.

The crime tech used a flashlight to read the name on the ATM card.

JACK REACHER.

CHAPTER TWO

The first time he felt the joy of killing, Archibald Sica was just eight years old. He was working on his uncle's farm an hour southeast of Guadalajara.

There was a well, with several long pieces of wood placed into the vertical shaft. The bottoms of the wood planks were buried in water. The tops of the planks were at the mouth of the well, which itself was raised and fashioned into a square out of cement. It was like a viewing area into the depth of the well.

It wasn't a deep well, just ten feet or so. The planks were twelve feet long, enabling a person to stand at the top of the well and use the plank to stir the bottom, or help retrieve something if it fell into the well.

And at the bottom of the well there was only a few feet of water. It was mostly used to collect rainwater.

And lizards.

In that part of the country, there were plenty of lizards. And they liked to sunbathe about halfway up the wood planks. When they got too hot, they would slide off, dip into the water, and then climb back out.

Sica's uncle enjoyed the lizards, and had insisted the planks be left in the well to allow the lizards easy travel up and down the well.

At eight years old, Sica was just a boy, and had a young boy's stamina for work. Which meant he took frequent breaks when he could manage to sneak away.

As he was doing now.

The boy was hot, sweaty and tired. They were in the midst of harvesting crops and his job was to tie bundles of marijuana and load them onto the back of a pickup truck. He couldn't stop sneezing and his eyes were bleary. Plus, his arms were itchy.

He was hungry.

And a little bit angry at having to do so much work.

So when he leaned over the edge of the well,

his forearms on the cement ledge, he studied the lizards. Some were bigger than others. Mostly green. A couple of them were a dark, mottled brown. There were slightly different tails. Some were long and straight, others were more upright, with a bit of a curl.

They stared ahead, surviving the heat just like everyone else.

Sica grabbed one of the planks and twisted it, then laughed as the lizards fell off into the water.

He was about to do the same to the others when he had an idea. He lifted the wood plank, which was very heavy for a boy his size, and raised the end from the water. He moved it over until its edge was directly above one of the fatter lizards with a curved tail.

And then Sica drove the plank downward.

The edge of the plank severed the lizard neatly in half. Blood squirted out onto the wood plank and the two halves of the lizard fell into the water.

Sica laughed.

Suddenly, he wasn't tired anymore.

He felt energized.

Happy.

He eyed the other lizards, nearly a half dozen on one of the other planks. He shuffled sideways, maintaining his grip on the plank. He raised it again and chopped downward six times, killing all of the lizards one after the other. They were either too tired, too lazy or too stupid to get out of the way. The boy marveled at how they could be so oblivious to their neighbors being slaughtered.

Where was their survival instinct?

Sica laughed again.

He repeated the action until every lizard in the well was chopped or smashed to death. The water had turned red, and chunks of lizard flesh floated to the surface.

The smell attracted flies who began to arrive at the top of the well.

Suddenly, the thrill of killing subsided for the boy and he realized what he had done. He dropped the plank and ran back to the field.

Later, word reached his uncle that the boy had murdered all of his pet lizards and Sica received a vicious beating.

But later, he thought it was worth it. The power. The pure joy of killing. Many years later he realized that scene at the well was a pivotal moment in his life. It helped him realize who he really was.

Now, some twenty-five years later, as he stared

across the room at the terrified young man, Sica thought again of the primal joy he'd experienced at the well.

He glanced over at the center of the basement room and the deep square hole cut in the middle of the floor. It, too, was about ten feet deep. But it was much wider to accommodate Sica's exotic pets.

Like his uncle, the young boy had developed a fondness for reptiles.

Specifically, alligators.

Now, he nodded his head and two of his lieutenants carried the boy by his arms to the edge of the opening. He cried and tried to scream, but the duct tape across his mouth held steady. His feet churned in the air. His body thrashed but he wasn't strong enough to break the grips of the much bigger men.

The boy was a thief.

And now, he would be an example.

Two other men brought the young woman to the edge of the opening. Her hands were bound, and her feet were hobbled together with two sets of handcuffs.

She tried to look away, but one of the men grabbed her by the jaw and twisted her face until she had to watch the boy in front of her.

Sica raised his hand and dragged an invisible blade across his own throat.

One of his men cut the throat of the boy and threw his body into the opening.

There was a splash, and then moments later, thrashing.

Sica listened, as did the other young men assembled for the viewing. They were part of the thief's crew.

The young woman vomited onto the floor and the men returned her to her seat against the concrete wall.

Tears streamed down her face and her chest heaved.

Sica wanted everyone in the room to learn from the display.

His hope was that the young woman would understand just how much trouble she was in.

And he wanted his crew to understand they had a choice.

They could be loyal.

Or they could be food.

CHAPTER THREE

Former FBI Agent Lauren Pauling held the gun steady.

She aimed for the heart.

But just for fun, she tilted the muzzle up and fired five rounds straight through the head. Without hesitation. And with deadly accuracy.

"Come on, Lauren," the voice next to her said.

Pauling took off her ear protection gear and thumbed the button to bring the paper target back to her.

It was a great grouping.

Five rounds neatly stitched into the forehead of the gun range's paper target bad guy.

Part of the requirement to hold a private investigator's license in New York was to stay up to date with firearms training and requirements.

Pauling loved to shoot. She spent frequent afternoons at the same indoor gun range just up the street from her apartment, and today, she'd invited a friend of hers, also a former agent, to the range.

Her friend's name was Haley Roberts and she now worked Internal Affairs for the NYPD.

"Head shots are for long distance," Haley said. "What were you trying to do, go all Hollywood on me?"

"I know," Pauling answered. "Sometimes, head shots are good therapy, though."

She ejected her spent shells and put the gun back into her case, which she slipped into her purse.

Roberts did the same and the two friends left the range.

They stepped out onto the busy street, where the sound of gunfire wouldn't be met with the same kind of casual indifference found at the gun range. At least, Pauling hoped not.

"Wine at my place?" Pauling asked.

"Nah, can't tonight," Roberts said. "Big meeting tomorrow with the chief about that thing."

Roberts was a tall black woman with an overbite and an athlete's body. Being a female and working Internal Affairs meant her popularity on the job was never very high.

But she was tough and strong. More importantly, she believed in what she was doing. Pauling admired her.

'That thing' was a department-wide bribe scandal that Roberts had managed to nip in the bud before it got out. Now, Pauling's friend was in charge of damage control and containment.

It was a big job and her friend was under a lot of pressure.

"Okay. Text me if you need any help," Pauling said as they parted.

It was a cool, late summer evening in New York and Pauling enjoyed the walk back to her apartment. The first touches of cold weather were just beginning to appear, and she made a mental note to take a look at her cold-weather wardrobe.

She made it back to her co-op near West 4th. The building was a renovated factory so her walls and ceiling were made of brick, at least two-feet thick. She opened her door and stepped inside. The apartment was light, bright and inviting. Even the smell, a vague sense of lavender, welcomed visitors.

Pauling set her keys on the kitchen counter

and stowed her gear in her bedroom closet before washing her hands and returning to the kitchen for a glass of wine.

She had leftover grilled salmon in the fridge but she wasn't terribly hungry. The living room was cozy with muted rugs, soft textures and dark woods. Pauling sank into a brown leather chair and debated about turning on the television, or filling the space with some soft jazz and just relaxing.

She ended up doing neither because her cell phone rang.

She fished it from her front pocket and looked at the number.

It wasn't one she recognized.

"Hello?" she said.

The voice on the other end was scratchy and gender-neutral.

It spoke in an even, measured cadence.

"Jack Reacher is dead."

CHAPTER FOUR

The shooter climbed higher along the face of the mountain. It was cold and a steady wind tore at the killer's pale face. Loose stones tumbled down the side of the hill and a hawk flew far overhead, hunting a field mouse.

With an easy confidence, the shooter made good time. Every step seemed to have a little extra bounce to it.

The shot had been a good one.

It occurred to the killer that not many people could have pulled it off. This thought process didn't stem from arrogance. Or a conceited ego.

It came from professionalism.

A cold knowledge that, like a machine, the mechanics behind another killing had meshed with robotic precision. Perfectly calibrated to factor in the wind. The drop in elevation. It hadn't been easy.

Back in the day, the shooter would have had a spotter who'd worked out a lot of the calculations.

Those days were long gone, though.

The sniper worked alone. And it was better that way. It was never good to depend on people, that's how mistakes were made. And in this business, the shooter knew, your first mistake was often your last.

The mountain leveled off and opened up into a deep meadow, filled with huge slabs of rock, long grass and a creek that ran through its middle. There were bear here, the shooter knew, and they tended not to like company.

There was no need to hurry. The body may or may not have been found yet, but that was now far away.

In this line of business it paid to train for endurance. Sometimes, like this one, the ability to exert oneself for extended periods of time was essential. But being in command physically was important for other reasons. A steady hand. Clarity of thought. The courage to kill.

The shooter continued on, weaving through a

dim trail that ran roughly to the main path nearly a quarter mile away. No trace was left behind.

That was certainty.

They could study bullet trajectory, try to pinpoint the shooter's location and search for forensic evidence.

But they would find none.

Oh, they would probably be able to figure out the location, maybe even point to some slight disturbances in the dirt or grass, but it wouldn't tell them any kind of story. Wouldn't give them the narrative they were looking for.

They weren't dealing with an amateur here.

Quite the opposite.

This wasn't the shooter's first mission.

That had been a long, long time ago. In a whole different part of the world.

The trail descended and the shooter branched off to his right, reconnected with the main path and soon found his vehicle.

It was the only one in the makeshift parking area.

After stowing the rifle and gear, the shooter checked the satellite phone.

No surprise there.

A message from the man paying the bills.

It was pretty clear.

This mission is not over.

CHAPTER FIVE

The dishonorable discharge prevented any kind of formal military recognition at Nate Figueroa's funeral. It was a simple ceremony, attended by a few people, on a cold, rainy day in Minnesota.

The thick sheet of gray reminded Michael Tallon of how lucky he was to live in the desert. The blue sky, present nearly every single day, was an affirmation of life.

Tallon had grown up in rural Indiana where basketball was everything. He'd been a natural athlete, but football was where he'd excelled. Although a competent student, he'd been bored with studies and classrooms, even though he was an avid reader outside of school. He'd been transfixed by stories of men in far off countries fighting, loving, and sometimes dying.

So he'd joined the military and never looked back.

Until now.

Figueroa had been his brother. Not by blood in the traditional sense, but by blood in the literal sense. They'd seen their share of battlefields, saved each other's lives multiple times, and returned back to their home country with plenty of scars, and enough money in the bank to allow them the freedom to pursue their life's passion.

For Tallon, it had been to continue what he had been doing but on a much smaller, much less dangerous scale.

For Figueroa, it had eventually been to fight his most epic battle ever. Against cancer.

It had been the briefest of battles. From initial diagnosis to the end in a matter of weeks.

Figueroa must not have seen it coming.

And when he did, it was too late.

Tallon hadn't even known his friend had been sick. The news hit him like a sucker punch.

Now, Tallon watched as Figueroa's family gathered after the funeral. A few with umbrellas, waiting for cars to arrive to carry them back to the house and celebrate what they knew about their son, brother and husband.

Tallon wouldn't be joining them.

He'd already offered his condolences.

Paid his respects.

Said his final goodbye to one of the finest brothers he'd ever known.

Tallon checked the sky again.

It was still a solid sheet of gray.

No sign at all that somewhere behind the wall of darkness was a sun, trying to break through, but failing.

Forced to simply bide its time.

CHAPTER SIX

Pauling sat on the couch in her living room, staring at the phone in her hand.

A voice had just told her Reacher was dead.

It was like being told the Earth was flat after all.

Impossible.

Jack Reacher dead?

Pauling felt a dull thud in the pit of her stomach. A void opened up within her and she was surprised by the reaction. It had been a fair amount of time since she'd seen Reacher, yet she thought of him often. Wondered where he was, what he was doing, if he was ever going to stop by and see her again. As always, it was a train of thought that always ended at the same place: not likely.

Reacher was a wanderer, a traveler, a rogue. It was a spirit and a frame of mind that naturally resisted constraint.

Some people were simply born for the open road. Reacher was one of them. Maybe the very personification of that innate wanderlust.

Now Pauling faced the possibility that he was gone.

Reacher dead?

"Who is this?" she said into the phone.

There was silence on the other end of the line.

On a most basic level, Pauling obviously knew that everyone dies. Some much sooner than others. Sometimes, death arrives as a surprise. Other times, it's the end to a long period of suffering.

No one is immune.

Yet the idea that Jack Reacher was dead just didn't sit well with Pauling. He seemed so immovable, like a cosmic force that just...*was*.

The most obvious questions came to Pauling's mind. How had he died?

An accident?

Illness?

The questions raced through her mind like bullets from a machine gun.

"Hello?" Pauling said into the phone, this time with an edge in her voice.

She listened.

Thought she heard someone shift slightly.

"The body's at a town called Pine Beach, on Whidbey Island, near Deception Pass," the voice on the other end of the line finally said.

Something about the voice triggered suspicion in Pauling. The voice was too perfect. Scratchy. Gender-neutral. A neat, even cadence.

It was mechanical.

As in, processed.

"Who the hell are you–"

Pauling knew she had little chance of getting her question across in time, and she was right.

The line made a popping sound and she was disconnected.

Pauling again looked at the phone in her hand. The number was blocked. She hit redial anyway but the call wouldn't go through.

She set the phone down in frustration and picked up her wine glass, got to her feet.

It was clearly a crank call. If Reacher was dead, she probably would have heard about it from someone in law enforcement. Her contacts or friends who knew she'd worked with Reacher before.

And if someone did call her, it wouldn't be done this way. Like some weird anonymous sex pervert.

And if it was a hoax, what was the point?

Did someone want to lure her to this town called Pine Beach? And was using the idea that Jack Reacher was dead to motivate her?

Or maybe she was convincing herself of a conspiracy because she didn't want to face a horrible prospect.

That Jack Reacher really was dead.

Pauling thought about her next move as she went into the kitchen and dumped the rest of her wine down the drain.

Sure, she could hop on a plane and be on her way.

But she was an investigator, first and foremost.

Occasionally, she had considered trying to track Reacher down. To see him again. But she never had, because she felt like she knew him well enough to understand that wasn't in his plans. She could have forced the issue, but there would have been no point.

Now, she had a reason to try to find him. A legitimate one, not born out of loneliness and, frankly, lust.

Hopefully, she would be able to find him.

Alive.

CHAPTER SEVEN

The shooter paid cash for an anonymous beige sedan and drove to northern California. It was better than flying. Easier than renting a car. The right dealership, the proper amount of financial persuasion, and a complete absence of paperwork.

It also meant that all of the shooter's gear could be used for the next job. Ordinarily, that wasn't the best way to go. Better to ditch a hot weapon from the last job, start fresh with the next one.

But time was tight.

Besides, the killer was used to traveling and rarely got hassled by cops. Just drive the proper speed limit, avoid doing anything stupid, and everything would be fine.

The fee for these two jobs was crazy money.

The kind that lets a professional in this particular industry take a couple of years off, or, properly invested, maybe even retire.

The shooter had no intention of doing that, however. Too much time off and rust sets in. The eyes don't stay as sharp. The reflexes start to slow.

In this business, that was how a person retired early, as in permanent retirement.

The rifle in the trunk was a factory model, paid for with cash and sans paperwork. The weapon was mostly factory with a few modifications. This made it not only cheaper, but almost impossible to trace. It was a well-known brand whose civilian models were very popular with deer hunters. Hundreds of thousands of the rifles were sold every year.

It was a fine weapon, with a smooth action, devastating power and perfect accuracy.

The shooter had just proven that on a lonely road on Whidbey Island.

It was a long day's drive but the shooter made it to his location, settled in and spent the night.

At the appropriate time the next day, it was time to fulfill the last part of the contract.

Now, the shooter sighted the target, adjusted for the very slight east-to-west breeze and waited.

It wasn't a difficult shot.

The shooter had made many, many more difficult ones under high duress. This was a soft target, no one shooting back. The only difficulty was evasion and escape.

But that wasn't a problem, either.

Civilian police forces weren't really designed to quickly identify and apprehend a long-distance shooter. Certainly not a professional one with a military background.

Overconfidence and arrogance were the twin engines on the flight to failure, however. A professional knew that. The wrong street cop showing up at just the wrong time could ruin everything.

So necessary precautions had been taken.

Always plan.

Always prepare.

Always be ready to walk away.

But today, there wouldn't be any walking away.

Especially for the target.

Everything was ready. The evacuation vehicle and route were in place, all designed to avoid any areas with security cameras. There would be no eyewitnesses.

And there would be very little evidence left at the scene. But the professional knew that on a microscopic level, there was always something that would remain.

But all precautions had been taken to make sure none of it could be traced back.

Now, nearly two thousand yards away, there was movement.

The shooter eased into position with steadied breathing and waited.

Fifteen seconds later, the trigger was pulled.

CHAPTER EIGHT

To do the necessary research, Pauling left her apartment, and crossed over to West 4th Street where her office building was just around the corner.

She climbed the narrow staircase to her second floor office suite. Pauling unlocked the door and went inside. There was a waiting room in the front and then a second room that housed her office, which consisted of a desk, a computer, two visitors' chairs and a low cabinet with drawers that doubled as file cabinets.

Everything was sleek, modern and upper tier corporate design. Not outlandishly expensive, but not cheap, either. Most of Pauling's clients were high-income types, and her office reflected that.

She fired up her computer, zipped through her

email and electronically filed anything outstanding.

And then she began to pursue Jack Reacher electronically.

There was really only one way, and she knew what it was.

Reacher carried an ATM card, a toothbrush, and a little bit of cash.

No way to trace a toothbrush or cash.

The ATM card, however, was another matter.

Pauling knew Reacher didn't spend much money on a daily basis. In fact, his biggest expenditures were coffee, and a change of clothes. The coffee he bought every day, the clothes, every few weeks or so.

Reacher lived easily and cheaply, always on the move.

Still, she figured he would need to replenish his cash occasionally, even though he hitched rides and stayed in cheap hotels.

Pauling estimated that if he lived frugally, he would still need to get cash at least once every few months, more or less depending on the level of his activity and where he was. If he was in a major city, it could be difficult to keep daily expenses down, as opposed to some small town in the middle of North Dakota where coffee and a huge breakfast came to a total of seven bucks or so.

It helped that Pauling had gotten to know Reacher on an intimate level, and even gotten a glimpse of his ATM card, so she knew which bank to sneak her way into. She hoped he hadn't changed banks for some reason. Pauling guessed he hadn't. Reacher was a guy who liked to keep things simple. If it wasn't broken, no need to fix it.

Armed with more knowledge than she usually had to work with, Pauling quickly slipped into the database of Reacher's bank. It was low-level hacking, essentially an open door left for Pauling by one of her former clients.

Pauling located Reacher's account with efficiency and noted his transactions. Small withdrawals, spread out sporadically every two to three months, ranging all across the country.

She noted with wry amusement, and maybe a touch of hurt feelings, that he had been near New York almost six months ago. But he hadn't reached out to contact her.

Oh well, she thought and continued to study the withdrawals.

Pauling let out a long breath.

His last withdrawal had been in Seattle.

Less than a week ago.

The mechanical voice on the phone had told her Reacher's body was near a town called Pine Beach, on Whidbey Island.

Pauling knew that Whidbey Island was in the Pacific Northwest, just north of Seattle, less than an hour by car.

For the first time, Pauling considered something that was difficult for her to even imagine.

Jack Reacher.

Dead.

CHAPTER NINE

Tallon pushed himself in the desert. It was his place of solace. His chair in front of a therapist. His temple.

The sun bore down on him with merciless intensity as he ran. The hills of Independence Springs were brown and barren to the naked eye. If one paused, life was abundant, it just didn't appear that way.

Tallon ran the long loop, a distance of nearly nineteen miles.

As with his body, his mind also ran free. And it turned to thoughts of Nate Figueroa. Tallon still couldn't believe his friend was gone. No warning. No word. Here one day, dead the next.

It happened before, of course. In his line of work, people died. Plain and simple. Some of them were men he knew slightly. Others, like Figueroa, were brothers-in-arms who'd fought, bled, and bonded on the battlefield.

It was never easy.

The experience always made Tallon take a step back and challenge his approach not only to work, but also to life.

The miles cruised by as Tallon's running rhythm comforted his thought process, made him feel like he could run forever. He'd made that mistake before, though. It was tempting to push on and add miles, but restraint in training was essential.

By the time he closed the loop and arrived at his predetermined stopping point, he was covered in sweat. His water was nearly gone and he walked the rest of the way back to his compound.

Tallon had carefully chosen the site that would come to be his home. It was a small ranch, or a casita, as the locals called it, roughly halfway between Los Angeles and Las Vegas. It wasn't visible from any main road or highway, and it afforded excellent protection.

The community was a modest size, but still big enough to provide anonymity, thanks to a fair percentage of the population being snowbirds who only flocked to the area during the winter months. Come April or May, they would lock up their homes or condos and head north.

Tallon lived at the place year-round. The hotter the better, in his opinion.

Building his casita had required a fair amount of time and a hefty budget, mostly because of the special requirements demanded by a man in his line of work.

There were multiple security cameras, some visible, some camouflaged. An elaborate security system with two backup generators. An underground armory, accessible only by a palm scanner.

There was a weightlifting room that occupied a space next to the garage and the landscaping had been chosen carefully.

Instead of arranging the plants to orchestrate a year-round bloom, Tallon's needs focused on preventing cover for an attacking force while also providing clear shooting lanes for someone inside the structure.

Tallon had also spared no expense on the communication system. There was a hardwired landline, buried. A wireless radio unit. Two satellite phones with multiple batteries and chargers. A hardwired communication system for cable and Internet, along with a satellite-based stream that could continue to feed the home information without power and if the physical cables were somehow severed.

The windows were bulletproof, the entry doors made of specific construction materials designed to withstand explosives and high-impact rounds.

It wasn't that Tallon had a large number of enemies. It was all about the high-level capabilities of people who could, in theory, seek to find Tallon for reasons counter to his health.

Now, before he entered the house, Tallon checked his security screens, and then used the facial recognition scanner to unlock the back door to the casita.

Inside, he took a long, hot shower before heading to the kitchen for an enormous glass of cold iced tea.

Tallon took the drink into his home office, and settled into a leather club chair that featured a laptop perched on a swivel desktop. As he sipped his tea, he perused the Internet, and checked his email.

Not much in the email folders, and even less on the news websites and military blogs he followed.

It wasn't until he was going to close his browser, that Tallon noticed his spam folder.

It had the number 1 in bold in parentheses.

There was a little line next to the parentheses that read 'empty now.'

Tallon brought his cursor over and was about to click on the 'empty now' but he didn't. His finger hovered there for a moment.

Many times, he would look back and wonder what would have happened, or what would not have happened, if he'd just emptied the spam folder without opening it.

But he didn't.

He clicked the folder and an email appeared in the main window.

It was from an address he had never seen before.

The subject line was empty.

The body of the email was simple.

They followed us. –F.

Tallon sat there, stunned.

F.

Figueroa?

CHAPTER TEN

The Senator from the great state of Oklahoma was Noah Raskins, the great grandson of a wildcatter and the spitting image of a riverboat gambler. He wore expensive striped suits, sported a thick moustache and had one of the largest and most valuable cowboy hat collections in the world.

He was in northern California for a conference with Oklahoma's Economic Development Council. It seemed someone had decided a vineyard in California might be an excellent investment for the state of Oklahoma. Wine was bigger than ever. All sorts of fancy wine subscription services were taking off, and some wine-drinking politician had a brilliant idea.

When he'd gotten the invite, Raskins had

smiled. He knew there would be no purchase of a California vineyard.

Not in a million years.

Raskins imagined the howling that would ensue if the purchase was made, once some enterprising journalist got ahold of it.

No, the state of Oklahoma would most definitely not be buying a vineyard in California.

However, the most important aspect of that for Raskins and the other men (no women allowed) had nothing to do with purchasing.

No, it had to do with research.

And for that, the state of Oklahoma would unequivocally pay.

The entire trip, lodgings, and per diem were all being footed by taxpayers.

The men assembled were going to have a great time, get drunk, and maybe see if there were any ladies available for some additional entertainment.

Raskins also had to smile because the vineyard was actually for sale. And it might even be purchased by some members of his group, but it would be handled privately, by a member or two of the council, with maybe a few silent partners, such as Raskins himself, through a private investment group with no public ties to anyone at the vineyard.

He almost laughed again. Research!

A bunch of good ol' boys sitting around a giant fireplace in some lodge in California, drinking wine and scotch, getting absolutely shit-faced. And it was all a taxpayer-funded boondoggle.

The spoils of victory, he thought to himself. All those years out pounding the flesh, making speeches, listening to "real" folk bitch about their problems. He'd put in his time, that was for certain.

The fact was, he hated real people. Oh, he had a great touch with the locals. They loved him.

But there was a reason they were "little" people. A lack of skills. A lack of intelligence. A lack of drive.

They were at their current station in life thanks to their own doing. He wasn't about to blame himself for being a cut above.

Way above, he corrected himself.

So what was wrong with a getaway to wine country?

Hell, half the senators in Washington hired hookers as "staff." Nothing like having Joe Taxpayer pony up the cash for your pussy. Now that was a little over the top, Raskins thought, even though he'd been guilty of the practice a time or two. Maybe three.

Now, as the tall Oklahoman stepped out onto the porch of the vineyard's lodge, he took a moment to soak in the fading California sun. It wasn't hot out here like in Oklahoma, he thought.

Not as humid, either.

In his home state, it didn't matter if you were in the sun or the shade, the heat and cloying dampness was the same.

Back home, he would be sweat–

A slight movement in the distance made Raskins pause. He had excellent eyesight. His pale blue eyes were notorious for being able to pick out distant mule deer on a hunt in the mountains.

So his train of thought was interrupted by something vague in the distance.

And then his mind was permanently interrupted by the bullet that crashed through the center of his forehead and blew apart most of his head.

Later, the mayor of a small town in Oklahoma who'd managed to get invited on the "business trip" to the vineyard, would remember Noah Raskin's cowboy hat. The mayor had been standing just inside the vineyard's lodge, watching Raskins stand on the porch like he owned the place.

He would tell the story for years to come, how Raskins' cowboy hat suddenly popped up into the air and hovered for the briefest moment, while the senator's brains were splattered all over the wooden floor.

No one heard the shot, they only saw its aftermath.

Senator Noah Raskins, dead on the porch of a vineyard in California.

Shot by a sniper.

His three thousand dollar cowboy hat?

Not a mark on it.

CHAPTER ELEVEN

Pine Beach. Deception Pass.

The names meant nothing to Pauling. She'd heard of Whidbey Island, only because she knew there was a military base there, and at some point she'd been in Seattle and someone had referenced the base.

But Pine Beach, the town where Reacher's body was found, was unfamiliar to her. Where it was in location to the military base, she had no idea.

Pauling sat in her office and contemplated the next move.

She certainly had no intention of hopping on a plane and flying across the country to find out this was all someone's idea of a sick joke.

Not when she had a cell phone and the

contact information for Pine Beach Police Department, Whidbey Island. It was on the screen of her laptop and she punched in the number.

After several rings, a male voice answered, sounding tired.

"Pine Beach PD," he said.

"My name is Lauren Pauling and I'm calling because I was notified that a body was found in or near your jurisdiction."

There was silence on the other end of the line.

"I was told the victim was identified as Jack Reacher," Pauling continued. "Can you confirm or deny this?"

"Uh, hold on," the voice said.

Pauling wasn't impressed so far with the Pine Beach, PD. But she reserved judgment. Maybe the guy was an intern.

There was an abrupt click on the line and Pauling was certain the operator had disconnected her, but then another voice spoke on the line.

"This is Chief Jardine," the voice said. "With whom am I speaking?"

The speaker was female, and Pauling could sense the annoyance in the woman's tone.

"Lauren Pauling."

A pause and Pauling heard the sound of pen on paper. Taking notes. Always a good idea. She was doing the same.

"You have some information for me?" Jardine asked. "Is that correct?"

Pauling almost smiled at the woman's attempt to put her on the defensive. "Not exactly. I received a call that a deceased person was found in your jurisdiction. ID'd as a man named Jack Reacher. I was calling to confirm."

There was a sigh on the other end of the line. "I'm afraid it doesn't work that way, Ms. Pauling," the chief said. "Are you family? Related to this man you mentioned?"

"Not exactly," Pauling admitted.

"Okay, well, even if parts of what you say may or may not be true, we would never give out any kind of information like that over the phone," Jardine said. "We do have some questions for you, though."

"I'm in New York, Chief Jardine," Pauling said. "I'm sure there's nothing I can tell you."

"Sure there is," the woman said, suddenly sounding cheerful. Almost like a chirp.

Pauling waited.

"For starters," Jardine said. "Who the hell is Jack Reacher?"

CHAPTER TWELVE

They followed us.

Tallon couldn't make sense of the message.

Who did?

He sat in front of his computer, the iced tea forgotten.

Behind him, the television was on, and the announcers were talking about the murder of Senator Noah Raskins of Oklahoma.

"I'll be damned," Tallon said. He'd never met Raskins, but he'd heard plenty of stories about him. A member of multiple committees on military issues, Raskins was known to most of the armed forces.

Not much was known.

It was clearly murder.

A gunshot from some distance.

A sniper? Tallon wondered. Now that would certainly ratchet up the intrigue.

From stories he'd heard, Tallon figured that if it was true Raskins was murdered it would either be from somebody he screwed in a shady business deal, or a woman he screwed on his desk in the Senate.

It was too early for any actual information and after about ten minutes the news coverage began to repeat itself, so Tallon shut off the television. He enjoyed the quiet more, anyway.

Besides, he wanted to wrestle some more with the email from Figueroa.

They followed us.

It made no sense.

Tallon and Figueroa had done a lot of work together. Both officially in the military, and unofficially for various employers.

They weren't mercenaries, per se. They had standards and never worked for anyone who was clearly on the wrong side of humanity.

But they had been very busy.

Their skills were always in high demand.

The thing was, it seemed impossible for Tallon to imagine anyone following them. They were nearly always strangers in a strange land.

Faceless. Nameless. Without a country. Without allegiances.

And had Figueroa actually sent the email?

He'd clearly been very sick. That was the thing with electronic communication like email, you didn't always know for sure who was on the other end.

He thought back to over a year ago, the last time he'd seen Figueroa.

It had been a bad mission, in a bad place, with some very bad people involved.

They followed us.

Tallon went into his kitchen, grabbed a beer and peered out into the dark desert landscape.

He thought about the missions he had shared with Figueroa. There were so many it was nearly impossible to count. They'd fought side-by-side in Africa, Indonesia, South America, Mexico and at various spots in Europe.

Most had been successful, others had resulted in an imperfect solution.

None of them had been abject failures.

The other thing that stuck in Tallon's mind was the idea that someone had followed them. Generally, the bad guys they targeted on missions weren't left alive. Harsh, he knew.

But dead men tend not to have the option of

following their killers around. Unless they're ghosts hoping to haunt guilty consciences.

Tallon didn't have a guilty conscience.

And he certainly didn't believe in ghosts.

One word repeated itself in his mind.

Impossible.

CHAPTER THIRTEEN

Back-to-back contracts were not the ideal way to work. Normally, there would be a need to take some time off, clear the head, get back in the zone. But this had been a special case. Or two special cases, as it were.

Although luck was never really involved in this line of work, the first project had been fortunate. Relatively easy, although there was hesitation to use that term when it came to the profession of killing human beings. The actual process might be simple, but the stakes were high, so it would never be considered easy.

But compared to other jobs, the first one had definitely been without complications. A lone man, walking near the forest. Multiple evacuation routes. Plenty of opportunity to scout the location, make sure no witnesses were present before, during or after. No security cameras.

Law enforcement nowhere nearby.

A good, clean kill.

The second one had been a doozy.

A much more populated kill zone. Plenty of witnesses. Several evacuation routes to choose from, however, most of them had a fair amount of traffic. Law enforcement was definitely present, along with the senator's private security detail.

It had been a huge planning process. It had required a trip to the winery, armed with the target's travel itinerary, and a thorough job of preliminary scouting. Then a return to the site of the second job to scout it, and execute the mission.

Afterward, it was back to the second project, and make the kill.

The intensity of the planning for both jobs, along with the added stress of the high-profile second target, had created fatigue.

But also an edge.

Whenever the job was finished, it always did the same thing.

Hole up in an expensive hotel, and book a high-priced escort from the most expensive service of its kind.

Quality was essential.

And worth the price.

Now, the blonde entered the hotel suite. He was young, but well-built, dressed in cotton shorts and a form-fitting short-sleeved shirt. Probably linen.

The shooter who had just assassinated a senator, smiled at the escort's reaction. He had probably been expecting an ugly, overweight business woman desperate for male companionship.

She must have been a surprise to him.

Small. Petite. Red hair and a slim, but rock-hard body.

He smiled at her.

She smiled back.

Walked toward him.

She had earned this prize.

And now, she was going to make sure he earned his money, too.

"Get on your knees," she said to him.

CHAPTER FOURTEEN

Lauren Pauling firmly believed in experiences over objects.

She was not the type to obsess over luxury vehicles, expensive jewelry (to a point) or engage in competitive real estate acquisition.

BSOs, a.k.a. bright shiny objects, tended not to hold much allure for her.

However, comfort was a different matter.

It had nothing to do with prestige, but when Pauling had worked for the FBI, travel was often highly unglamorous. Budget-friendly, as her coworkers liked to say. Cheap hotel rooms. Second-rate rental cars. Less than stellar restaurants due to a small government per diem.

So now, when Pauling traveled on business, it was her business. And she gladly paid for comfort.

Nearing fifty, Pauling was in great shape and stretched her legs, enjoying the extra room in first-class. An unopened bottled water sat on her tray table, and she toyed with the idea of ordering a Blood Mary, then decided against it.

Instead, she took out her laptop and fired up her browser.

Pine Beach was a small community on Whidbey Island, which sat in Puget Sound just north of Seattle. Pauling had been to Seattle many times, and had even driven north on I-5 into Vancouver, Canada. Beautiful, rugged country, she recalled. She'd never been on Whidbey Island, though.

Was it where Jack Reacher died?

Pauling shook the thought from her mind.

Too soon to jump to conclusions. She had to admit though, the remoteness and ruggedness of the place would have drawn Reacher to it. She could imagine him hitchhiking along the single highway that cut through the middle of Whidbey Island. Looking for a diner for a strong cup of black coffee. Maybe someone in trouble who needed help.

Reacher always looked out for the little guy.

It was one of the things about him that fascinated her. It just seemed like there weren't men like Reacher around anymore.

He was one of a kind.

While Reacher was more than happy to stick a thumb out for a ride, there would be no hitching rides for Pauling.

She would land in Seattle, get a rental car and make the drive. She checked her watch. By her estimation she would be in Pine Beach around dinnertime.

It would give her an opportunity to talk to Chief Jardine face-to-face, as the phone conversation hadn't been very effective.

Later, she would check into her hotel room and grab a bite to eat.

Pauling connected to her airline Wi-Fi account, for which she paid a premium. Her plan was to take a quick peek at the best restaurants in Pine Beach.

Instead, a breaking news article popped onto her screen.

Senator Noah Raskins had been assassinated.

Pauling looked at the photo of the man.

She knew him.

For a brief, fleeting moment, she remembered that he had been a prominent part of certain military committees and her mind connected it with the body of a man who may or may not be Jack Reacher.

Pauling saw in the story that the senator had been shot in California.

She subtly scolded herself. There was no way someone killed Jack Reacher in Washington and then shot a prominent senator the next day.

No way.

For starters, she had no idea if the body was Jack Reacher. And secondly, she had no idea if he'd been hit by a car, or stabbed, or fallen off a cliff.

So there was no reason to try to connect the two.

Pauling laughed at herself. What the hell? Was she becoming a conspiracy theorist?

She shut her laptop.

Maybe it was time to have that Bloody Mary after all.

CHAPTER FIFTEEN

It was no accident that the wealthiest city in Europe was home to a group of men and women who called themselves the Zurich Collective.

They had formed themselves decades ago and seen some changes throughout their existence. Members had come and gone, mostly due to death. It was rare for an individual to leave while healthy and even more uncommon for them to leave on their own volition.

Members joked the only way out was feet first.

While the organization had seen some changes, its current lineup was its most powerful, ever. Which was an impressive feat, given that past configurations had accomplished feats including altering the global economy, manipulating outcomes in world wars and overthrowing a dozen governments in countries spanning the globe.

The current group was neatly divided into two constituencies.

The first were the ultra wealthy. Titans of commerce, heads of multinational companies, independent sellers of black-market goods and services.

The second group wasn't quite as wealthy as the first, but were paid huge sums by various employers to protect mutual assets and business interests.

They shared a level playing field within the association, however.

Save for one.

Her name was Gunnella Bohm, and she was a towering figure both literally and figuratively. Standing 6'3" tall with broad shoulders, solid hips and a hawk nose, she ran the Zurich Collective with a precision that rivaled the region's world-renowned watchmakers.

Other than her legendary sexual appetite, Gunnella Bohm was known for her extraordinary wealth and passion for increasing that wealth at all costs. She consumed power like she consumed lovers; with great vigor and with a goal of wringing everything useful from her target before moving on.

Her wealth was both inherited and earned. Her father, a German industrialist, had been stripped of a great deal of his assets due to his sympathies for the Nazi party. However, he had been able to squirrel away nearly a quarter of his wealth by hiding it in various banks scattered throughout mostly South America.

When he died, as his only heir, Gunnella Bohm reassembled that small slice of the family pie and proceed to grow it with a shrewdness and ruthlessness that far surpassed her father's reputation for both.

She had also replaced his spot on the Zurich Collective and it soon became apparent to all that even among them, she was something special. Within ten years of joining the collective, she was made its presumptive head.

Now, she turned from the enormous window that looked out over Lake Zurich and faced the others in the room. They were seated along a long table made of tempered glass. The walls were white, the video screen at the end of the table was sheathed in chrome. Several glass pitchers of water were placed in intervals along the length of the table, but no one had bothered to accept a glass.

"That brings us to America," she said. "Gregory. Give us your situation report."

Heads turned toward a petite man sporting a silk suit and a delicate face. He had black hair just beginning to pepper with gray and he spoke with a highly articulated, high-pitched voice.

"Our objective was achieved with no negative consequences," he said. "I continue to monitor the situation, but as of now I anticipate no issues."

"Is the scale of the initial investigation what you expected?" Bohm pressed. Other heads along the table raised slightly at the follow-up question.

It was never a good sign.

"Of course," Gregory said. "When a senator is murdered, they pull out all the stops. But initial reports continue to indicate the lack of evidence. Investigators are stymied and I see no reason why that should change."

Gunnella Bohm studied Gregory's face.

She had spent a lifetime perfecting the art of interpreting facial and body mechanics. Something in Gregory's pursed lips made her wonder if he really did have everything under control.

Immediately, Gunnella Bohm made plans to safeguard the situation.

Any deviations from the plan in the United States would need to be dealt with quickly, and if needed, with violence.

It was the only way.

There was simply too much at stake.

CHAPTER SIXTEEN

"Shoot him," Figueroa looked at Tallon.

"No, please," the man seated on the ground said, with his hands cuffed behind his back. He was sweating, and his eyes were wide with fear. But both Tallon and Figueroa saw beyond the fear. They saw something else.

Resistance.

Arrogance.

Cunning.

The fear was real, Tallon knew. He just wasn't sure if their captive was afraid of them, or his boss.

Ferdinand Sica.

Gunfire chattered nearby and Tallon and Figueroa both swiveled, Tallon's gun still pointed at their captive's forehead.

"Where is he?" Tallon asked the man on the ground.

"Shoot him," Figueroa repeated. "He's not going to tell us."

An explosion rocked the ground beneath them, and over the tops of the trees ahead, a thick column of black smoke rose into the sky.

"He'll be on the chopper by now," the man said, shaking his head. And then he smiled. "You stupid gringos will never catch him."

Figueroa stepped back and cracked the man on top of the skull with the butt of his rifle. The man toppled over onto his side.

"Jackass," Figueroa said to the unconscious man.

Tallon cursed under his breath. He raced ahead, knowing the team was counting on them to cut Sica off before he could get to any form of transportation.

Tallon was fairly sure the man had been bluffing. They had done a thorough job of scouting and there was virtually no way Sica could have made it to the chopper already.

As he ran, he reconsidered their objective.

There were only six members of the squad assigned to this mission, and Tallon feared the amount of gunfire he'd heard was not good news. He also recognized the sounds for what they were. The team all had similar weapons, and much of the gunfire was not coming from them. Which meant their opposition was still alive and armed.

Not good.

Smoke filled the air, more gunfire erupted and another explosion sounded off behind the fortress. The sky, already overcast, now held clouds of smoke and Tallon's nostrils burned with the scent of fire and gasoline.

A chopper's engine whined above the din and Tallon increased his pace, running to the left of the compound's concrete wall.

He rounded the corner, Figueroa hot on his heels.

Tallon saw three armed men waving two small figures toward a chopper. One of Tallon's men was already down, and he couldn't see the others.

Tallon lifted his rifle and felt a hammer blow to his shoulder that spun him around and dropped him to the ground. He continued to roll, heard and felt the bullets tear up ground behind him.

Figueroa was down on one knee, firing at the chopper.

Tallon fired as well, saw the three armed men now down, and he poured his rounds into the chopper, watching the helicopter's glass dome shatter underneath the rounds, and the two smaller figures were down on the ground, as well.

Suddenly, there was silence.

A burning sensation tore at Tallon's shoulder but he

ignored it as he got to his feet and ran toward the chopper. Figueroa was behind him.

The figures on the ground were dead. Blood everywhere. Body parts still smoking.

Tallon went to the two smaller individuals who'd been running toward the chopper.

The first was their target, Ferdinand Sica. The biggest active narco trafficker in the world.

Now dead.

The second figure's face was covered.

Tallon brushed the black scarf aside.

Caught his breath.

A girl.

CHAPTER SEVENTEEN

Pauling had her choice of vehicles in the premium, members-only portion of the car rental lot. As a member of the loyalty program, there was no waiting at the check-out counter.

You went to the rental car lot, saw your name on a board, and were free to pick any vehicle in that area.

The keys were already inside.

Along with the paperwork.

Pauling made her way to the designated area where an Audi SUV caught her eye. All-wheel drive probably wasn't a bad idea out here, considering the mountains.

She threw her bag into the back seat, got

behind the wheel and exited the parking structure after showing her ID.

The Pacific Northwest's reputation for gray skies and clouds proved to be well-earned. There was a layer of gunmetal across the dark sky. The Seattle skyline faded into Pauling's rearview mirror as she headed north toward Whidbey Island.

After she threaded her way through the glut of traffic near the airport and then downtown, Pauling was free to let her mind wander as the roads opened up.

She hoped this was all a big misunderstanding, that the person they had in the morgue was not Jack Reacher.

One, she hated the thought that Reacher was gone. Somehow, she had always envisioned a scenario where she would see him again. Probably foolish, but maybe not. She was former FBI. He was a former Army investigator specializing in homicides. They had ended up working together on a criminal case.

It happened once.

It could happen again.

Pauling just wasn't ready to accept that Reacher was gone. The idea that he was out there somewhere, armed with nothing but an ATM card and toothbrush, gave her comfort. Injustice was everywhere. Every small town, big city, wherever people had to interact with other people, someone was probably getting taken advantage of. It was the way the world worked.

But for the lucky few being oppressed or victimized, Jack Reacher made things right.

Pauling struggled to stop her train of thought. Failing to keep an open mind, she was already convincing herself this was a fool's errand. A hoax.

She almost laughed at herself. Dropping everything, flying across the country based on very little information. On the bright side, maybe she could wrap this up in a couple of hours and not waste too much more time.

Pauling figured she could get to the bottom of the mystery, and then maybe zip down to Portland for a few days to visit her sister. It would be good to see her little nieces and nephews again. Maybe the little town of Pine Beach had some cute shops she could find a couple of toys for the kids. Wasn't it an aunt's job to spoil the kids?

Traffic was light as she pushed the Audi north, eventually swinging to the west and crossing onto Whidbey Island. The road was a narrow two-lane highway when she got to Deception Pass, a stunning bridge over a strait separating Whidbey Island from the next piece of land over. The water churned below, and steep cliffs opened out onto a wide expanse of water, bluffs and trees.

It was a sight, and Pauling felt a slight tinge of vertigo as she drove along the bridge, the feeling of emptiness beneath her.

The road wound through the rugged hills and eventually it flattened out and soon she was pulling into the town of Pine Beach.

It was on the water, naturally, and featured a main street that ran parallel to the widest part of the harbor. Evergreens surrounded the area and in the distance, a mountain range neatly framed the expansive view. On the water, a variety of boats, both pleasure and working, were either docked or in transit. Gulls flew overhead and the faint smell of fish filled the air.

Pauling had programmed in the police station's address and she found it at the end of town, set back from the water several blocks, set on a wide patch of land that was probably donated to the city. Not valuable in the least for anything commercial. Down the street from the police station were two other municipal buildings. One of them was a library, the other a small elementary school.

She pulled into a visitor parking spot, got out, and went inside.

It smelled like a library, a little bit musty, with an overlay of artificial evergreen scent, which amused Pauling. Why not just open a window?

A front desk, not separated from the lobby, sat facing the front door. No bulletproof glass here, Pauling noted. Not a lot of highly violent offenders coming in and out of the police station every day, she surmised.

Pauling stepped up to the desk, which was unmanned. She glanced around, wondering if she'd caught someone on a bathroom break.

"Can I help you?"

A uniformed officer glanced out from behind a filing cabinet.

"I'm here to see Chief Jardine. Lauren Pauling."

The face disappeared from view and Pauling heard the sound of a file drawer being rolled shut and moments later, a side door off the lobby opened.

"Follow me," the cop who'd been behind the filing cabinet said. He was young and his pants looked short, as if he'd just completed a growth spurt.

Pauling followed him down the hall and then

he pointed to an office with glass walls and an open door. The cop veered left, and Pauling stuck her head in the door.

"Chief Jardine?"

A woman with dark hair, cut short, glanced up from a computer.

"You're Pauling?"

"Yes."

Chief Jardine nodded. Pauling studied the woman's face. It was all sharp angles and the eyes were small but shone with an intensity that seemed out of place in the low-key atmosphere of the office.

Jardine straightened up in her chair, took a long, appraising glance at Pauling.

"What do you say we start with the body?"

CHAPTER EIGHTEEN

As much as he wanted to do it over the phone, Tallon knew that wasn't an option. He reversed the flight he'd made days ago, and headed back to Minnesota.

The streets and neighborhood of Figueroa's family looked the same as from the funeral, but much more sad with all of the people gone.

The presence of many was the point of funerals, Tallon supposed. A way of coping with loss.

Now, returning to the place of grief, the quiet was especially powerful.

He parked his rental in front of the Figueroa house and walked to the front door. It was a modest structure, a craftsman-style bungalow with a wide front porch and a center gable that looked out onto the street. There were two chairs and a cocktail table on the porch near the corner. Tallon pictured his friend sitting there with his father, drinking beers, talking about some of Nate's exploits.

Now, the chairs were empty, and wet with the rain that had passed through the area.

The doorbell appeared to be broken so he knocked. It was early evening. Well after the day's work should be done but also at a time where interrupting dinner might be a possibility.

It was cold. The damp chill in the air seemed to penetrate Tallon's clothing.

He had packed quickly and the chilled Minnesota air cut through the thin denim jacket he had on. If he'd taken a little more time and not made such a hasty departure for the airport, he would have added a few more layers to his suitcase.

The front door was solid wood, not surprising on a house that had to have been built not much less than a hundred years earlier. It was a densely populated neighborhood. The homes were small but tidy. Lawns were cut. No signs of peeled paint. A neighborhood with pride.

The heavy door opened and Tallon found himself looking at Figueroa's father. A shorter, stockier version of his friend, with gray hair and a face that had aged since he'd last seen it, just a few days back.

"Help you?" Charles Figueroa asked.

"I'm Michael Tallon, I was a friend of Nate's," he said. "I was here just a few days ago for the funeral."

Recognition dawned on the older man's face.

"Oh, yes. I remember you. I'm sorry, come in," he said. He stepped aside and Tallon entered the home.

"Coffee? I know it's late, but you look like you're cold."

"Yeah, I'd love a cup, thanks," Tallon said. He followed the older man down the hallway into the house. It was well-kept. Area rugs, dark wood floors and comfortable furniture. In the kitchen, Charles Figueroa grabbed two cups, filled them, and gestured toward the living room, where he took the center spot on a leather couch, and pointed Tallon toward a club chair.

"What can I do for you?" the older man asked.

Tallon took a deep breath. He'd thought about this on the plane ride and had decided that the best way forward was to be honest.

"When I got back home after the funeral, I found a strange email from Nate," Tallon said. "It simply said 'they followed us.' I'm kind of confused by it, because it appears that it was sent after Nate had passed away. So I'm wondering if someone else may have sent it, and if you know who that might be." He had printed off a copy of the email and handed it to his old friend's father. Charles Figueroa looked at the sheet, read it several times and handed it back.

"Well, I know that's Nate's email address," the older man said. "I got the hang of email a few years back. But I don't know what that message might have meant. And I don't know who might have sent it, if it wasn't from Nate."

Tallon recognized honesty when he saw it.

"Nate may have sent it," Tallon said. "There's a way to schedule emails to go out after you've written them. I don't know how to do it, but I know it can be done. I'm just not sure why Nate would have done that."

The old man shrugged his shoulders, waited for Tallon to continue.

"Had anything happened before Nate became ill? Had he said anything or anyone was bothering him? Some issue that he was having?" Tallon asked. "I'm really sorry to ask, but this message really came out of the blue."

Charles Figueroa glanced down and to the left before he spoke.

"Oh, there are always issues in a family," he said. "Always."

Tallon nodded. It was hard for him to identify with the notion of family.

He was an only child, and both of his parents were gone. He really didn't have much in the way of family, which is why the military had become a second home for him.

"I always considered Nate my brother. I hope he felt the same about me," Tallon said. And then waited.

"Nate has a sister up in Seattle," the older man said. He let out a long breath. "She called him and asked for help. He went out there and when he came back, he wasn't the same. Something was wrong. And then that was it."

Tallon's first thought was, *why didn't he call me?*

It was a selfish reaction.

"Nate's sister. Is she okay now?"

The old man looked up from the area rug he'd been studying.

"That's just it. No one can find her."

CHAPTER NINETEEN

The morgue was located in Coupeville, the seat of Island County, just a stone's throw from Pine Beach.

Jardine had verified Pauling's identity and background before she agreed to take her to the morgue, which was housed in a long, low-slung building that reminded Pauling of an elementary school.

Except this one had drawers for dead bodies, instead of pencils and erasers.

Chief Jardine vouched for her at the various security checkpoints and eventually, they made their way to the basement where a gurney was brought in to a viewing room.

"This one's going to be tricky," Jardine said. "You won't be able to do any kind of facial recognition, if you know what I mean. We couldn't even get dental records."

"So what do you want me to do?" Pauling asked.

"No surviving family members, so if you can at least recognize the body, that would be a good thing," Chief Jardine said. "At least it would be a place for us to start."

"How am I supposed to identify him if there's nothing of him...left?"

Jardine shrugged her shoulders. "I don't know. Maybe there were birthmarks? Scars? Some identifying marks on his body?"

Pauling was tempted to make a joke but it never really formulated in her mind. It had to do with the fact that she was intimately familiar with Jack Reacher's body. Had actually pictured it many, many times in her mind since their last time together. Maybe too many times.

"I can try," she said.

A man in a white lab coat pulled the sheet from an incredible specimen of the male body. A huge upper body with broad shoulders and chest, long, thick arms, down to a relatively narrow waist with big, strong legs.

The sheet was kept over what remained of the body above the neck.

From where she was standing, Pauling could see the chest and pec area. She knew Jack Reacher had various scars on his body. She had run her fingers, and maybe even her lips, along their patterns some time ago.

Pauling studied the body before her with great care. Jardine didn't say a word. The man in the lab coat just waited. Somewhere, a voice shouted outside the room and then it was silent again.

"May I take a closer look?" Pauling finally asked.

Chief Jardine gestured toward the body. "Be my guest."

Pauling walked closer to the body. Studied the legs. The waist. The flat stomach. The incredible chest and shoulders. The arms were enormous.

The dimensions seemed right.

She studied the scars.

Closed her eyes, tried to picture what she remembered of Reacher.

And then she opened them.

"It's him," she said.

CHAPTER TWENTY

Tallon was angry.

And hurt.

But they were emotions on which he rarely ever dwelled.

And this was no exception.

The fact that Figueroa, his de facto brother, hadn't told him about the illness was one thing. That, he could understand, to a degree. Illness, especially something like cancer, sometimes caused people to retreat into themselves. So Figueroa hadn't called him to let him know about his condition.

But Figueroa's sister was missing?

And he hadn't called Tallon to enlist his help?

Why not?

What could have possibly prevented him from doing so?

As he packed, he found solace in the act of compartmentalizing objects, and he transferred that approach to his emotions.

Having spent the vast majority of his adult life in the military, Tallon's way of living made packing for trips on short notice a matter of routine.

Within hours of his return from the Figueroa household in Minnesota, he had his SUV loaded with gear and supplies for the drive to Whidbey Island.

He could have simply hopped a plane from Minneapolis and flown directly to Seattle, but something told him it would be a good idea to bring along the kinds of resources that are prohibited on airlines.

Arming the compound was the most time-consuming task. It wasn't as simple as punching in a code on an alarm panel by the garage door. Tallon had special compartments and storage areas in the house that required extra steps to secure. Once he finished those, he activated the motion-detection system linked to a series of hidden cameras. The images were available for him to view on his smartphone, if he so desired.

Finally, loaded with food, water, clothes and a small but effective selection of weapons carefully stashed in a special section of his SUV, Tallon set out for Seattle.

It would be a lonely drive for much of the time. He would skirt Death Valley before eventually connecting with I-5 in northern California and from there, it would be a relatively straight shot through Oregon to Whidbey Island.

Plenty of time for him to think through what he'd learned in Minnesota.

It was a puzzle.

And not a good kind of mystery. His friend was dead and before his death, had been dealing with a problem. A problem he felt hadn't required Michael Tallon's assistance.

The road rose as it neared the mountains and Tallon felt the reassurance as his vehicle's beefy engine surged ahead, even sped up as the incline increased.

It was mid-morning and the sun was up, the sky was a clear blue, and in the distance Tallon could see a hawk circling far overhead.

As he drove he cycled through a variety of scenarios, trying to better understand what kind of trouble Figueroa's sister might have been in, and how he would have approached it.

There just wasn't enough information for him to put any credence into his ideas. There was a good chance he would get there and it would turn out to be nothing. Maybe the sister had met some guy Figueroa hadn't approved of, and now she'd run off with him. End of story. Or maybe the sister had been surprised by a trip to Europe and hadn't had time to let everyone know.

Stranger things had happened.

If it did turn out to be a simple case of miscommunication, it would mean Tallon made an eleven-hour drive for no good reason.

Except driving down lonesome highways was something he enjoyed. He relished the open space. The lack of confinement. The anonymity.

Besides, it was his duty to find Figueroa's sister and make sure she was okay. Even though his friend hadn't asked him to.

Figueroa would have done the same for him.

The miles and hours flew by. Traffic remained sparse.

Soon, he was blazing through Oregon, then navigating his way up the Washington coast before finally hitting some urban congestion around Seattle. But it was well after rush-hour and he made short work of it.

He'd settled on a reasonably-priced hotel and

self-parked the SUV. He brought his gear up to his room and checked his phone.

There was one unopened email.

He checked the sender.

Figueroa?

Impossible.

He opened it.

There was one word.

Sica.

CHAPTER TWENTY-ONE

There wasn't much to choose from in Pine Beach for lodging. Pauling had secretly hoped she would be on her way back to Seattle right then, but it was a no-go. After the scene in the morgue, she wanted to stay.

And drink.

She wasn't normally a drinker, but suddenly she wanted to feel the warm buzz from a couple glasses of wine. Or maybe a good, strong martini.

In any event, she found an overpriced but quaint hotel on the water and checked into her room, showered, and changed into jeans and a fleece pullover. Down by the bar there was a fireplace with a pair of leather chairs and a rough-hewn table. She ordered a dirty martini at the bar, sunk into the chair and when her drink was handed to her, she drank half of it in one long pull.

The fire was fake. A gas flame with artificial logs looking like a discarded prop from a B movie.

Oh well.

Why have a real fireplace in a location like this? Where would you get firewood? It's not like the area was surrounded by towering pine trees or anything.

Sarcasm wasn't the place to go, Pauling thought to herself. Besides, it was kind of pointless when it was an audience of one.

Pauling took another drink of the martini and thought about what she'd seen. Not good. Not good at all. It had taken a very powerful rifle to do that kind of damage and create such difficulty in being able to identify the body.

The sight of that body, Pauling thought. She gave an imperceptible shake of her head, thought about her past with Jack Reacher.

They were good memories but in light of this situation, they felt like bad thoughts.

The last of her martini went down the hatch and Pauling popped the olive into her mouth. It had been stuffed with blue cheese.

It was good, but she couldn't have another one.

The server noticed her and Pauling asked for a glass of chardonnay.

Chief Jardine had seemed to be satisfied with her identification of Reacher. They'd exchanged business cards and Pauling was honest in telling her she was going to stay put for the night and probably leave in the morning.

Pauling wondered what it was like to be a female police chief in a place like this. It had the look of a town that would be filled with rugged lumberjacks on the weekends. Plaid shirts. Lots of facial hair. Plenty of drunk-and-disorderlies.

Rough-hewn folks who probably liked to get rough on the weekends.

Then again, Jardine seemed like she could take care of herself. A hard woman who looked like she'd seen her share of challenges and stared them down until they turned tail.

It had been that way for Pauling in the Bureau.

Most of her colleagues had been decent men, but there was always an old-school personality somewhere, sometimes even lurking in someone very young. Attitudes toward women were learned early. It took a lot of life experience to change those beliefs. She almost wished Jardine was here to compare notes.

Her chardonnay arrived and Pauling sipped, feeling the first effects of the martini. It was like putting on something made of silk. Smooth. Comforting. Luxurious even.

As Pauling watched the fake flames flashing in between the artificial logs, she thought about illusion.

Deception.

And trickery.

Yes, Chief Jardine had been satisfied with Pauling's assessment in the morgue.

Which was fine, Pauling thought.

Even though it had been complete bullshit.

CHAPTER TWENTY-TWO

S*ica?*

Sica was dead.

Tallon stared at his screen. It made no sense.

Figueroa was dead, too. Who was sending emails from his account? And why?

Tallon needed to get his blood pumping and clear his head from the long car trip and from sitting too long. It dulled the senses.

He needed to clear the cobwebs.

He unpacked, found his swimming trunks and went down to the hotel swimming pool where he swam laps for forty-five minutes, until the water was practically worked into a froth. He toweled off, went into the hotel's small fitness center and pumped iron until the moisture from the pool had evaporated and was replaced with sweat.

Back in his room, he showered and threw on a pair of athletic shorts and a T-shirt and sat down in front of his computer.

During his workout, he'd let the situation marinate in his mind. He had formulated and tossed aside several different plans of action, until he'd settled on what he was about to do.

Tallon opened his laptop and connected to the hotel's Wi-Fi and sent three emails, pounding them out on his keyboard like machine gun fire.

The first went to the pathologist who performed Figueroa's autopsy, requesting a copy of his report. He fudged a little, implying he'd been hired by the family to look into the matter. Not true. But not totally untrue, either.

The second was to a friend of his who ran a sideline business hacking into other people's computers. He forwarded the email he'd just sent to the pathologist, and asked his friend if the answer was negative, could he get the report for him anyway.

The third email was to Figueroa.

Or, more accurately, to whomever was using his email account.

He kept it short and simple.

You're not Figueroa. Who are you?

CHAPTER TWENTY-THREE

When her eyes began to half-close with fatigue, Pauling signed out of her tab and left the bar area. She passed through a small dining area set up to take advantage of the view of the harbor.

Nautical themes were everywhere, with paintings of old clippers and even a wall tapestry made with fish nets and an anchor.

Pauling skipped the elevator and used the thickly carpeted steps. The hotel was only three stories and she climbed the stairs easily, thinking about her plan for the next day. She had a lot to do, and wanted to get an early start.

Down the hallway, she passed a hotel employee probably doing turn-down services. A couple of the rooms had used room service trays sitting outside, holding water glasses and silver dish covers, usually with a used napkin placed on top and discarded condiment jars.

Pauling got to her room, used her key card and opened the door.

A girl was sitting on the edge of the bed. She jumped to her feet and Pauling instinctively reached for her gun, but realized she wasn't carrying one.

"No, it's ok!" the girl said. "I just need your help."

She was young, her eyes were wild with fear.

Pauling stepped into the room, but held the door open, and glanced around the entryway into the rest of her room. The bathroom was empty as was the rest of the space.

The two of them were alone.

Pauling crossed quickly to her bag and made sure her gun was still there.

It was.

"Who are you and how did you get into my room?" Pauling kept her voice steady. But she hated surprises.

"My name is Maria," the girl said.

Pauling guessed she was in her late teens. Skinny, with big expressive eyes. Clearly Hispanic heritage, with dark black hair pulled back into a tight ponytail. She had on jeans and a sweatshirt.

"My cousin works here as a maid," the girl said. She sat back on the edge of the bed. Her hands were in her lap and she was wringing the life out of them. "You used to be the police, right? Now you help people?"

"How do you know anything about me?" Pauling asked.

She shrugged her shoulders. "It's a small town. Is it true? Do you help people?"

Pauling was tempted to lie.

"My brother is missing," the girl said. "I can't go to the police."

"I know the police here," Pauling said. "They're very good. I can't help you or do any better than they're doing."

"That's not what I've heard about you," the girl persisted. "You worked for the FBI, right?"

"Jesus," Pauling said. "This town isn't *that* small. How do you know all this and exactly why can't you go to the police?"

"My brother was in Seattle," the girl said, ignoring Pauling's direct questions. "Whoever took him or killed him did it in Seattle. The local cops here won't do anything. They'd be like little people in that big city. Or they'd end up like that guy they found out on the road. By the woods."

The young woman had a way of talking that told Pauling she wasn't a native English speaker. An odd cadence. She also had a thin, sallow appearance. Either a drug user, or malnourished for a different reason.

Pauling was still considering her comment about the dead man out by the woods, when the girl reached into her pocket.

Pauling had her gun in hand and the girl nearly screamed.

"No, it's okay," she said. From her pocket she withdrew a photo.

"Here. Here's a picture of him. My brother."

The girl handed her a small photo, worn but still in good condition. Pauling took it and looked.

There were two men.

The man on the right must have been the girl's brother. Not only because he looked like her, but Pauling knew the man on the left.

Michael Tallon.

CHAPTER TWENTY-FOUR

Sleep refused to grant Tallon's request. It hovered on the edge of his periphery but remained firmly out of his grasp and left him staring at the ceiling, thinking about Figueroa and the mysterious emails.

When his phone buzzed on the nightstand next to him, he was relieved. Tallon glanced at the screen, smiled and answered.

"Lauren Pauling," he said. "I was just thinking about you." And then he added. "I'm in bed."

"What a coincidence," she responded. "I'm in bed, too. And *I'm* thinking about *you*."

Tallon didn't believe her, but he liked her answer.

"Really?" he said, recognizing that it wasn't

standard operating procedure for Pauling to flirt. She tended to be a little more direct.

Tallon could picture her, and the sound of her voice always made him happy. Or at least, made him feel better. It was that kind of great voice possessed by jazz singers who frequently light up.

"Yes," Pauling said. "What's new with you since our last case?"

He chuckled softly. That was an understatement. Their last case had been a doozy.

"Working," he said. "You?"

"Same. In fact, I just spoke with a young woman who said her brother is missing," Pauling said. "And when she showed me a photo of him, you were there, too."

Tallon sat up, swung his feet around to the floor.

"You're kidding me," he said. "Was her name Figueroa?"

"Yes," Tallon said, and he heard the surprise in her voice. "Maria. You know her?"

"No, but I knew her brother well."

"Knew?"

He sighed.

"He died last week. Cancer."

"I'm sorry."

"The weird thing is, their family told me that

Figueroa's sister was missing," Tallon explained. "And that he had come out here to Seattle to find her."

"Wait a minute. You're here? In Seattle?" Pauling asked.

"Yeah," he said. And then it dawned on him. "You are too?"

"Sort of. I'm on Whidbey Island," she said.

"Business or pleasure?"

"Unpleasurable business."

"Having to do with this girl?"

"No," Pauling said. "Completely separate. Maria somehow found out I was here, my background, and surprised me with a visit. I honestly don't know what to think. And it's awfully strange that you're involved."

"Do you have a way to contact her?" Tallon asked. He was already up and getting dressed.

"Yeah, a cell phone. Are you going to call her?"

"Tomorrow. But right now I've got something else to do."

"Like what?"

"Like, drive to Whidbey Island."

CHAPTER TWENTY-FIVE

After Maria left her room, leaving only a cell phone number and virtually no other information, Pauling got a few hours sleep.

She was up early, not feeling rested at all, but still managed to hit the hotel gym and put in a good workout. Afterward, she showered, dressed and grabbed a cup of coffee from the hotel coffee bar.

In her rental car, she drove out of Pine Beach, along a lonely road virtually devoid of traffic. The staggeringly tall pines towered over her on either side of the strip of asphalt, occasionally parting to reveal distant mountains tinged with layers of deep blue.

As she drove, Pauling thought about the original phone call she'd received, the one back in New York. How it had alerted her to the discovery of the body and the Jack Reacher ID.

Who had that been?

Chief Jardine certainly hadn't called her. She hadn't even known who the hell Jack Reacher was, let alone Lauren Pauling.

Maria Figueroa hadn't called her. If she had, why would she have bothered with the anonymity if she was planning on surprising her in a hotel room a couple days later?

She was in Pine Beach, people had clearly noticed her presence, yet no one had stepped forward taking responsibility for the phone call.

So who had it been?

The coffee was strong and delicious, just the way she liked it. The road crested in front of her and she topped out, saw a long ribbon of highway ahead of her. It was the kind of road she imagined Jack Reacher loved.

She could picture him, putting one foot in front of the other. Nowhere to go. No one to see. Just endless space and possibility.

Pauling thought about what she'd told Jardine.

It's him.

She'd said it with a conviction that she didn't feel. There was no real way to know, of course.

Yes, the body was right. The scars were wrong, though. Not correct, and not in the right place.

And they appeared to be recent.

Pauling had said what she needed to say, because to suggest otherwise would lead to more questions. If she'd said she didn't think it was Jack Reacher, then what? It would lead to more questions and require more of her time tied up in bureaucracy.

If it wasn't Reacher, that meant someone had gone to some fairly drastic measures to deceive the police.

Why?

Who would do it?

And the first person who came to Pauling's mind was the obvious one.

Jack Reacher.

Maybe he'd wanted to fake his own death for some reason. She couldn't come up with a logical motivation, but one never knew. It would be easy enough. Plant his own ATM card on some big lug that looked like him, and disappear forever.

Except, Reacher had already sort of disappeared.

Why would he feel the need to go to this extreme?

What Pauling needed was time. Which is why she lied to Jardine.

By asserting to Jardine that the body was Reacher, it gave her the freedom to investigate on her own.

Starting with the crime scene.

She'd seen the report in Jardine's office, and knew that the shooting had taken place near mile marker 34 on the same rural road she was now on. It was a no-brainer. As soon as she saw the information in Jardine's office, it was a foregone conclusion. Of course she would look at the crime scene.

Pauling drove on, the only car on the road, and after nearly an hour she started to question her method. But as soon as she doubted herself, the crime scene tape came into view, and Pauling pulled her rental car to the side of the road.

She shut it off, pocketed the keys, and looked around.

There was a man.

With a gun.

CHAPTER TWENTY-SIX

Tallon arrived on Whidbey Island in the early morning hours. He crossed the bridge at Deception Pass and studied the terrain. He'd spent a lot of time in mountains both in the United States and abroad. What struck him about this area was the lushness of the foliage. The Pacific Northwest was a place of impressive beauty and Tallon was able to set aside the reasons for his trip to the area and take a moment to appreciate his surroundings.

But only a moment.

His first call was to Maria who stated she couldn't talk and asked to meet at an address she texted him.

His next call was to Pauling, but the call went to voicemail.

Tallon filled his SUV at a gas station with a huge plaza attached. He went inside, bought a coffee and a breakfast sandwich that was piping hot and as soggy as a used beach towel.

Tallon ate and considered his options.

He checked his phone for any response from either Figueroa's pathologist or his hacker friend, but no one had reached out.

Tallon wadded up his breakfast sandwich wrapper and tossed it into the garbage can nearby.

He had put the address into his phone for the location of the rendezvous with Maria and he would have to be there soon.

It gave him an unsettled feeling.

Figueroa gone.

The strange appearance of his sister in Pauling's room. And perhaps most of all, the appearance of Pauling in the same area, working a separate case.

The confluence of actions made him glad that he had driven to Seattle, as opposed to flying. There were things in his vehicle he would need before he met with the girl.

Now, he drained the rest of his coffee, got into the SUV and drove it around back, behind a semi truck that blocked any view of his actions. The huge truck also blocked any of the security cameras he'd spotted at the back of the station.

Tallon went into the back of his SUV, unlocked the compartment beneath the false bottom and lifted the lid.

Tallon studied the guns. He'd brought a 9mm semiautomatic pistol, as well as a military shotgun outfitted with a pistol grip and plenty of ammo for both. He also had two tactical knives and a Kevlar vest.

He left everything in its place except for the 9mm handgun, which he fitted into a holster concealed beneath his untucked shirt. He closed the compartment and locked it.

Tallon got back behind the wheel and headed out to meet Maria. The location wasn't far away, and in less than a half hour he was pulling into the address at the end of his navigation route.

It was a store at the end of a deserted street. It was a sad combination of retail down on its luck, with a lot of abandoned residential homes.

Depressed was the only word that could describe the locale.

Maria had told Tallon he should drive to the back of the building matching the address she'd provided. It looked like a convenience store, but the windows were painted black and the door was shut. It had security bars across its front.

To the right of the store was an empty parking lot.

Tallon took it all in, and then followed the directions Maria had given him. He drove past the store where a second parking lot, also empty, sat. At the rear of the property was a thin patch of grass with a dead tree and a picnic table.

The picnic table was occupied.

By a young woman.

Alone.

Tallon parked the SUV and approached her.

"Maria?" he said.

She turned and Tallon knew immediately she wasn't Figueroa's sister. She looked nothing like him, and he immediately recognized the presence of drug addiction. The young woman was thin, with dark circles under her eyes and the glassy-eyed look of someone not in her right mind.

The young woman smiled at him and he saw her eyes lift slightly over and to the right of his shoulder.

He turned.

A group of four men had emerged from the back of the building. They were all dressed in similar fashion. Baggy pants, black T-shirts and tattoos covering most of their exposed skin.

Gangbangers, through and through.

One was carrying a baseball bat. Another had a section of lead pipe.

And one had a knife.

Tallon studied their tattoos.

He'd seen quite a few in his time and these were the type he'd seen once before.

In Mexico.

Which meant one thing.

Sica.

CHAPTER TWENTY-SEVEN

"Can I help you?" the man with the gun asked Pauling. His uniform told her he was Pine Beach PD. His baby face told her he was probably new to the force, a young patrolman assigned to keep an eye on the crime scene until further investigation could be conducted. He looked bored.

"Not really, but thank you," Pauling said. She gazed up at the steep bluff to the left of the road.

"May I see some ID, ma'am?" he asked.

Pauling nearly rolled her eyes, but she handed him her driver's license. He was pasty, with a buzz cut and a uniform that looked too small for him. Or maybe he'd gained weight recently and hadn't had time to buy a new one.

"This is a crime scene," the young patrolman said as he handed her back the license. His voice and chest were both puffed up.

"Really? What happened?" Pauling asked.

He shook his head.

"Probably be best if you moved along," he answered. "Nothing to see here, anyway."

Pauling spotted the nameplate above his left breast pocket.

Shepard.

"So I assume the shot came from up there?" she asked, and pointed toward the bluff. To the right of the road, the embankment fell away as it curved slightly upward.

"I can't comment on that, ma'am," he said. He seemed to realize that she knew more than she should. It occurred to him with a realization that arrived in slow motion. "Are you the one that identified the body?" he asked. His pasty skin turned a little pink.

Pauling smiled.

"Yes, I did."

"Chief Jardine mentioned you," he said. Now his voice had a little edge to it. "But she didn't say you were going to stick around and...do whatever it is you're doing."

He finished the sentence awkwardly, and shuffled his feet to work out his discomfort.

"Yeah, I didn't mention that," Pauling said. "Just curious is all."

"Uh huh," he said, his voice less than convinced.

"There a way up there?" she asked him.

He frowned. Clearly, she wasn't paying heed to his suggestion that she move along. But Pauling also saw the conflict.

"I actually just came out for some exercise, wanted to find a good hiking trail," she said. "Is there one back there? I'd like to check out the view."

It was a good compromise. He could help her out, without breaking any kind of rule that would get him in trouble.

"There's a parking area about a quarter mile up to the left. From there, you can pick the eastern trail and it winds up there," he said. "Don't go where there's yellow tape, though. Otherwise, I'll have to come up there."

"No problem, Shepard," Pauling said. "Thanks and I'll see you around."

She got back into her car and drove ahead.

As soon as she was around the bend, Shepard

took out his personal cell phone and dialed a private number.

"She's here. Now would be a good time to grab her," he said.

CHAPTER TWENTY-EIGHT

There's always a leader.

An alpha male, surrounded by subservient betas.

Usually the tallest one.

But he isn't always the guy who's going to go first. Sometimes it's the opposite.

The smallest, weakest member of the pack usually has the most to prove and the eagerness to go along with it.

Tallon immediately spotted the leader. Not the tallest, but clearly the strongest, with broad shoulders bulging out of a wife beater shirt, a flat face and dull eyes. No fear, but also no eagerness. He was all business.

The unacknowledged leader was in the middle, and at opposite ends were the weakest of the group. Two of them already several full steps ahead of the pair in the middle.

Unlike the guy in the middle, their eyes were alive with excitement. Bloodthirsty and also tinged with the need to perform. This was perfect for them. Four on one. A surefire victory.

They were anxious to get started, demonstrate their worth by beating a lone man, clearly outnumbered, and demonstrate their value to the group. It was like a home game against a clearly overmatched opponent.

To lose was to bring shame to everyone involved.

Tallon considered drawing his gun and shooting them, but he figured they were armed, to a certain extent, beyond the baseball bat and the lead pipe. He didn't want to be the first one to start shooting. They clearly felt they could handle the situation without resorting to guns as well.

A tactical mistake, but perfectly understandable.

Tallon was more than happy to keep guns out of the equation for now. Mainly because he wanted information.

So he let them come, and turned his back on the girl for the moment. He figured she wouldn't do anything just yet. It wouldn't surprise him if she had a little pistol. Maybe a tiny .25 semi-automatic in her purse. Nothing to be concerned about at the moment. She certainly wouldn't shoot first and guns like that were notoriously inaccurate. The odds of her hitting him were extremely low.

So Tallon waited, knowing that the low men on the totem pole would act first.

And they did.

The two on the ends darted in. One went high and the other went low.

In theory, a decent approach.

An inexperienced fighter might be temporarily frozen with indecision. Do you duck or jump? They were counting on him to do just that, which would provide the perfect opportunity for them to take a baseball bat to his shins and a lead pipe to the temple.

Game over.

Unfortunately for them, Tallon took a third option.

He lunged forward, rendering both of their swings ineffective. To swing a bat and connect with a target required distance. Once inside the bat's arc, power was greatly diminished.

Tallon grabbed the handle of the baseball bat

with his left hand, and drove an elbow into the face of the guy with the lead pipe. He felt or heard the man's nose squash beneath the blow.

Tallon continued his momentum, pulling the baseball batter forward and he spread his left leg out, tripping his assailant, forcing him to the ground.

The man's grip on the bat loosened and Tallon wrenched it from his hands and drove the butt of the bat into his temple. Much better use of a club to drive it forward on a straight path. Just as much power with a higher degree of accuracy and effectiveness. The man with the broken nose was still conscious so Tallon utilized the bat again, this time with so much force that he actually felt the man's skull give way. Experience told him that it was probably a blow from which the man would not survive.

Tallon turned and the leader, along with the last of the group, had suddenly realized their odds had shifted quite dramatically.

Any pretense of a quick and savage beating was gone. The man next to the leader glanced at his superior, as if he was asking what he should do.

Tallon knew that any hesitation was deadly in a fight like this.

The leader of the group was already going for his gun.

However, it's one thing to pull a gun when you've got all the time in the world. Maybe when you're showing off for a friend, or practicing in front of the bedroom mirror.

It's an entirely different matter when there's another human being less than twenty feet away who's doing the same.

Tallon was smooth and confident and his 9mm was out and firing while the leader of the group had barely managed to get a big shiny semi-automatic out of his baggy pants. It was probably a great weapon to wave around at a party when you're full of malt liquor and bragging about how you're going to kill rival gang members, not so great when you're trying to extricate it from your sagging blue jeans when a man directly across from you is beating you to the draw.

Tallon's shots shredded the leader's chest, painting the man's wife beater shirt with blossoming flowers of red blood.

The second man's gun was nearly coming on line when Tallon's bullets hit him in the chest and throat. He got off one shot as he was falling backward, a bullet harmlessly flying directly toward the sky.

For a brief moment, Tallon didn't move as he watched the two gang members complete their fall to the ground. His gun remained in his hand, but he knew they were both dead.

Tallon glanced down at the first two of his assailants and they were completely inert, too.

He turned, expecting to see the girl with either a gun or knife, coming at him.

But he was wrong.

The girl was gone.

CHAPTER TWENTY-NINE

The parking lot was little more than a clearing in the grass that ran about four car widths across.

At some point, someone had thrown in a few bags worth of loose gravel to prevent the grass and weeds from reclaiming their territory. It hadn't worked. There was a lot of green overtaking the gravel. Before long, nature would win.

The lot was empty, and Pauling pulled her rental car into the middle of the space. She got out, locked up, and wished she'd brought some bug spray.

The air was damp and the sun wouldn't be able to cut through the dense pine trees. A perfect environment for mosquitoes and biting flies.

Pauling spotted two trailheads, one to the north, the other slightly back toward the direction she'd just come. That would be the one the shooter had used.

She paused, thinking it through.

Had the shooter parked here, as well? Seen the lone man on the road? He then would have driven past him, hurried into position and taken the shot. A simple sequence, most likely accurate. But not the only plausible scenario. Pauling needed more information.

She considered the setting.

It was definitely a remote location. Traffic virtually nonexistent. No one to see the murder. Hearing it would be a different matter. Sound carried well in the mountains due to the thinner air.

Pauling wondered if Chief Jardine had been thorough in canvasing the area to check if anyone had seen a car parked in this spot around the time of the murder. There were no residential areas nearby. Tough to knock on doors when there weren't any houses. But had someone heard the shot? Pauling made a note to check on whether or not there were any active hunting seasons. If not, a gunshot would certainly catch someone's attention.

She wondered how long the man had been walking on the road. Had he come from Pine Beach? If so, that was at least two hours walking on the road. Surely someone would have passed him.

And a man with a physique similar to Reacher's would not go unnoticed.

Pauling made a mental note to see if Jardine had posted any descriptions of the man in the morgue. 6' 5" with massive shoulders and arms corded with muscle. Walking. Alone.

Someone must have seen him.

Pauling realized she was avoiding going into the woods so she walked ahead, took the trail and was soon climbing vertically on a path covered mostly with pine needles and loose stones.

Along the way, she kept her eye out for anything that didn't fit, but she had little hope. It rained here every day, practically. If the shooter had left behind any evidence, the chances were slim it had still survived intact.

The nature of the kill was interesting, too. Downhill shots were always a little tricky and the more she climbed, the more convinced she was there was more investigating to do. Her initial assessment of Chief Jardine was one of competence, but perhaps lacking in experience. Pauling could help with that.

She climbed and the trail twisted left, toward the road. Pauling soon discovered the site.

There was an enlarged area cordoned off with yellow crime scene tape. The pine needles were scattered and what grass had managed to grow in the space was heavily trampled.

No doubt the shooter had retrieved the shell casing, or casings. She assumed it had been one round fired. A head shot that had clearly gotten the job done. But she made a mental note to follow up with Jardine.

Pauling studied the ground.

Had the shooter been standing? Or had he gotten down on the ground, in a true sniper position to take the shot?

No way to know now, Pauling thought, as she studied the highly contaminated crime scene. There was clear evidence that someone, most likely Jardine and her officers, had trampled all over the site. The grass was matted down and the dirt underneath was slick and muddy.

Where the trail widened it created a ledge that wasn't big enough to be called an overlook, but would have provided enough room for a single shooter to get comfortable. It was less than a quarter mile from the parking area, so the killer would have needed to be fairly confident no one would be coming along the trail.

Concealment would also have been possible, to a certain extent.

The shooter hears someone coming along the trail, slides off the edge of the embankment and he's not visible from the trail.

That is, if he heard someone coming.

Pauling glanced down, over the ledge.

Maybe some disturbance visible, maybe not. Impossible to tell and even if someone had been there, how would she know if it'd been the cops or the shooter? She didn't have a personal crime lab to analyze fibers.

She looked down the line of sight to the road.

By her estimation, Pauling put the distance at roughly eight hundred yards. Not an exceedingly difficult distance for a good rifleman, but not a cakewalk, either.

Downhill.

Wind shear from the bluff could be unpredictable.

The distance said less about the shooter's ability, and more about his confidence.

When he set up here, he had no problem with the length of the shot or the gusting winds that swirled enough to affect the trajectory of a bullet.

A breeze picked up speed behind her and pine boughs above her swayed in a delayed reaction. Pauling realized that not a single car had passed since she'd been occupying the vantage point.

With nothing else to analyze, Pauling turned and headed back toward her car. She watched as she walked, looking for anything discarded or missed by the Pine Beach PD, but she found nothing. Either they'd collected everything, or there'd been nothing left by the perp, which was Pauling's guess.

Back at the clearing, she walked toward her rental car as she heard the sound of a vehicle approaching.

Surprised, she glanced up as a black SUV slowed.

The windows were tinted.

Pauling had her door open, and watched the SUV.

It had slowed even more.

And now, it stopped.

CHAPTER THIRTY

She was satisfied, in every sense.

Over the course of a week she had made a clean kill on a tricky downhill shot, assassinated a senator, and fulfilled her every sexual desire to the fullest extent possible.

It had been a successful sequence of events for the shooter known to her employers and fellow mercenaries as Grace.

The name was an inside joke.

Not her real name, of course.

She'd chosen it for the multiple meanings. Grace under pressure. To grace someone with her presence. But mostly, hoping her victims prayed for grace before drawing their last breath.

Now, she watched as the gates to Sica's

compound opened, and she drove forward, to the main house.

When she parked and got out, she felt the eyes of Sica's bodyguards on her. Grace could read their minds.

This was the assassin?

A petite, red-haired woman who barely weighed a hundred pounds soaking wet?

But then they saw her face, the lack of fear, the utter lack of emotion and she could see their appraisals instantly shift.

Grace was shown inside to a study that smelled vaguely of marijuana and whiskey. Sica stood before a floor-to-ceiling window that looked out on a wide expanse of green grass, patrolled by two men with machine guns.

Sica turned to look at her and his face was partially obscured from view by the slight haze of smoke. There was no surprise registered on his face. Grace knew that Sica had done his homework. He also most likely knew it was very dangerous to meet in person. Not for her.

For him.

If things ever went sideways, anyone who saw her face would become a marked man.

A bodyguard stepped into the room and took up a space next to the door.

That was okay.

Grace wasn't here to take out Sica. No need at this point, not with another fat paycheck that was most assuredly on its way to her.

Besides, this was the wrong place and the wrong time.

If it came to that.

If that moment ever did arrive, though, it would be relatively easy despite the little man's paranoia. Paranoia without intelligence amounts to ineffective busywork.

Grace watched the little Mexican drug boss and waited. He pulled a cigar from his shirt pocket and offered it to her.

She shook her head.

"You don't smoke?" Sica asked.

"I'll get enough secondhand, thank you."

He took a long drag on his cigar and blew the smoke upward.

Grace waited.

Sica smiled at her.

"You like movies?" he asked. "Big Hollywood... what do they call them? Blockbusters?"

Grace didn't bother to respond.

"I do," Sica continued. "And when I see a good one, I'm happy. You know why? Because I know there's going to be a sequel. Always. There is always a sequel. I know, I know," he said, holding up a tiny little hand. "Usually they're not as good. But still, I enjoy them. That's what we have here. A sequel."

Grace nodded. She knew that was why she was here. There was a huge payday to come, all she had to do was hope this little man got to the point. And soon.

"Part one of your job was completed to everyone's satisfaction," Sica said. "However, the next step that was to be completed by others, did not get done. I need you to do it."

Sica produced a sheet of paper, folded into a small square. He handed it to Grace.

"A word of advice?" Sica said. "You seem like a very confident woman. That is good. I sent four confident men to complete Phase 2. None of them came back."

Grace's face remained impassive.

"That was a bad sequel," Sica said. "Like Jaws 2. I think you will do very well with the third in the series. Like the Indiana Jones movies? Remember? First one was great. Second one not so good. Third one excellent. And the fourth was a disaster, but there won't be a fourth in our little adventure, will there?"

Grace replied simply. "No."

"Let me show you something," he said. Sica walked past her and she followed, through the foyer to a side door that led down to a large subterranean room with an open square in the middle.

Sica walked up to the edge and pointed down. Grace glanced into the pit, saw the alligators at the bottom.

If he was trying to intimidate her, it didn't work. She'd already heard about Sica's little pet collection.

"I call them my evidence processors," he said. "Better than a deep grave. My enemies become alligator shit." He laughed, a high-pitched little giggle.

"One more thing," he said. Sica led her back upstairs to a bedroom. He opened the door and Grace saw a young woman chained to a bed. The young woman's face was a mask, her eyes blurry and unfocused. Heavily sedated.

There was something familiar about the face, and Grace instantly knew who the girl was.

"She's the sister of one of the men who murdered my brother and his daughter in Mexico," Sica said. "I'm using her as bait. Once you complete your part of the job, she'll go for a swim. Do you know what I mean?"

Grace nodded. She knew exactly what he meant, because she had worked with Nathan Figueroa once, a long time ago.

This would be the part where he threatened her, Grace thought. Imply that if she didn't fulfill her part of the deal, she too would end up in the pit.

But he displayed a little more intelligence than she had given him credit for and he implied the threat rather than directly stating it.

It didn't matter, she thought, as she walked out of Sica's compound.

She allowed a small smile to appear on her face.

Grace had known all along that Sica's phase 2 plan wouldn't work.

Because she knew Michael Tallon personally.

Oh, yes.

She knew Michael Tallon very, very well.

CHAPTER THIRTY-ONE

Pauling watched as the black SUV with tinted windows came to a stop. She had the door of her rental car open, and her hand slipped inside her jacket to the butt of her gun.

The SUV idled for a moment, and then pulled away.

Pauling debated about following, but decided against it. She had arranged to meet with Tallon at Pine Beach.

She got into her rental car, fired it up, and made her way back from the direction she'd come.

Once in town, she parked and spotted Tallon outside the restaurant where she'd suggested they meet.

"Made-from-scratch biscuits," he said, pointing at the sign in the window.

She laughed. "Men always think of food first," Pauling said. They hugged and Tallon's body felt warm and hard. As always, she felt the flash of physical attraction to him. He wasn't what you would call a handsome, leading-man type, but he was attractive in a rugged kind of way.

They went inside and Pauling ordered scrambled egg whites with a biscuit and honey on the side.

Tallon chose coffee and a biscuit.

After some small talk and catching up, Tallon said, "So tell me how you ended up out here."

Pauling filled him in on the mysterious phone call saying Reacher was dead, and then the story about a dead body believed to be Jack Reacher. Pauling knew that Tallon wondered why she had gotten a plane so quickly to come out and investigate, but he didn't bring it up.

"So you have your doubts that it's actually him?" he asked.

"I'm not convinced," she said. "In fact, I'm fairly certain it isn't him. I just haven't shared that with the local police yet, but eventually I will. I just wanted some freedom of movement for the time being."

"And you still don't know who called you about it?"

"No."

"Well, someone wanted you out here," he said. "It stands to reason it's the same party responsible for the murder, right?"

"Most likely," she said.

"Who else?" Tallon asked. "It's not like the local police would place some mysterious call asking for help. First of all, they wouldn't ask for help, and if they absolutely had to, they wouldn't hide it. Too much red tape these days."

The waitress brought their biscuits and placed them on the table and topped off their coffee.

"A certain level of sophistication is on display here," Pauling said, taking a forkful of egg white. It was bland. She added some salt and pepper.

"Yeah," Tallon said. "You don't manufacture a fake ATM card very easily. Unless they stole it."

"From Jack Reacher?" Pauling asked, raising an eyebrow. "I don't think so."

Tallon cut a section of biscuit off with his fork. Chewed.

"Damn, these are good," he said. "I should have ordered two."

"The sophistication angle is an interesting one," Pauling said.

"Sure," Tallon agreed. "I mean, forget the ATM card. How the hell did they know about your history with Reacher? Didn't all that happen in New York?"

"It did."

He stabbed another chunk of biscuit with his fork. "Do you have any enemies in this part of the country? Someone who would want to lure you out here with a jacked-up story about Reacher? No pun intended."

Pauling took a sip of coffee.

"Not that I know of. I've got a sister in Portland, but she's a civilian. Nothing to do with me or my background.

"What about you?" she asked.

Tallon told her about Figueroa, his missing sister, and the gangbangers.

"So you don't think the woman who was in my hotel room is actually his sister?"

"No," Tallon said. They had already mutually described the woman and arrived at the conclusion that the woman in Pauling's hotel room had been the same woman on the picnic table who'd orchestrated the ambush.

"So if she wasn't Figueroa's sister, who is she?" Pauling asked.

"Great question," Tallon said.

Pauling ran through some scenarios in her mind, none of them making much sense. Something nagged at her and suddenly it occurred to her.

"If they knew about my history with Reacher, they probably know about my history with you," she said. "Or, put another way, they know about *your* history with *me*."

They both watched each other as the implications reached home.

"What if the goal wasn't to lure me out here?" Pauling asked. "What if the point was to lure *you*?"

Tallon's phone buzzed and he looked at the screen.

"Shit," he said.

"Problem?"

"Maybe part of the solution," he said. "It's the pathology report on my friend Nate Figueroa," he said. Pauling watched as he scrolled through a message on his phone.

"Any surprises?" Pauling asked.

"Yeah, you could say that."

He signaled for the check from the waitress.

"Nate Figueroa didn't die of cancer," Tallon said.

The waitress placed the check on the table and Tallon threw down a twenty.

"He was poisoned."

CHAPTER THIRTY-TWO

Zurich, Switzerland

Gregory stood before Gunnella Bohm and struggled to maintain eye contact. Partly because he knew she wasn't happy. And partly because she was nearly six inches taller.

"Is this about our friend in Seattle?" Bohm asked him. Of course, she already knew the answer to the question. She just wanted him to know that nothing he could say would come as a surprise.

"Yes," Gregory said. "It appears that one of

the Department members has been doing some extensive freelance work."

"Freelance work is their livelihood, Gregory," she countered, just to see what he would say.

"True, however certain projects require preapproval, of which she did not obtain."

Bohm raised an eyebrow.

"Grace has always been fiercely independent," she said. "One of the things I admire about her."

Gregory cleared his throat. "Independence in contractors can become a liability, which I believe is now the case."

Bohm turned her back on him and studied his reflection in the window. He didn't move. She knew he wouldn't.

"Your next step?" she asked him.

"The best way to handle an issue in the Department, is to let the Department take care of it themselves," Gregory said. "Under my direction, of course."

"Is that a logical assumption?"

"I believe it is," Gregory answered.

She turned and faced him.

"The Collective is not something that does things on hunches and whims. Our actions are direct, concrete, and therefore consistently effective. Only those who demonstrate those same abilities have a place here."

"My course of action will have the result needed with maximum efficiency."

Bohm smiled at him.

"Who in the Department are you going to utilize?" Bohm asked.

"Moss."

Bohm nodded. It was who she would have chosen if she'd been in the same position. Of course, she would never have allowed herself to be in this position in the first place. Gregory hadn't directly errored, but sometimes errors of omission were the worst kind.

"Timetable?" Bohm asked.

"Immediate."

"Collateral damage?"

"None."

Bohm didn't believe that, and she suspected Gregory didn't believe it, either. But it was the right answer.

"Deliver your next update twenty-four hours from now," she said.

The door beyond slid open, triggered by the remote control in her pocket.

Gregory turned to leave.

"One last thing, Gregory," Bohm said.

He glanced back at her.

"The Department must come out of this situation stronger, not weaker. Any negative effects on The Department will greatly disappoint me."

He nodded and left.

Bohm slid the door shut and picked up her phone.

CHAPTER THIRTY-THREE

Pauling and Tallon left the café.

He was going to check into the same hotel as Pauling and they would join forces.

It only made sense.

They parted on the sidewalk. Pauling walked along the street and while her biscuit had been good, she knew she would have to spend a little extra time on the treadmill during her next workout.

Maybe she and Tallon would work out together.

She smiled at the thought. What *kind* of workout that might be, who knew?

Pauling allowed herself the thought of how nice a romantic rendezvous with Tallon would be.

She found him very attractive and unless her radar was completely off, she sensed that the feeling was reciprocal. Hell, he'd flirted with her on more than one occasion.

As she walked, she glanced in the display windows of stores along the street. Mostly nautical knickknacks and tourist stuff. A local art gallery. A used bookstore. A brewpub proudly featuring craft brews of the Pacific Northwest. Maybe she would try that later.

A little physical affection would be nice, she thought, as her mind returned to Tallon and their shared hotel.

It had been awhile since her last relationship, with an investment banker who spent most of his time on his yacht, sailing the world.

She'd spent a week with him in the Mediterranean, stopping at ports for good food, great wine and beautiful scenery.

Eventually, though, she'd gotten bored with both the trip and the banker. Plus, when she suggested they take things more casually he had responded by proposing to her. A curious reaction and the opposite of what she had just requested.

So that had ended, and there really hadn't been anyone since.

Now, she checked her phone as she walked to

her rental car. There were several messages from friends back in New York, along with some case updates in her email.

She would have plenty of catching up to do when she got home. Maybe she would grind through her email back at the hotel so when this was all done she wouldn't face a mountain of unresolved issues back in New York.

Pauling unlocked the rental car and slipped inside. She fired up the engine and was about to put it in gear when a cloth was slapped over her face and an arm reached from the back, clamping across her upper body.

She struggled, dropped her phone, and tried to reach her gun.

But her vision blurred and then she saw nothing.

CHAPTER THIRTY-FOUR

The first to arrive was the only American in the Department. His name was Moss, and as he strolled through the Seattle airport, he looked like a man on a casual business trip. Tan jeans, a T-shirt beneath a lightweight sport coat, with a briefcase and single strolling suitcase.

He looked neither young, nor old. Short, brown hair that may or may not have had a touch of silver.

While his age wasn't apparent, his physical condition certainly was.

Lean, but powerful. A former athlete, maybe, who'd never stopped competing.

Moss was unhurried, but walked with a

purposeful stride. The kind of guy who always arrived at least ten minutes early to a meeting.

The single suitcase was all he really needed, because he knew the Collective had shipped everything he needed ahead of time. The car was already parked short-term, and when he stowed his suitcase, he was satisfied to see two bags already in place.

The Collective was highly efficient.

Having an unlimited budget didn't hurt, he knew.

As always, though, it came down to intelligence. The more information the better. And the right kind of information.

Moss left the airport, headed toward Whidbey Island.

He'd never gone after another member of the Department.

It was highly unusual and carried with it a great deal of risk. However, the folks back in Zurich had doubled his normal fee. He failed to mention to them that he knew his target, personally.

He smiled.

Moss would have been happy to kill the bitch for free.

CHAPTER THIRTY-FIVE

Tallon sipped from a small black coffee and wondered where Pauling was.

He'd dumped his gear at the hotel, and ducked around the corner for some caffeine. The carbs from the biscuit had made him feel a little sluggish.

Now, he logged onto the café's Wi-Fi and checked his phone.

Nothing.

It was a little strange.

They had just talked a few hours ago, and agreed to meet at the hotel. He thought for sure she would either be working out or, more likely, just working. He knew that Pauling's company was very successful and high-end. He was sure running a business like that placed a lot of demands on her time and attention. Still, it was unusual for her not to communicate.

Tallon wondered where she might have gone.

A man and a woman walked into the coffee shop, vehemently discussing what sounded like a pending real estate offer. Something about a condo and whether or not a chandelier was included. It seemed like, according to the woman, if the chandelier wasn't included then the deal was off.

Tallon watched the street, waiting.

He considered his options and how long he was willing to wait.

When his phone rang, he saw the blocked number.

"Tallon," he said.

"I'm with Lauren Pauling," a woman's voice said. "Join us in an hour at the address I'm about to text you."

The call disconnected and then beeped with the incoming text message.

Tallon clicked on it and it automatically opened his map app. The address was forty-five minutes away, near Deception Pass, but in a remote location, far from any town.

He left the café, retrieved some items from

his room and soon had the SUV pointed toward the address he'd been sent.

Tallon knew that voice.

He couldn't quite place it.

But it was someone he knew.

As he drove, he tried not to concentrate on it too much.

He hoped it would come to him.

And soon.

CHAPTER THIRTY-SIX

Pauling came to and quickly realized two things. One, her arm was numb because it was handcuffed to an iron pipe.

And two, her ass hurt.

She was sitting on a cement floor and from the musty smell, she assumed it was a basement.

There was no one around.

Her cell phone was gone. Her head hurt, but she knew it was from the chloroform and not because she'd taken any blows to the head.

It was important to stay positive.

She wasn't scared. She'd been taken hostage once before, but that was totally different because Jack Reacher was involved.

Now, she didn't have Reacher to rely on.

A door opened above her and two people descended, pushing a third in front of them.

Both of them were small.

One man.

One woman.

In front of them, was a girl.

Pauling instantly knew it was Figueroa's real sister, not the imposter who'd no doubt been working for the man in front of her.

The woman was small, but wiry. With bright red hair and pale skin. Her eyes passed over Pauling and registered nothing.

The other person was a tiny man with dark skin and jet black hair. Mexican, if she had to guess.

Two heavyset men descended the staircase and used a set of handcuffs to chain the girl next to Pauling.

"This is her?" the Mexican said, pointing at Pauling. "She's old!"

"Screw you, pal," Pauling said.

The little Mexican walked toward her and kicked her in the stomach. She saw it coming and managed to twist enough to block some of the kick.

"You trying to hurt me with those size 5s?" she asked.

A small smile tugged at the red-haired woman's mouth and then it was gone. She glanced over at the little Mexican man who looked like he was going to try to kick Pauling again.

"So much bait," the man laughed. "I'm glad you agreed to doing it here. I think it's for the best. Still, all this for one man. Overkill, no?"

The red-haired woman didn't answer.

The little Mexican man walked over to an opening in the floor and looked down and then he looked at Pauling.

"They're going to love a taste of you," he said. "After my men have had their fill."

"Whatever, oompa loompa," Pauling said. The same little smiled showed briefly on the red-haired woman's face.

The Mexican looked confused. "Oompa lompa? What is this?"

He looked at the red-haired woman who didn't answer.

"Google it, asshole," Pauling said.

The pair left then, climbed the stairs and Pauling heard the click and lock of the door.

She turned to the young woman beside her.

The girl was unconscious. Pauling wished she could lift her hand and check her pulse, but it was impossible.

"Hey, it's okay," she said.

The girl didn't respond.

Pauling struggled to maintain her breathing, admitting the kick hurt a lot more than she let on.

The little man had said the bait was all for one man.

She knew what he meant.

And wondered what Michael Tallon was doing.

CHAPTER THIRTY-SEVEN

There was a time for planning.

And a time for action.

Tallon believed strongly that the moment called for less planning and more action.

Of course, instinct told him what he was going to find. Pauling had already figured out the situation. She had started to uncover it when they were at the café.

While it was true Pauling had been lured out here, it wasn't the end game. They had used her as insurance to get Tallon in their crosshairs.

And he thought he knew why.

The thing that tied it all together was Figueroa.

And Sica.

Not Alberto Sica. Because he was dead.

Gunned down by Tallon, Figueroa, and the rest of their crew.

Unfortunately, they'd killed Alberto Sica's daughter, too. Firefights have a way of getting out of control.

That one had been no exception.

There had long been rumors that Sica had family who'd fled to the United States. Tallon was now sure that they were the ones behind this. They had somehow managed to poison Nate Figueroa, and figured it would be easier to kill Tallon by luring him into their territory.

Now they had Pauling.

And probably Maria Figueroa.

Tallon knew what was in the compound he now faced. A gate. Multiple bodyguards. Sica himself. And probably a hired killer or two. Maybe even the same one who'd shot the Reacher lookalike.

No, the time for planning was over.

The next step would be a direct approach.

Literally.

His SUV was reinforced with a crash bar at the front, as well as a rear guard. But the crash bar in front was connected to the entire frame of the vehicle. With a full tank, it was a heavy vehicle.

And he put the big vehicle in high gear, four-wheel drive, and pressed the accelerator to the floor. The road leading up to the gate was slightly downhill and it helped him reach nearly eighty miles per hour before he hit the gate straight on.

No airbag deployed because he'd removed it during the vehicle's customization. The gate was blasted off its hinges and one of the sections screeched down the side of Tallon's SUV as he plowed through it and straight toward the front door of the compound's main building.

He continued straight ahead, the SUV pulling hard to the left because either there was something pinned to the vehicle or because the frame itself was knocked out of kilter.

It didn't matter because the engine was powerful enough to drive straight up onto the front porch and barrel right into the front door.

Not surprisingly, the door didn't hold and the SUV was in the middle of the building's main room where gunfire erupted.

Tallon flung his door open and rolled from the truck immediately after the front door gave and the SUV skidded to a stop, its engine smoking and transmission grinding to a halt.

He rolled away from the vehicle as it shuddered on, and he came up with his gun in hand.

The first targets were easy.

Mexican gangbangers, Sica's men, no doubt. They were not trained to be attacked and they were in the process of directing their fire toward the vehicle.

They sprayed it down with hundreds of bullets.

Complete overkill.

Only one of the men seemed to realize the driver was no longer in the vehicle.

He was the first man Tallon killed.

His own gunfire was lost in the thunderous noise.

After Tallon dropped the first of Sica's men, he took out three more in quick succession. None of them had seen him and their attention was on the vehicle or their weapons as they paused to reload.

When all three dropped, though, attention turned to Tallon.

By then, he had already scrambled to the left of the entrance, taking cover behind a metal bin containing firewood ready to be burned in the fireplace.

Bullets dinged off the metal. Metal shards combined with wood chips rained down on him.

Tallon crawled to his left again and spotted

two of Sica's men trying to flank him around the crashed SUV.

He shot both of them, two sets of double taps to the chest.

And suddenly, the cabin was silent.

Tallon ran to his right, around the back of the SUV and came face-to-face with Sica. The little man had a huge machine gun he was trying to bring to bear.

Tallon was much faster.

He knocked the gun down, placed the muzzle of his pistol against Sica's forehead and pulled the trigger.

The little man dropped to the floor and suddenly, Tallon was facing a woman with bright red hair and an arm around Pauling's throat.

She had a gun to Pauling's head.

"Hey," the woman said. "Tallon. Long time no see."

"Nowhere to go Grace," Tallon said.

"We miss you in The Department," she said. "It's not the same without you."

"That was a long time ago," Tallon said. "Besides, it was hard to know who you were working for." He nodded his head. "No amount of money is worth being employed by scum like that."

"Speak for yourself," Grace said.

Tallon looked at Pauling. She returned the gaze with a frank expression. Not scared. Just waiting.

"You going to kill her?" Tallon asked Grace. "And Nate Figueroa's sister, too? Two innocent women? That's what you've become?"

"The girl's downstairs," Grace said. "Alive."

"How magnanimous of you," Tallon replied.

"A contract is a contract, though," Grace answered. "I honor all of my contracts, which includes you, and her."

Tallon saw Grace's finger tighten on the trigger but he knew there was no way he could pull his gun in time.

And then suddenly, he didn't have to.

Because Grace's head exploded in a shower of blood and brain tissue.

Moss stepped out from behind her, holding an automatic with a silencer attached. Smoke curled from the weapon's muzzle.

Pauling had fallen to the floor alongside Grace, but now she scrambled forward, toward Tallon who lifted her to her feet.

He looked her over.

"Are you okay?" he asked.

"Yeah. Jesus, who was that woman?" she asked, glancing down at what was left of Grace.

"She was bad news."

The man with the gun stepped over the dead body.

"Pauling, this is Moss," Tallon said. "Moss, this is Pauling."

"Can't believe I had to bail you out again," Moss said to Tallon.

"I'm getting Maria," Pauling said.

Tallon looked at Moss.

"They sent you here?" he asked.

Moss nodded.

"Was she your only contract?"

Moss smiled, glanced at the SUV in the middle of the room.

"That was quite the entrance," he said.

CHAPTER THIRTY-EIGHT

Two days after the shootout at the cabin, Tallon and Pauling sat with Moss at the same coffee shop where Tallon had been sitting when he'd gotten the message from Grace that she had Pauling.

"Doctors say Maria's going to be okay," Pauling said, and put her phone away. "It didn't look like they'd gotten to her yet."

Tallon nodded. "Her father is flying out this morning to bring her back to Minnesota. He's very glad she's okay, considering what happened to Nate."

Moss shook his head. "Nate was a good guy." He paused. "Zurich gave me the background information, if you want to hear it," Moss said.

"Who's Zurich?" Pauling asked

"Probably better if you don't know," Tallon said. "A small group of people over in Europe who run The Department, which is what we called ourselves. At least, when I was still in it." He glanced at Moss. "You guys still call yourselves that?"

Moss shrugged. "Unofficially."

"So tell us," Pauling said.

"The operation to take out Alberto Sica was a success, but they also killed his daughter."

Moss paused, giving Tallon the opportunity to chime in.

He stayed silent.

"Alberto's brother, Archibald, was here, in Seattle. When he found out about his brother and niece, he hired Grace to kill a Reacher lookalike and send word to Pauling. They figured by bringing her out here, they could lure you in."

"So who was the guy they killed?"

"A bare knuckle brawler known to some folks in the underground. So when word was sent out looking for people who matched Reacher's description, his name came up."

"So I'm guessing when the people in Europe found out Grace was freelancing, that's when they sent for you," Pauling said to Moss.

"Grace was off the reservation. Had been

going that way for a long time, apparently. She shot the senator because apparently he was threatening to expose one of the people in Europe. That person then hired Grace, who not only took on the job of the senator, but also Sica's highly lucrative contract. Same general area. Two birds with one shot, kind of thing."

"So they found out they had two people off the reservation. Grace, and someone on the inside," Tallon said.

"That's when Zurich sent me in," Moss said. "They already knew where Grace was. So they sent me the coordinates. That's how I got there about the same time you did."

"How did people in Zurich know?" Pauling asked.

Tallon glanced at Moss, then back at Pauling. "They know everything. Their resources are unmatched."

Moss glanced at his watch. "Speaking of resources," he said. "I've got a plane to catch."

He stuck out his hand to Pauling and then to Tallon. "Any time you want to come back to The Department, we can always use the help," he said.

Tallon held up his hands.

"I'm retired," he said.

Moss laughed and left.

Pauling looked at Tallon.

"Department of what?" she asked.

Tallon shrugged his shoulders. "Murder."

He drained the rest of his coffee.

"Now what?" Pauling said.

"My room is paid through tomorrow," he said with a grin. "Why don't we put it to good use?"

Pauling smiled, finished her coffee.

"Took you long enough to ask."

CHAPTER THIRTY-NINE

ZURICH, SWITZERLAND

The body had been in the chilly waters of Lake Zurich for at least twenty-four hours before a visiting investment banker in a water taxi spotted it floating a hundred yards from shore.

A call was made and the police arrived. They promptly loaded the body onto their boat where it was decided there was no need to call a medical examiner to the scene because the cause of death was obvious.

Two bullet holes in the center of the dead man's forehead told the story.

From her perch high above Lake Zurich in the Collective's conference room, Gunnella Bohm watched the police boat motor away with the body of her former colleague.

Gregory had made several mistakes.

The fact was, his first lapse in judgment had already earned him a death sentence, the errors that followed simply provided additional support, albeit that evidence was completely unnecessary.

Once the decision to remove an individual from the Collective had been made, there was no going back.

Gunnella Bohm was well aware of Gregory's impending fate long before she officially ordered his removal from the Collective. It was both an instinctive sense that the man was not going to last, as well as a decision based on fact. Every member of the Collective was under various levels of surveillance, depending upon their experience, risk level and Bohm's ongoing assessment.

Gregory had been a holdover from her father's regime. A mistake that she never would have made.

The sins of the father, she thought.

Now, the sun was setting and the police boat was out of sight. The sky above the water took on the color of amber as the arrival of another crisp evening took shape over Lake Zurich.

Gunnella Bohm stepped back and pressed a nearly invisible button recessed along the edge of the large window. A white metal screen silently rolled down from above and covered the window, leaving the conference room as black as night.

By then, Gunnella Bohm was already gone.

GET MORE JACK REACHER NOW!

Book 3 in the USA TODAY BESTSELLING SERIES!

CLICK HERE TO BUY

AN AWARD-WINNING BESTSELLING MYSTERY SERIES

Buy DEAD WOOD, the first John Rockne Mystery.

CLICK HERE TO BUY

"Fast-paced, engaging, original."

-NYTimes bestselling author Thomas Perry

ABOUT THE AUTHOR

Dan Ames is a USA TODAY Bestselling Author and winner of the Independent Book Award for Crime Fiction.

www.authordanames.com
dan@authordanames.com

ALSO BY DAN AMES

THE JACK REACHER CASES

The JACK REACHER Cases #1 (A Hard Man To Forget)

The JACK REACHER Cases #2 (The Right Man For Revenge)

The JACK REACHER Cases #3 (A Man Made For Killing)

The JACK REACHER Cases #4 (The Last Man To Murder)

The JACK REACHER Cases #5 (The Man With No Mercy)

The JACK REACHER Cases #6 (A Man Out For Blood)

The JACK REACHER Cases #7 (A Man Beyond The Law)

The JACK REACHER Cases #8 (The Man Who Walks Away)

The JACK REACHER Cases (The Man Who Strikes Fear)

The JACK REACHER Cases (The Man Who Stands Tall)

The JACK REACHER Cases (The Man Who Works Alone)

The Jack Reacher Cases (A Man Built For Justice)

The JACK REACHER Cases #13 (A Man Born for Battle)

The JACK REACHER Cases #14 (The Perfect Man for Payback)

The JACK REACHER Cases #15 (The Man Whose Aim Is True)

The JACK REACHER Cases #16 (The Man Who Dies Here)

The JACK REACHER Cases #17 (The Man With Nothing To Lose)

The JACK REACHER Cases #18 (The Man Who Never Goes Back)

The JACK REACHER Cases #19 (The Man From The Shadows)

The JACK REACHER CASES #20 (The Man Behind The Gun)

JACK REACHER'S SPECIAL INVESTIGATORS

THE JOHN ROCKNE MYSTERIES

DEAD WOOD (John Rockne Mystery #1)

HARD ROCK (John Rockne Mystery #2)

COLD JADE (John Rockne Mystery #3)

LONG SHOT (John Rockne Mystery #4)

EASY PREY (John Rockne Mystery #5)

BODY BLOW (John Rockne Mystery #6)

THE WADE CARVER THRILLERS

MOLLY (Wade Carver Thriller #1)

SUGAR (Wade Carver Thriller #2)

ANGEL (Wade Carver Thriller #3)

THE WALLACE MACK THRILLERS

THE KILLING LEAGUE (Wallace Mack Thriller #1)

THE MURDER STORE (Wallace Mack Thriller #2)

FINDERS KILLERS (Wallace Mack Thriller #3)

THE MARY COOPER MYSTERIES

DEATH BY SARCASM (Mary Cooper Mystery #1)

MURDER WITH SARCASTIC INTENT (Mary Cooper Mystery #2)

GROSS SARCASTIC HOMICIDE (Mary Cooper Mystery #3)

THE CIRCUIT RIDER (WESTERNS)

THE CIRCUIT RIDER (Circuit Rider #1)

KILLER'S DRAW (Circuit Rider #2)

THE RAY MITCHELL THRILLERS

THE RECRUITER

KILLING THE RAT

HEAD SHOT

STANDALONE THRILLERS:

KILLER GROOVE (Rockne & Cooper Mystery #1)

BEER MONEY (Burr Ashland Mystery #1)

TO FIND A MOUNTAIN (A WWII Thriller)

BOX SETS:

AMES TO KILL

GROSSE POINTE PULP

GROSSE POINTE PULP 2

TOTAL SARCASM

WALLACE MACK THRILLER COLLECTION

SHORT STORIES:

THE GARBAGE COLLECTOR

BULLET RIVER

SCHOOL GIRL

HANGING CURVE

SCALE OF JUSTICE

FREE BOOKS AND MORE

Would you like a FREE book and the chance to win a FREE KINDLE?

Then sign up for the DAN AMES BOOK CLUB:

For special offers and new releases, sign up here

A MAN MADE FOR KILLING

SET IN THE REACHER UNIVERSE
BY PERMISSION OF LEE CHILD

DAN AMES

USA TODAY BESTSELLING AUTHOR

Published by Slogan Books, Inc., New York, NY.

FREE BOOKS AND MORE

Would you like a FREE copy of BULLET RIVER?

Then sign up for the DAN AMES BOOK CLUB:

For special offers and new releases, sign up here

AUTHOR'S NOTE

Although A MAN MADE FOR KILLING is the third book in the Jack Reacher Cases series, it is the first chronologically.

The time period is after Lauren Pauling appeared in Lee Child's THE HARD WAY, but before she has met Michael Tallon.

A MAN MADE FOR KILLING

THE JACK REACHER CASES

BOOK #3

by

Dan Ames

It is much more difficult to avoid wickedness,
for it runs faster than death.

-Socrates

CHAPTER ONE

The body washed ashore in pieces.

Each successive wave brought fresh evidence of a unique horror inflicted upon what was once a young woman.

When the tide receded, hours later as dawn began to break, the first of the gulls appeared overhead.

Simultaneously, a man emerged from the early morning fog. He ran with a slow purpose along the beach.

His name was Michael Tallon.

He was used to death.

He'd seen it in Iraq. Then again in Afghanistan. And in a few other places in the world he wasn't allowed to talk about.

Even here on San Clemente Island, a remote

barrier island off the coast of California, he knew he wasn't immune to it. It was here that special forces personnel often spent a great deal of time. Sometimes they came here to train. Other times, it was their first stop back from duty overseas. They came here first because it was a safe place to begin the decompression process. Not safer for the special forces, safer for the people around them.

Still, even among professionals, accidents happened. And other things did, too, that weren't always accidents.

Running on San Clemente Island was not to be undertaken lightly. The island was quite large, nearly twenty-five miles long and five miles wide. It had been used as an artillery range by Navy ships for decades. Now, it was a place shared by many different groups of the military. Some who knew each other. Some who didn't.

And the public hardly knew about the place at all.

The ground was still full of ordnance, some of it unexploded.

Tallon was a pro and he had spent a lot of time on the island. He knew when and where to run.

One of those spots was along the Western

coastline of the island. It was hard to get to and you could see where you were putting your feet.

So now, he turned up his pace as he neared the halfway point of his out-and-back run.

The morning sun was barely up and it was cold, yet sweat glistened on Tallon's forehead and his legs were slick.

San Clemente Island really didn't have a beach per se, simply larger outcroppings of rock with patches of sand here or there. This section of the island was the closest to being an actual beach and Tallon powered his way down the sand to the edge of the water.

As he slowed to a stop he noticed a large pile of sea cabbage, a frequent deposit found on the rocks. But a flash of white caught Tallon's eye and he went closer to the clump.

His breath slowed and he felt the warmth of the sun as it began to burn through the faint morning mist.

Tallon stopped.

He realized the small pile wasn't cabbage at all.

It was the shredded remains of a torso.

A female torso, as he recognized the sight of one breast that remained intact on the body.

He let out a long breath and looked around.

There was no one else here.

Tallon stepped closer to the remains and noted there were more deposited in a rough line along the remains of the outgoing tide.

He could make out chunks of human flesh. A severed limb that was most likely an arm.

Shark.

The island was surrounded by great white sharks, Tallon knew. You often saw them from the plane that brought personnel out from Los Angeles. Flying overhead you could frequently see the huge sharks, never swimming together, but on the prowl for the sea lions that made their home at various points along the shore.

The wounds on the torso were clear. Shredded skin that could only be a shark. He didn't know if it was a great white or not, but whatever it was had done its damage.

The rest was a mystery. There were no surfers out here. No one swam for recreation. Hell, even the Navy guys were careful about going in the water.

And then Tallon's breath caught in his throat.

Because he was looking at the foot that was partially covered with sand.

Peeking out of the sand was the top of a tattoo.

The ink on the skin was a rendering of a bird's wings.

Tallon let out the breath that he had been holding.

A chill went through his body.

He knew who she was.

CHAPTER TWO

"Jack Reacher needs your help."

Those were the words that had brought Pauling from New York to northern Wisconsin to meet with one of the wealthiest men in the country, Nathan Jones.

Now, Pauling drove her rental car, an SUV, up the long, winding drive to the sprawling log home that looked out over Barrel Lake. It was a private lake with only one home located on its shores.

It was a classic log home, but on a grander scale than most had ever imagined. It had a towering entrance with twin posts and a large steeped roof. There was an intricate carving above the front entrance, bigger than most double garages.

Pauling parked her vehicle on the circular drive, just past the entrance. Barrel Lake was reflected in the dozens of panoramic windows facing out from the house. A steady breeze blew in from the lake and in the distance, she saw a few whitecaps. The wind had picked up, and the fishing wouldn't be as good.

As Pauling walked to the front door she considered Nathan's call.

Her first thought was surprise that Jack Reacher needed help from her. More accurately, that Jack Reacher needed help, period.

Reacher was a guy who could handle anything on his own.

And most likely, had.

Still, Pauling was intrigued enough to meet with Nathan Jones. He had promised first-class accommodations and a week's worth of pay just to meet with him.

Pauling had done her research.

Nathan Jones had made a fortune in the paper business, the lumber business and the stock market, in that order. Not only did he own Barrel House, the name of his estate that referred to his love of blues music, but he had an apartment in Manhattan and a penthouse condo in the Florida Keys.

Pauling walked up to the deck that had sweeping views of the lake, and noticed her reflection in the huge bank of windows and sliding glass doors.

She was still in great shape. Over the years she'd had a lot of self-defense training and in addition to traditional workouts, she frequently dropped in on martial arts classes to keep her reflexes sharp.

The woman looking back at her was in good shape, with light, blonde hair cut short but stylish, a lean face with startling green eyes hidden behind a pair of Ray Ban aviator sunglasses.

Pauling peeked inside the house through the sliding glass doors.

Nathan Jones stood in the great room, looking out toward the lake, with a glass of whiskey in his hand. He waved Pauling inside.

"Hello," she said.

"Lauren Pauling, thank you for coming on such short notice."

"Thank you for the invitation."

"Can I get you something to drink?"

"Sure," she said. "Whatever you're having."

He nodded and went to a sideboard where a decanter of whiskey and several glasses sat.

Pauling studied him as he poured her drink.

Nathan was a big man, with broad shoulders and just a bit of gut beginning to hang over the edge of his pants. But he had a fine head of silver hair, ruddy cheeks, and the presence of a man who was used to getting things done. And getting them done his way.

Nathan returned with a drink in hand. He gave it to Pauling and then took a seat in one of the big chairs that flanked the main window looking out at the lake.

Pauling chose a chair across from him.

"So you said Jack Reacher needed help," Pauling said.

"Yes," Jones said. "I asked him to do a favor for me, and now he says he needs your help."

Pauling shook her head.

"Hard to believe, but I'll play along," she said. "What does he need help with?"

"It's about my daughter, Paige," Nathan said. "I'm sorry to be blunt, but she's dead."

"I'm sorry for your loss," Pauling said.

"What happened?" she asked.

"They say she drowned," Jones answered. He took a drink of liquor. "The story is she drowned and then sharks attacked her. Or vice versa."

His voice trembled briefly before he regained his composure. Pauling noted the sarcastic emphasis Jones had placed on the word *story*.

"She was working on San Clemente Island," he said. "Studying the Shrike. It's a kind of endangered bird."

"San Clemente?" Pauling thought the name sounded familiar but she couldn't place it.

"It's one of the Channel Islands off the coast of southern California. Owned by the Department of Defense."

"Was she working for the government?"

"No. That species of bird is endangered. Paige was working for the Bird Conservatory. They have a whole program out there to basically protect the bird population and try to get it to grow."

Pauling took a sip of Scotch. It wasn't her kind of drink, but it gave her a little time to think.

"When did this happen?" she asked.

"Six weeks ago."

Pauling straightened in her chair.

"Six weeks ago?"

"Yes. It took me awhile to determine the quality of the investigation."

"The police are investigating?"

"That's just it, they aren't."

Suddenly, Pauling was struck by where the conversation was going.

"I see," she started to say.

"It's all bullshit," Jones finally blurted out. He had seen the realization in her face.

"What's bullshit?"

"Everything the cops told me," Jones said.

"That she drowned?"

"Paige didn't drown," Jones said, his voice as harsh as sandpaper. He tossed down the rest of his Scotch and banged his glass down on the table next to his chair.

"She was murdered."

CHAPTER THREE

Pauling wasn't sure she had heard right. She figured Nathan Jones was a pragmatic man. A mourning parent often had the inability to think clearly.

Pauling chose her words carefully. She had seen more than her fair share of death and killing. It was instinctive to believe that accidents just can't happen – that a loved one can't be dead just by a cruel twist of fate. It gave comfort, in an odd way, for family members to believe that it had been a part of someone's plan.

But she had her doubts about this one.

"Why do you say that?" she asked.

He held out his thick hands and grabbed his pointer finger.

"One. Paige was not a swimmer. Not even

close. The only time she ever enjoyed getting in the ocean was in the Caribbean," he said. "And even then, she liked to stay shallow where she could see the bottom. When we went snorkeling she absolutely did not want to go out into deeper water."

"I can see that," Pauling said.

"Hell, half the time when we were traveling she didn't even want to swim in the goddamned hotel swimming pool. No way she would have gone out into that water. No way in hell," he said. His face was flushed and his voice had grown in both volume and intensity.

Pauling knew instinctively that what he was saying he unequivocally believed to be true.

"Two," Nathan continued. "We did some research. That water around San Clemente, at that time of year, is absolutely freezing. It's ice cold. There's just no way in hell Paige, who didn't like the water all that much to begin with, would suddenly decide to swim in fifty degree water. Absolutely no way in hell that was happening."

That made sense to Pauling. She'd spent more than her fair share of time in southern California. The water was usually pretty cold.

"And three, that water around the island is not conducive to swimming," Nathan concluded.

"First of all, there are a ton of sea lions around the island so there are about a bazillion sharks. And not the little bitty ones like you see in Florida. I'm talking the big boys. Great whites. Even the Navy guys who train there don't like to swim. And two, the water isn't very clear. In some spots it might be. But in most, it's not. So you tell me, would a girl who doesn't like to swim suddenly decide to jump in water that's ice-cold, murky, and full of sharks?"

To avoid answering, Pauling took another drink of her Scotch.

"No," Nathan said. "Absolutely not."

"What if she had gone out on a boat? Fallen off the boat and then drowned?"

"Whose boat?" Nathan countered. "Why didn't they alert the authorities? I checked, there were no missing boats during that time period. No sailboats gone missing. Plus, Paige had been working on the island."

"So what do you think happened?" Pauling asked. Nathan Jones had already done a lot of thinking and researching.

He finished off his glass of liquor before speaking. "What I think is that someone killed her and dumped her body out in the ocean and then let the sharks destroy the evidence."

Nathan slammed his empty glass down onto the table next to his chair.

"In fact, that's not what I think happened. That's exactly what happened. I know it more than I've ever known anything in my life."

He pointed his thick finger at her.

"That's why I got in touch with Jack Reacher. And now I need you to go out there and help him."

Jones leaned forward, the intensity coming off him in waves.

"You and Jack Reacher need to find the bastard who killed my daughter."

CHAPTER FOUR

"Here's why you and Reacher are the perfect pair to get the bottom of what happened to my daughter," Nathan said.

Pauling figured Nathan Jones was a master of negotiation so she sat back and listened.

"First of all, you're highly intelligent." He smiled at her. "Top of your class. Every Ivy League school wanted you. Second, you have an impressive background with some experience dealing with the military. Reacher's resumé speaks for itself in that regard."

He looked out the window at the lake. An eagle flew low looking for a fish. It careened back upward. No sign of prey.

"You're the right gender as well," he said.

"This place is about as male-dominated as you can get. If I only sent a man in there, it would become a bullshit testosterone macho contest. You can infiltrate much more effectively than some swinging dick like Reacher. The fact that you're beautiful will only help matters. The two of you will make a perfect tag-team."

To anyone else, it would have sounded sexist, but Pauling understood the man before her. His mind didn't work that way. He was all about strategy and aggression. Nothing more, nothing less.

"Reacher is already there, doing his thing. As far as your role, I've worked out an arrangement with the Bird Conservatory, thanks in part to their regret over what happened to my daughter," he said, his voice dripping with sarcasm. "It probably doesn't hurt either that I made a huge contribution to their fund awhile back."

Pauling sighed.

Nathan Jones was a force of nature.

He gestured toward the backpack and held up the envelope.

"Here's everything you'll need," he said. "A copy of the bullshit police report. Travel arrangements. Plane tickets. Dossiers on some of the individuals you'll meet. Phone numbers. Contact lists. Email addresses."

He put the envelope back into the pack.

"There's also a satellite phone, preprogrammed with my number and Blake Chandler's number. Blake is my computer guy."

Nathan Jones continued. "There's even a specially programmed laptop which has some uplink capabilities, courtesy of Blake. He'll be in touch with you if you need anything. There's also twenty grand in cash. Use it if you need it. And I will pay you for your time, double your normal fee. No matter how long it takes. Does that work for you?"

Pauling really hadn't planned on taking the case. She was overworked already. But the idea of working with Reacher again was too good to pass up.

"Yes," she replied.

"Great. Read through everything. We can fly you out there as soon as you're ready."

He got to his feet. Spoke softly, his voice trembling.

"Find out who killed my girl."

CHAPTER FIVE

The tiny log cabin located on Acorn Lake was just a few miles from Nathan Jones's sizeable domain. The cabin had been rented for her, just for the meeting with Nathan Jones.

Now, Pauling pulled the Land Rover into the gravel driveway, parked, got out and unlocked the cabin's front door. She walked inside and set the backpack Nathan had given her down on the couch.

The cabin consisted of one room that contained an open kitchen, a living area with a wood burning fireplace, a small dining table, and a loft with a bed. The only other room was the bathroom just off of the kitchen. The walls were knotty pine. The giant picture window facing the lake provided all of the cabin's decoration.

Pauling went to the refrigerator and pulled out a bottle of Chardonnay. She poured herself a glass, dug out the envelope from the backpack and walked out onto the cabin's front porch. Two weathered Adirondack chairs sat facing the lake. She took the one nearest the door, sat down and set the folder in her lap.

She took a drink of wine and studied Acorn Lake.

It was much smaller than Barrel Lake. The water wasn't as clear and there were more widespread weed beds. Trees towered along the lake, dropping their acorns into the water, giving the lake its name. They also caused the water to turn darker.

It was hard not to feel compassion for Nathan Jones and a a wave of sadness for his daughter.

She also felt an eagerness and excitement to see Reacher again. Had he changed? What was going on that he needed her help? And did he really need her help or did he just want to see her again?

As she gazed out at the lake, saw the sky turning from blue to dark red at its edges, she thought about the situation.

Pauling looked down at the envelope in her lap, opened it and pulled out the thick sheaf of papers.

The travel documents were first, with airplane tickets and a hotel reservation in Los Angeles. She glanced at the dates. Yes indeed, he wanted her leaving as soon as possible.

Pauling put the travel papers back in the envelope.

Next, she skimmed the contact list and the instructions for using both the sat phone and the laptop.

The dossiers she didn't even glance at. Those she could read later.

The police report was only two pages long. A clear case of drowning. It appeared as if no other detective work had been attempted.

Finally, she pulled out a leather journal. When she opened it, a photograph fell out. A note was attached that told her it was Paige Jones, a year ago, standing at the top of an old wooden tower that had been built to look out over a sinkhole in the state forest a dozen or so miles from Barrel Lake.

Paige had been a beautiful girl. Dark hair, startling blue eyes, and an enigmatic smile.

She opened the journal and saw another note. It was Paige's journal.

It wasn't a diary, but rather notes from the field on habitat and wildlife. There was no date on either inside cover.

Pauling put the journal back in the envelope and studied the mirrored surface of the lake.

The sun was setting, and a tangerine sky was now sporting subtle shades of purple. It would disappear behind the trees in less than a half hour.

Pauling gently nudged backward and the sound of the rocking chair creaking on the wooden porch seemed obscenely loud.

Another eagle, maybe the same one from Barrel Lake, appeared over the treetops and dove toward the surface of the water.

This time, it dove sharply and its claws tore through the water.

When it surged upward, it had a fish in its talons.

It reminded her of Jack Reacher, and a saying her old boss often used.

A true hunter never stops hunting.

CHAPTER SIX

She wasn't surprised to receive a call from Nathan Jones. He'd probably made a large part of his fortune by being able to read people. And as good as Pauling's poker face was, when she'd learned that Reacher needed her help, she was already in.

"Blake will pick you up at six a.m. sharp," Nathan said. "Plenty of time since your flight doesn't leave until nine-thirty. He'll return your rental car later."

Pauling had glanced at the itinerary and knew that from the small airport in northern Wisconsin she would fly to Milwaukee and then from there to Los Angeles.

"I have to be honest with you," Pauling

explained. "I don't feel there's a high probability of success on this."

His response was immediate. "Something like this you don't play the odds," he said. "You make them. I have a sense of how you like to work, Pauling, and my guess is it's a lot like mine."

Pauling wasn't so sure of that herself, but she had to admit that Nathan Jones was no doubt a highly driven person. And she'd been labeled with that term from time to time herself.

"Every wall you run into you see as a temporary obstruction," Nathan continued. "Your first instinct is to go right through it. If that doesn't work, you find a way around. But then you go back and remove it anyway, just in case you have to come back that way."

Pauling smiled at the compliment. It made a sort of sense to her and it was a statement she couldn't disagree with.

"Walls and bridges, sometimes they have to be destroyed," she said.

"Now you're really sounding like me," Nathan said with no small amount of satisfaction. "Good luck and stay in touch. Make your first progress report whenever you feel like you have something you want to share. This is your show, not mine."

It was her hope to find out everything she could within two weeks at the most. If she hadn't learned anything by then, Pauling figured spending even more time there wouldn't accomplish much.

At least, that was her goal. Maybe she could do it in two days and be back.

A lot of it depended on Jack Reacher.

A light rain had begun to make its way across the lake and now it was pattering against the cabin walls. Pauling built a fire in the fireplace, the last one she would probably enjoy for awhile and sat down on the couch.

Suddenly, she had an intense desire to talk to someone. Anyone. Pauling looked at her phone. There were a few people she could call, including her sister, but she decided against it.

Instead, Pauling dug out Paige's journal from the backpack and opened it.

She read through the first few pages which consisted of notes regarding ground cover and a bunch of long, complicated names in Latin. Maybe once she was on the island she could talk to someone who would be able to interpret for her.

On the fourth page, there was a beautiful drawing of a bird. It was perched on a thorny branch. Next to it, there was the body of a mouse.

The mouse had been impaled on one of the tree's thorns.

Beneath the drawing, Paige had written three words.

The Butcher Bird.

CHAPTER SEVEN

In the morning, Blake arrived and Pauling threw her things into the SUV. She climbed into the passenger seat.

"I grabbed you a coffee," he said. "Black, right?"

"Thanks, yes," she said. "Where did you get it? Isn't the nearest Starbucks about a hundred miles away?"

"I picked it up at the mini-mart at the edge of town. It's not great, but not bad, either. I was going to get you some jerky too and maybe a baseball cap with a drawing of a hunter standing over a deer with the caption *the buck stops here*."

Pauling blew on the coffee and took a sip. Not bad. Nice and strong the way she liked it.

Blake pulled out onto the dirt road, eventually

making it to the rural highway where he was able to notch the speed up significantly.

"By the way, I meant to compliment you on your poker face," Pauling said. "We fished together all day and you never once mentioned Nathan's plan."

A sheepish expression came across Blake's face. "Honestly, I didn't know his plan and he didn't really tell me. It was more of a technical request. But once he started asking me to do specific things with documents, phone numbers, addresses and email addresses I started to guess it was going to involve you."

"I'm just giving you shit, Blake." She felt bad making him explain himself.

"Oh," he said, looking relieved. "You know Nathan. No one wants to get on his bad side."

There was an awkward silence between them.

"You're not asking where I'm going and what I'm doing because you don't want to know, right?" she guessed.

Blake drummed his thin, pale fingers on the steering wheel. Pauling guessed he'd been spending a lot more time in his office on the computers than in the boat fishing.

"It wouldn't take a genius to guess it has something to do with Paige. But exactly what you're doing and how you're going to get involved in it, well–"

"Do you want to know?"

"You tell me," he answered. "I don't want to know if I'm not *supposed* to know."

"Okay," Pauling said. "To put an end to this goofy conversation, I'm going to say it's on a need-to-know basis and right now, you don't need to know exactly what I'm doing. But I believe you're going to be a resource for me. Did Nathan at least explain that?"

"Yeah, he kind of mentioned it. Again, in a general sense."

"Okay, we're in agreement then," Pauling said. "Although depending on what I find, the level of your involvement could change quickly. How's that?"

"Fine with me," Blake said. "I've been in the dark most of my life. I like it there."

Pauling laughed. She loved Blake and how self-deprecating he always was. It was refreshing from the host of alpha males she had always been forced to deal with.

They talked a lot about former high school friends and what they were doing as the rain abated and a few tentative shafts of sunlight appeared in the horizon. The landscape changed from thick trees to gently rolling hills and eventually they found the airport.

It was a single building with a few parked cars in front. Behind the building, they could see the runway and an airplane that appeared to be idling.

"I think that's Nathan's private plane," Blake said.

Pauling got out of the Explorer and hoisted her backpack onto her shoulder. Blake retrieved the one rolling suitcase she was bringing.

That was it.

"Be careful," Blake said.

"I'll shoot first and ask questions later."

Blake hugged her.

"I would expect nothing less."

CHAPTER EIGHT

The flight was going to be so short Pauling didn't bother breaking open her backpack to do any more investigating. Nathan's private plane was going to take her to Milwaukee, and from there, she would catch a commercial flight to Los Angeles.

So she simply enjoyed the scenery on the small plane, felt some of the despondency that had begun to sink in now fall away as the aircraft lifted off.

Beneath her, Wisconsin's green rolling hills flattened out into traditional quadrants of farm fields. Occasionally, a stand of trees had been planted to serve as windbreaks.

It seemed they had barely leveled off before

the pilot announced they were beginning their descent.

The plane touched down and she was escorted across the tarmac and back into a terminal where a commercial flight was boarding for Los Angeles.

She took a quick detour to get a bottle of water and a bag of nut mix.

Pauling preferred to stand while waiting for the plane to board and soon she was in the first-class line and then promptly showed her seat.

No one sat next to her and the fight attendant asked her if she wanted a drink. She was about to say no, then changed her mind and asked for a Bloody Mary. Why not?

Eventually, the boarding doors closed with first class still half-empty, even after the few upgrades had taken place. The seat next to Pauling was still empty and she moved her backpack from the foot space in front of her and plopped it into the seat next to her.

Pauling sipped her Bloody Mary, which tasted surprisingly good and closed her eyes. She thought about trying to sleep but she was too well-rested.

Pauling opened the backpack, pushed aside Paige's journal and instead took out the file with background information on San Clemente Island.

Whatever researcher Nathan had hired to provide background for her had done a very good job. The information was presented in a very neat and orderly fashion.

San Clemente Island sat sixty-eight miles off the coast of California and was part of the Channel Islands. It was twenty-one miles long and nearly five miles wide.

Native American remains dated to at least ten thousand years ago, and the island had been named by a Spanish explorer who'd discovered it on Saint Clement's Feast Day, hence San Clemente.

The United States military acquired the island in the 1930s, mainly as a ship-to-shore firing range. Training continued on the island to this day.

Tell me about the birds, Pauling thought as she skimmed through more of the island's vital statistics.

Finally, she got to the part she'd been looking for.

In the midst of the biggest live firing range the military owned, an endangered bird lived. The Shrike of San Clemente. At one point, it had become one of the rarest birds in the world with only fourteen living individuals left.

When it was put on the endangered species list, the Bird Conservatory among others rushed in and began efforts to protect it. The military was immediately forced to cease some of its more "disruptive" activities and now worked in tandem with the naturalists to protect the bird.

Probably after some bad public relations, Pauling figured.

She read the last page and slipped the papers back into their folder and the folder went into the backpack.

She closed her eyes.

Imagine that. A rare bird in the middle of a live firing range on an island populated by what sounded like plenty of Special Operations soldiers.

And right in among all of that?

Paige Jones.

Beautiful.

Intelligent.

And apparently vulnerable.

Despite her conviction that dozing was not an option, Pauling began to drift off to sleep.

Had Paige Jones met Jack Reacher? If so, how had this happened? Pauling figured that Reacher had arrived after the murder.

Maybe because *of* it.

One final thought entered Pauling's mind.

She wondered if Paige Jones ever had any inkling of the dangers surrounding her on San Clemente Island.

In Pauling's sleep, no answer came.

CHAPTER NINE

It was a smooth landing but Pauling was wide awake before the rubber hit the road. They taxied into their parking spot and soon she was off the plane, through the terminal and when she descended via the escalator, she caught sight of a driver holding up a card emblazoned with her name.

Pauling almost laughed. When Nathan Jones arranged your travel, no expense was spared.

She approached the man holding the placard bearing her name, showed her identification and he took her out to a black Cadillac Escalade.

Fresh from the terminal, she stepped out into the southern California air and smiled. It was so much warmer and less humid than back in Wisconsin.

She climbed into the back while the driver put away her bags.

"From one airport to another," the driver said. He smiled at her from the rearview mirror.

"No rest for the wicked," Pauling answered.

He put the big SUV into gear and they wound their way out of the airport before merging onto Sepulveda. They were heading south and Pauling knew from what Nathan had given her that the airport she would be going to wasn't exactly official. There were a number of planes and pilots that were pre-approved by the military people on San Clemente. It wasn't possible to get there without permission in the first place. Every plane had to have its manifest approved by the authorities on San Clemente Island.

Nathan had strategized that the best way forward was to have her listed as an employee of San Diego State who was volunteering her time with the Bird Conservatory. If anyone wished to take the time to run her identity, it would show the cover story Nathan had concocted; that she was an IT specialist. More of a general troubleshooter, really. That distinction would help her avoid anything too technical should an issue arise.

The good news, and the reason Nathan had chosen that role was that Pauling had learned quite a bit about computers, and had spent the majority of her workday on one at the FBI.

But she was not an IT specialist by any means.

She didn't really expect to have to defend her cover story that much anyway. She had gotten the sense that the bird people were constantly in the field while her story was that she would be checking and updating the main computer system in their office. And she could be vague enough about geeky computer code stuff to bore anyone to tears.

They headed south and Pauling soon recognized the area south of Los Angeles. Manhattan Beach. Long Beach. The sight of industrial areas and loading docks.

It was the part of Los Angeles tourists never saw and pictures of which never graced the front of postcards sent to the old folks back home.

They made their way past strip malls and the occasional factory, with quick glimpses of tiny residential neighborhoods choked with parked cars packed tightly on the street bumper to bumper. Here and there groups of men stood on street corners and the occasional shopkeeper sweeping the walk in front of an ethnic grocery store.

The driver turned onto a street that looked

more to Pauling like an alley than an actual traffic lane, eventually arriving at an impressive gate topped with razor wire. The driver said something into the intercom and the sturdy gate, sporting wheels on the bottom, rolled apart and the driver pulled the SUV ahead to an open aircraft hangar. He parked, helped Pauling with her bag and thanked her when she slipped him a twenty.

Hell, she had twenty grand in cash. The least she could do was be a good tipper.

Once the Escalade drove away, Pauling went into the open hangar.

There was a man with a clipboard and a walkie talkie on his hip. He was probably in his late thirties or early forties, brown hair with a touch of gray at the temples. He had on cargo pants and a jacket that was military green.

Behind him was a vintage airplane on display. Pauling wondered if it was one of the original Pan Am airplanes that were pre-WWII.

She was glad it appeared to be open to visitors.

She approached the man with the clipboard.

He looked up.

"Lauren Pauling?" he said.

"Hello."

He stuck out his hand. "Josh Troyer," he said. "I'm the flight coordinator for NASSCI."

A puzzled expression on Pauling's face made him chuckle.

"Naval Air Station San Clemente Island," he said. "We're really fond of acronyms around here."

"Got it," she said. Government speak was nothing new to her.

"You've got about twenty minutes if you want to grab a coffee or something," he said. "Facilities are over there." He pointed to public restrooms as well as a set of vending machines.

"Okay," Pauling said. "Is that exhibit open for viewing?" she said, pointing to the ancient plane. "I'd love to get a glimpse inside."

"Sure," he said. "An original DC-3. Built in 1930 or so. Yes, you can see the inside. After all, it's what you'll be flying in out to the island."

CHAPTER TEN

They carefully weighed and stowed Pauling's gear and showed the same care for everything else that went onto the plane. Apparently they needed to be meticulous when it came to loading the old aircraft.

Troyer introduced her to the pilot, a man named Brock Jamison. He looked to be a little younger than Troyer. Slim, with dark hair and intense blue eyes. When he smiled, his teeth were jagged and crooked, ruining what would have been a strikingly handsome man. Pauling guessed he was a civilian pilot otherwise the military's dental plan would have taken care of those teeth.

"Hope you're not used to flying first class," Jamison said. She noticed that he actively worked to hide his teeth. He smiled only with his lips and at times it looked more like a grimace.

"No divas here," Pauling said. "How long is the flight?"

"Little over an hour, depending on wind," Jamison said. "Plus, top speed isn't very fast." He gestured at the plane behind them. "But she'll get us there. Hopefully."

Troyer made a sign of the cross and then both he and Jamison chuckled. It looked like a little comedy routine.

It turned out, they were just getting started.

Pauling boarded the aircraft with the other passengers.

The interior was something else. It had been done up almost as some kind of Las Vegas lounge act. Velvet seats, velvet curtains over the windows, and purple carpet. The lights along the row between the seats were done in rainbow colors and there was rock music playing in the background.

All this airplane needs is a stripper pole, Pauling thought.

As the other passengers boarded, she tried to figure out who they were by their appearances, but it wasn't easy.

The military people were obvious, of course.

She saw two people in Navy Seabee uniforms, one man and one woman. If Pauling recalled correctly the Seabees were the construction arm of the Navy.

There were two men wearing ties who looked like engineers. They had already broken out their laptops and appeared to be going over spreadsheets.

An entire group boarded the plane but Pauling had no idea who or what they might be. It was mostly guys, dressed in tan camo pants and Nike t-shirts. There was a woman, also dressed more in athletic gear than military gear.

Once everybody had found a seat, and nearly every seat was taken, the plane began to taxi toward the runway.

Troyer appeared from the cockpit, pushing a small cart. On its surface were bottles of beer along with an ice bucket in which a bottle of white wine had been placed.

"May I interest anyone in a beverage?" he said. The passengers erupted in applause. Pauling laughed and took a beer, just to join in.

As Troyer made the rounds, Jamison appeared, which made Pauling wonder, who exactly was in control of the plane?

"As some of you may or may not know, San

Clemente Island is one of the Channel Islands and home to a very robust population of sea lions." He had a martini glass in his hand and gestured with it as he spoke.

Pauling continued to look out the window as the plane flew, wondering exactly when autopilot had been invented and hoped that it was after the manufacture date of the aircraft. That, or maybe one had been retrofitted.

Either way, she hoped someone was paying attention.

"The sea lion's main predator is a teeny weeny fish called the great white shark," Jamison continued. He sipped from his martini and pulled out the olive and chomped it down.

"They literally surround San Clemente Island and attack anything in the water within a few feet of them," he said. He tossed down the rest of his martini and Pauling hoped that his title of "pilot" was ceremonious at best and there was really someone else who would fly the plane.

"With that in mind, today's entertainment on the short flight out to the island is a little film made by my good friend Steven Spielberg," Jamison continued. "It really made his reputation as a filmmaker and most of all, accurately captures the dangers surrounding San Clemente

Island, especially if this old gal doesn't quite make it." He patted the ceiling above him.

"Enjoy the flight, folks!" he said and beamed at the passengers who half-heartedly raised their drinks in a mock toast.

Jamison disappeared behind the curtains that blocked the view to the cockpit, and Troyer returned the cart (now empty) to a spot just in front of the first row. He locked it in place and then joined Jamison at the helm.

On the video screens spaced periodically above the seats, the opening of the movie JAWS began to play.

Pauling smirked and drank her beer.

Well, she thought, *it was a great film.*

CHAPTER ELEVEN

The shark on the screen was not alone.

As they approached the island, Pauling saw a huge, dark shadow languidly cruising less than a quarter mile from the island.

As if reading her mind, Jamison's voice spoke over the intercom.

"There's one of our native San Clementians as we speak."

Everyone found a window and watched the huge shark cruise its patrol.

Pauling couldn't help but think of Paige, and wondered if this was the same shark that may have gotten to her. All of the humor and jocularity of the flight instantly disappeared.

She drew the curtain on her window closed and thought about the job ahead.

There wasn't much to her cover. An IT specialist. Helping the bird people.

It could be done.

The descent was loud, slow and jarring. When they landed, it seemed like they went on forever, but Pauling knew the runway was actually very short. And she had read that the flight conditions themselves were very dangerous. High winds. Short runway. Small margin of error. Despite their bad comedy show, Pauling figured that Jamison and Troyer were probably very good at what they did.

Eventually the plane came to a stop and they disembarked. A young man in military clothing unloaded the gear and had it waiting for them on the tarmac. Although 'tarmac' was far too grandiose a word. The runway was cracked asphalt and another metal shed served as the airport's headquarters.

Pauling found her bags and carried them into the metal shed.

It reminded her vaguely of the small airport in northern Wisconsin, but this one was even more rustic. The vending machines were older. The floor was dirtier. And the smell was, well, *stronger*.

"Pauling?" a male voice said behind her.

She turned to find a curly-haired man, brushed with gray, wearing wire-rim glasses, a thick barn coat, blue jeans and Sperry boat shoes.

"Yes?" she said.

"My name is Dr. Abner Sirrine."

Pauling shook his hand, noting the soft grip. He made no move to help her with her bags. She thought he looked nervous.

"I'm parked right outside."

He turned and Pauling followed him to a filthy, older model Jeep Cherokee. It was white underneath a layer of dirt and grime.

Dr. Sirrine got behind the wheel.

Pauling loaded her bags into the backseat and then climbed into the front passenger space. The interior of the jeep was just as dirty as the outside. Gum wrappers, chunks of mud and grass, an empty Diet Coke can.

"So I guess I'll take you back to our HQ."

His voice was soft and tentative. She thought he sounded like a college professor or a high school biology teacher.

"Actually, can you give me a quick tour of the island?" Pauling asked. "Just to help me get my bearings."

She smiled at Dr. Sirrine and thought he

seemed to relax a bit. In that moment, she understood why he was nervous. As always, she weighed the pros and cons of alleviating the tension. Sometimes it worked in your favor. For now, she decided to help him out.

"What were you told about the work I would be doing while I'm on the island?" she asked.

He gave her a look that was a cross between guilt and panic. "Well, no one would tell me exactly. Something about computer systems which is kind of odd because ours is really old and basic. Not much to analyze, really."

Nathan had told her she would be given a solid cover and she hadn't been on the island for more than a few minutes and someone was calling bullshit. Not a great start.

"That's part of it," Pauling said. "To study what you have and possibly make some recommendations on how to upgrade it or scrap it altogether and get something new."

"I see."

"And it's not just computers. My role is really to analyze the technology you're employing and prepare a report on how things can be improved and made more efficient. That's why I'll be involved in all aspects of what you're doing out here."

She thought he was going to protest so she quickly added, "Just as an observer, though. I'm not a biologist so I'll just try to stay out of your way."

This was also Pauling's way of letting him know that she would be needing to talk to everyone. From top to bottom.

"So what can you tell me about the island, Dr. Sirrine?" Pauling asked.

She'd already done her homework, but she got the sense that this was the kind of man who liked to hear himself talk, especially when it came to educating someone. Perhaps a female was also an inspiration.

"Fascinating history, really," Dr. Sirrine said.

Pauling chuckled silently.

Bingo.

CHAPTER TWELVE

"The earliest remains are from nearly ten thousand years ago. Most scholars believe it was the Tongva Native Americans with some influence from the Chumash as well."

They rounded a sharp curve and Pauling braced herself. Maybe it wasn't such a good idea to distract Dr. Sirrine. His driving skills couldn't afford it.

"From there the next stage was the Spanish conquest. A man named Juan Rodriguez Cabrillo discovered the island but it was named by a later explorer, Sebastian Vizcaino, who arrived on the island on the Feast of St. Clements Day. Hence the name."

"They must not have stayed around very

long," Pauling said. "They didn't build anything. Not even a church?"

Dr. Sirrine shook his head. "No, the island is too far from the mainland."

Pauling watched a seagull fly over the jeep and in the distance, she saw a military helicopter.

"The most fascinating part of the history of the island though isn't the people, it's the animals," Dr. Sirrine continued. "Although, I admit I'm probably not terribly objective."

Pauling was listening but she was stunned by the scenery. It was nearly apocalyptic. Very little shrubbery. Dirt roads that seemed to disappear over the edge of a cliff. Just bare land, the ocean in the background and sky. Fascinating. And surreal. She realized she'd never seen a place like this before. Anywhere.

"Feral animals, to be more specific," Dr. Sirrine continued. "It seems that some of the early peoples, or settlers after the Spanish, had goats. And when they left, a few of the goats remained. And naturally, the animals did what animals do. They ate and they reproduced. And ate some more and reproduced a lot more. At some point there were ten thousand goats on the island and not a stitch of green. No grass. No shrubs. No trees. Nothing."

It made sense to Pauling. To her, it looked like the landscape hadn't really recovered. The whole place felt like a Mad Max movie setting, on an island in the middle of the Pacific.

"So when the military bought the island, they had to get rid of the goats." Sirrine smiled and waggled a finger in the general direction of the windshield. He was really loosening up now. "They didn't kill them. Oh no, the public found out somehow and caused a huge uproar. So they had to airlift them off the island!" He laughed. "Can you believe it?"

"Operation Goat Removal," Pauling said.

"Yes! How bizarre!" Dr. Sirrine said. "And that's the whole story of why I'm out here. But there's plenty of time to tell you about that." His voice had taken on an edge of mystery.

"Habitat destruction?" Pauling said. "That's what led to the decline of all animal populations, right?"

Dr. Sirrine's eyes widened behind his glasses. "Yes, exactly. You've done your homework."

He sounded impressed and disappointed that he had been denied the answer to his mystery.

"I always took my homework seriously," Pauling said. Which was total bullshit. She had rarely done her homework when she was a student, preferring the all-night cram sessions fueled by pressure. It had been a game to her. It was only when she'd gotten a real job that she finally realized the need for daily focus.

"So now we're approaching the south end of the island?" she asked.

"Yes, this is where you'll be doing some field-work with the team. That is, if you really want to understand what we do."

"Yes, I do."

They drove in silence for several miles. Pauling was astounded continuously by what she saw. The landscape was like a huge tract of ocean front real estate that had yet to be discovered by the hotel people.

She could picture a Four Seasons Resort springing up or a tropical resort every mile or so. They would import tons of royal palm trees. They would have to make the island look lush and fertile, in a commercial sense. And that could certainly be accomplished, with a big enough landscaping budget.

But none of that would happen, after all, because the island was owned by the military. Pauling knew that the U.S. government was the biggest single owner of real estate in the country.

Dr. Sirrine continued to drive and Pauling was

aware that he performed the task much better when he wasn't talking. However, she was here to gather information.

"So how many people are on your team?"

"Well, the number is fluid. People are constantly coming in and out of here due to the nature of their careers. We have some summer grad students, people on fellowships, volunteer observers and students who are only available for a semester or two. So there is actually a very high turnover, although we do everything we can to maintain some kind of continuity."

It was not what Pauling wanted to hear. She had hoped there would be more of a locked-room type of situation, so she could narrow the investigation as quickly as possible. But if people were coming and going on a regular basis it would make her job more difficult.

"Have you been working with Jack Reacher at all?" Pauling asked.

Dr. Sirrine looked at her. "Who?"

Pauling shook her head in reply.

"I'm going to turn here," Dr. Sirrine said. It was a strange little intersection. A sign to the right said RESTRICTED and there was a gate across the road. Although, with four-wheel drive, it seemed it would be relatively easy to drive around it.

"There are quite a few of those around." He glanced at her. "They don't look like much, but you have to pay attention to what they're saying. There are people with guns and live ammunition everywhere. If a sign says not to enter, take their advice and don't enter."

They continued on as the sun began to set. The ocean looked beautiful in the dying light.

"Is every sunset as spectacular as this?" Pauling said.

Dr. Sirrine looked up and out at the water.

"You know, I never really noticed."

CHAPTER THIRTEEN

The road wound off to the side where a collection of buildings sat on a small rise. They were a combination of cinder block and aluminum. The main building had a row of parking spots in front of it. It was the cinder block building.

Above the main entrance was a wooden sign with the words THE NEST burned in by hand.

Dr. Sirrine pulled into the first parking spot next to the main building, and shut off the jeep.

"Welcome to The Nest as we call it," he said. He held up his hands. "Don't shoot me for the bad pun. Someone long before me came up with it."

"I like it," Pauling said.

"Bring your stuff in here and we'll figure out where you're staying," he said.

He went to the back of the jeep and grabbed his gear which consisted of a battered, brown leather backpack.

Pauling brought her gear through the door that Dr. Sirrine held open for her.

The space was one large room. Off to the left, a full kitchen with a counter and a refrigerator and a few tables surrounded by plastic chairs.

The floor was industrial tile, plain white. The walls were standard beige and the ceiling was a classic dropped number that looked like it had come from an elementary school from the 1970s.

Directly ahead was a small living-room type area with a couch, love seat, and some mismatched chairs facing a large screen television that had been directly mounted to the wall.

Off to the right was a doorway that led to a hall.

Dr. Sirrine led her down the hallway where there were rooms spaced at lengthy intervals, with dark wood fiber doors that seemed more appropriate in a shoddily built office building.

The same tile floor was in place, and the hall smelled vaguely of disinfectant.

They came to the end of the hallway and one

door remained.

"Ah yes, here you go," he said.

He used a key to open the door and then he flicked the light on inside and handed the key to Pauling.

"Home sweet home," he said.

Pauling stepped past him into the room. There was a dresser with a mirror above it. The dresser was made of flimsy particle board and it seemed to sag crookedly against the wall like it was too tired to hold up the mirror any longer.

There was a bed with a steel frame and no headboard. A mattress was on top of visible coiled springs and a stack of sheets and blankets were on top of the mattress.

A tiny bathroom was on the opposite side of the room.

There was a closet built into the wall across from the bed that looked like it could hold a half dozen t-shirts and not much else.

And next to the dresser was a desk that must have been rescued from a middle school that was about to be demolished.

"Well, someone will probably be throwing together some kind of meal in the next hour or so," Dr. Sirrine said. "If you want to settle in and then come on up to the main room you can feel free. Nothing formal happens. But I think when someone is joining us, there is usually a meal."

"Okay, thank you. I will," Pauling said.

Dr. Sirrine backed out of the room and she could hear his footsteps down the hall.

Pauling unpacked, which took no time at all. She stuffed most everything into the shoddy drawers of the dresser, and hung a few things up in the tiny closet with a single bar.

At least the room was spotless. Someone had thoroughly cleaned the place since its last inhabitant. Pauling suddenly wondered if this had been Paige's room. She made a mental note to ask.

Finally, she unpacked the laptop, phone and all of the chargers and power cords that she would need and placed them all on the desk. There was an outlet just behind the desk and Pauling was glad she had thrown in a power strip. She plugged everything in.

Lastly, she took Paige's journal out of her backpack and tossed it onto the bed. She would read it before she went to sleep tonight.

One last stop into the bathroom where she splashed water on her face and then she closed the door, locking it behind her.

It was time to meet everyone.

And hopefully find Jack Reacher.

CHAPTER FOURTEEN

Pauling smelled the food first. She thought she detected onions, peppers and maybe a dash of cumin. If she had to guess, she would predict tacos were going to be the main course at tonight's dinner. Mexican food, for sure.

She came around the corner and saw a woman with dark hair, black glasses and a gray t-shirt standing over a large frying pan. The woman looked up at her.

"Hi," she said and smiled, revealing a row of teeth, tinged slightly red by the glass of wine next to her on the counter.

"Hello," Pauling responded. "Smells good."

"My standard chicken fajitas," the woman said. "If you see me cooking, odds are that nine out of ten times I'll be making fajitas. Kind of a one-hit wonder."

The woman put down the wooden spatula she had been using to stir the contents of the frying pan and stepped out from behind the counter. She thrust her hand out toward Pauling.

"I'm Janey Morris," she said. She was a small woman with pale skin and had the look of a nerdy librarian.

"Nice to meet you, I'm Pauling."

Janey smiled. "Abner said you'd be arriving today. How was the flight in?" Janey moved back to the pan and started to stir around the fajita ingredients.

Pauling looked around for a bottle of wine but didn't see one. She wouldn't mind a cocktail right about now, she thought.

Pauling noticed a second pan with a few tortillas warming.

"The flight was interesting," Pauling said. "I thought the plane was an antique for display purposes only. Didn't realize I'd actually be flying in it."

"I did the same thing," Janey said. "It was kind of cool. I felt like I was in an old Humphrey Bogart movie. And the guys are so funny. It was a really cool experience."

"They're funny the first time, but the routine gets old," a voice said from the living area. Pauling turned, realized she hadn't noticed the person sitting on the couch.

He was tall and thin with a face that sported an enormous jaw and big ears.

"Pauling, this is Ted. Ted, this is Pauling," Janey said, making the introductions.

Ted put down the book he had been reading, came over and shook Pauling's hand. Probably the kind of kid who was told by everyone to play basketball but was terribly uncoordinated. It was a hunch, but Pauling figured Ted wasn't very athletic.

"Want a beer?" he said.

"Sure."

While Ted went to the refrigerator Pauling said to Janey, "Is there something I can do to help out?"

"You can shred some cheese if you want," Janey answered, pointing at the chunk of cheddar on the counter next to a well-used grater. Pauling started the process while Ted handed her a bottle of beer. She raised the bottle, said 'cheers' and took a long drink. Still a little tired from the trip, the beer tasted great. Ice cold.

"Do you normally all eat together?" Pauling asked.

"Hell no," Ted said. "This place is chaotic with everyone on different schedules. We all kind of chip in and grab food or cook whatever's in the fridge. Abner does most of the supply ordering, so we're stuck with whatever's around. It's not like there's a grocery store around the corner."

Just then, Dr. Sirrine emerged from the hallways behind the kitchen. Pauling had a strange notion that he'd been standing there listening and now decided to come into the room. She wasn't sure why she felt that way, but it felt right.

"Yes, I'm in charge of the ordering," he said. "And this is the most important part." He held up a beer from the fridge and also gestured toward some chilled bottles of white wine in the door's shelves and a vast array of red wine on the counter to the left of the fridge.

"Not everyone drinks here," Janey said, rolling her eyes a bit at Dr. Sirrine and Ted. "These guys make it sound like we're a bunch of lushes. But since there isn't a whole lot to do around here after the work is done, let's say that most of us enjoy the cocktail hour on a fairly regular basis."

"Cocktail hours, would be more accurate,"

Ted said, putting emphasis on the plurality of the word.

He chugged his beer and got another, raised an eyebrow in question at Pauling. She smiled and shook her head. Her beer was still pretty much full.

"So you're here to help with our computer systems?" Janey said.

Pauling heard Ted snicker under his breath.

A quick glance at Janey's wide and expressionless face made Pauling groan inwardly because the picture of innocence was total bullshit. Nathan's efforts to place Pauling here secretly hadn't worked. Pauling instantly knew that no one had bought the cover story.

"That, and more," Pauling said. The rest of them seemed to wait for her to explain, but she didn't. It wasn't a lie. And the tone in her voice conveyed the message that she didn't care what they thought. She was going to do her job and do it right.

Clearly, the message got through because Ted's smirk dropped immediately from his face and Janey quickly became more interested in her meal preparation.

And suddenly, Dr. Sirrine was gone.

CHAPTER FIFTEEN

After dinner, the fajitas were surprisingly tasty, Pauling stopped at the bulletin board in the hallway on the way to her room. There were various schedules posted, some Dilbert cartoons and a few articles on the Bird Conservatory, mostly pertaining to funding issues. There were also a few military articles about various internal notices regarding construction projects on the island.

Pauling went down to her door, unlocked it and stepped into her room. She suddenly had a flashback from college. It felt like a dorm room to her and reminded her of her freshman year at the university. Her roommate had been a strange girl from Oklahoma who spent most of the year at the health clinic on campus. A true hypochondriac. For Pauling during that freshman year, it had been like not having a roommate at all. She remembered initially trying to do everything she could to help the poor girl. It had been a roommate's duty, after all. But by the fifth or sixth mystery illness, Pauling realized the girl was just coping with the transition to college the only way she knew how.

After that recognition became clear, Pauling barely even asked the girl what was going on or how she was feeling.

Now, Pauling locked the door behind her. She glanced at the satellite phone and the computer on her desk and thought about calling Nathan Jones to try to get more information on Jack Reacher. Where was he? He was supposed to get in touch with her once she was on the island, but so far, there had been no word. And she had no way of contacting him.

So instead, Pauling thought about the investigation.

The police report had been a major disappointment. No report, really, at all. No investigation, certainly. It had been deemed a drowning and that was that.

Still, she knew she was going to have to confront the police at some point, if she could dig up some kind of information to get them interested.

But right now, her plan was going to be straightforward. She was going to try to figure out with whom Paige had spent the majority of her time while working here. Once she identified that person, Pauling would go after him or her hard and try to garner as much information as possible. Once she had a better idea of Paige's closest circle, she could rule them all out and go back to Nathan with the most likely answer; that Paige really had drowned.

It was Pauling's opinion that no human being ever really understood another. It was an impossible assumption. Understanding required full knowledge. And no one had full knowledge of another human being. It simply didn't exist. There were things spouses, married for decades, still kept from one another. There was no expiration date on secrets. Pauling suspected that Paige, just like every other human being ever to exist on the planet Earth, had had a few secrets of her own. Nathan was convinced that his daughter was one thing, but the truth was, she was probably that along with a few other things. The world was only black and white in fancy art galleries showcasing the latest avant-garde photographer's work.

In the real world, there were as many different shades of reality as there were people who perceived them. Hell, half the time people had trouble admitting to themselves who they were, how could anyone expect them to be honest with others?

Pauling stretched out on her single bed, amused that her feet nearly hung over the edge and that her mattress felt like a glorified piece of plywood. She stared at the dropped ceiling tile, noticed a brown water stain at the corner of one of the sections.

She pulled Paige's journal off the table next to the bed and opened it to where she'd left off.

The contents continued to be field notes, broken up only occasionally by a sketch of certain plants, or a lizard. Paige had also included observations on the weather, amount of sunlight, and levels of moisture in the soil. There were quite a few notations on specific birds, naturally, most coded in a combination of letters and numbers that were indecipherable to Pauling. She made a mental note to show the codes to Dr. Sirrine and see if he could decipher them for her.

She was just about to close the journal when a section of text centered on the page as opposed to all of the other writing that was flush left caught her eye.

It was four lines, written in the same block letters that Pauling had come to appreciate as the penmanship required of a scientist.

Pauling read the words with great interest.

Smooth blue oceans of calm
hidden currents twisting
vestiges of desert guns
here but still there too

She read them two more times and then closed the journal.

One of her literature professors in college had told the class that in his opinion great poetry by itself meant nothing. That there was no internal message required. Rather, the value of a great poem was that it could mean something different to each person who read it. That even if a poem did carry a specific thought, originated by its author, the greatness of the writing was that it had the potential to be interpreted emotionally on a highly individual basis.

A lot of students disagreed, and Pauling knew

that some of the other professors argued just the opposite. It was their belief that a good poem conveyed a very specific idea or emotion, one the poet intended to convey with precision.

But the theory of multiple possible interpretations had always stuck with Pauling.

And now, she wondered about the four lines Paige had penned.

It could be about the ocean.

It could be about time.

It could be about the shifting tides of memory and perception.

Or, it could be about a man with blue eyes just back from serving overseas in the military.

CHAPTER SIXTEEN

It was a horrible night.

She went from being freezing cold to insanely hot. There were bad dreams, along with explosions.

Her eyes snapped open.

She was covered in sweat.

And the explosions weren't just in her dreams. They were outside her window.

She sat up and listened.

Dr. Sirrine had mentioned that the military trained a lot at night. And sure enough, the gunfire was loud and intense. One of the explosions was so close it rattled the walls.

She got out of bed and went to the bathroom, filled a cup with water and drank deeply.

Eventually, she went back to bed and slept for

a few hours but when she woke up in the morning, she felt more tired than when she'd gone to sleep.

After an ice-cold shower, Pauling went to the kitchen area and discovered that while there was no organized breakfast, someone had at least made coffee.

It was the large, aluminum tower coffee pot that Pauling associated with banquet halls and church basement get-togethers. She poured herself a cup and walked over to the living area, to the window that overlooked the cliff's edge and the ocean beyond.

She had to laugh.

This would be primo real estate anywhere else. If, instead of a set of buildings belonging to a wildlife group, it was a six bedroom house in La Jolla, Malibu or Miami with this kind of ocean view it would be worth tens of millions of dollars and owned by a movie star, a professional athlete or a business mogul.

Here, it was just taken for granted.

Outside, behind the main building, Pauling noticed a pair of horseshoe pits and a gas grill. It appeared that was the extent of the entertainment options.

"So I hear you're going out with me today," a

voice said behind her. She turned and saw a tiny man, stocky, with a shaved head and chubby cheeks. He had on jeans, hiking boots and a shirt with a vest that had about twenty pockets.

"Gabe Rawlins," he said. He stuck out a thick hand with stubby fingers and Pauling shook it. The hand was warm, almost sweaty, but the grip was like iron.

"Lauren Pauling," she said.

"I see you've got the most important thing for today. Coffee. Lots and lots of coffee."

She smiled. "It's not going to be terribly exciting, is that what you mean?"

Gabe put his hands on his hips and considered her question.

"Let me put it this way. I've had more people fall asleep on me than a hooker at a narcolepsy convention."

He waited for her reaction with obvious expectancy and when she chuckled, he beamed at her.

"You probably had preconceived notions of what bird people are like," he said. "Which is fine. Because I had a preconceived idea of what a computer geek who was coming to help us out would look like. And boy was I wrong."

Pauling didn't take the bait and easily side-stepped the trap.

"So what exactly is on our schedule today?" she asked. Gabe's face gave away his disappointment at not being able to comment on her appearance, which Pauling knew he was hoping to do.

"Sitting, watching birds and taking notes," Gabe said. "All day. If we really want to get crazy maybe we'll take some soil and plant samples. But I don't want to get your hopes up."

She smiled. "It actually sounds sort of interesting."

"Wow, you're a cheap date," Gabe said.

Again, he looked to her for a reaction and she gave him none.

"Why don't we meet outside in five minutes or so?" he said, glancing at his watch. It was an oversized piece of hardware that must have been able to tell him every scientific measurement there was to make.

He left and walked down the hallway behind the kitchen where Dr. Sirrine had gone. Pauling figured that the men were on one side of the building and the women were on the other. Once again, she couldn't help but compare it to a college dorm.

Pauling went back to her room, grabbed a fleece jacket and a windbreaker. Her plan was to dress in layers while she was here. It seemed like the kind of place where weather could change on a dime.

When she got outside Gabe was already in the truck, an old white Ford with the engine idling. She climbed inside, smelled coffee and cigar or cigarette smoke. Maybe even the hint of marijuana.

Gabe put the truck in gear.

"Just so you know, I tend to say a lot of inappropriate things, but my goal is to never offend," Gabe explained. "So just let me know if I've crossed the line. I'm a bit of a failed comedian if you hadn't already noticed."

"Get out of town," Pauling said.

Gabe grinned at her. "I like you. I think we're going to get along just fine."

CHAPTER SEVENTEEN

A light mist began to cover the windshield and Gabe had to use the wipers to clear it.

"We're going to head to the southwest side of the island, near a place called Horseshoe Canyon. We've got a small bird group there and today's task is to try to determine how well they've been feeding and if there's been any noticeable change in habitat growth."

"Okay."

"We'll start at an observation post but depending on what we see, we may venture into the habitat in order to take some measurements."

They drove on and Pauling was again struck by the landscape. So foreign it almost felt alien. They weren't on a gravel road anymore, this one was plain dirt and she was glad the truck was four-wheel drive. She could imagine some serious storms out here and with the road being little more than mud, a loss of traction could be devastating. Especially as there wasn't a single guardrail on the entire island.

Thankfully, Gabe was a better driver than Dr. Sirrine but sometimes the road went right up to the edge of the cliff and there was nothing between them and the ocean save for a steep cliff of jagged rock. If you lost control and went over the edge there was nothing to stop you from a horrific fall into the ocean.

Twenty minutes later Gabe pulled up to a spot that was marked off from the road. There was a wooden pole stuck into the ground next to something that looked like an overgrown mailbox. A garbage can with a metal lid and a lock and chain was next to it.

Gabe got out and Pauling followed him.

He opened the box and she saw a stack of papers, binders and various implements that looked like they belonged in a hardware store.

Gabe slid one of the binders into his backpack, a sturdy thing made of green burlap.

"Okay, let's go," he said.

He turned and trundled off onto a well-worn

foot trail and Pauling walked along behind him. She was glad she had packed a sturdy set of hiking boots. It was cool but not cold. Just a slight chill in the air exacerbated by the slight mist.

Pauling was also glad she'd dressed in layers and only now wished she'd thrown in a baseball cap for good measure.

Well, next time, she thought.

The trail wound down away from the ocean and thick ground cover quickly grew in height.

There were isolated stands of trees, mostly scrub oak and one time Pauling heard something scurry away from them into the underbrush.

Eventually, they made their way to an area roughly six feet by ten feet, cleared, with a trap spread out and an overhang made of tent poles and thick camouflage netting.

It was a lean-to and Gabe slid into one side and Pauling took the other.

Gabe pulled out an enormous set of binoculars and began to scan the surrounding tree lines. He stopped occasionally to make some notes. He grunted a few times at what he saw.

Pauling sat with her knees up and her arms hugging her legs. She wasn't sure what she was looking at.

"What are you looking for?" she asked.

"Seeing if they're eating," Gabe answered. "That's the big thing. When the bird population almost died out it was because they were starving. The goats and the military had decimated all of the habitat and their prey was almost completely gone. Nowhere to hide, that kind of thing."

Pauling remembered that Dr. Sirrine had told her some of the same details.

"Oh yeah, they're eating well today," Gabe said, looking through the binoculars.

"How can you tell?"

"Take a look."

He handed her the binoculars.

"Okay, look straight out toward that stand of trees."

Once she got herself oriented Pauling was able to bring the group of small oak trees into focus.

"Okay, look at the top of the tree," Gabe said. "And then go down about one branch level."

"Got it," Pauling said.

"Now do you see the lizard impaled on the branch?"

She scanned and was about to say no but then she saw it. She gave a sharp intake of breath. A lizard had literally been skewered onto a vertical, dead branch. A small bird with black and white feathers was picking at its flesh, tearing it away in chunks with its beak.

"You didn't know how the Shrike of San Clemente hunt and eat their prey?" Gabe asked, an amused expression on his face.

"No," Pauling replied truthfully, her voice soft.

"They go after small vertebrates like that native lizard and dive bomb them," Gabe said. His face was alive with a bizarre kind of enthusiasm. "They strike them in the head with their beaks and knock them unconscious. After that, they take them up and impale them on a branch and then slowly pick away at the meat. It sometimes takes days for them to eat one."

"Interesting," Pauling said.

"That's how they got their nickname."

Pauling lowered the binoculars and looked at Gabe.

"What nickname?"

He smiled at her, an odd expression in his eyes. It momentarily gave Pauling a chill.

And then she remembered the name from Paige's journal.

"The Butcher Bird," she said.

"Exactly," Gabe agreed.

CHAPTER EIGHTEEN

The afternoon saw a slight break in the light rain and the sun even came out briefly before being swallowed once again by a wall of gray in the sky.

Gabe continued to make notes in his field journal, alternating between his binoculars and a camera equipped with an extremely long lens.

"A picture's worth a thousand pages of notes," he said, shaking his hand, tired from writing in his field notebook. Pauling had noted that his handwriting was very similar to Paige's. All caps, block letters, neat and readable. A scientist's penmanship.

Eventually he put away the camera and the binoculars and checked his watch.

"Not a great day to go out and collect

anything. Too wet. And with some of the population still actively feeding, not a good idea to disturb them too much."

There was something about the island and its abandoned-planet vibe that was getting to Pauling. It had a sense of lawlessness to it. That observation gave her pause, and she wondered about Paige and the psychological effects, long-term, of being out here. Could it drive someone to murder?

There was a very definite sense of lawlessness here. No highway patrol. No speed traps. No local cops. What, were they going to be pulled over on the way back to the bird headquarters? A suspicious vehicle pulled over by Johnny Law?

Not hardly.

Pauling wondered if that mentality existed for others and to what degree? If there was somebody on the island with bad intentions, a bad guy, how much did they feel they could get away with? Pauling was sure there was a military police presence here, although she imagined it wasn't very large.

In the reports from Nathan, she knew that civilian law enforcement was handled by the Los Angeles County Sheriff's Department, but their nearest office was on Catalina Island, which was some twenty miles away. Which meant there was no civilian police force on San Clemente at all.

She thought back to Nate's reports about the discovery of Paige. It had immediately been deemed a drowning. But how long had it taken the cops to arrive from Catalina Island? A few hours? A day or two? And who watched over the body during that time?

"You look lost in thought," Gabe said.

"Just thinking," she said. "This place seems conducive to thinking. Daydreaming. Wondering."

"It does," Gabe agreed. "I've done fieldwork in a lot of places but nowhere as isolated as this. It's an unusual place."

"It seems almost a little dangerous," she said. "I heard on the plane ride over here that a girl drowned."

Gabe nodded. "Yeah. Her name was Paige. She was a good scientist, very meticulous with her notes and observations."

"How did she drown?"

Gabe shrugged his shoulders. "No one really knows. The ocean is dangerous around the island, a lot of wicked currents."

"I would never get in that water," Pauling said.

"Screw the currents, I'd be worried about the sharks."

Pauling suddenly thought of Paige's poem. It wasn't about Gabe. Gabe had brown eyes.

"We should get back," Gabe said, a bit too abruptly for Pauling's taste. "I think Abner said something about giving you a tour of the place. Fascinating, I'm sure," he said with a forced smile.

They gathered their gear and climbed back into the truck. As they drove, Pauling gazed out at the sea and wondered again what kind of psychological impact there would be if a person had to work here day after day, month after month.

She realized almost immediately how it could make someone feel.

Lonely.

Pauling realized she would feel a lot better if she could find Jack Reacher.

CHAPTER NINETEEN

"Ah, there you are," Dr. Sirrine said when she and Gabe entered the main building. He was at the table, working on a laptop with a can of Diet Coke next to him.

Dr. Sirrine snapped his laptop closed and got to his feet.

"I want to give you an overview of the rest of the place so you have a better idea of how this whole thing works."

"Sounds good," Pauling said. "Also, is there a place where military police have an office?"

Dr. Sirrine looked strangely at her.

"There are no military police on the island," he said. "But I can take you to the headquarters of the military folks."

"Ok, let's do that after the tour," Pauling said. Certainly the military folks would know where Reacher was.

Dr. Sirrine looked at his watch. "Take five minutes or so to put away your gear and meet me back here," he said.

She went to her room, unlocked it and threw her gear on the bed. Pauling went into the bathroom and splashed some cold water on her face and brushed her teeth.

Pauling went back to the lobby and Dr. Sirrine led her out of the front door of the building. They followed a stone path around to another long, low aluminum-sided structure.

He opened the door and Pauling was surprised to find the space flooded with a ton of natural light.

She looked up, saw that huge chunks of the ceiling had been cut out and filled with jerry-rigged skylights. They weren't real skylights, but homemade versions built with wood framing and a type of acrylic or hard plastic, mixed in with intersecting sections of camouflage netting. The skylights were clearly not made of glass.

"Hard polypropylene," Dr. Sirrine said, noticing her upward gaze. "Someone tried conventional skylights a few years back and they were destroyed either by a storm or some wayward mortar shells. No idea which story is true."

Pauling wasn't sure if he was kidding or not. After some thought, she realized he wasn't. He wasn't the kind of guy to joke around.

"This is our nursery," he said. He gestured toward multiple rows of unique structures made with a combination of wood, chicken wire and more camouflage netting. Small trees were growing in the space and some of the enclosures were built around segregated shrubbery.

"We've managed to foster several dozen birds and bird families here," he said. "It's been crucial to the repopulation of the island."

They walked through the space and Pauling noted the precision with which the area had been filled out. Everything was neat and clean and well-organized.

"Ted does a great job here, with some assistance from Janey," Dr. Sirrine said. "But Ted's main job is the nursery and he's a natural."

He led through a set of doors at the far end of the building and they passed under an overhang and directly into the next structure.

"This is the herbarium," Dr. Sirrine said. "This is Janey's domain."

Gone was the purely aluminum shed and in its place was a greenhouse of similar size and dimension. When they stepped inside, Pauling immediately felt the cloying moist heat. With the high amount of natural light and the quality of the air, she figured Janey was successful in her efforts.

There were plants along the middle row of tables and various stands, pots and assorted plantings, all fed by a mist of water that rotated in intervals throughout the rows of plants.

"The first step in understanding the decline of the Shrike was to understand the decline of the habitat," Dr. Sirrine said. "The environment was made of native plants, trees and wild grasses. There hadn't really been any introduction of foreign plant life. Once we understood what happened to the native species and what was still happening to them, we would have our first clue as to what was going wrong."

He looked up.

"Oh, there's Janey now," he said.

Janey set down a garden hose and approached them. She had on an old sweatshirt and there was dirt on the side of her face. Her hair was tied back into a short ponytail.

"Hi Abner," she said. "Hey, Pauling."

"How are things going, Janey?" Dr. Sirrine

asked.

"Good, we had a bit of a fungus problem on the *Castilleja grisea* seedlings but I think I was able to eliminate most of it."

"Excellent."

"How was your first day in the field?" Janey asked Pauling.

"It was actually very interesting," she said evenly. "I'm enjoying learning more about the kind of work you do out here. And the Shrike is a fascinating bird."

Janey nodded but Pauling could sense the skepticism in her. Why was this young woman so cynical? Or perceptive, in this case?

"Gabe behaved himself?" Janey asked with a small grin.

"More or less," Pauling answered.

"Some of us are going up to the Salty Crab tonight to grab a drink if you want to come," Janey said.

"Sure. Sounds good." Pauling was anxious to see it. Reacher wasn't exactly a sit-at-the-bar kind of guy, but there weren't any diners on the island, as far as she could tell.

"It's the only bar on the island," Dr. Sirrine added. "The military guys are there all the time so consider yourself warned."

CHAPTER TWENTY

"There she is," Gabe said. "The world's hottest computer repair person."

They were all standing by the front door, ready to go to the Salty Crab.

"Who was the runner-up?" Pauling asked.

Gabe didn't have a comeback and Ted laughed under his breath.

"Let's go," Janey said in the silence.

"Thanks for waiting," Pauling said.

"No problem," Janey answered and she led the way out the door. They climbed into the same dirty white jeep Dr. Sirrine had picked her up in.

"Is Dr. Sirrine coming?" Pauling asked.

The others chuckled.

"You really have to start calling him Abner," Ted said. "It's throwing me."

"He might join us later," Janey said.

"No, he won't," Gabe answered, shaking his head. "He hardly ever goes there anymore. He doesn't like the clientele."

Gabe's voice became sarcastic at the word.

"The military guys?" Pauling guessed.

"And girls," Ted said. "There are a few women but not many. They can be just as obnoxious as the guys. Abner prefers quiet when he drinks."

Janey visibly stiffened at the way Ted worded the phrase and Pauling wondered if there was more to the story. She would have to figure that out.

It took them less than ten minutes to get to the Salty Crab. From the outside, it looked just like every other structure on the island. A utilitarian, single-story building made with aluminum siding and off-the-rack windows and doors.

There were a half-dozen vehicles in the parking lot, most of them pickup trucks emblazoned with some sort of military emblem or another.

When they exited the jeep, Pauling could hear the music inside.

Gabe paused and turned to Pauling.

"Needless to say, this isn't your average dive bar," he said. "Since this is your first time here all

I'll say is to be careful. Some of these guys might be just back from overseas and if they've seen some of the really bad stuff, they aren't necessarily in a great frame of mind."

"And the ones who have been on the island for awhile are generally as aggressive as hell," Janey said.

"She means horny," Gabe countered.

"Got it," Pauling said.

Ted led the way inside.

The door opened into a large room that featured a dozen long wooden tables flanked by heavy wooden chairs. There was a bar with a single bartender manning the operation. A short row of bar stools faced the bar, only one of them occupied.

There was a jukebox in one corner, and a few pinball machines in the other.

Across from the jukebox were two pool tables, one of them being used by two young men in t-shirts and jeans. They stared openly at Pauling.

"They smell fresh blood," Ted said, his voice dry.

A waitress brought a pitcher of beer and four glasses. Ted did the honors and poured everyone a glass.

"To Pauling. May her stay on the island be memorable and productive," Gabe said.

"Cheers," Janey agreed.

They all drank. The beer was cold and tasted fresh. She figured if there was one thing the military guys demanded, it was good booze.

"So what do you think of the Crab?" Janey asked. She peered at Pauling over the rim of her glass.

"It reminds me of a bowling alley," she answered honestly. It really did. The wood floor, scratched and marred. The basic tables. The beer signs, the juke box, the pinball machines.

"Circa twenty years ago," she quickly added.

Gabe laughed. "It really is a place stuck a couple of decades in the past."

"Well, that didn't take long," Janey said.

Pauling heard a voice speak behind her.

"Do we have a new birdie in the nest?"

It was one of the pool players. Up close, Pauling realized he was huge. At least six foot five, two-fifty, with giant shoulders and a narrow waist. He had a tattoo of barbed wire around one of his biceps.

"Clever," Gabe said.

"You want to play some pool?" the big guy said

to Pauling. His partner was waiting back at the table.

"No thanks," Pauling said. "Just going to have a drink with my friends. But have you seen Jack Reacher around?"

The big guy looked at her with an odd expression.

"Who?" he asked.

"Never mind," Pauling answered.

The big guy nodded his head and looked at the rest of them like Pauling had just said she was going to dive into a trash dumpster.

"Suit yourself," he said.

He sauntered away.

"Who's Jack Reacher?" Janey asked her.

"Some guy I know who's supposedly working out here on the island."

There was a brief moment of silence and then Ted said, "Get used to it. The attention." Ted lifted his chin toward the military guys.

"At least they didn't use their favorite line," Janey said. "When you turn them down."

"Yeah? What's that?"

Janey smiled.

"Well, here on the island, the men outnumber the women something like fifty to one. So the guys hit on every woman here, pretty much. But when you reject them, they like to remind you that if it weren't for the scarcity of available women, they probably wouldn't be interested in you."

"Wow, that was nicely put," Gabe said.

"That's not what they say," Ted explained. "They have a phrase they love to use."

"Spit it out, guys," Pauling said.

Janey turned to her.

"They like to say, 'You're only a plane ride from ugly.'"

CHAPTER TWENTY-ONE

Pauling swung out of bed, made her way to the shower and let the hot water beat down on her. She toweled off, dressed in jeans, a sweatshirt and hiking boots and went into the kitchen area.

The giant coffee pot had already worked its magic and Pauling poured herself a cup. She carried it outside and walked along the edge of the property's border, stopping occasionally to look out at the ocean. It was a cool morning with a gauzy layer of clouds hovering above the sapphire blue water. A bird flew overhead, followed by the sound of an automatic weapon firing off rounds.

Morning on San Clemente Island.

So far, not a single person had heard of Jack

Reacher. Pauling wondered about Nathan Jones and his motivation for bringing her out here.

Ultimately, it didn't matter. Pauling was hooked. She wanted to find out what had happened to Paige Jones on this weird, mysterious island.

One way or another, she would get answers.

With or without Reacher.

Eventually, she finished her coffee and headed back to the Nest.

She walked inside and saw Dr. Sirrine – Abner – sitting at the table with a short, squat fireplug of a man with a head of steel cut hair and a face that looked like a slab of cement.

The man had on a dark blue t-shirt with a gold crest over the breast pocket and a pair of khaki pants with multiple pockets. He had on camouflage hunting boots.

"Pauling," Abner said. "Someone here would like to meet you."

She put her cup of coffee on the counter and walked over to them. Both men stood and the short one stuck out his hand.

"Ma'am, I'm Commander Wilkins," he said. His voice perfectly fit his gravelly appearance. "But you can call me Bill."

"Hi Bill, I'm Lauren Pauling."

The man smiled, but he did it more with his eyes than his mouth. His face was leathery with deep creases. He had blue eyes and Pauling could see the lively sense of humor behind them.

"The boys up at the Crab didn't know your name," Wilkins said. "But you sure fit the description."

Ordinarily, a statement like that would be followed by a leer. But somehow, Wilkins pulled it off and Pauling didn't sense any creepiness.

Now it was her turn to smile.

"So are you Commander of San Clemente or something else?" she asked.

"Yes," Abner stepped in. He sounded nervous, as if Pauling might say something to upset Wilkins.

"Bill is in charge of everything, and everyone, on the island. Technically." Abner added that qualifier at the end, probably referencing the bird personnel. Wilkins wasn't in charge of them. Of course, being in charge of someone and having power over them are two different things.

"Great," Pauling said. "Do you have any idea where I can find Jack Reacher?" she asked.

"Jack Reacher? I don't know anyone by that name," he answered.

And Pauling felt like she finally had her answer.

They all sat down at the table.

"I like to come out and catch up with Abner whenever he's got someone new on his team," Wilkins explained. "Communication is the key to everything we do. So if something ever comes up, I know we're all on the same playing field and I know who the players are."

"Do things come up often?" Pauling asked, making sure her voice sounded as innocent as possible.

"What do you mean?" Abner interjected.

Wilkins just smiled at her. He knew exactly what she meant.

"Well," Pauling said, "It sounded like you were saying that if there's a problem between the bird people and the military, you like to know who everyone is ahead of time."

It was a guess, but Pauling figured that's why the commander was here.

She had no doubt that the men from the bar last night had talked about her. And at his age, she figured Wilkins wasn't here to ask her out on a date.

"No, not much comes up out here," Wilkins said. "No real problems between the two groups of people. Unless you count my two divorces," he said, followed by a wink.

"You're serious, aren't you?" she asked, knowing he was.

"Afraid so," Wilkins answered. "I could never keep my hands off of those pretty birdies. Should've known better," he shook his grizzled head.

Pauling wasn't taken in by his *aw shucks* attitude. He looked like the kind of guy who wasn't really an administrator. In his day, he'd probably conquered some territories all by himself. A Special Ops guys for sure.

"It really is an interesting dynamic," Pauling ventured. "Some of the deadliest military personnel in the world cuddled up with a group of scientists. I'm sure it could make for some unique issues."

"Over the years all of the bugs have been worked out," Abner said. "Everything has always run very smoothly, at least since I've been here."

Wilkins nodded. "Abner keeps his folks in line, and I do the same with mine. We're all professionals."

Wilkins got to his feet.

"Well, I've got to get going," he said. "Pauling, if you ever want to come up to my HQ I'd love to give you the cook's tour of the island and show you what we do here. That is, if Abner ever stops working you like a dog. He's a real slave driver, I hear."

Abner chuckled and shook his head.

"I would like that, Bill," Pauling said.

And she meant it.

CHAPTER TWENTY-TWO

"Has there?"

Dr. Sirrine had just started to get up but Pauling stopped him with the tone of her voice. She was at the coffee pot and she raised her head at him to see if he wanted some. He held up his hand to say no. She filled her own and sat down across from him.

"Has there what?" he answered, without conviction. Pauling could see his reticence a mile away.

"Has there ever been any problems between the naturalists and the military people?" she said, spelling it out for both of their benefit.

Dr. Sirrine let out a long sigh.

"Yes and no," he finally said.

"What does that mean?"

He sat back and folded his hands across his stomach, and seemed to look past Pauling out toward the island beyond.

"As far as the military folks see it, this is their island," he explained. "They only humor us because they have to and they don't want the bad press back home to talk about them destroying an endangered species."

"That makes sense."

"But make no mistake," he continued. "They feel the work they do is the only work that matters here. They think what we do, running around taking care of these little birds and the little trees and shrubs they depend on is a big joke."

Pauling nodded. She'd worked with a lot of military guys and knew that what Dr. Sirrine was saying was true.

"As far as the military thinks, the work they do keeps the country safe," he continued. "They're providing us with the freedom we need to live our lives. It's the most important job in the world and they believe we take it all for granted."

There was some truth in that belief, Pauling thought.

"And because of that," Dr. Sirrine said. "We ought to get down on our knees and thank the Lord every day for the guys with guns who take care of us."

"So they think they're better than us?" Pauling asked.

"Yes."

"Above the law?" Pauling probed. She knew the answer, but wanted to hear what Dr. Sirrine thought. After all, he had worked closely with Paige and any insight into his view of the world would help her investigation. If nothing else, it would help point her in the right direction.

Dr. Sirrine shrugged his shoulders.

Pauling was surprised that there wasn't any anger in his voice, considering the net of what he was saying.

"On the one hand, as an American, I believe what they do is essential to our survival as a country. Our peace, our prosperity, our very way of life. Absolutely," Dr. Sirrine said. "On the other hand, losing a species, any species, for eternity, is a pretty big deal, too."

"In other words," Pauling said, "It doesn't have to be one is more important than the other. They both can co-exist."

"Yes, that's how I see it," he said. "But they don't."

Pauling considered what he was saying.

"So I asked you if there had ever been any problems between us and them. You said yes and no. What did you mean by that?"

"My point is that if there is a problem, whoever from our side that's involved is usually promptly escorted off the island," Dr. Sirrine said. "End of problem."

"I see."

"Luckily, I've been here for a number of years and the biggest problems tend to be when people drink too much and they get into arguments. Even then it usually doesn't get physical because we're obviously overmatched."

Pauling thought of the huge guy from last night. He could have pulverized Ted, Gabe and Dr. Sirrine with one hand tied behind his back.

"What about problems between men and women?" Pauling asked. "Whenever you have a shortage of women and some hot-blooded young men who may or may not be returning or going to a battlefield, you could have some pretty big problems."

"Like I said, it hasn't happened yet," Dr. Sirrine said. "Or at least recently. Because everyone is very careful, especially on my team. I've made it a priority for everyone who works for me to understand that with absolute clarity. And you should be, too."

"Was Paige careful?" she asked.

It looked like Dr. Sirrine had been punched in the solar plexus.

"What kind of question is that?" he asked. His face was pale and she could see the anger in his eyes.

"I'm asking you if Paige ever had any problems with people in the military here on the island."

He looked at her a long time and finally let out a deep breath.

"No," he said. "Not to my knowledge." Which, for some reason, struck Pauling as something someone would say in a court of law. As if they were on trial. And it was a phrase a lot of people used when they weren't really telling the whole truth.

Dr. Sirrine got up and walked to his hallway, shutting the door behind him.

From what she understood, Dr. Abner Sirrine was one of the world's leading experts on Loggerhead Shrikes and, in particular, the San Clemente Shrike.

Which was a good thing.

Pauling got up and dumped the rest of her coffee into the sink.

Because he was one of the worst liars she'd ever seen.

CHAPTER TWENTY-THREE

Pauling went back to her room, changed out of her jeans and hiking boots into a pair of sweatpants and trail-running shoes. She grabbed a map of the island and found Janey in the herbarium.

"Is this a good place to run?" she asked, using her finger to trace a route on the map. She had done some research on the plane and knew that the trail ran along the beach where Paige's body had been found. Any evidence was long gone, of course, but she wanted to see the place with her own eyes.

She watched as Janey appraised the route.

"Yeah, that's fine," she said and tapped a finger, one with dirt packed beneath the fingernail, toward a horizontal line on the trail.

"Just do NOT cross that line," she said. A speck of dirt remained on the map where Janey's finger had been.

"That's where they do their private training, the endurance testing and some live fire trial exercises," Janey explained. "Some of the guys they occasionally get in are young. Most are seasoned but it always seems like someone's either a bad shot or there's the occasional ricochet."

Janey's eyes seemed to linger on the area of the trail where Paige had been found.

"I'll look at it as an adrenaline boost," Pauling said. "Who knows, maybe I'll run faster."

Janey looked like she was going to say something but stopped. She turned away, then changed her mind and turned back.

"Be careful," she said.

Pauling said she would, folded the map up and put it in the pocket of her sweatpants and set out on a run once she got back out on the main road.

The road was called Perimeter Drive and naturally it ran along the contour of the island. The entrance to the footpath was less than a mile from the Nest.

It was strange to be working out without music but Pauling wanted to be able to hear anything that was going on. Especially if she heard rifle fire that sounded like it might be a hair too close.

Once she was warmed up she set out at a slow jog, enjoying the feel of the moisture in the air, the soft sea breeze that always seemed to be blowing.

She found the turnoff and went down the path, a trail of hard-packed dirt and small stones.

It skirted the edge of the cliff and she had to remind herself that if she went over the side, no one would find her for a long time.

She lengthened her stride, glad to be running again. When she'd worked at the Bureau she'd run every day and had come to crave the exercise, her antidote for stress.

Pauling ran easily, eating up the miles, lost in the stark beauty of the scenery. She had once run on the beach in Malibu and not only was this breathtaking in its unique way, she had this all to herself.

There was nothing marking the area where Paige's body had been found but Pauling recognized it right away from the photographs in the documents Nathan had given her. She slowed to a walk and went to the water's edge.

The air seemed to turn colder all around her and this close to the water she felt its immense power. The waves crashed into the surf with thunderous regularity she could feel in her knees. Pauling put her hand down and the water was ice cold.

No way Paige would swim in this stuff.

It was not the calmer water of a hotel swimming pool, either. It was a churning type of sea with thick waves, sea lions and kelp out in the distance. It didn't even seem right to call it a beach. This was the real deal. The Pacific Ocean in all its unspoiled beauty and ferocity.

Nathan was right.

Paige would never have gone willingly into this water.

"Watch yourself," a voice said behind her.

Startled, Pauling turned.

A man, also in running gear and slightly out of breath with a fine sheen of sweat on his forehead stopped a few feet from her.

He was strikingly handsome and his perfect teeth gleamed in the gray air.

"There's a hell of an undertow just a few feet out," he said. "If it grabs ahold of you, you don't have a chance."

He stepped closer and a slight chill ran through Pauling's body.

He had the most beautiful pair of blue eyes she had ever seen.

CHAPTER TWENTY-FOUR

"I'm Michael Tallon," he said. He stuck out a hand and Pauling shook it. It was warm and strong but not wet. She had a feeling her hand was sweaty. On his other wrist was an impressive watch, with a thick face and steel bracelet.

"Pauling," she said. "Thanks for the warning."

"It's deceptive," Tallon responded. "The undertow. Guys are always surprised when we get them in the water and it starts pulling at them."

"What do they do?"

"We teach them to swim diagonally, as opposed to directly against the undertow. You have a better chance of swimming out of the current that way. We've had some strong swimmers take it on. And they lost every time."

For a moment, they both stood and looked out at the water.

"It's a Ball," he said.

Pauling looked at him.

He lifted his wrist. "My watch. You were looking at it. A Ball Engineer Hydrocarbon NEDU. NEDU stands for Navy Experimental Dive Unit."

"So you're Navy?" she asked.

"Sort of," he responded.

"And there was the girl who drowned here, right? This is where they found her body?"

Tallon stiffened at the question, and for a moment the nice guy was gone. His expression had hardened and his mouth had formed a thin line.

"Yeah," he said. "And they didn't find her. I did."

"You found her?" Pauling asked, wondering if the name Michael Tallon had rang any bells with her. Had it been in the police report?

"I run here practically every morning," he explained. "It was not good."

Pauling was about to ask him if he had known Paige, but he cut her off with a quick question of his own.

"So you're with the bird folks?" he asked. There was a small smile on his face.

"You look like you already know the answer to that. What, the guys at the Salty Crab?"

He nodded, a bit sheepish.

She shook her head. "Don't you guys have anything else to do than talk about every new woman who shows up at the bar? What, have you got a web cam there?"

He laughed, and Pauling was struck again by his good looks.

"Hey, I know we just met, but are you hungry? I was going to the cafeteria to get some lunch."

A bit abrupt, but Pauling had to admit, she was hungry. And, more than a little intrigued.

"Sure."

They agreed that Tallon would pick her up at the Nest, so Pauling went back and changed out of her running gear and jumped in the shower. Afterward, she toweled off, threw on a pair of jeans and a fleece pullover and went back outside to find Michael Tallon waiting for her in a military jeep.

She climbed inside, just as Dr. Sirrine appeared in the doorway. He looked at her with an odd expression on his face. Pauling waved, and

Dr. Sirrine waved back as Tallon pulled away from the Nest onto Perimeter Drive.

"Have you eaten at the cafeteria yet?" Tallon asked.

"No."

"Well, the good news is, it's the best food on the island," he said.

"And the bad news is that it's the only food on the island?" she guessed.

He laughed. "Yeah, you've heard that one, huh? Well, technically, the other food on the island is the bar menu at the Crab. Which is actually better than the cafeteria, but the Crab's not open yet."

"The Crab's not open?" Pauling asked. "That puts a pretty big hole in the entertainment options for the guys, doesn't it?"

"It does," Tallon admitted. "If there is a silver lining though, it's that the cafeteria actually has a salad bar that's at least serviceable. Everything else there, well, I would tread with caution."

They followed the road down to a slight valley and Pauling saw a cluster of military buildings, one of them actually made with brick as opposed to the island's ubiquitous aluminum siding. The brick building also had real windows that looked out across the road to the ocean.

Tallon pulled the jeep into a parking space in front of the brick building and shut off the car.

"This is it," he said.

Pauling followed him inside and saw the long bank of counters serving an open space filled with tables and chairs. Across from them was a bank of food stations, complete with sneeze guards and another station that looked like it dispensed soft drinks.

It smelled like a mixture of meat and cabbage.

"Just for fun, go take a look at the food at the buffet," Tallon said.

She swung by and saw only three of the ten or so metal trays had food in them. And each one was a mysterious meat swimming in a slightly different colored gravy.

Pauling quickly joined Tallon at the salad bar. He had a plate and tray ready for her.

"I'm a big fan of mysteries," she said, accepting the tray from him. "But in book form. Not when it comes to food."

"I'm surprised you didn't run out the door," he said.

He laughed and she was struck again by those blue eyes. She wondered again if they were the eyes Paige had written about in her journal. Pauling cautioned herself not to push it. Let things happen naturally and the answers would come.

The salad bar would have been considered average back on the mainland, but out here it looked fantastic to Pauling. She took a mixture of lettuce, some chickpeas, shredded parmesan, olives and sunflower seeds. Finally, she added a light drizzle of olive oil and balsamic vinegar.

Tallon picked out a smaller table next to a window. The view was dynamite, Pauling noticed. She would never get tired of the expanse of ocean just above the horizon.

"So tell me about finding Paige," Pauling said. If he was surprised that she knew Paige's name, he covered it well.

Tallon shook his head. "Pretty bad. I mean, I've seen a lot of things, considering what I do. But, it wasn't good."

"Is that because you knew her?" she asked. It was meant to throw him off guard and it worked. Even though it was a guess, Pauling's instincts told her she was right.

Tallon looked at her, his face difficult to read.

"No," he finally said. "I didn't recognize her. It's just there's a difference between seeing a soldier who's been killed. They chose to be in the fight, whether they're the good guy or the bad guy. But a civilian is always very difficult. A very different experience."

She listened as he explained how he contacted the commander of the island, and showed the investigating authorities where the body was.

Pauling noticed that he hadn't confirmed or denied that he had known Paige. She decided to let it go, for the moment.

"So was it a shark attack?" she asked.

"Sure looked like it," he said. Which wasn't really answering the question.

"Did you think she was swimming?" Pauling asked, and then pointed out at the ocean. "Out there? Water's awfully cold. The dangerous undertow. Sharks."

He shrugged his shoulders. "I don't know."

Pauling munched on some of her salad and then put down her fork and took a drink of water.

"So how did you know Paige?" she finally asked.

"I didn't really," he said. "Just saw her a few times at the Crab, maybe bought her a drink. I don't remember."

If he was lying, Pauling couldn't tell. Plus, she had no way of knowing for sure that Paige's journal was referencing Michael Tallon. It stood to reason there was more than one man on the island with blue eyes and maybe even then it wasn't someone on San Clemente. What if Paige had been remembering someone from her past? From before San Clemente Island?

"I already know the answer, but do you know if Jack Reacher is around?"

Tallon's face took on a puzzled expression.

"Reacher? Why would he be here?"

"You know him?" Pauling was surprised. She'd expected another negative reply.

"Not really, but I know of him. He's Army, though. An MP, right?"

"He was," she said. "He's out now."

"Then he definitely wouldn't be here. But I can tell you that if he was here, I would definitely know it."

He squinted at her.

"Why are you looking for Reacher?"

She looked out the window.

"I'm not," she said.

CHAPTER TWENTY-FIVE

Something was different.

Pauling noticed it the minute she stepped through the door. It wasn't that it looked different to her, it was a scent she didn't recognize.

It was the smell that tipped her off and it was an odd observation considering she'd only been here a couple of days and was still getting used to her surroundings.

But it wasn't the kind of vague change that could have resulted from someone mopping the hallway floor and the smell coming into the room under the door.

It was more a sense of something having been disturbed and their presence lingering.

What had they been looking for?

The journal.

Paige's journal. Pauling crossed the room and grabbed it from the night table, anxious to see if there was anything about it that would tell her if it had been read. It didn't look any different. Nor did it feel unusual and she saw no signs that pages had been removed. Of course, there was no way for her to determine if it'd been read or photographed or scanned for that matter.

She hadn't really been here that long, but the act of someone breaking into her room felt like an invasion of privacy. Pauling had the shitty sense of being victimized. Even though the room felt as if it belonged to somebody else, the whole thing unsettled her.

Considering that when Nathan first hired her for this case she had thought the idea of foul play was all in his imagination. Pauling had genuinely believed that her investigation would produce confirmation of an accident.

Nothing more.

But seeing the water and feeling how cold it actually was on her bare skin, seeing the energy of the waves, how wild and how desolate it was had all shocked her.

The idea of Paige going out for a swim seemed ludicrous to her.

And now this. Someone, she was nearly positive, had gone through her belongings, searching for something.

How curious could someone be to actually break into the room of a new employee of the Bird Conservatory?

Sure, there were extremely nosy people everywhere on this earth. However the unwelcome invasion also made sense if the person looking through her stuff was the same one who had something to do with Paige's death.

The image of Dr. Sirrine standing at the door watching her drive off with Michael Tallon suddenly flashed across Pauling's mind. It would have been the perfect opportunity for him, or someone else, to run back to her room and find a way in. Maybe they had an extra key.

For the first time Pauling wished she had been able to bring her gun. But the rules had been clear: no firearms brought onto San Clemente Island.

How ironic on an island surrounded by armed men she was defenseless other than her intellect and an ability to fight. She closed and locked the door, changed into a t-shirt and sweatpants and laid on the bed. She thought about lunch with Michael Tallon. It'd been pleasant and almost refreshing to talk with somebody other than the people from the Nest.

Or was it just that he was a very good-looking man and she was lonely?

Pauling would have to be very careful from here on out. And she decided that the break-in made it the perfect time for her to take the investigation to the next level.

CHAPTER TWENTY-SIX

In her previous life Pauling was all about the dossier. Hunting, compiling information, targeting, creating psychological makeups; it was all about what she had done for a living.

And she was good at it.

Nathan, being Nathan, had supplied her with an extensive collection of background information. She had pored over those files but they provided mostly surface information. Pauling needed more. She needed the kind of information that wasn't available on public databases.

Pauling opened up her laptop and connected to the Wi-Fi, then joined the network called BirdsnestOne.

Even though the laptop was encrypted, Pauling was fairly certain that somewhere someone was watching what she was about to type. She only hoped that they weren't watching too carefully.

So she wrote a chatty email to Blake completely unlike her regular tone of voice and told a rambling story about how much fun she was having and listed off the people she met in a witty way.

But, in the process, she was sure to include both the first and last name.

For instance, she talked about the interesting Dr. Abner Sirrine. She told him about a funny story going to the Salty Crab with Gabe Rawlins, Janey Morris and Ted Fargo. Her lunch with Michael Tallon was included along with a description of meeting Bill Wilkins, Commander of San Clemente.

And then at the end of her note to Blake she talked about the one drawback to the island was a sense of sensory deprivation and a lack of information.

Blake already knew what she was doing here. He knew what her mission was. But she wanted to leave no room for misunderstanding. She needed to find more about the people she'd met and Blake was a shortcut.

She fired off the email and then closed her

browser. She spent the next hour creating specific files for each person on the list. Pauling wrote down everything she knew about each person, described her interactions with each person thus far, and then left room for information from Blake. She intended to continue to investigate and each new piece of information would be added to the appropriate dossier.

It was how she liked to work and would make things easier when she was trying to formulate theories on what may or may not have happened.

Finally, she closed her laptop.

It would take some time for Blake to read her email and do his investigations.

In the meantime, she would continue to dig. And, in the process, hopefully find out who had broken into her room.

CHAPTER TWENTY-SEVEN

Pauling walked into the kitchen, opened the fridge and saw a bottle of white wine with a cork in it. She filled a glass three quarters full and walked to the picture window in the living area.

Outside, she saw Janey sitting on the picnic bench looking out at the ocean. Pauling saw an opportunity because if Paige had talked to anyone out here it would've been a woman. And if Paige had been friends with Janey, Janey would be the perfect resource to get more information.

Pauling opened the door, stepped outside and felt the cool ocean breeze, tasted the salt in the air. It had rained earlier in the day and now the grass was wet and the sky had a tinge of orange from the early day shower.

“Mind if I join you?" Pauling asked.

Janey turned and looked at her. She had an odd expression on her face as if she'd been thinking about something that had deeply upset her.

"No, no problem," Janey said.

Pauling took her glass and sat on the picnic table next to Janey. She didn't say anything, just joined her and looked out toward the water.

"I just saw a great white shark make a snack out of a sea lion," Janey said, her tone very matter-of-fact.

"Does that happen very often?” Pauling asked. “Early evening they start feeding, right?”

"Oh, it happens all the time but you’re lucky to see it. Then again, you see a lot of things out here,” Janey said.

Pauling wondered what she meant by that. She noticed Janey had a glass of wine in her hand, too.

"Did you know Paige Jones very well?" Pauling asked.

Janey laughed.

"You aren't really here to look at our computer systems, are you?" Janey said.

"Well, I am collecting data if that's what you're asking," Pauling said.

Janey laughed again. "Okay," she said.

Pauling saw a dark shadow pass about 600 feet from the shore. It cruised slowly and at first she thought it was a school of fish and then her breath caught in her throat.

"Is that the shark?"

"It sure is."

Pauling watched as the shadow slowly disappeared.

"I didn't know Paige very well, actually," Janey said, finally answering the question. "We talked occasionally being the only women here at the Nest. But we were both very private people and the conversations never really got too personal."

"Did you see anything out of the ordinary? Anything that made you think somebody would have wanted to hurt Paige?"

Janey shook her head. "No. I didn't see anything out of the ordinary," she said. "But honestly, everything out here is abnormal. This is an unusual place. I mean, think about it. A group of people obsessed with a tiny bird. Academics, really, who spent most of their lives with their noses in thick textbooks studying arcane patterns of wildlife." As she talked, she gestured with the wineglass in her hand. "And now, out here, they're surrounded by men who, for the most part, have a very basic education but extensive knowledge of how to kill people, shoot guns, blow things up and make their enemies disappear."

Janey finished her outburst and looked at Pauling. She was smiling, but there was a strange energy behind it, powered by emotion.

Pauling hid her curiosity by taking a sip of wine.

“So I guess the question is, since you’re out here and asking questions about Paige, do you think it wasn’t really a drowning?”

“No, I’m not saying that, nor do I have any evidence of that,” Pauling answered. “I'm just curious about what happened. What was she really doing out there? This doesn't seem like the kind of place a young woman who doesn't like the water would decide to go out and swim."

"Some of us thought the same thing," Janey said. "We tried to tell them but nobody seemed too interested in our information."

Pauling already knew there wasn’t anything in the police report about interviews with Paige’s co-workers.

“Was there anything you can think of?” Pauling asked, sensing there was a lot more Janey had to say. She just didn’t seem to be ready to divulge.

"Look, I can tell you this," Janey said. "It did seem like there were an awful lot of nights where Paige didn't come home. Back to the Nest. Now no one here is a babysitter or a warden. And in fact, there is a rich history of young women coming here to study birds ending up getting a very close-up study of the anatomy of some of these young military guys."

"I see," Pauling said.

"There isn't a lot to do on this fucking island," Janey said. "I couldn't blame her. If that many guys were to hit on me, I probably would spend a lot fewer nights here too."

She got to her feet and tossed the rest of her wine onto the grass. Pauling wondered if she didn't want to drink anymore, or if the conversation had caused her to lose her desire.

"Okay, I've got to go tend to my plants. Good luck collecting your data," she said. She smiled at Pauling and it was a friendly smile, but with an edge.

Pauling was glad they had connected. Janey left and she looked out at the ocean, at the broad expanse of silver water stretching toward the distant horizon.

Instead of the beauty of the image, Pauling found herself looking in the water for shadows.

CHAPTER TWENTY-EIGHT

The wine tasted really good so Pauling afforded herself another glass. She sat outside and watched the sun slowly sink below the horizon. The sunsets were spectacular here. When the case wrapped up, if it ever did to anyone's satisfaction, she was going to miss the sunsets. Pauling highly doubted she'd see any again so stunning.

Pauling went back inside to the corkboard that held the keys to the conservatory's vehicles and selected the white jeep that Dr. Sirrine had picked her up in when she'd first come to the island.

She went outside, fired it up and there was a rap on the window that startled her. She jumped.

"Hey, are you going up to the Salty Crab?"

Gabe Rawlins looked in at her, a big grin on his cherubic face.

“Yeah, hop in," Pauling said.

Gabe opened the door and slid into the passenger seat. Pauling pulled out of the driveway of the Nest and minutes later they arrived at the Salty Crab, parked and went inside. There were a few guys sitting at various tables, another group of men shooting pool.

Gabe and Pauling went to the bar, each ordered a beer and sat down near one of the picture windows.

"So what do you think of this whole thing so far?" Gabe said.

"What do you mean?" Pauling answered.

Gabe shrugged his shoulders. “Oh, I don't know," he said. "I guess I'm just wondering since you're new to this and you just met everybody what do you think? Anything strike you as odd? What do you think of all these people? Dr. Sirrine? Ted? Janey?”

Pauling smiled. "Everybody seems cool," she said. "I guess the big question is what do you think of everybody? You‘ve been here longer than I have."

Gabe took a long drink of his beer, which was already almost empty. He had pounded that beer fast. "To be honest I think you got a bunch of second-rate scientists stationed to this outpost because they're losers." He nearly spat the words at Pauling.

"I appreciate you being direct."

"More like being honest," he said. He stood with his empty bottle and Pauling tossed down the rest of her beer. She'd better slow down or she'd get trashed. Best not to try to match Gabe beer for beer.

Gabe went and brought two more beers back to the table.

When he sat down, Pauling asked him, "So how well did you know Paige?"

He shrugged his shoulders as if it was a subject he was tired of discussing. "I hit on her a couple of times," he said. "She wasn't interested, if you can believe that," he said, his voice rich with sarcasm.

He nodded his head toward the military guys sitting over at the tables and playing pool. "She seemed more interested in those kind of guys. You know, ripped bodies, raging hard-ons and IQs in the 70s."

Pauling reconciled the answer with what Janey had told her. Gabe put his beer down on the table and toyed with the napkin underneath it.

Gabe looked up at the man who had suddenly appeared at their table. He was a young guy in a t-shirt and jeans with tattoos covering both arms. He was carrying a tray with three Dixie cups on it.

"Just thought you two might like something stronger than your beers," he said, but his eyes were locked on Pauling. He ignored Gabe completely.

"How thoughtful," Gabe said.

"My name's Tom," he said, and stuck his hand out toward Pauling. She shook it and then picked up one of the Dixie cups.

Pauling hadn't done a shot of liquor in years but she raised the Dixie cup toward Tom and Gabe and tossed it down.

Tequila.

Not her favorite.

Pauling was starting to feel lightheaded.

Tom was looking at her and she realized she hadn't said her name.

"I'm Pauling," she said.

"We were kind of in the middle of something, Tom," Gabe said.

Tom ignored Gabe.

"Thanks for the shot," Pauling said. "But we were talking about some private stuff."

Tom smirked at both of them and then joined his buddies at their table, all of them turning and looking openly at Pauling.

She looked down and saw a slip of paper with a cell phone number on it next to the tray.

Pauling waited until Gabe took a drink of his beer and his eyes were tilted to the ceiling to slide the slip of paper into her hand.

“Want to get out of here?” she asked.

"Sure."

They went up to the bar and got four beers to go which Pauling didn't know was a possibility. They walked out to the jeep and Pauling gave the keys to Gabe.

“You better drive,” she said.

They got inside and Gabe immediately cracked a beer.

“Can I show you something totally bizarre?” he asked.

“Sure,” she said. “Why the hell not?”

CHAPTER TWENTY-NINE

"They call it Rag City," Gabe said.

They had wound their way around the island in the dark, the only light provided was from the headlights, but with the nature of the twisting road, it was easy to become disoriented.

Of course, the alcohol and pot didn't help, either, Pauling mused. She was starting to feel a little carsick. Or just plain sick.

Pauling had no idea where they were or where they were going. It seemed as if Gabe had come to this place quite a few times because he knew exactly how to get there despite the lack of road signs.

"I thought we weren't supposed to wander off from the main roads," Pauling said. "Aren't there guys with guns training at night all over the place shooting their guns and blowing shit up?"

Gabe chugged the rest of his beer. He turned to her.

"Sure, that's what makes this little outing so interesting," he said. "I've always found the idea that I could be shot at any moment kind of invigorating. It gets the juices flowing."

Gabe slammed on the brakes and they skidded to a stop. A cloud of dust overtook them. Gabe left the headlights on and the twin beams of light shot through the dust cloud and illuminated some vague shapes in the distance.

Pauling got out of the jeep and in the dim light saw something that shocked her.

It was a town.

An actual little city block.

Although it was dark she could certainly make out the rows of buildings, the narrow streets running between them, and the size of the place to make her feel like it was a real community.

Sans any people.

"What the hell?" she said.

Gabe laughed. "Come on, I'll show you," he said.

He grabbed himself a new beer and offered one to Pauling but she didn't take it. She'd had enough. She was already walking a little unsteadily on her feet.

Gabe confidently walked ahead and was even whistling a tune. It sounded like a Cat Stevens song.

They walked around the edge of the first building and found themselves in the middle of the street. Pauling's eyes were adjusting to the darkness and combined with a sliver of moonlight, she could see pretty well.

"They use this for training," Gabe explained. "This is supposed to look like a little neighborhood in Iraq or Afghanistan. Except without all of the bad guys."

They strolled up the street and there was enough light so Pauling could see a few feet inside the buildings. They were empty except for structural elements like support beams and staircases.

"How big is this place?" Pauling asked.

"It's really just a couple of city blocks. But they keep adding on to it all the time," Gabe said. "You can hear the engineers up here working on it constantly. The rumor is they had some FBI guys out here last week."

Pauling almost wondered out loud if she would recognize any of them.

"Yeah," Gabe said. "Try to watch where you

step. Supposedly there's unexploded ordnance all over the place."

"Great," Pauling said.

"Hey, I want to show you something," he said.

He turned down one alley and then another and went into a building. He used the flashlight app on his phone and waved it around the middle of the room. There was a couch and a couple of chairs. Pauling's foot scraped the floor and a bunch of brass scattered around the space.

Empty shell casings, she realized.

Gabe sat down on the couch and she could see him drinking a beer thanks to just a touch of moonlight filtering in through one of the windows. Although there wasn't an actual glass window but rather a square opening in the wall of concrete.

Pauling went and stood by the couch and suddenly felt Gabe's hand on her ass. She took a step away.

"Hey," she said.

"What? You got a great ass," he said. He laughed a little and drank again from his bottle of beer. "Here we are, alone in the big city, it's so romantic."

"Thanks, but–"

"But what?" Gabe stood and walked toward

her and she held her ground. He went to put his arms around her and she put her hand directly on his chest and pushed him back.

"Gabe, I don't know what you had in mind by bringing me up here but whatever you're planning, it isn't going to happen," she said.

There was silence from him and then he turned and hurled his beer bottle against the concrete wall where it shattered. Little bits of glass rained down on the concrete floor and their echoes filled the air.

"Christ, I hate this fucking place," he said.

And then he was gone. Pauling waited a moment and then walked out of the building and into the alley. She saw no one. She tried to make her way back to the jeep but took a wrong turn and ended up walking the long way around the building. She heard an engine rev and tires spinning out.

When she got to where the jeep had been parked it was gone.

She stood there, waiting.

What could she do?

Suddenly a jolt of electricity went down her back. When Gabe had flashed his cell phone camera in the room there'd been a brief glimpse of some graffiti on the wall, and in the darkness the image popped back into Pauling's mind.

It hadn't sunk in because a moment later she was fighting off Gabe.

Now, she raced back to the building recognizing it in the dark as best she could. She went into the room and used her phone's flashlight on the wall.

It wasn't there.

She thought for a moment and realized she might not be in the right spot. She had to go back and figure out exactly where Gabe had been standing.

Pauling retraced her steps and did it again. This time the light illuminated some writing on the wall. She walked toward it with her flashlight app slowly gaining in intensity until she stood before it.

She examined the wall and her breath caught in her throat.

PJ was here.

Paige Jones.

CHAPTER THIRTY

Gabe came back.

Pauling wasn't surprised, she had pretty good instincts when it came to people and he seemed like the type who would come to his senses. Plus, he was a little drunk and a little high, but Pauling didn't think he was cruel.

He pulled up and she opened the door.

"Sorry about that," he mumbled as she climbed in. "I just got a little crazy. You know, sometimes those guys at the Crab just piss me off and I wonder why I'm not more aggressive. And then something like this happens and I know why."

"You just had on your beer goggles," she said. Gabe chuckled and they pulled out of Rag City with a spray of dirt and gravel.

"Seriously, it won't happen again," Gabe said. Pauling knew he believed himself, but she knew it wasn't true. In a day or two Gabe would forget it and go back to being his sexually frustrated self.

Back at the Nest, they said their good nights and Pauling went to her room, undressed and got into the shower. She felt woozy and unstable. She couldn't remember the last time she'd had so much to drink.

The hot water felt great and she let it pound onto her face and neck. Afterward, she toweled off, brushed her teeth and collapsed onto her bed. She hadn't learned a whole lot, but tomorrow morning she knew her head would recognize the effort.

As she closed her eyes, she thought of the graffiti she'd seen at Rag City.

PJ was here.

When had Paige been there? And with who? Gabe? And how often had she gone? Just the once, and the novelty of being there had inspired her to leave her mark?

There were plenty of questions and no answers.

It did make Pauling think, though. Janey had just said that Paige often didn't return home at night. And it had been made clear to Pauling that certain parts of the island were off-limits. So while it made perfect sense that a wannabe rebel like Gabe had sneaked into Rag City, it was somewhat surprising to Pauling that Paige had done the same thing.

It made her wonder how many other things about Paige she didn't know. Human beings weren't just people, they were unique collections of secrets.

In the morning she awoke with a surprisingly mild hangover. In the kitchen, she put some sugar in her coffee and carried the oversized mug back to her room.

She fired up the laptop and drank coffee while she waited.

Gabe must have made the coffee because it was strong as hell. She was glad she'd cut it with some sugar otherwise it would have been nearly undrinkable.

Immediately, she felt her blood start to pulse and the small headache was already gone.

Her screen had come to life and now she looked at the email Blake had sent her.

There were a ton of attachments he had put into a zip file. But his instructions were clear: immediately open the folder marked "Sirrine."

Pauling did as instructed.

She scanned the first few lines and leaned back in her chair.

"Holy shit," she whispered.

CHAPTER THIRTY-ONE

The first thing Pauling saw was the headline of a newspaper clipping.

Respected Professor Forced to Resign Amid Sex Scandal Rumors

The article continued:

Renowned Ornithological Professor Dr. Abner Sirrine announced his resignation yesterday from California State College. School administrators were alerted to a sexual abuse complaint filed by one of Dr. Sirrine's students. Although investigators found the results inconclusive the administrators felt that due to the severe nature of the complaint, Dr. Sirrine should be forced to resign.

Pauling continued to read the background Blake had supplied. She set aside the scandalous stuff and went to a biography from one of Dr. Sirrine's earlier employers.

It told her that Abner had graduated from a prestigious private school on the East Coast and then went to Dartmouth where he graduated magna cum laude. He immediately began writing papers and gaining recognition for his insights into bird migrations, in particular the birds of southern California. These papers had ultimately led to his being offered the position at California State College, where he'd been an instructor for decades.

Pauling learned that after his resignation, Dr. Sirrine went off the grid before he reappeared for the Bird Conservatory. Pauling wondered if the reason he was accepted for the job was that he wouldn't have any underage females working for him.

That made sense to Pauling. She continued to read the material from Blake on Dr. Sirrine until she had completed nearly everything.

Before she dug into information on the others she thought about what she'd read.

Could it be that Dr. Sirrine had anything to do with Paige's death?

On the surface, it seemed absurd.

Dr. Sirrine was like a goofy old uncle. Additionally, his physicality was less than impressive. He didn't look fragile necessarily, but he certainly wasn't much of a physical specimen.

Pauling saw no way in which Dr. Sirrine could overpower Paige.

Unless of course Paige had been under the influence of something, knowingly or unknowingly. Pauling thought of her escapades the night before. But nothing she had seen in Dr. Abner Sirrine suggested he would've killed Paige.

But if there was one thing she had learned at the FBI, it was to never underestimate the potential for evil in the human heart.

CHAPTER THIRTY-TWO

After Pauling ate breakfast and had a couple more cups of coffee, she decided to skip the field trip Dr. Sirrine had planned for her and instead commandeered the jeep and drove it directly to the commander's office.

She parked in the little gravel parking lot outside a civilian-looking building that looked more a real estate agent's office than military headquarters.

Pauling walked inside and saw two offices. One was empty and the other was occupied by Commander Bill Wilkins and seated in a chair across from him, Michael Tallon.

Pauling decided to be bold and ignore

protocol so she walked right up to the office and stood outside the doorway.

Wilkins looked at her and his expression made Michael Tallon turn and look over his shoulder. When he saw Pauling, he smiled.

"Hey! Pauling, how are you doing?"

"I'm doing fine. How are you? Hello, Bill."

“Pauling,” Wilkins replied.

"Couldn't be better," Tallon answered. “Are you here to see me or this old salt?"

"The old salt," she said.

“No problem, we were just finishing up,” Tallon said. “I’ll talk to you later, Bill.” Tallon got to his feet, nodded at her as he walked past and then stopped.

"Hey, have you ever gone diving for lobsters before?"

"No, can't say that I have," Pauling answered.

"Great. Let's do it. You can’t come out to San Clemente and never go lobster diving. It’s a rite of passage."

“Sounds interesting,” Pauling said.

“I’ll pick you up tomorrow morning.”

He walked on and Pauling turned to Commander Wilkins.

"Is he serious?" she asked.

Wilkins nodded. “Yeah, I'm afraid so. I try

not to eat too much lobster, as good as they are. High in cholesterol."

Pauling took the chair in which Tallon had been sitting.

"So what can I do for you?" Wilkins said.

"Well, you offered to give me a tour of your part of the island so I thought I would finally take you up on that," she said. "Or is now a bad time? Is this the kind of thing you schedule?"

"I did, in fact, have a couple things on today's calendar but when a beautiful woman like yourself offers to spend some time with me, I'm not gonna turn her down," Wilkins replied. "I may be old but I haven't lost my faculties."

He snatched up a set of keys and gestured for Pauling to follow him.

"So who actually provides law enforcement for the island?" she asked, knowing the answer but wanting to see what he would say. "Is it the military police or your own guys? Or is there an outside police force whose jurisdiction the island falls under?"

"You get right to the point, don't you?" he said, glancing at Pauling. "Technically, we fall under the jurisdiction of the Los Angeles County Sheriff's Department whose nearest precinct is actually on Catalina Island. Have you ever been to Catalina Island?"

Pauling thought about it. "Yes, I have been on Catalina but it was a long time ago when I was a little girl."

Wilkins led her outside to a small blue pickup truck and he took the wheel. She slid into the passenger seat. The truck smelled like coffee and cigarettes.

"We're not a very big operation," he said. "We only have a couple hundred people here usually. Mostly guys rotating in for training and rotating out. The people who are here on a full-time basis tend to be the Seabees who are the construction people from the Navy. Of course the kitchen staff are year-round. The maintenance people are year-round, too."

Wilkins drove her from one end of the island to the other, pointing out the various locations of training sites. Most of them were not much to look at.

As they drove, she occasionally spotted groups of men jogging.

The tour took less than an hour and Pauling didn't see anything that surprised her, or that she hadn't seen before.

The most interesting thing to note was what Wilkins hadn't shown her.

Rag City.

Eventually, they wound up back at Wilkins' office.

"So were you shocked when the body of Paige Jones showed up?" she asked.

"Absolutely," he said casually, as if she'd asked him about the weather report. "We see training accidents all the time. Some of them are fatal. But the birdies? Nothing ever happens to them. It was a shame. I'd met her, saw her occasionally at the Crab. A beautiful girl."

Pauling nodded.

The phone on the desk rang. Pauling almost chuckled. Who had landlines anymore?

"You'll have to excuse me," he said.

"Thank you for the tour."

He nodded to her as he picked up the phone.

CHAPTER THIRTY-THREE

She found Dr. Sirrine standing outside the herbarium. He was examining a new batch of seeds that had been collected that morning.

Pauling took in his appearance, which was the same as always. Khakis, a barn jacket, worn leather boat shoes and a field hat.

"Any exciting discoveries?" Pauling asked.

Dr. Sirrine shook his head.

"No, but it's been a dry season and the ground cover isn't doing as well as we'd hoped," he said. "But it's not horrible. Plenty of camouflage for our favorite birds' food."

"That's good," Pauling said. "Hey, do you have a minute? I'd like to talk to you about something."

Dr. Sirrine put down the seeds he'd been studying and glanced at her.

"This sounds serious."

Pauling didn't respond.

He pointed to a bench near the back of the building. They walked to it together and sat down.

"What did you want to discuss?" he asked.

"I've read the newspaper articles about your departure from California State College," Pauling began. "I guess I wanted to hear your side of the story."

Dr. Sirrine sighed and rubbed his hands on his thighs, brushing off some dirt and loose grass he'd collected during his research.

"What makes you possibly think I would want to talk about that?" he snapped. "It's ancient history."

"So do the newspaper stories tell the whole truth? Or is there more to the story?"

"Truth and reality are two different things," he explained, a tone of condescension in his voice. "They told their truth, and I have mine. The reality depends on which lens you're standing behind."

"Spoken like a true professor," Pauling said. She paused, and was amazed at how right at home she felt. She'd interrogated some bad people in her life. The naturalist sitting next to her was severely undermatched.

"How much does the Bird Conservatory know?" Pauling asked.

Pauling sensed Dr. Sirrine's back stiffen at the mention of it.

"Is that a threat?"

"I don't know," she answered. "Do you feel threatened by the idea of me talking to them? Or do they already know your full history?"

In other words, Pauling thought, *yes, it's a threat all right.*

Body language oftentimes speaks several volumes louder than verbal speech. When Dr. Sirrine's body seemed to fold in on itself, Pauling knew she had cracked him.

"There was nothing, absolutely nothing, untoward," he finally said. "The fact was, she had been my student, but wasn't under my tutelage when we began seeing one another. She was eighteen. I was thirty-eight."

A truck drove by on Perimeter Road and Dr. Sirrine waited for its sound to fade.

"I was lonely, she was in need of adventure. For a brief time, we found solace with each other."

His voice had warmed, and Pauling instinctively knew Dr. Sirrine still had feelings for the woman.

"But as is so often the case with these things, it ended badly," he explained. "For someone my age, I knew these things happened. She was young, and didn't know how to handle it, so she lied and said the relationship had begun six months before it actually did. When she was seventeen. She knew what would happen to me. And it did."

"Did she ever recant her story?" Pauling asked.

Dr. Sirrine shook his head. "No, she changed her story, repeatedly. But she never recanted the fictional start date. However, each time she told the story she added in new details, mostly regarding my depravity. It was almost like she felt she couldn't tell the same story over and over. She needed to spice it up each time. Needless to say, the damage to my teaching career was irrevocable."

Pauling leaned back against the bench. She folded her arms across her chest.

"What did you think when they found Paige's body?"

His laugh was full of cynicism. "I naturally

thought of myself. I figured someone would eventually come calling, questioning me regarding my whereabouts, that kind of thing. I figured it would be the police."

"And did they?"

"They talked to me about her, but I had nothing to tell them. And they only asked about her in the context of a drowning. They clearly felt foul play wasn't involved, and frankly, I felt the same way. That is, until you arrived. And then I began to wonder who had hired an investigator, and why."

Pauling ignored the bait.

"Did they ask about your past?" she asked.

"No."

He looked directly at her.

"You're the first."

CHAPTER THIRTY-FOUR

When Pauling was finished talking with Dr. Sirrine and he had gone back to the Nest, she heard movement behind her and a door banged shut. She got up from the bench and walked around to where she heard the sound. There was a door that must have been a side entrance to the herbarium.

Pauling went inside and Janey was standing at a rolling table, working with some soil samples.

Pauling wondered if Janey had been trying to listen in on her conversation with Dr. Sirrine.

And if so, why?

"Do you enjoy your work here?" Pauling asked, as she walked up to watch Janey.

Janey spoke quickly, almost nervously. "I enjoy

what I do, but not much else. You know, when I came here a lot of people at the Bird Conservatory said the work was rewarding but you'll live in isolation. There's nothing to do there, they said. You'll lose contact with friends and family and being able to do social things. And I found out they were right."

It had all come out in a gushing torrent and Pauling suspected Janey had been listening to her conversation with Dr. Sirrine. She'd been a little too eager to fill the void.

"But you do enjoy the work?" Pauling asked. "Are you achieving things professionally?"

Janey stopped what she was doing and turned to Pauling, almost as if she hadn't fully realized she was there until that moment.

"Do *you* enjoy what *you're* doing?" Janey asked. Her tone was verging on anger. Pauling was surprised. What had she done to piss off this woman?

"Are you achieving things that you want to achieve in a professional sense?" Janey persisted. Some of the snark had gone out of her tone, but Pauling sensed there was a lot of emotion behind the question.

Pauling knew what Janey was getting at. She was obviously thinking that Pauling was snooping around about Paige's death. *But why would that upset her?*

"I find my work challenging," Pauling said. "But I feel that what I do is very important."

Pauling followed Janey as she carried a tray of seedlings and put it under a grow light.

"I wanted to thank you for telling me about Paige and some of her habits," Pauling tried, softening her tone as much as possible. "I was wondering, was there anything else you can think of? Anything else that happened to Paige while she was out here? Anyone who might've wanted to hurt her?"

Janey frowned. "No. I did remember one thing though, and I meant to tell you. One morning I saw Paige at breakfast and her face was puffy and red and there were marks on her throat. It was hard to tell what they were though. There are a lot of strange pollens out here and sometimes we have allergic reactions. Not to mention all kinds of spiders and flies and mosquitoes. We're constantly getting bitten," Janey said. "But there was a part of me that wondered if someone had slapped her around a little bit. Maybe even put their hands around her throat. Then again, I figured I might have been paranoid or something. And it wasn't my place to ask."

"So you didn't ask her about the marks?" Pauling asked.

"Not right away, but eventually I sort of did. A couple of times. But she never wanted to talk about them, and she never told me what happened. As far as I know she never told anyone."

Janey set down the tray of soil as if it was a punctuation mark on what she said. And then she walked away.

CHAPTER THIRTY-FIVE

Pauling spent a fitful evening going over the material Blake had sent her, updating her dossiers on everyone involved and then eventually falling asleep.

She had a bad night's sleep punctuated by a nightmare in which she was stranded in the desert facing a pickup truck with a huge machine gun installed in the truck bed, manned by a terrorist.

When she awoke, she got her coffee and found Michael Tallon waiting for her.

She'd forgotten about his offer to take her diving for lobster.

"Ever had lobster for breakfast?" he asked. His blue eyes shone like beacons and Pauling realized once again how incredibly good-looking he was.

And then she caught herself. She was here to investigate Paige's death. Not to meet a handsome military guy.

She wasn't sure why she had accepted the offer in the first place. But it occurred to her that Paige's journal had referenced a man with blue eyes. And Paige had washed up on the shore as if she'd been out swimming.

So when a man with blue eyes invited her out for a diving expedition she felt, as an investigator, she had to say yes.

Because in the back of her mind, she couldn't help but wonder if this was exactly how Paige had met her unfortunate demise.

An innocent offer from Michael Tallon.

Pauling didn't think it would be the case, but she also felt like she needed some insurance.

Besides, she still had no idea if Paige's poem was even about Michael Tallon, or if it was about a man at all. It all depended upon the interpretation.

Before she left, Pauling sent an email to Blake, letting him know that she was going out on a dive boat with a Michael Tallon. She made it sound like a casual mention in a frivolous email and refrained from specifically asking Blake to do anything.

Pauling also made a concerted effort not to mention how angry she felt that Jack Reacher was nowhere to be found. Nathan Jones would have to give her a proper explanation when she got back.

They took Perimeter Road down to the military's shipyard. There were some boats with machine guns on them and Pauling was again reminded of her dream.

"Those are called RHIBS," Tallon explained. "Rigid Hull Inflatable Boats."

He pointed over toward another set of two boats that were bigger and held more machine guns. "Those are called Mark Vs."

Tallon parked the vehicle and they made their way down to the pier where Tallon led her to a boat that looked like a glorified barge.

"Yeah, this isn't as sexy as those other boats but it'll get the job done," he said. "This is our backup boat for dive training. Right now there's hardly anything on it which makes it perfect for us to go look for some lobster."

It was a small vessel maybe 25 feet in length but at least 15 feet wide. There was a little pilothouse and then there were rows of oxygen tanks on the side along with dive gear.

"Why don't you untie us while I fire up the engines?" he said.

"Aye aye, captain," she said.

Pauling went to the bow and stern of the boat and undid the thick ropes holding the barge in place as she heard the rumble of what she assumed to be a big diesel engine get going.

They slowly pulled out of the harbor and into an immediate chop. The barge didn't exactly rise and fall with the waves as much as plow through them, occasionally bumping and going sideways.

Pauling made no move to put on a life jacket, nor did Tallon. Of course, for all she knew, Tallon could have been a Navy SEAL. His Ball watch, the NEDU, meant Navy Experimental Dive Unit. Maybe there was more to that story than he'd indicated.

"The best place is about a mile out. There's some structure and the season's right."

He had come out of the pilothouse, leaving the barge on some sort of autopilot, she guessed.

"Have you done any diving?" he asked.

"A little," she said. "I was certified once awhile back on a Caribbean vacation."

"Well, the good thing is the water clarity out here is fantastic, so it shouldn't be much of a problem."

He gave her a wet suit and they geared up.

"What about the sharks?" she asked.

Pauling still hadn't decided if she was going to do this or not. A lot of it depended on Tallon's answer.

"They won't bother you," he said. "It's the middle of the day and I've done this a thousand times. Now, if it was midnight, no, I wouldn't be doing this."

Not exactly what she wanted to hear, but at least he sounded honest.

They pulled out into the open ocean and occasionally Pauling glanced back at San Clemente. It already looked so small, she found it hard to believe she was living on it temporarily.

Ahead, there was a large stone outcropping with a strange white cap. There were thousands of birds on the rock, or in the air above it.

"Bird Shit Rock," Tallon said.

"Lovely," Pauling replied.

By the time they got most of the gear ready, Tallon glanced up and said, "Great, we're here."

He shut the engines off and somewhere an anchor splashed into the water.

They did tests for each other's air and then dropped into the sea.

Pauling was fascinated with the color of the water. And she was also terrified of the sharks she'd seen.

Tallon led the way, swimming down to a structure covered in green. Pauling noticed Tallon had some sort of large glove on his hand.

Suddenly, a lobster shot out of the structure and Tallon caught him expertly with the glove. He stuffed it into a bag on the side of his hip.

He gestured toward Pauling and gave her the glove. She slipped it on, realizing it was some sort of hockey goalie's glove.

A lobster scooted out in front of her and she grabbed it with the glove, but it squirted out from her grasp and got away. She repeated this several times.

Tallon made a gesture to her that looked like he was saying she needed to squeeze harder.

The next lobster that came she did just that and this time, it stayed in the glove.

Tallon slid it into his bag and she gave him the glove back. She had caught one. That was good enough for her.

Pauling watched while Tallon caught a few more lobsters and then she was startled when a sea lion zipped between them, going for Tallon's lobster catch.

He was able to maneuver quickly enough to avoid the thief.

They surfaced and climbed back onto the barge.

"Well done, Pauling," he said.

"Thanks, you were pretty handy with that hockey glove. Although that sea lion almost had an easy feast."

"Yeah, it's sort of a game with them. Sometimes I'll feed them a couple for their troubles."

Pauling stripped out of her gear and helped Tallon stow the lobsters in a cooler filled with ice.

Tallon pulled a couple bottles of beer from another cooler she hadn't even noticed.

They sat on the end of the barge, the warm sun blasting down on them and the chill she'd felt from the water quickly went away.

She felt warm, safe and the beer was perfect.

They clinked bottles.

"To fresh lobster," Pauling said.

"And good company."

CHAPTER THIRTY-SIX

"You in the mood for a burger?" Ted asked her when she came back to the Nest after her lobster-diving expedition. By now, it was early evening and Pauling was tired from her day on the water.

She was still thinking about Michael Tallon and what Janey had told her about Paige.

"A burger?" she asked.

"Yeah, at the Crab," Ted said. His mop of black hair was hanging over his eyes and Pauling had a negative reply on the tip of her tongue.

But she bit it back. She and Michael had grilled the lobsters on the boat and had them for lunch and she wasn't really hungry.

"Sure," she said. "I just need a couple of minutes first, is that okay?"

"Yeah, I'll grab a beer while I wait."

Pauling went back to her room and quickly changed her clothes.

Something told her this was going to be different than her outing with Gabe. Gabe wore his heart on his sleeve and was consumed with lust.

Ted was quiet. Bookish, almost.

She joined him in a white jeep and they drove to the Salty Crab.

Pauling was beginning to wonder how many more times she would have to go to the bar.

But she wasn't ready to completely write off the Crab just yet; besides, getting people to drink tended to help an investigation. The drunk man's tongue speaks the sober man's mind, right?

Ted parked and they went inside.

Pauling also understood the sensory deprivation that naturally occurs on San Clemente Island. It has to. There are no shopping malls. No row of restaurants. No residential neighborhoods with kids playing in the yard. All there is on the island is a foreign landscape, nearly completely devoid of trees, and beyond it, ocean.

The Crab served a useful purpose. Seeing other human beings, talking to them.

And fried food.

They got a table near the kitchen, both ordered cheeseburgers with french fries.

Pauling already felt vaguely ill. She hadn't had a salad since her lunch with Tallon and her diet had become a steady supply of meat and carbs. And booze.

Her mind briefly drifted back to Michael Tallon. She wondered where he was and what he was doing.

"Christ, I'm so hungry," Ted said. The food was delivered in red plastic baskets. Again, it reminded Pauling of greasy spoons back in the day.

Pauling ate her burger and had to agree with Ted, it was good. But she couldn't eat like this much longer.

Someone bumped into her from behind.

Pauling turned and looked into the sweaty, greasy face of a woman. At first, she thought it was a man. But when the woman looked down at her and said, "Fuck outta my way," Pauling could tell it was a woman.

Her arms were huge, and one of them sported a barbed wire tattoo around the impressive bicep.

The woman sat down a few tables away from Pauling and Ted.

"Uh-oh," Ted said.

Pauling and Ted tried to focus on their cheeseburgers. Pauling's was only half-eaten. Ted had demolished his but was picking at his fries. Pauling drank some of her beer when a shadow fell across the table. She looked up and saw the woman who had bumped into her staring down at her.

"Who the hell are you?" the woman asked. Pauling could smell the alcohol on her breath and her pupils were totally dilated. She was clearly drunk.

"My name is Pauling. What's yours?"

"Oh great, another little birdie to fly around and bug the shit out of me," the woman said, ignoring Pauling's question.

"Look, we're just trying to have some cheeseburgers and a beer and then we're gonna get out of here," Ted said. "No need for any problem here."

"You goddamn right there's not gonna be a problem," the woman said, her voice thick and slurry. "In the future, you bitches stay away from me."

She left and went back to her table. There was a guy at her table. He was big with a bulging pot belly and a dirty t-shirt.

"I think those are the construction people,"

Ted said. “They tend to be kind of rough. A lot of times they're worse than the military guys."

"Yeah, why did she have such a problem with me?" Pauling said.

"Because you’re competition," Ted said. “I have a feeling that when the guys are drunk, even on this island where there's hardly any women and the guys are all horny, she probably still has problems getting laid.”

“Shocking with that winning personality of hers,” Pauling said.

“And look at her,” Ted said, glancing over Pauling’s shoulder.

“I’d rather not.”

“What you lookin’ at?” The man with the big gut stood up and pointed at Ted.

“Holy shit,” Ted said.

The man’s chair scraped across the floor.

“Hey, come on guys!” a voice called from another table. A man stood and Pauling recognized him as the pilot from the plane that brought her out to the island. He was sitting with his co-pilot and a military guy she hadn’t seen before.

“Give me a round for that table!” he shouted at the bartender and then walked over to Pauling’s table. He stuck out his hand.

"Brock Jamison, I flew you out here. Along with my partner over there, Josh Troyer."

He nodded at the table with the construction couple, who'd suddenly gone quiet.

"It's kind of like that Asian philosophy of how if you save someone's life you're responsible for them," Jamison said. "That's how I see it. When I fly you out here, my job isn't over."

He laughed and Pauling was glad he was there. She and Ted were probably no match for those two.

"Come on, Jamison, quit trying to be a hero," Troyer said, and approached the table. "It doesn't suit you very well."

He looked at Pauling. "I remember you. Didn't we just fly out here a couple days ago? And you're causing problems already?" He winked at her.

Brock Jamison had returned from the bar with a tray of tequila shots. He took them over to the construction workers' table and they spoke quietly.

Pauling glanced over and they were looking at her, scowling. But the big guy had sat back down.

Jamison returned to their table.

"You can either come and sit with us or you've probably got about ten minutes before those new shots of tequila wear off and they start looking for a fight again."

Ted stood. "I think we're going to go," he said.

Pauling decided not to push her luck.

"Thank you for that," she said to Jamison and nodded her head toward the loud-mouthed drunkards.

"My pleasure," he said.

Pauling and Ted headed for the door. As they veered wide around the construction workers' table the woman looked up at Pauling.

"Watch it, birdie or you'll fly away forever."

CHAPTER THIRTY-SEVEN

Pauling decided to go for a walk, although it wasn't really possible to go for a true, aimless walk. Not unless you wanted to get shot by a sniper or step on a land mine.

No, she had to settle for walking around the birders' compound.

She said good night to Ted and walked around behind the main building. The cheeseburger, even though she'd eaten only half of it due to the interruption by the manly female construction worker, sat heavy in her stomach.

When she got off this island, she was going to eat nothing but salads of mixed greens for a month straight. And plenty of green tea. Plus, she would work out every damn day. Hardcore.

She walked under a sky filled with stars, an

absolutely windless night and the sound of the surf pounding below. As she walked, she thought about Paige.

The first image that came to mind was that of Paige getting her ass kicked by the woman Pauling had just met at the Salty Crab. She made a note to find out who the woman was, her name, and talk to her, preferably when the woman wasn't drunk and belligerent. She didn't know if the woman was never *not* drunk or belligerent, but she would find out.

She walked past the herbarium, past the maintenance shed with the trucks and the gas pumps. The road sloped down and she followed it, careful not to re-emerge onto the road. That was definitely not the place to be. Here, on the south side of the complex, she knew the military generally didn't train.

However, she had no intention of taking a chance.

In the distance, she heard the high-pitched howl of what she assumed was a fox. They had once been extremely prevalent on the island, but had seen their numbers dwindle over the years. The population was stable, though, and in no danger of extinction.

Pauling walked on, wanting to walk faster but

aware that she had a limited range of travel. She would have to do laps–

Slap.

She stopped in her tracks.

The sound of something hitting flesh. It sounded like a hand. Like someone had slapped someone's face.

She waited.

Slap.

It was to her left. Past the maintenance buildings, toward a tiny shed used for storage. Now, she saw a small light visible only from this side of the building.

She walked toward it, careful not to make a sound.

Slap.

Pauling walked ahead, her ears straining for any voices.

In the corner of her vision, just around the edge of the tiny shed, she saw a foot. Its laces were pressed into the ground, as if the owner was kneeling.

Pauling widened her approach, and the scene came into view.

Dr. Sirrine was on his knees behind Janey, his pants down and his naked ass exposed to the moon.

Janey's lower half was naked, her buttocks visible as Dr. Sirrine thrust into her and slapped her naked ass.

Pauling stood, frozen.

"You like that, don't you?" Dr. Sirrine said, his voice a growl.

"Yes, harder," Janey said.

Pauling had seen enough.

She turned and tripped over a discarded set of plumbing pipes. She fell on her face in the long grass.

Pauling heard the sound of feet scraping in the dirt and the rattle of a belt buckle. She ran toward the Nest, ducking around the larger maintenance building and then beelining it for the Nest.

She made it inside and hurried to her room, let herself in and shut the door.

She left the light off.

It was a strange sense of guilt, but she simply didn't want Dr. Sirrine and Janey to know that she had seen them. But it made her head spin. She'd figured there would be some cases of romance between the men and women who worked at the Nest, but she never would have figured on Dr. Sirrine and Janey. The age difference. The personalities.

But most importantly, she wondered how it affected her investigation of what happened with Paige.

Had Dr. Sirrine, who made every effort to appear morally superior, made advances on Paige? He'd clearly made them, and succeeded, with Janey.

There was no way Paige would have acquiesced to Dr. Sirrine.

But again, Pauling knew when it came to human beings, one could never really be sure of anything.

CHAPTER THIRTY-EIGHT

In the morning, Pauling grabbed a cup of coffee and the keys to one of the pickup trucks.

She no longer felt the need to ask. As she drove, she thought about island fever, that feeling of claustrophobia some people succumbed to. She wasn't there yet, but the sense of isolation was strong.

Now, she drove ahead past the cafeteria building and around the administration building to where she'd been told by Gabe the maintenance staff was housed.

The maintenance department most likely included the construction workers.

Pauling smiled at the idea of waking up the construction woman from the night before. It would be great payback for the woman's boorish behavior. Pauling hoped she was hungover and feeling terrible.

She would have some fun with it, she decided.

There was an open two-story aluminum-sided garage set back from a driveway with a sign that read "Maintenance."

Pauling pulled the truck into the driveway, parked it and went inside.

The smell of diesel fuel was strong, and she heard the clang of metal.

There appeared to be no one in the front half of the garage. She walked toward the back, eventually seeing a desk with an ancient computer sitting on top of it.

Her friend from the bar was sprawled on a couch that had been pushed up against the wall.

Her face was pale and she had a Gatorade in her hand.

She looked up at Pauling. Her bloodshot eyes narrowed.

"What do you want?" she asked.

"I'd like to talk to you."

The woman shook her head.

"I've got nothing to say," she said, her voice sounding like sandpaper. "If I said something last night you don't like, go ahead and complain to my supervisor."

The guy from the Crab with the pot belly and dirty t-shirt stepped into the space from a doorway off to the left. He still had on the same shirt.

"There he is now," the woman said.

He had a giant iron wrench in his hand.

Pauling smiled.

"No complaints about last night," Pauling said. "I had fun. I actually wanted to ask you about Paige Jones. She worked with the Bird Conservatory here."

"She the dead girl?"

"What's your name, by the way?" Pauling asked.

"I'm Deb. And no, I don't remember her."

"Shit, you don't remember anything," the guy said.

"What's your name?" Pauling asked him.

"The hell should I tell you?" he said. His eyebrow was raised and he was hefting the wrench with apparent pleasure.

"Why not?" Pauling answered.

He nodded as if that was a good enough response for him. "I'm Donnie. I don't remember her, but I heard one of the birdies died. Was that her? And that's why you're asking around?"

"Paige was a very beautiful girl, dark hair." Pauling produced the photo of Paige that she'd brought along.

"Shit yeah, I remember her," Donnie said. "Great ass. Those military guys ate her up."

"Literally," Deb said. She and Donnie high-fived.

"Did you ever threaten her like you did me?" Pauling asked.

Donnie dropped his hands by his side like he was about to brawl. Deb's head popped up and she winced, as if the movement hurt her.

"Probably," Deb said. "But I sure didn't kill her if that's what you're asking. Christ. The booze sometimes makes me shoot my mouth off, that's all."

"Any idea who might have wanted to hurt her?" Pauling asked.

"Hurt her? I thought the dumb bitch drowned," Donnie said.

"What a touching eulogy," Pauling said. "Answer the question. Was anyone after her?"

"Hell, all those guys were after her," Deb said, sorrow and disappointment audible in her voice.

"Maybe she screwed one of them over. They all got fragile egos."

"Big egos and little dicks," Donnie said, puffing himself up and looking at Pauling.

"How would you know?" Deb asked.

She and Pauling looked at Donnie.

"Piss off, both of you," he said and walked back out the door. Deb laid back on the couch and put a towel over her face.

"Fly away, birdie," she said.

CHAPTER THIRTY-NINE

Pauling got back into the pickup truck, pulled out into the driveway and made it to the intersection with Perimeter Road, next to the maintenance sign.

Another car drove by and behind the wheel she saw Michael Tallon. His face registered no surprise but he hit the brakes hard and nearly skidded to a stop. He put his car in reverse and backed up in front of her. Pauling pulled out onto the road so they were side by side. She rolled down her window and he did the same.

"What are you doing out here?" he asked.

"Oh, I was just looking to see if they needed a full-time mechanic. You know I'm a real grease monkey."

"Hmm, I didn't realize that. Wait here," he

said. He pulled his car off onto the shoulder, put the hazard lights on and ran around to the side of her pickup. He opened the door and hopped into her passenger seat.

Pauling put the truck in gear and pulled off onto the shoulder.

"I've been meaning to ask," Tallon said. "What is it you do with the bird people again?"

She drummed her fingers on the steering wheel. "Why?"

He shrugged his shoulders. "I seem to recall you telling me you had something to do with computers."

"Yeah, I believe I said something like that," she said. Pauling wondered where this was coming from. He hadn't asked her any of these kinds of questions when they'd gone diving. Maybe he hadn't wanted to spoil the outing.

He furrowed his brow as if he was trying to reconcile that idea.

"It just seems like you remind me of a certain kind of person," he said.

"Oh yeah, what kind of person is that?"

"Well, you know I did a lot of work in Special Ops," he grinned at her. "Still do, occasionally, maybe."

Pauling knew that was the case, she'd guessed that the minute she'd met him.

"We did a lot of missions all over the world and I worked with a lot of different people," he continued. "You don't seem like a boots-on-the-ground kind of person, too much. But you do remind me of some people I worked with. There were a few folks who helped plan strategy, you know, more of an analysis kind of thing. You remind me of them. I don't know, it's just a feeling.

Pauling wondered if he knew who she really was, because he had described what she'd done at the FBI. And was he asking her this because he already knew it to be true? Had they dug into classified files and found out who she really was?

For a brief moment Pauling thought about telling him the truth. But then she changed her mind.

"Don't you have somewhere you need to be?" she asked, a bit abruptly.

Tallon laughed, opened the door and got out of the truck. He leaned on the doorframe and looked at Pauling. "Maybe one day you'll tell me who you really are." He tapped the roof twice and walked back to his car.

Pauling drove away.

He's right, she thought. One day I probably will.

CHAPTER FORTY

Pauling drove back to the Nest and saw Ted unloading a bunch of gear from the back of his truck. She parked, went over and lent him a hand. There were cardboard boxes of various shapes and sizes, some heavy, some light.

"What's in this?"

"Mostly supplies," he said. Pauling grabbed a box and followed Ted around to the back of the building and started stacking the boxes near a table.

They went back and forth making trips from the truck to the stack and it took them nearly half an hour to completely unload the vehicle's cargo.

"Did these just come in on the plane today?"

"Yep," Ted said.

They finished and sat down at the table. "That was a good workout," Pauling said. Ted grabbed them each a bottled water from somewhere.

"So Ted, how well did you know Paige?"

"Give me a break," Ted said, his even demeanor dropping and going right into Angry Ted.

"You know, I know you're asking everybody about this and I know you're going around trying to find a bunch of stuff out. Why don't you just leave the dead alone? If you aren't going to, at least just leave me alone about it, okay?"

Ted's face had gotten red and Pauling knew it wasn't from the exertion of unloading the gear. "I had nothing to do with anything related to Paige. Okay? I hardly knew her, I barely even talked to her. She went out every night. She had a lot of boyfriends and I'm not judging. But you don't have to investigate me if that's what you're doing."

"I'm not investigating you," Pauling answered evenly. "I'm just wondering if you knew anything about her."

Ted snorted. "Oh bullshit, Pauling. We've all talked about you and we all know you're not remotely involved with computers or anything else. So just give me a break, okay?"

It had all come out like a torrent and Pauling watched as Ted caught his breath and took a drink of his bottled water.

"You seem very emotional about this, Ted," she said, her voice calm and controlled. "I'm actually not an investigator, but I do believe when you find somebody who adamantly doesn't want to talk about something usually there is more to the story."

He slammed his bottled water down and it spilled onto the table.

"Enough with the psychobabble! Jesus Christ!" he thundered at her. "Thanks for helping me with the boxes. Now just leave me alone, okay?"

He stormed off out of the building.

Pauling grabbed her water and tried to figure out why Ted was suddenly so emotional about her questions.

Something he had said struck her.

Leave the dead alone.

It suddenly gave her an idea and she realized she should have done it already.

CHAPTER FORTY-ONE

Back in her room Pauling fired up her laptop. She sent a message to Blake asking him if he could hack into the Los Angeles County Sheriff's Department website and track down the autopsy records for Paige Jones.

There had been a note in the paperwork Nathan had given Pauling regarding how an autopsy had been performed but that it had been inadequate to the state of the remains. But now Pauling wondered if an autopsy had at least been attempted, maybe they'd recorded something. Anything would be helpful at this point.

It might have seemed a strange request to ask Blake to hack the LASD, but Pauling knew Blake had once hacked into another law enforcement website and that one was linked to the federal government.

So she figured getting into a much smaller organization should be easier.

Pauling also remembered that Dr. Sirrine had set up the afternoon for her to go into the field with Ted.

Oh, that should be fun, she thought. Pauling figured Ted would take one look at her and cancel the outing.

It didn't matter because Pauling didn't want to spend the afternoon with Ted. She realized instead that she really needed to go and speak to the investigator who had overseen the examination of Paige upon the discovery of her body. According to Commander Wilkins, the investigating authority was on Catalina Island.

Pauling thought about how she could get there.

She knew there weren't flights to the island. She knew she just couldn't catch a ferry there, either. All transportation to and from San Clemente Island had to be sanctioned by the military.

What you really needed was a friend with a boat.

A small smile crept onto her face. Michael had given her his cell phone number and told her that the military had a small tower on the island which let people call each other on San Clemente, but that it wasn't strong enough to reach people on the mainland.

Pauling sent a text message to Michael asking him if he'd ever been to Catalina Island.

He texted back right away. *Sure. Have you?*

A long time ago.

He wrote back: *Weather is supposed to be great tomorrow. Low winds. We could grab a boat and go.*

She accepted the invitation she had forced, and then put her phone down. Back on the laptop, she went onto the Los Angeles County Sheriff's Department website. Under the administrative section of the website Pauling found the detective in charge. She emailed him asking him if she could talk to him tomorrow and she included her cell phone.

The next morning, Tallon came and picked her up in the truck and they went down to the marina. He had authorized a boat that had been civilianized, meaning all of the weapons had been taken off and it was mostly used as a transport vessel.

They set out from San Clemente Island and it

took them an hour to get to Catalina. They pulled into the harbor and found a spot to tie off the boat.

"What do you want to do first?" Tallon asked her.

"I'm starving. How about we get some food?"

They found a restaurant that was perched over the water with fantastic views of the hundreds of sailboats anchored. It really was a beautiful harbor with the hills surrounding the water, and the community itself cascading down the hills settling on the water's edge.

Picture-postcard.

During lunch, Tallon talked about the rich history of Los Angeles celebrities coming out to Catalina Island for weekends of debauchery. Pauling was pretty sure she knew what he was getting at.

She feigned deep interest in her grilled shrimp salad.

After lunch Pauling said to Tallon, "Why don't you go off and explore on your own, while I do some shopping? We can rendezvous for drinks at happy hour."

He smiled at her. "If you want to get rid of me for a couple hours all you have to do is say so," he answered.

She gave him a kiss on the lips for an answer and it tasted good.

CHAPTER FORTY-TWO

Pauling turned and walked up the hill leading to Main Street.

She found a little office for the sheriff's department and went inside.

"Is Officer Johnston here?" she asked. The guy looked up at her.

"He's at lunch." The man's eyes slid over to the clock and Pauling saw that he noticed it was 2:30 in the afternoon.

"He should be back anytime now," he added.

There was a seat across from the reception desk and Pauling sat. The guy at the desk looked at her and then turned in his chair. Pauling knew he was texting Johnston to let him know that he had a visitor.

Pauling looked around the space. It was a

cross between a tourism office and a cop shop. There was a dolphin on the wall with the letters LASD across its side. Another wall showed photos of the harbor and next to them were a pair of shotguns locked into a rack.

The windows were open and Pauling saw no sign of air conditioning. She could smell the ocean.

Ten minutes later Officer Johnston walked in. He was a slim black man and he glanced down at Pauling.

"Are you Lauren Pauling?" he asked.

"I am."

"Paul Johnston," he said. "I got your email, come on back."

Pauling followed him to his office and they both sat down.

"So you wanted to ask me about Paige Jones?" he said.

"Yep, I sure did."

"Why would I want to help you?" Johnston asked, his tone easy and relaxed, in contrast to the nature of his question.

"Why wouldn't you?" she responded. "Don't you want to find out what happened to her? Are you totally convinced it was a drowning?"

Johnston's face remained blank. Pauling

figured he was probably a pretty good poker player. He dug out a folder from a file cabinet, flipped it open, read for a bit, then snapped it shut.

"Look, we're what you would call a kind of satellite office," he said. "We got the call to liaison with the military guys. The remains were sent to the lab. And the results came back indicating death by drowning, followed by a shark attack. So the case was closed."

Pauling started to ask a question but he held up his hand.

"I spend most of my day dealing with drunks, shoplifters and two-bit drug dealers, mostly weed. And people just ripping off the tourists here. My bosses are back in Los Angeles. If you've got a problem with the way it was handled or just don't like the results, I suggest you take it up with them."

He swiveled in his chair and put the folder back in his file cabinet.

"That's it?" Pauling asked.

"Yes. Now kindly leave my office and let me take care of Catalina Island. If you've got some kind of crazy ass conspiracy theory, take it up with my supervisors back on the mainland."

He stood and Pauling walked out of his office.

She emerged on the street and was dazzled by the bright sun and the reflections off the water.

Pauling knew she was making progress.

Johnston's overheated performance was just that, an act.

He knew more than he wanted to admit.

CHAPTER FORTY-THREE

She and Michael decided to spend the night on Catalina Island. Pauling knew it was probably a ploy just to get her into bed, but she also realized that she didn't really have a problem with that plan.

They ate at a restaurant on the square. She chose a big salad with grilled vegetables. She figured it was a chance to add some greens to her diet that had largely been missing since her time on San Clemente.

Tallon got a grilled swordfish steak.

"How did your afternoon go?" he asked, a smile on his face, and a little gleam in his blue eyes. Pauling suspected he knew pretty much what she was doing.

"Oh, you know, a lot of stuff is so overpriced out here, but I found a few things."

"Meet anyone interesting?" he persisted. "Have any good conversations?"

She nearly smiled, but also knew that Tallon was still very much a suspect, even though her intuition was telling her he wasn't.

"You know how it goes, I'm sure," she answered.

"What do you mean?"

"There are people who love to talk and there are people who love to have their little secrets," she said and met him with a direct stare until he looked away.

She left it at that and he didn't pressure her for more information.

They went to a bar and had a few drinks and soon she felt a little drunk. At one point, he got her onto a dance floor and they did some kind of butchered cha cha.

They left and went to the hotel.

"Do you want to come up to my room for a little bit?" Tallon asked her.

"A little bit?" she asked.

"It's just an expression," he said.

"I appreciate the offer but I'm tired and a little too loopy to make that decision right now."

The truth was, she was thinking of Paige and wondering if she'd been in this same position.

She gave him a kiss on the cheek and went to her room.

Alone.

CHAPTER FORTY-FOUR

They left early in the morning while the sea was calm and made it back to San Clemente quickly. Pauling didn't say much on the short trip back and neither did Tallon.

They docked the boat and Tallon dropped her back at the Nest where Pauling found an envelope that had been slid under her door.

It simply said: *Rag City. Ten o'clock tonight. I know what happened to Paige.*

There was no signature.

She spent the day reading through the files Blake had sent her. She'd already read them through several times, but she went through all of them, looking for things that she might have missed and adding thoughts and observations to her dossier.

But nothing jumped out at her.

The Dr. Sirrine/Janey angle was interesting but she couldn't help but feel it had nothing to do with Paige. Still, she couldn't rule it out.

By the time she was done updating her documents, it was late afternoon and she realized she was exhausted. She laid on her bed, closed her eyes and napped.

When she awoke, it was night and she had an hour before her rendezvous with her mysterious source at Rag City.

She thought about precautions. She had no gun. No weapon of any kind. She considered calling Tallon and having him serve as backup, but she didn't want to do that.

Finally, she decided to send Blake an email so that at least one person on Earth knew where she was.

When the time came, she commandeered one of the trucks and made her way to Rag City. It took her longer than she'd expected, until she realized that the only time she'd been there before was when she was both high and a little bit drunk. After a half-dozen wrong turns, she finally found the place.

She parked and waited.

The note hadn't said where to meet. For some reason, she felt safer in the truck.

She waited, and ten o'clock came and went, and then ten-thirty. Pauling debated about driving back to the Nest.

But then a text message appeared on her phone from a blocked caller.

Come to the Town Square, in the apartment building. Don't worry, you are safe.

Yeah, right, Pauling thought. She also wondered, how did the person know that she was aware of Rag City? Gabe was the only person who knew she'd been there.

Unless someone had been watching her.

Well, she wasn't going to back out now.

She got out of the truck and walked into the middle of Rag City.

Pauling remembered the basic layout, and soon made her way to the structure that was meant to resemble an apartment building in the middle of Baghdad.

She stepped from the street up to the sidewalk, but she forgot about how much higher it was than in real life and stumbled. She fell to one knee and the cement wall where her head had been exploded, raining chunks of rock and dust down onto her.

She rolled forward and dove inside the building as another rifle shot tore up dirt in the street where she'd just been.

Inside the building, behind the wall, more shots punched through the cement.

It was a big rifle, Pauling realized. Maybe a high-powered sniper rifle like a Barrett. The kind that chambered a .50 caliber bullet.

In a flash, Pauling realized what a horrible situation she was in. Trapped inside a building at night with most likely a Special Ops sniper targeting her.

And she had no weapon.

CHAPTER FORTY-FIVE

She was well and truly screwed.

Pauling knew firsthand the kind of equipment Special Ops snipers employed. Night vision goggles. Infrared. Scopes that could see the hair on a gnat's ass from a thousand yards.

She was in a world of trouble and cursed herself for not being better prepared.

Stop it, she told herself.

Make a plan.

The first thing she did was to get lower on the ground. Even the best scopes and night vision couldn't see through cement walls like the ones that were surrounding her.

It was her guess that the sniper had already started to move to a new location, maybe even coming into the building. If that happened and she was here, there was almost no way out.

So she had to move.

Pauling belly crawled across the floor toward the back of the room hoping there was some sort of backdoor and that the sniper wasn't going to be coming in that way.

Would she even be able to hear him?

Those guys moved in total silence. Still, she knew that the ground outside consisted at least partly of gravel and dirt. Which made for at least a slight possibility that the shooter might make some noise.

So she stayed still and listened.

Nothing.

And then, she heard the softest whisper of sound. Not a footstep. Certainly not on gravel.

It had sounded like fabric.

The quiet whisper of fabric on fabric. It had come from the front of the building.

Pauling raised herself up on her hands and knees and crawled toward the barely discernible window of darkness in the rear corner of the building that she hoped and prayed was a doorway.

She made her way to it.

Pauling continued forward and then one of

her hands went past the floor and she fell out of the building. She landed on the ground and it was solid packed dirt. Luckily there was no sound as she slid all the way out of the building onto the ground outside and crawled so she wouldn't be visible through the doorway.

If the shooter came in the front and looked, even with infrared, he would not be able to see her body as long as she stayed low, so Pauling again belly crawled along the exterior of the building foundation, grateful there were no loose stones.

And then she was away from the building and into a stand of ice plants. Pauling got to her feet and began to run, hunched over, slowly, as she could barely see anything in front of her. Certainly nothing beyond arm's length.

Forward was the only thing she knew, away from the building and the shooter.

Her face hit stone and pain slapped her in the face. Pauling felt blood trickle from her nose into her mouth and the taste was both coppery and dusty.

She felt with her hands and eventually came to the edge of the structure. She leaned around, feeling foolish because she couldn't see anything anyway–

Cement exploded just above her head accompanied by the sound of a shot.

She turned again and ran. With no idea where she was going she raced at full speed. It was a terrifying run. All the shooter had to do was get around that building and if he had a night scope could easily put a round right between her shoulder blades. She tensed as she ran, waiting for the blow–

Suddenly, she was airborne and falling.

Too late, Pauling realized she'd run right over the edge of the cliff and something viciously struck her on the shoulder and she rolled. A stabbing pain pierced her side along the hip and she rolled again, bounced, felt branches scratch at her face and her knees scraped rock.

Finally, she came to a stop.

Her body screamed in agony, blood was wet on her face and she wondered how far she'd fallen.

If the sniper stayed on the edge with his night scope he would be able to pick her off easily. Pauling knew she needed to get under some sort of cover. And then she heard the faint sound of waves crashing and she instantly recognized her location.

She had stood at this very edge with Gabe and

she remembered the large rock outcropping near the ocean.

Her mind raced back to that night with Gabe, which had been moonlit. Now, it was pitch black.

Pauling scrambled ahead, certain that any minute a bullet was going to crash into her and blow her body apart.

Her feet hit water and she remembered the crevice of rock that opened up onto the beach, with deep ledges on either side.

The water was ice-cold but at least she wasn't visible. Pauling forced her way through the water and around the edge until she was under a little ledge. At least now she was out of the water and hidden, but she was cold and hurt.

Instinctively, Pauling appreciated that there was no way the sniper could get into the water and to her without making a sound.

No one was that good.

The thought of the shooter entering her sanctuary motivated her to feel around until she found a good, fist-sized rock.

If her attacker came into the water she would hear and clobber him on the head. Not the most sophisticated of strategies and with little chance of success, but it was all she could come up with.

Pauling waited, keeping her mouth open as

cold began to seep through her bones so her teeth wouldn't chatter.

After several minutes she thought she heard something. The sound of a boot, maybe something hitting water and then she heard a soft laugh.

Pauling waited, but no one came after her. She lost track of time, put the rock down and folded her arms across her chest, trying to generate heat.

She was going to stay here until daylight.

If she didn't die of hypothermia first.

CHAPTER FORTY-SIX

Blake studied the requests Nathan had sent to the investigator's office regarding information on Paige's death. They had released some initial findings and documents but not the autopsy results even though Nathan had specifically requested that. It appeared the official response had been that the state of the remains prevented any meaningful findings.

But, like Pauling, Blake wondered if that meant they hadn't found anything at all. Had they tried?

Blake realized that hacking the server of law enforcement was not a great idea, even though he'd done it before. The challenge, naturally, was that law enforcement had the means to investigate hacks as a criminal violation. Companies had to first prove the hack on their own and then go to the authorities. Which was why hacking the authorities themselves was a much riskier proposition.

However, the email correspondence between Nathan and the clerical branch did give him a window.

It was much easier to hack into email than into confidential servers.

So that's what he set about to do. Using the main email address he was able to reach the email server and after several hours of digging, Blake located an email from one of the investigators to another investigator with an attachment. It appeared the attachment might contain information from Paige's autopsy.

Blake got in and was able to download the attachment. He then sent the full document to Pauling via his own encrypted system knowing full well that she was on an island controlled by the military who were no doubt monitoring electronic communications. Especially Pauling's.

He used a basic encryption code that he knew Pauling would understand right away and that would throw off at least a preliminary glance from anyone on San Clemente Island. It wouldn't stand up to serious scrutiny, but he hoped it would go through as is.

It did.

CHAPTER FORTY-SEVEN

Pauling never felt as cold and tired as she did the minute she woke up.

The sun had just started to peek into the crevice of rock where she had crawled, and the change in light had no doubt roused her.

She stretched her limbs and they audibly creaked. Her face felt stiff and her lip seemed puffy. She remembered running into a wall.

At least she was dry, although her feet still felt a little wet. Maybe that was why she was still so goddamned cold.

Pauling climbed down from the ledge and realized that she could walk to the left out onto another lower shelf of rock that led to part of the beach.

She started to walk out into the full sun but

stopped. She peeked around the ledge first looking for any sign of a sniper or rifle and understood how foolish that was.

Those guys could be two feet in front of you and you would never know it. But still, she scanned the horizon and saw nothing so she stepped out into the full sun, grateful for the warm at the same time bracing herself for a shot that never came.

Pauling hiked along the water's edge until she found a trail that led back up the cliff. She scrambled her way up and got to the edge and saw she was a quarter mile down from Rag City.

She slowly worked her way around the rocky terrain until she came to the road and hoped there was a car but none appeared, so she walked on until she got back to the Nest. She opened the door, walked in and the first thing she heard was Janey who let out a little gasp.

"Oh my God!" Janey whispered. "Pauling! Are you okay?"

Pauling gave her a half-hearted thumbs up and walked past her, staggered back to her room and flopped on the bed, then rolled over and pulled the covers on top of her. She closed her eyes and within minutes was sound asleep.

She had another dream that took place in the

desert. This time, a gunman was chasing her and in the distance, she could see Paige, waving to her. Pauling ran, but just when she was about to reach her, a bullet hit her in the back and she fell face down in the desert. Her mouth was filled with grit-

Pauling woke up, and her mouth was dry. She was sore all over and she briefly relived what had happened at Rag City. She remembered the shots, being chased and falling off the edge of the cliff.

Pauling got up, went into the bathroom and looked at her face. No wonder Janey had reacted the way she did. Pauling looked just like what she was. A woman who'd been chased, shot at and had taken a few major tumbles.

What a mess.

She had scratches on her face and when she lifted her shirt saw a bruise the size of a baseball on the side of her hip.

That's really what hurt the worst. But in retrospect, she was glad. If she'd landed on that rock just a little bit higher she would be looking at about three or four cracked ribs. Who knows, if she'd been really unlucky, maybe even a punctured lung.

And then she probably would've died out there.

Overall she was lucky.

It just didn't feel that way.

Pauling had met her fair share of Special Ops soldiers. When they took a shot, they rarely missed. She dabbed her cuts with a warm washcloth and soap, wincing in pain as she scraped the dried blood from each wound.

It was true, Special Ops guys were the best in the world. So why had the shooter missed? She thought about it. It was night. Pauling was running. Hiding. They wouldn't have been easy shots to make.

Another possibility arose in her mind.

Maybe the shooter hadn't wanted to kill her. Maybe his shots had gone exactly where he'd wanted them to. Near her. Just over her head.

They weren't intended to kill.

Maybe he'd just wanted to scare her.

When she was done cleaning herself she took a hot shower and got dressed. She took several Tylenol and washed them down with tap water. Immediately, Pauling felt a lot better. Still not one hundred percent, but seriously improved.

She thought about reporting the crime, but what would she say? The first question asked would be about what exactly she was doing in Rag City.

Would they really buy a mysterious message about a rendezvous?

Something told her the military guys wouldn't really care. They would chalk it up to a birdie making a big deal out of nothing. Probably scared by nearby gunfire that had nothing to do with her.

Pauling went out to the kitchen, thankful that no one was there. She poured herself a big cup of lukewarm coffee and went back to her room. She opened up her laptop and checked her email.

Only one message.

From Blake.

Pauling opened the attachment and began to read the autopsy on Paige. There was the usual preliminary information but about halfway through the report, the examiner noted several marks that he couldn't attribute to shark bites.

He simply labeled them indeterminate.

She wasn't trained to read autopsies but it did seem to her that there were a lot of marks on Paige's body labeled as inconclusive. If Paige had truly drowned and all the damage been done by sharks, shouldn't every mark on her body be labeled as such?

Pauling made the immediate decision and she

fired off multiple emails, one to Blake and another to Nathan's attorney stating in no uncertain terms that Paige's remains should be immediately exhumed and sent off to a pathologist she had worked with in Washington, DC.

He was retired now but he had been the best in the business. In the email to Nathan, Pauling stressed that he needed to move heaven and earth to get the remains exhumed immediately and overnighted to the pathologist. She wasn't satisfied with the autopsy.

And she knew Nathan wouldn't be either.

Pauling picked up the satellite phone and called Nathan.

“Pauling,” he said when he answered.

“How secure is this line?” she asked. Pauling didn’t want to waste a lot of time speaking in code.

“Fairly secure,” he said. “But one can never be too careful.”

She sighed. She then told him what had happened but avoided using names as much as possible.

“I never had any doubt,” he said when she finished giving him the details.

“I know you didn’t,” Pauling replied. “I feel

I'm still a long way from finding out exactly what happened, but what I do know is that we're a lot closer than we were a week ago."

"That's for damn sure," he said. "I knew you were the right person for the job. Call me the minute you hear from the examiner. Those inconclusive marks are going to be the key."

"Of course. We'll talk about Jack Reacher when I get back," she added.

"Have you been working with him?" he asked. His tone sounded very hollow.

"No," she replied. "No sign of him. In fact, no one's ever heard of him."

"Do you want other backup?" Nathan asked. "You've got snipers shooting at you for Christ's sake. What if I sent in another person undercover who could act as your bodyguard?"

She could tell by the tone of his voice that he knew it was a bad idea and that it was really a token offer.

"No, I'll just have to be more careful. Besides, if another new volunteer showed up here, I'm sure no one would do any more talking. Then it's a full-on, blatant investigation. At least now I've got some doubt on my side."

"You're right," he said. "Keep me posted."

They disconnected and Pauling thought about those inconclusive marks on Paige's body.

She wondered why the investigators hadn't been surprised by the autopsy results either.

Maybe they hadn't wanted to be.

CHAPTER FORTY-EIGHT

The next day Pauling checked the bulletin board to see who was working where in the field. She saw that Ted was operating in the south field, one of the few places she had yet to visit. Pauling put on her walking shoes, got a big bottled water from the fridge and set out. Her body was still stiff and sore, especially her hip, but walking under the sun she soon felt much better. Her face wasn't showing any lingering effects of its meeting with a cement wall.

It took her nearly an hour and a half of hard walking to get to the observation post.

Pauling wondered how she was going to handle Ted, since the last time they'd chatted he'd practically taken off her head.

She stood at the observation post, opened the box containing field notes, and began to flip through them. As she expected, they meant virtually nothing to her and she saw that Paige hadn't written anything.

Suddenly she heard voices coming from the trail and she assumed it was Gabe and Ted.

Ted emerged from the field first and behind him was a man as young as Ted but whom Pauling had never seen before.

Both men stopped in their tracks. Deer in the headlights. Pauling noticed Ted's hair was especially messy and the young man's shirt was pulled out of his jeans.

Before they'd spotted her they both had a relaxed happy look on their faces and Pauling knew instantly what they'd been doing.

Suddenly it all made sense to Pauling.

Ted's surprising anger with her over pursuing the investigation. He'd attacked her with vigor and now she

knew why.

He'd had a very dangerous secret to protect.

Pauling knew that homosexuals in the military were really not welcome. Officially, policies had begun to change but unofficially, gay men in the military was still an uncomfortable subject for a whole lot of people. While Ted wasn't in the armed services, it appeared his companion was. So Ted was no doubt protecting him.

"What you doing out here?" Ted said.

"I've never been out here before," Pauling answered, her voice relaxed and cheerful, as if she hadn't put two and two together. "I was curious to see this area and figured maybe I could help."

The young man stepped past Ted and wore an easy smile on his face. He stuck out his hand.

"I'm Jim," he said. Pauling shook hands with him and Jim turned to Ted.

"We should get back, he said. "I've got to start work in about a half hour."

Ted's gaze lingered on Pauling for a moment and then they walked past her.

She stood there in the sun, pretending to flip through the field notes.

Pauling waited the requisite amount of time to make sure Ted and his companion were well on their way and then she put everything back in place, turned and began the long walk back to the Nest.

This little island is just full of secrets, she thought.

CHAPTER FORTY-NINE

Pauling had been right about Nathan, but in a way she had also been wrong.

He had, in fact, moved heaven and earth and probably spent a prodigious amount of money greasing the right hands. But it took him more than three days to get the remains exhumed and sent off to the medical examiner of her choice, Dr. Milton Killibrew.

Dr. Killibrew had been one of the most famous pathologists in all of law enforcement. Pauling had gotten to know him when she was at the FBI.

They had worked together on a particularly vicious case and Pauling and Dr. Killibrew had bonded. She had even gone to his retirement party where he'd said that if she ever needed any help he was always available for her. Pauling laughed as she remembered him saying that he didn't golf, fish or like the beach.

He just liked to work.

When the first message came through via email encrypted, Pauling opened up Dr. Killibrew's report.

It began with the usual disclaimer that this was just preliminary and that he planned to spend at least several more days with various body parts under the microscope to get a better understanding.

Once she'd gotten past the obvious vital details, he confirmed shark bite marks and agreed that there were several wounds that were inconclusive. But it was the last thing on the report that caught Pauling's attention.

It had also obviously intrigued Dr. Killibrew.

The renowned pathologist described discovering a very small piece of lung that had been hidden in a mass of cartilage and bone. He stated that under the microscope it appeared to him that the level of salinity and oxygen could lead to only one basic conclusion.

Again he provided a bevy of disclaimers but in

the end he said he would be willing to testify to a 95% certainty rate. The conclusion made Pauling sit back.

Paige had been dead before she went into the water.

CHAPTER FIFTY

M*urder.*

There was no other explanation.

Pauling sat back and thought about her next steps. The investigator's name was on the report. And it belonged to the Los Angeles County Sheriff's Department, but not the officer on Catalina Island. The report had been generated in Los Angeles proper.

She toyed with the idea of emailing or calling him, but then she quickly dismissed it. She knew she would get nowhere on the phone or online.

It was time for a different tactic. She thought it through and came up with a plan. She went to her things, dug through to the bottom where she had hidden Nathan's stash of money and peeled off three thousand dollars worth of bills.

Next, she commandeered a truck.

She drove up to the airport and waited for the plane from the mainland to come in. It arrived every day of the week except Wednesdays, Saturdays and Sundays. Its usual arrival time was early afternoon, but that could sometimes change depending on weather but with a clear sky and no sign of storms, Pauling was confident it would land at its regular time, in about a half hour.

She used the time to think.

If Dr. Killibrew's finding was true, it meant beyond almost all certainty that Paige had indeed been murdered.

There could be no other explanation for how she had been dead before she went into the water.

That would mean she hadn't drowned.

So if she had already been dead, how did she get in the water?

The easy answer was a boat. Somebody who had access to a boat most likely killed her, took her out into the middle of the ocean and dumped the body.

Of course, there were a lot of military guys who had access to the boats. And probably quite a few who used them even if they weren't authorized. So it was a pretty big pool of possibilities.

Still, there was only one person she knew who had both a boat, and a beautiful set of blue eyes.

Michael Tallon.

CHAPTER FIFTY-ONE

The plane landed and Pauling stood up. She went to the window and watched the half-dozen passengers disembark. They all appeared to be military personnel.

The engine gradually shut down and the pilot, Jamison, got off the plane but stood outside talking to some of the military guys.

The flight coordinator came into the building and went into the office just off the main room. Pauling remembered him from the bar when Deb had tried to pick a fight with her. She remembered his name was Troyer. Josh Troyer.

Pauling walked over to the doorway and looked at him. "Hey, when is the next flight out?" she asked

Troyer looked up at her. He shook his head. "That ain't how it works," he said.

"I know," Pauling said. "But I really have to get to Los Angeles as soon as possible."

The flight coordinator shook his head. "We're going later today but you know there's a two-week waiting list to get on the flight plus all of the paperwork. You're usually looking at almost a three-week wait before you can get on the plane. This isn't exactly Delta Airlines."

Pauling walked over to him and slid the bundle of cash out of her jacket and put it on the desk.

"Consider this an expedited rate," she said, "for a round trip."

Troyer looked at the money, then glanced over at the guys on the tarmac. Finally, his gaze returned and settled directly on Pauling.

He smiled.

"Good news," he said. "We just had a cancellation. There's now an open seat on the last flight out today."

Pauling glanced down and saw that the three grand had disappeared from the top of the desk. She smiled.

"What time do we board?"

CHAPTER FIFTY-TWO

The seats on the plane were empty, but the cargo hold was full. Pauling saw the boxes and crates, along with what looked to be some machine parts, packed into the hold at the rear of the plane.

Jamison waved at her from the fold-out stairs. She carried her pack and climbed into the plane.

"No comedy routine today," he told her. "Pick a seat. Any seat."

Pauling noted that the plane was completely empty.

She sat in the first seat across from the door opening and tossed her pack into the empty seat next to her.

"It'll be a quick flight," Jamison told her. He winked at her and she could tell from the expression on his face that Troyer had cut him in on the deal. He would have had to otherwise there would be no explanation.

Pauling was beyond excited to be back in the real world. She couldn't wait for her regular cell phone to work again. And she really wanted to spend the night in a hotel and sleep in a real bed. But that would all depend on what she found out.

They finished loading and Troyer climbed aboard. He nodded and grinned at Pauling, then went into the cockpit and closed the door.

The engines revved and very quickly they were airborne. Pauling looked out the window as San Clemente Island fell away beneath her.

The plane banked and she saw the rolling waves of the Pacific. A few minutes later, they passed over Bird Shit Rock and Pauling saw a large, dark shape a hundred yards from the outcropping of land.

A great white, for sure. She shivered involuntarily, thinking of her diving for lobster with Michael Tallon. She could've been a tasty snack for that shark.

The flight was short and the landing smooth.

Once on the ground, Pauling took a cab to the Los Angeles County Sheriff's Department, located in the Hall of Justice. Pauling briefly thought of some kind of superhero reference.

She went inside and found her way to the department in charge of accidental deaths. After all, that was what Paige's death had been ruled.

Ultimately, she found herself seated across from a tired-looking man with dark circles under his eyes and a neatly trimmed beard. He had a white shirt with a collar that was just starting to show signs of staining.

"Paige Jones, let me see," he said. His name was Gianfranco and he thumbed through a file cabinet looking for the name.

At last, he pulled out a folder and set it on the desk between them.

He flipped it open.

"Drowning," he said, "followed by shark feeding."

Gianfranco looked up at Pauling.

"So what are you investigating, exactly?" he asked.

"I don't think it was an accident."

He sat back in his chair and smiled at Pauling.

"I've got twenty detectives working overtime on a backlog of cases. Even with that, we look at every case. If there had been any indication foul play was involved, it wouldn't have wound up in that file cabinet. Trust me."

Pauling thought about what he'd said.

"Is there any other reason it would have wound up in that file cabinet?"

His big, dark eyes peered out at her.

"It seems like the investigation was not very thorough. Rushed, almost," Pauling said. "And when I spoke with one of your colleagues on Catalina Island, I felt like I was practically thrown out of his office."

Gianfranco gave her a tired smile. "You seem like a sharp lady," he said. "Can you think of any reason a cop on Catalina might handle a death on San Clemente a bit gingerly?"

"The military, of course," she answered. "If they were involved in limiting the investigation. But why would they care about Paige Jones drowning?"

"I'm sure they didn't care then and I'm sure as hell they don't care now."

"Wait a minute, you're not making any sense," Pauling said. "You're contradicting yourself."

"No, I'm not. What I'm saying is they probably didn't care any more or less about your relative's death. But they don't want anyone investigating anything out there. Do you know what I mean?"

Pauling did understand him.

"You've been out there, right?" he said.

"Yes."

"Then you know as well as I do there is a ton of clandestine shit going on. You've got FBI guys out there, CIA, Spec Ops. Who knows, maybe they've got a part of the island where they torture terrorists."

"I don't think so," Pauling said. "But the point is, they don't want anyone asking. At all. Period. So there must be some sort of unofficial standing order that if anything happens on San Clemente at all, the military will actually handle it and you guys take a back seat."

"I would deny that with my last dying breath," he said.

Maybe she had been wrong, she realized. Maybe there hadn't been any interference run on Paige's death specifically, but it was just standard operating procedure for anything that happened.

Gianfranco seemed to read her mind.

"That island is bad luck, though," he said.

"What do you mean?"

Gianfranco closed the folder and put it away before Pauling could sneak a glance at it.

"We had a girl a year ago come back here to L.A. from that island, get in a car and disappear. Never found again. She's a cold case now."

Pauling couldn't keep the awestruck expression from her face. How could no one else have known this?

"I want her name," she said.

"Why?"

"Because maybe she knew Paige," Pauling said, winging it. "Maybe looking into her background can help me put together a cohesive description of what happened, if nothing else."

Gianfranco eyed her warily, pulled the folder back out and said to her, "Donnellon. Emily."

He put the folder back in the cabinet, shut it and locked it and then scooped up his coffee cup in one smooth motion.

"I hope you're not forgetting what we just discussed," he said.

"Oh, I'm not."

"Great. I'll show you out," he said.

CHAPTER FIFTY-THREE

Pauling put in a quick call to Blake and had him run the name Emily Donnellon, making sure she would get the right one. Pauling could have used some of her services back in her office in New York, but since Blake was free, she chose him.

He called her back within minutes.

"Good news," he said. "She lived in the Valley. Went to UCLA. Her parents still live in the family home, according to utility records, combined with her school records."

He gave Pauling the address.

She took a cab to a car rental company, rented a sedan and drove directly to the Donnellon family home, a split-level ranch with a GMC SUV in the driveway.

Pauling parked her car and knocked on the door.

A woman looked out, then unlatched the door.

"Can I help you?" she asked.

"Mrs. Donnellon?"

"Yes."

"My name is Lauren Pauling and I'm looking into the death of Paige Jones. She died on San Clemente Island. I understand your daughter Emily disappeared after returning home from the island?"

It all came out quickly but Pauling figured it was the best way to do it.

"Please, come in," the woman said.

She led the way to a living room. It was immaculate, with an upright piano against one wall, a seating area with a couch and chairs facing a gas fireplace.

Mrs. Donnellon sat in one of the chairs and Pauling sat across from her on the corner of the couch.

Pauling briefly studied the woman. She was probably in her late fifties or early sixties, with a stylish haircut and a trim body. She looked a little bit like a California beach bunny, all grown up and doing well.

"Do you think they're related?" the woman asked.

"I'm not sure, Mrs. Donnellon," Pauling said.

"Please. Call me Julia."

"Julia, I'm not sure because frankly I just found out about your daughter. I've spent the past couple of weeks on the island trying to find out what happened to Paige, and no one even mentioned it. Which surprises me."

Julia Donnellon shrugged her shoulders. "Maybe they don't know. Emily only spent a week out there and she landed here in Los Angeles. It was after that she disappeared."

"Did she come home? To this house?" Pauling asked.

"No. No one saw her."

"Who was the last to see her?"

"When the passengers disembarked they were all checked off at the airport. That was the last time anyone saw her."

"Were the police able to find anyone who picked her up? A friend? Did she call a cab? Taxi companies record most of their calls and obviously keep track of who picked up fares and where."

Julia Donnellon shook her head. "No, they

contacted all of the cab companies but no one could find evidence of picking her up."

"So she was last seen at the airport."

"Yes. They used her cell phone records to see that her phone was turned on when she landed. But then she didn't make any calls or send messages afterward. And then she disappeared and the phone was never used again."

"So she couldn't have called a friend or a cab, then?" Pauling asked.

"We figured she didn't have to call. Sometimes there are cabs just waiting at the airport to pick up a fare. That's probably what happened."

Pauling thought about the small, military airport with its secured gate. Not a place a cab driver would hang out looking for fares.

"Do you have a photo of your daughter I could look at?"

Julia Donnellon got up, left the room and came back with a photo in a frame.

Pauling looked at the girl in the picture. Blonde. Blue eyes. Very pretty.

Not exactly like Paige, but in the ballpark.

"Beautiful," Pauling said, and handed the photo back.

Mrs. Donnellon set the photo on the coffee

table between them. Pauling felt like the girl was looking up at the both of them.

"Now what?" Julia asked.

Pauling stood. "Thank you for talking to me. I'm going to fly back to San Clemente Island and see if I can talk to some people who might have known both Paige and Emily. See if there is any kind of connection. Is there a phone number where I can reach you if I have any questions?"

The woman jotted down a number and gave it to Pauling.

"Good luck," Julia Donnellon said, her voice heavy with sorrow and fatigue.

"If you find out what happened to Paige, maybe you'll find Emily."

Pauling nodded.

She didn't have a good feeling about it, though.

CHAPTER FIFTY-FOUR

Pauling was never a big believer in coincidences. And something felt very wrong about the situation. Two beautiful girls, one dead and one missing?

It just didn't add up.

How was it no one on San Clemente Island felt the need to mention that Paige wasn't the only young woman to have possibly been harmed?

Was it that they didn't know?

Or were they trying to hide it?

Obviously, it wouldn't play well for the reputation of the Bird Conservatory to have young women continually experience harm while working for them. Or, in this case, just after.

Nor would it be good for the military people

on the island. There was certainly a fraternity there of men who protected their own.

It wouldn't be the first time a group of men had covered up crimes against women to protect their own.

Pauling mulled all of this over as she returned the rental car and took a cab to the little airport. She noted that there were no cabs waiting to pick up fares.

There was no excitement over the idea of going back to San Clemente Island, but now Pauling had a whole new set of questions to ask. There was a surge of adrenaline, though, at the prospect of confronting Dr. Sirrine, Wilkins, and even Michael Tallon.

Had Tallon known Emily Donnellon?

If he was all about seducing beautiful women, Emily would have fit the bill. She had been a breathtakingly beautiful young woman.

Pauling also wasn't looking forward to going back under what they call the cone of silence. A lack of Internet and lack of cell phone coverage was conducive to a feeling of disconnectedness. Even though she had the satellite phone and could communicate with Blake via email, a sense of isolation was pervasive on the island.

Pauling made her way to the old airplane and

walked up to Troyer, who was overseeing the loading of more cargo.

He turned to her. "There she is," he said. "Our lone passenger."

She took her seat as they finished loading the plane. Once her gear had been stowed, Pauling sat down and pulled out her phone. It might be the last time she had quick and easy access to her email.

She checked her mailboxes and saw a message from Dr. Killibrew. Attached was a Word document with a more thorough analysis of Paige's autopsy.

The plane hurtled down the runway and then lurched into the air. Pauling momentarily put her phone down to hold onto the arms of her seat. It was windy, and the old plane creaked and groaned as it gained altitude.

Once it was calmer, she got the phone back out and opened the document.

The fourth paragraph made her gasp out loud. It stated:

...Subject appears to have suffered from a full body concussion initially misdiagnosed as blunt force trauma. A more accurate diagnosis

with a higher degree of accuracy would state that the trauma was consistent with suicide jumpers...

The phone dangled in Pauling's hand.

Suddenly it made sense.

When Paige had been placed into the ocean she had already been dead.

But what she suddenly realized was that Paige hadn't been tossed into the water from a boat.

She'd been dropped from somewhere much higher.

And no one had seen Emily Donnellon once she'd gotten off the plane.

Pauling knew why: she'd probably never gotten off the plane in the first place.

At least not on land.

The realization sunk in and then she felt the cold, razor-sharp edge of steel placed against her throat.

"Whatcha reading there, honey?" the voice asked.

CHAPTER FIFTY-FIVE

"I was reading all about your handiwork," she answered through gritted teeth.

"Yeah, how so?" Troyer asked.

He stayed behind her.

"Pretty slick," Pauling said. "Find your victims, get them on the plane alone, have your fun, then dump them into the ocean. More specifically, a part of the ocean full of hungry great white sharks."

She heard him chuckle.

"Lean forward and put one arm behind your back," he said.

Pauling had no choice but to comply.

"It was you at Rag City, wasn't it?" Pauling asked.

"Yeah, we get bored when we have to overnight on the island."

From the cockpit, Jamison appeared. He smiled back at them, and he had a small pistol in his hand.

"It's a .22," he said, reading her mind. "I can shoot you, but it won't go through the fuselage. The perfect caliber for this sort of thing."

Pauling felt the knife removed from her throat, and then cold steel snapped around her left wrist. The snap of the handcuffs closing seemed to echo in the airplane.

"She was asking about our fun shooting at her in Rag City," Troyer said.

"I'm a helluva shot," Jamison said. "Missing you was easy but I tried to get as close as possible. For the effect."

"How'd you put the note under my door without being seen?" Pauling asked.

"Easy. The Nest is empty all the time. That's how we searched your room, too."

"Put your other hand behind your back," Troyer said.

"Whoo boy, I've been waiting for this ever since we flew you out here," Jamison said.

"That's pretty pathetic," she said. "Can't compete with the military guys, huh? 'Cuz they're young and athletic and you're middle-aged and soft?"

She wanted to piss them off, get them to momentarily forget their cool, and she desperately wanted at least one hand free.

However, she knew methodical killers rarely made mistakes. It was when they were distracted that they failed to think things through.

Jamison slapped her.

It was a quick hard move and it rocked her head back. She tasted blood.

Troyer used the slap to grab her arm and snap the cuff on it.

Pauling spit the blood out at him. "What a great idea," she said. "Kill them on the plane. No witnesses. Plenty of time to get rid of evidence. Hell, you could even doctor the flight records to make it look like they landed in Los Angeles."

"Oh, they landed all right, just not on terra firma," Troyer said. His voice sounded cool and collected. Jamison still looked flushed, pissed off at what she'd said.

"Can't they track your flight records?" Pauling asked, stalling for time. "I'm assuming you put the plane on autopilot while you have your fun?"

"Oh, we just divert due to weather for awhile. No big deal," Troyer answered.

"Yeah, you look like you'd be pretty quick in the sack," Pauling said, meeting Jamison's eyes. "Little-dicked buddies spurned by women, right?"

Something snapped in Jamison's eyes and he slid the pistol into his pants and lunged at Pauling.

She lowered her head and butted him in the sternum, then spun and grabbed for the pistol with her hands behind her back. Jamison grabbed her and they tumbled together onto the floor.

Pauling was lucky. She landed on top of the gun and was able to get ahold of it. However, she was pinned on top of it and couldn't budge it, so she squeezed the trigger.

The sound was an explosion and Jamison screamed. Troyer jumped off of her and she lurched forward, getting the gun out of Jamison's pocket and she aimed it blindly behind her and down. She pulled the trigger multiple times and then spun as Troyer reacted.

He came at her but she shot. The bullet went high, catching him in the throat. He stopped, and then staggered. Pauling lowered the pistol and fired two more times until the hammer clicked on empty.

Troyer fell, the front of his shirt a bloody mess.

Pauling looked down, behind her, and saw that one of the bullets she'd fired into Jamison had gone in under his chin and come back out through his left eye.

They were both dead.

Even worse, the plane was tilting down and Pauling had a moment to wonder if one of the bullets had gone into some wiring or fuel lines.

She looked to the cockpit and saw through the windshield a sky of blue.

Except there was a wave in the sky.

And then she realized the blue wasn't the sky, and the wave was real.

The plane crashed into the ocean and Pauling's world went black.

CHAPTER FIFTY-SIX

Cold.

Pauling's world went from black to cold. And then to bright white. Foam filled the airplane as it creaked and heaved in the cold ocean water.

Her hands still locked behind her, she struggled to her feet. The crash landing had snapped a wing off and taken a chunk of the fuselage with it. The sun burst through the opening, along with a steady roar of ocean water.

Suddenly, the sun was gone, replaced by a glow as the plane sank beneath the surface of the water. Pauling instinctively dove toward the opening, unable to use her arms, instead, kicking with everything she had. She made it through the opening just as the plane heaved to the right. She felt something stab her left leg and then she was kicking upward.

Her head broke through the surface and she gasped, taking in a huge lungful of water.

She bobbed under, then back up. She rolled to her side and then to the other.

To her right, she had glimpsed the top of Bird Shit Rock. She rotated her body and rolled onto her back, and began kicking furiously.

Her leg was burning and she had the sickening realization that she was probably bleeding.

Not a good thing with sharks everywhere.

Pauling was tempted to try to stop and confirm if she was bleeding, but what would be the point? She continued to kick and twist to remain on her back.

She was sure at any moment something huge would crunch through her legs.

It took her an agonizingly long five minutes to reach the outskirts of Bird Shit Rock.

In those last few seconds she was absolutely positive something was going to bite off her legs.

But it never did.

She heard the waves splashing on rock and maneuvered herself into an opening between two jagged thumbs of rock. She could barely keep her head up to see, and each time the sea rewarded her by smashing her face with a vicious wave.

Pauling choked on the ocean water but crabbed sideways, getting her feet beneath her and working her way around until she could stand and climb higher onto the outcropping.

She was safe, out of the water, but she was bleeding. The back of her leg was crimson and blood had seeped down, covering her foot.

Pauling wondered how long she would have to wait. The sun felt good on her skin as she shivered and closed her eyes.

CHAPTER FIFTY-SEVEN

"How long were you out there?"

Pauling looked up at Nathan.

"A couple of hours," she said. "The military air traffic control guys saw the plane disappear. They sent a helicopter out and they found me."

"You were lucky," he said.

"I know."

He sighed.

They were in a hospital room in Los Angeles, flown directly there by the search and rescue team. She'd had a mild concussion and some bruised ribs. The jagged cut on her leg had taken twenty-seven stitches.

In a few hours she would be released and able

to head back to Wisconsin on Nathan's private jet.

Not that she was all that anxious to get back on an airplane.

"You did it," he said.

"A lot of luck was involved," Pauling said.

"Those bastards got what they deserved," Nathan said. In some ways, he looked more tired and older than when she'd last seen him. But there was something different in his eyes, too. A sense of closure, maybe.

Justice.

"There may be more than Paige and Emily," Nathan said. "The cops are scouring their files for any other missing women. They think they've already found one."

Pauling knew they would. Jamison and Troyer had gotten very good at what they were doing. And they'd gotten that good through practice.

Plenty of practice.

"I owe you an apology," Nathan said. "I'm sorry about using the Jack Reacher story to get you to take the case. I had read about your background and knew you were the perfect person to find out who killed Paige."

Pauling let it go. She wasn't happy about it,

and she'd almost died, but she wasn't going to tear into Nathan Jones now.

There was movement in the doorway and Pauling saw Michael Tallon looking at her. He had a clutch of flowers in his hand.

"Well, I'll see how soon we can get you out of here," Nathan said. He nodded at Tallon as he left the room.

"You know if you'd wanted to see Bird Shit Rock up close all you had to do was ask," Tallon said. He gave Pauling a sheepish smile and put the flowers on a table at the foot of the bed.

"Pretty impressive, what you did," Tallon said.

"Thanks," Pauling answered.

"How long was I a suspect?" he asked, with a twinkle in his eye.

"Not very long," she answered.

"Before you trusted me," he said.

"Who said I trust you?"

"You don't?" he made a big deal of looking shocked. "What do I have to do to earn it?"

She glanced out the window and then looked back at him.

"I've got a few ideas in mind."

AN AWARD-WINNING BESTSELLING MYSTERY SERIES

Buy DEAD WOOD, the first John Rockne Mystery.

CLICK HERE TO BUY

"Fast-paced, engaging, original."

-NYTimes bestselling author Thomas Perry

FREE BOOKS AND MORE

Would you like a FREE book and the chance to win a FREE KINDLE?

Then sign up for the DAN AMES BOOK CLUB:

For special offers and new releases, sign up here

BOOK ONE IN A THRILLING NEW SERIES

A Blazing Hot New Mystery Thriller Series!

CLICK HERE TO BUY

ABOUT THE AUTHOR

Dan Ames is a USA TODAY Bestselling Author and winner of the Independent Book Award for Crime Fiction.

www.authordanames.com
dan@authordanames.com

ALSO BY DAN AMES

The JACK REACHER Cases #1 (A Hard Man To Forget)

The JACK REACHER Cases #2 (The Right Man For Revenge)

The JACK REACHER Cases #3 (A Man Made For Killing)

The JACK REACHER Cases #4 (The Last Man To Murder)

The JACK REACHER Cases #5 (The Man With No Mercy)

The JACK REACHER Cases #6 (A Man Out For Blood)

The JACK REACHER Cases #7 (A Man Beyond The Law)

The JACK REACHER Cases #8 (The Man Who Walks Away)

The Jack Reacher Cases #9 (The Man Who Strikes Fear)

The Jack Reacher Cases #10 (The Man Who Stands Tall)

DEAD WOOD (John Rockne Mystery #1)

HARD ROCK (John Rockne Mystery #2)

COLD JADE (John Rockne Mystery #3)

LONG SHOT (John Rockne Mystery #4)

EASY PREY (John Rockne Mystery #5)

BODY BLOW (John Rockne Mystery #6)

MOLLY (Wade Carver Thriller #1)

SUGAR (Wade Carver Thriller #2)

ANGEL (Wade Carver Thriller #3)

THE KILLING LEAGUE (Wallace Mack Thriller #1)

THE MURDER STORE (Wallace Mack Thriller #2)

FINDERS KILLERS (Wallace Mack Thriller #3)

DEATH BY SARCASM (Mary Cooper Mystery #1)

MURDER WITH SARCASTIC INTENT (Mary Cooper Mystery #2)

GROSS SARCASTIC HOMICIDE (Mary Cooper Mystery #3)

KILLER GROOVE (Rockne & Cooper Mystery #1)

BEER MONEY (Burr Ashland Mystery #1)

THE CIRCUIT RIDER (Circuit Rider #1)

KILLER'S DRAW (Circuit Rider #2)

TO FIND A MOUNTAIN (A WWII Thriller)

STANDALONE THRILLERS:

THE RECRUITER

KILLING THE RAT

HEAD SHOT

THE BUTCHER

BOX SETS:

AMES TO KILL

GROSSE POINTE PULP

GROSSE POINTE PULP 2

TOTAL SARCASM

WALLACE MACK THRILLER COLLECTION

SHORT STORIES:

THE GARBAGE COLLECTOR

BULLET RIVER

SCHOOL GIRL

HANGING CURVE

SCALE OF JUSTICE

Made in the USA
Middletown, DE
16 December 2022